AVODAH OFFIT

SIMON & SCHUSTER
New York London Toronto Sydney Tokyo Singapore

SIMON & SCHUSTER
Rockefeller Center
1230 Avenue of the Americas
New York, New York 10020

Designed by Bonni Leon
Manufactured in the United States of America
1 3 5 7 9 10 8 6 4 2
Library of Congress Cataloging-in-Publication Data
Offit, Avodah K.
p.   cm.
1. Sex therapists—California—San Francisco—Fiction.
2. San Francisco (Calif.)—Fiction.   I. Title.
PS3565.F384V57   1994
813'.54—dc20   93-36227   CIP
ISBN: 0-671-87436-5

FOR SIDNEY OFFIT
MY TEACHER, MY STUDENT, MY VERY BEST FRIEND

PROLOGUE 1992

What is real and what is virtual? Where does fact end and story begin? And which world does one truly inhabit, the rough crust of the earth or the regions of the mind that can create heaven, hell and narrative?

My mother's presence has always inspired these questions. Merely listening to her, being impaled on the quick thrust of her martyrdom or her vengeance, can send my imagination on journeys in search of a way to transform her pain. I discovered early that I could be near her and far away at the same time, physically close to her but mentally beyond her in my own world of love united, peace achieved, pardons granted. I could soar across space to a land where I was the agent of order and joy.

But yet she held me captive with her sagas. Her story is the beginning and end, the alpha and omega, of mine. My mother's most improbable tale is of how my father betrayed her and how she punished him for it with death. "I killed him," she says, describing how she murdered him, in effect, by allowing him to die without access to medical salvation. For my mother always won her battles—against natural disasters, human perfidy and, especially, the mismanagement of justice. She spent all her conversational energy on defining herself as victorious warrior. Her life events are the stuff of myth. My mother won her final revenge against men by recounting the simplest of acts: she removed the emergency call-button from my father's reach as he lay dying of ventricular tachycardia in the hospital.

She tells this adventure with death again and again, enjoying her power over life, knowing that no accusation, no indictment will ever be made, whether or not it's true. She is telling it now, in an early version, as we assess my father's jewelry in a box on the bureau and look at his clothes, neatly lined up in the closet. For work or play, he wore only lightweight worsted suits, either pinstriped or woven in a muted plaid. As chief engineer of New York City's Bureau of Waterways, having worked his way to that position through intelligence, dedication and legendary honesty, he always presented a dignified appearance. My mother will relish her tale of retribution against this Agamemnon until she, too, dies.

My father must have felt the first beating rush in his chest on becoming aware of my mother's arrival as the other woman was leaving his bedside. He'd been doing well, too; he'd practically recovered from the initial heart attack. They'd taken the box—the telemetry box—from around his neck. He didn't even need to be monitored anymore! My mother tells me, degrading every detail, that the woman was old and dirty, although she still had a good figure. Her scalp was raw from bleach. Her coat was a peach-colored rag. Her painted nails were chipped and cracked. Her lipstick bled into the washboard lines of her skin. Her perfume ruined the air. This filthy woman, this foreigner, asked him for money and he was *giving* it to her, a thick envelope full of cash, just as my mother arrived. My mother saw the whole thing, watched the woman kiss him on the mouth and clatter out of the room in her frayed high heels. . . .

What clothing did I want? Could I wear the jackets of his suits? Women today wore men's clothes. Maybe his pants would fit my husband or my son. It was too bad my brother was dead, he would probably be a doctor by now, he could have worn them. I should certainly take the jewelry. A pocket watch. A pair of cuff links, real gold. And his Brooklyn College graduation ring.

She had confronted my father immediately. Why was he giving cash to strangers? Who was she? She certainly seemed to know him. What was a streetwalker like that doing in his hospital room, taking money? He didn't answer, but she persisted—she never gives up—no one can resist her inquisitions or deprive her of her rights. It was hers to know. As heaven was her witness, she had to protect herself, me, her grandchildren. . . .

My father had coughed, breathed hard and stared out the window. Finally he sat up straight in his bed—he could always sit so straight—and told her to shut up, he'd had a mistress almost all his married life and she knew why, but he hadn't needed a woman for years, he'd given her enough money to keep her away, and that was the end of it. No one would ever see her again.

It's part of my profession to hear women rage and mourn their husbands' adulteries. Often I sympathize. As often, I have only professional empathy. I hear them out. The entitled want to kill the other woman. The self-effacing want to kill themselves and sometimes do. Unless their legacy is poetry, no one talks about it afterward. . . . There are some women who take adultery as an occasion to destroy their families, to tell the children the sins of the father and try to win allies. A few hardy competitors joust with the hidden opponent and deliver the best sex ever, for a while. Others are delighted to be relieved of the noxious act and withdraw entirely, so long as the day laborer comes home for dinner. Almost no woman sees her spouse's adultery as a signal of distress, a request for more (or less) attention. And only a few discerning women perceive their anger to be at the man, himself. Too often, it's at men in general. At that whole half of the universe about which my mother was fond of quoting George Eliot even before the revelation. "A man's mind—" she would say, "what there is of it—has always the advantage of being masculine." She had read *Middle-*

march and *Romola* in high school. She was radical, even by today's standards.

What about his shirts? And his hats? He wore very good hats. Gray felt, with a ribbon band. Thick leather inside, no discoloration. He never perspired, my mother insists. The man never let the sweat out. But he had been sweating in his hospital bed. Plenty. The water had poured down his body. He was paler than the sheets. He couldn't breathe, either. I should really take the jewelry. Who gave it to him, anyway? Didn't Harry, my first husband, give him the cuff links for his fiftieth, the watch at sixty? He never wore them, we should know that. He wasn't going to let his children retire him with a watch. Were we trying to tell him his time was up? We should know that he had a long way to go, a long way. Didn't I want some of the clothes? Anything?

No. I didn't want anything. Yes, I did, the cuff links and the watch. . . . The medical terms for the sequence of events were scrolling through my mind: pallor, diaphoresis, dyspnea, cyanosis, mental confusion, death. Had she seen it all? Had she seen the blood waves pulsing in his neck, had she seen his fingers fumbling along the sheets in search of help, had she seen him reaching for air, for oxygen, for the elixir of another awful moment of life? Had she seen it the way I could see it in my mind, the suffocation in the fluids of his own body? I asked if she had seen it all. Did she see him die?

Of course not. She had dropped the clamp and cord on the floor and walked out. She'd sat in the reading room until the doctor came to get her. The doctor said she didn't have to make a decision about resuscitation, wasn't that a relief.

I'm sure she didn't see him die. I don't know whether she killed him. My mother avoided death. She didn't stay to see my brother die when he was sick. She never went to violent movies. If her religion had included looking at the bleeding Christ on the cross, she couldn't have done it.

Maybe that's why she could say she killed. Why secretly, in some unmentionable chamber of my soul, I was freed by her confession. She could conceive what I can hardly imagine because I know I die with other people. I do not feel immortal the way she does. I do not live her magical, eternal life. And yet, I am angry, too. Every time she tells the story, I want my father dead as much as she did. I want them all dead, all the betrayers. But I don't have to murder. My mother has sinned for me. I pardon him. I pardon her. I pardon us all. And I'm free. Free to love.

PART ONE

SEX AND MORTALITY

Toni

1

To: dr zion   SUBJECT: new person
6.20.91

Well, thank you very much for directing a *PATIENT* this way! It's
more than all my former "friends" in New York have done—not
even one of my network buddies attempted to help me start a
practice here in San Francisco—so please know that your extension
of self into my world, as well as the long stretch of your sentences
over 3,000 miles, is vastly appreciated. . . .

And you will see, you will see, you will be rewarded for your
effort at installing the software and learning to send e-mail to me
because there is something archaic, deep and mysterious about the
transmission of words through cyberspace (my new hobby, preoc-
cupation, interest); i don't mean to impose it, to force it on you,

even though i've done just that, but thank you for indulging a fledgling passion for esoteric forms of communication.

The greater gratitude is due you because in "real" as compared to "virtual" reality, dr charles varnhos, a friend of your husband's, has sent me/us a patient: her name is *TONITA YEI* (i have her permission to use it), and her chief complaint (as we used to write on the first line of all those physical exams) very strongly suggests vaginismus. In her own words, "I'm too tight. No one has ever been able to get in."

The demographics are that toni is 32 years old, single, native american, part swede, and *EXTRAORDINARILY* attractive! She had a complete hysterectomy for uterine sarcoma last year and says she was discharged as "cured" and "clean" after some hormones and a short course of chemotherapy.

I found this difficult to believe. No radiation? A touch of chemo? Some surgeon with a sadistic sense of kindness was avoiding the spoken word. . . . she was probably riddled with metastases even though she looked healthier than bran flakes, but dr houston, her surgeon, confirmed that she is, for the time being, as well as anyone else on earth! Only problem: soon, or sooner or later, the sarcoma may recur and then it could kill her with a sacrificial vengeance, though meanwhile none of the traditionally more aggressive treatments have proved statistically to have an advantage.

So here is this hyperbole of a woman who probably never would have gotten to see a psychiatrist if she didn't complain that her vagina hurt; no one would think to suggest that possibly she'd have a need to explore the experience of having a sentence of death by torture at some unspecified time, no, instead she complains of vaginal tightness, probably during examination, and this liberated oncologist sends her to a new *sex therapist* he's hardly heard of?

What now?

marc

To: Dr. Martell   SUBJECT: Sarcoma
   6.21.91

I've discussed Tonita Yei's sarcoma with my husband (Elia's a pathologist) and he agrees that you have to consider her whole and healthy. She hasn't been mistreated. And she may be an interesting woman, a good sex therapy case, if there are no complications. I'm looking forward to hearing more and I'll do my best to monitor your work!

Warmly,
Aphra

To: dr zion   SUBJECT: education
    6.24.91

I've read your short textbook on treatment so i know the sequence: first teach vaginal contraction and relaxation (Kegel exercises), then instruct in bearing down (like Lamaze), finally suggest insertion of the patient's own fingers, first one, then two or three.

QUESTIONS: 1. Why teach bearing down?
                 2. Why patient's own fingers? Why not her partner's?
                 3. What has all this got to do with love?

marc

To: Dr. Martell   SUBJECT: Sex therapy
    6.25.91

When a woman bears down, she *opens* her vagina. That's why bearing down helps to deliver a baby.

And when a woman can insert her *own* fingers, she's in charge. No one else is intruding. Some women are more emotionally disturbed by intrusion than others.

As for love, we don't try to teach it in sex therapy. When it's there already, we hope better sex makes it stronger.

Gently,
AZ

To: dr zion   SUBJECT: vaginismus
    7.1.91

Keeping things out. . . . letting things in. . . . toni's vagina is a metaphor for the whole bloody world, I think! Shut it up/keep it closed/squeeze it tight: nothing gets through and you feel no pain. It's a defense as anna freud would have said: isolation expressed as a symptom that's a sign of the times.

I don't think toni is a candidate for simple sex therapy, at least not right now. . . . she's complicated, although in a peculiar way she's not disturbed. *I'm the one with the problem!* She disturbs me and i don't fully know why. . . . it may be i've never heard anyone discuss sex so openly; i know i'm supposed to be focusing on the disorder but i hear the *woman* and she's talking to *me*. . . . is my imagination supposed to have been sanitized in medical school? But it's more than this woman's appearance: it's her lack of flirtatiousness, the candor that conceals her shyness, her way of talking in that low slow precise resonant unembarrassed voice about men's cocks and cums and classic pricks—these things quicken my gonads—i think they'd quicken the dead.

I'm really not sure what to do. . . .

marc

To: Dr. Martell   SUBJECT: History
  7.1.91

Your writing is graphic, vivid even, but I need to know more about Toni—her background, her family relationships. . . .

Patiently,
Aphra

To: dr zion   SUBJECT: toni
  7.2.91

Toni has a lot to keep out; her vaginismus is more than legitimate: she can't even count the number of men who've tried to get at her, *including her alcoholic father and her brothers!* I have a passion for native americans but they're left only with oases of health in a desert of sickness. The way she was raised, in the hell of l.a., toni should have been a wizened dwarf! How she developed her height, her straight white teeth, her firm cheekbones, is a small miracle, not to mention—i have to be oh-so-careful not to mention—the rest of her, and maybe the sarcoma represents all the evil—the abuse collected and lurking in her body—either now totally removed by the operation or waiting to emerge and destroy her all at once.

She's such an odd mix: part mystic, part impenetrable whore, part vast unexplored intelligence, part nothing at all where her feelings should be. . . . she finished high school and then a classy los angeles madam picked her up, taught her manners, and rented her out at $400.00 an hour in the british escort tradition. . . . she says men paid that much for *oral sex only*—for the right to push her long black hair aside and watch her—that's how she met reilly, who is her keeper now. Reilly is some kind of industrial crocodile with a heart of gold: he pays my fees, he allows her to have a boyfriend (which she doesn't have), he sends money to her mother, and he buys her anything—anything she wants short of major forms of transportation like airplanes and boats—i want to get him to pay his way right out of having a mistress!

So there's no point in doing sex therapy right now; there's no one she wants to sleep with and she doesn't really want to open up to herself, at least physically. . . . the reason she came to a sex therapist rather than an ordinary psychiatrist was that she thought someone in the sex business would understand her better—be less shocked by her—than someone on the outside, which might be true, but she's run into a *naive subject*. I think i need special help. . . .

marc

To: Dr. Martell   Subject: Therapy
    7.2.91

She's probably suffering a depression that will emerge as she talks to you. Women who deny their emotions about having paid sex often suffer severely. Go slowly and gently—be kind and supportive—and as long as we're not doing sex therapy, I'm willing to wait for the next patient.

Agreeably,
Aphra

To: dr zion   Subject: complications
    7.3.91

Something is going on with me—i really need my own psychiatrist and i really can't afford one right now—it's a miserable irony to be in the shrink business and not to be able to afford a good shrink! no one will take you on free, either, or even half price; it's different from other medicine.

These past few days i can't go to sleep at night without thinking about toni. . . . i try to imagine how i'll instruct her sexually once we

deal with her emotional trauma and she meets the right man, but i
know damn well she's too damaged ever to meet the right person
and, besides, the right man is me, or so i think when i'm awake in
the middle of the night. I found myself thinking about how right i
am for her sunday afternoon, too, when i was sitting with my wife
trish and my little daughter patti in our roof garden, and we were
all drinking lemonade, and you could see the blue bay water past
the white pots and red geraniums that line the sky over our parapet.
. . . You see, toni is technically a virgin. I've never made love to a
virgin. . . . i think/i try not to think/i am in a thinking/not thinking
state. . . . if i had her, if she had me, she'd turn out just fine. . . .

I know i won't make love to her; i know i have to get past the
fantasy but, aphra zion, how do you do that? When i practice regular
psychotherapy, the sexual material emerges slowly and i have
plenty of time to get control, but because it started as sex therapy,
all that came out so fast. . . .

communicate soon,
marc

To: Dr. Martell   SUBJECT: You
   7.3.91

When a psychiatrist—no matter how analyzed—begins training
in sex therapy, all sorts of submerged fantasies surface. I'll help you
to deal with them as much as I can, but I'd be much more comfortable doing this face to face.

Warmly,
Aphra

To: dr zion   SUBJECT: return
   7.4.91

I'm coming back to new york next year—trish wants back; she's
spending this year on a long distance quest for the right job, but
even if she stays, there's a good chance—the way things are going
—that i'll leave. (The spirit of independence moves me today.) So
if nothing else, maybe you could listen to me write about toni; it's
important for me to get hold of what could become an obsession,
what is, in fact, already an obsession. . . .

m

To: Dr. Martell   Subject: Exploring Toni
   7.4.91

What makes it so compelling to "get in" to such a difficult place?

Take care,

Aphra

To: dr zion   Subject: re: question
   7.12.91

Sorry about my long absence from e-space . . . and thank you for taking me on with that important, insightful question, thank you very much, but i don't know the answer; i'm too involved in toni even to think about myself. . . . she takes up all the room in my mind, like a channel blocker, stopping other passages. . . . do you know that she reads *books* while she waits for her session? Do you know what she reads, this woman with hardly a high school education? She reads stephen hawking and james gleick, she reads *The Quantum Self,* she reads books on shamanism, religion, existentialism, tantra—her mind is working all the time! No magazines, no pop feminism, no how to do it all in your free time—that *excites* me—you know what trish the harvard business school grad reads? After the financial stuff for work, she reads vogue, vanity fair and decorating books, not to mention what slick surfaced garbajio she flips through at the hairdresser and in airports. . . . toni carries her books around in a little schoolgirl satchel/backpack combo; i like that, i can't help it, i could be pygmalion to that. . . . it's all there! What do you think?

m

To: Dr. Martell   Subject: I think
   7.14.91

I think Toni's closed vagina keeps her keeper out and a lot else besides. It should remain closed until Toni wants to open to someone. So continue to explore your own reactions. And you *must* elicit her feelings, even if they're buried deep.

Aphra

To: dr zion   SUBJECT: re: it's been good
   7.22.91

   I feel like we've had a one-night stand: aphra zion asks the first
of the sphinx's four questions and the traveler disappears. . . . toni
is gone! Zap! Out of sight! She's left for bali. Reilly decided to take
her there for a rest. She says she'd rather stay here and talk about
her misery with me, and she doesn't know why she'd rather tell me
about her misery than go to bali, but reilly wants to give her a good
rest—he thinks it will keep her cancer away—a couple of *weeks!*
The vaginismus is unimportant to him; he'd just as soon she stayed
closed. Reilly's pretty smart, i think: this may be his way of defeating
her therapy to keep her from getting away from him. . . . anyway,
she's flown and here i am yet again without a new patient, sex or
otherwise. She promises to come back—i think she will—but once
fringe characters disappear, they're usually gone forever. . . .
   What now? You know, i don't express my gratitude often enough
—i always had a special connection to you—i think you felt it for
me, too. . . . i'm really sorry i'm not back in new york, training in
your presence, with proper patients; i've even had some fantasies
of lunches and gallery grazing with you—next year—

                                                     yours,
                                                     m

To: Dr. Martell   SUBJECT: Exploration
   7.25.91

   Even if Toni flees treatment, you should continue to explore
yourself in relation to her. If she returns, you'll be prepared, and if
she doesn't, you'll bring more experience to your other cases. . . .
   Why do you need to conquer resistant spaces? You've had
enough therapy to know where to look for answers. . . .

                                                     Aphra

To: dr zion   SUBJECT: you
   7.28.91

   I wish i were back in new york, and i also wish i could be your
patient right now, but before we go much further, we should
change our names—for privacy—so take a look at the initial set-up
and you'll see where you can enter up to 5 names above your real

one. I'm going to be e-man from now on, electric, neither he-man nor she-man. . . . What about you?

marc

To: E-man   SUBJECT: Names
  7.28.91

I tried Godot but I couldn't be anyone except Godot15. There were fourteen others. So I chose Go-dot. It's enough like Godot to make me feel invisible.

A.

To: go-dot   SUBJECT: dotty
  7.28.91

If you mean go-dot, as in moving pixels, the dots that make up the picture, right on!

m

To: E-man   SUBJECT: Dots
  7.28.91

That's what I mean. Write on.

Go

To: go-dot   SUBJECT: 1st question
  8.11.91

Why do i have to get in? I've thought about this for two weeks now (sorry about the hiatus, but i know your first priority isn't thinking about me). I've tried to remember what went on in my therapy, which was once a week for two years, ten years ago, but nothing much emerged from that except my divorce from my first wife.

My therapist did say i had a compulsion to rescue people— fantasies that were either a result of wanting to save my mother from my father's neglect or of wanting to bring back my older brother, who died in an accident when i was three. . . . my therapist also tried to imply that i had a lot of guilt because i ambivalently wanted my brother gone, but how could you know that if you are three years old and what you remember (is it all they ever talked about?) is a great happy light, bright blond curls and radiant blue eyes over the cribtop, a mouth smiling with its small, perfect teeth. . . . the rest is lost. . . . i can't remember whatever it is, and whenever i try to contemplate my past right now, i wind up in my mental bed with toni; she still preoccupies me.

And then, whenever i'm sitting and looking out on the bay and thinking, my wife trish bombs in and asks what the hell am i doing when at *least* i could be watering the plants or taking our daughter patti for a walk in the stroller or *something* since i don't seem to be earning money anymore and it's up to her to support the family these days.

And i go into the shouting litany about how i had a *perfectly fine practice* in the city, but she needed to make a lateral move out west for a year because it looked like the eastern office of her company was falling apart—illegally hogging the bond market—so here we are. I follow her like a good twentieth century man, and now i'm the *goddam doormat* for someone else's greed and stupidity.

When i think about it, i married her because i need a strong, tough, aggressive, bright (more than bright) woman, and i saw trish as ms bessemer steel, taking on the whole male financial establishment and coming up roses. . . . she far outdid the old diana riggs in my fantasy. . . . i used to imagine that the world could perform all sorts of aberrational acts on her and she'd come out unscathed, lively, tough and feisty, the *INDESTRUCTIBLE WOMAN.* She liked playing it tough, too. My fantasy didn't create her out of entirely whole cloth.

But now she's everything i never wanted in a wife: she whines, she haggles, she nags; she says I don't understand why you don't . . . and you never . . . and I can't stand it when you . . . she doles out money as if i'm pawning my services; she has no time for me and blames me for having too much time and no time for her—she has programs and schedules—i became a psychiatrist so i could arrange my own time (within limits), but she has it all laid out for me. Dr z, is it productive for me to be telling you all this?

e-man

To: E-man   SUBJECT: You
8.13.91

Why did Trish turn suddenly from all-good mother/father to all-bad mother/father? What made you see her as depriving? Why do you need an indestructible, infinitely nurturant parent as a fantasied lover? Were your own parents so fragile, distant, miserly? Must you keep testing?

Go-dot

To: go-dot   Subject: sorry
     8.18.91

I know i'm shirking; i'm being a terrible supervisee/patient(?), but don't you have to ventilate before you can think, before you can say why and how anything at all happened? Yes, my mother was fragile, my father was distant and miserly, you hit it with your first shot, but i don't want to think about them.

I'm feeling such intense pain, i can hardly function; i feel as though everything is being torn from me. I have an image of myself starving to death in hell and that's pretty close to reality because trish has stopped nurturing me in every conceivable way: most of all, with *food.* I wouldn't mind if she stopped cooking as a statement, a stand for equality. . . . even though i'm ten or fifteen years younger than you are, i was brought up in a tradition of women serving men (it's hard to erase those early years), but i'm willing—eager—begging to discard my shards of machismo!

Trish has decided not to cook just for spite, she's retaliating—patricia the patrician—starving me because i'm not bringing home money, that's all the woman is about: *money!* It's her life's work: *MONEY*!!! And she's perverse; she says: what's the use of cooking all your vegetarian slush, which isn't even edible unless it's fresh out of the wok, when i can't even figure out what time you're coming home?

Well, i don't come home at any one time and i've been taking any patients i can get, any time they want to see me because i can't afford to be selective: i'll take anyone, any time between seven in the morning and ten at night; if trish wants me to make money, i can't do it on her investment banker hours. (I know investment bankers work hard, but she's incredibly efficient: gets out no later than four every afternoon!)

As earth mother, trish has turned into an underground relic—she even burns the tofu—it takes real work to burn tofu. . . . i can't tell you how strong feeding is for me; nurturing is important to my genes, i think: i'm an anthropological artifact from when women did the gathering and men went out to hunt.

She's hurting me, she's hurting us, she's on a rampage. . . . Are you there? Do you read me? What do you think?

e

To: E-man   SUBJECT: Yes. . . .
  8.18.91

If you were my patient, what I would say now is "M-hm." But compared to that soft sound, the written version seems desolately inadequate. I wish there were a cipher that could deliver my feeling to you. . . .

On the other hand, I have some gender bias about your attitude. Should Trish have dinner waiting, even though you don't give her clear signals about what time you'll be home? And why must she cook? You have some strong menu ideas of your own. Act on them? Or are you too angry? Or is that too simplistic a question?

Go-dot

To: go-dot   SUBJECT: anger
  8.18.91

How did you guess? I'm mad, as in incensed—pissed off! She's brutal. I don't even exist for trish anymore—she must think she lives alone, the way she never does a dish, never straightens the futon or hangs up her clothes or sorts out her necklaces or collects her dirty pantyhose, not to mention sweeping the floor or cleaning the toilet or changing patti.

Sure, a worker comes in once a week to do the heavy stuff, but i'm talking about simple neatness; trish says she's no patrician—far from it—she reminds me she's from appalachia, white trash with an anomalously great brain that i used to admire; i used to be proud that she wasn't much good at the middle-class ethic, which is true. She and her sisters lived in a trailer with their slovenly mother, all of them sitting there in the old black and white pictures, poking at the ground for vegetables and waiting for the chicken to lay an egg not too far from the front door. . . . they didn't know about putting things away; they didn't have anything to put away.

But trish was a star at school, the teacher took an interest in her genius, she went to college on scholarship, but when she gets stubborn she goes back to her old ways, she knows how to lay it on me.

Why am i being punished? What have i done to deserve being hungry and neglected in my own home?

marc

To: E-man   Subject: M-hm. . . .
  8.18.91

Go on. . . .

A.

To: E-man   Subject: Hm. . . .
  8.31.91

Hm? I didn't hear from you. Did I hear from you? Did I miss you? It's been 13 days, 8 hours, 23 minutes and 4 seconds since your last message according to the Compu-Mail electronic timer. (There are three clocks on my desk and one on the wall. Lately I've taken to wearing an old pocket watch as a necklace pendant, in addition to my Swatch. Not that all these timepieces mean I'm particularly prompt. They're more to help me not to forget the time, which I'm always losing.) Which leads me, by some mysterious indirection, to suggest that you and Trish consider marital therapy. Have you thought about it?

Flustered,
Go

To: go-dot   Subject: Hm, marriage. . . .
  9.1.91

FYI we had pastoral counseling last year for four months. Trish couldn't stand the counselor; she felt his technique (or his mind) was so slow-moving that by the time we graduated from therapy we'd go directly to heaven, and after no miracle had happened in three sessions, she wanted out. . . . besides, she didn't like being trapped in "my" territory (she thought the counselor kowtowed to me because i'm a psychiatrist. . . . they had a fight over that and the therapist "suggested" we look elsewhere for help); now she thinks therapy's a crock—won't go near it.

And as far as you and time are concerned, i had a dream that left me in such a rage at you that when i woke up i couldn't even write to you even though i knew that you didn't deserve my anger, but i couldn't seem to get free of it.

Through a keyhole i could see you lying in a bed. You were apparently sleeping; your back was toward me and your body was much rounder and fuller than i'd thought it was. The door was locked and i was so enraged that i couldn't "get in," i wanted to break the door down with my shoulder, but you kept sleeping and sleeping and sleeping. . . .

That's all there was to it. You see, when my conscious mind can't work on a problem, my unconscious takes over. I want to be a good supervisee/patient/friend, whatever i was, am, will be—i don't want to stop—i'll go into therapy if i can convince trish, but it's probably hopeless—the marriage may be hopeless—do you interpret dreams, herr doctor?

> cheers,
> marc

To: E-man   SUBJECT: Dreams
  9.1.91

I'm keeping you out and I'm asleep at the job. But my guess is that I'm not the original sleeper. Who is she?

> Aphra

To: go-dot   SUBJECT: toni
  9.11.91

My associations have had to hold for another day. . . . toni returned from bali and she actually made an appointment to see me!! When she came she looked worn, quite depressed, not rested at all. Bali had a negative effect on her: when she started to talk she became agitated, she couldn't sit still. I asked her if she could define anything that was wrong. She hesitated as if i would think she was crazy and then she told me that in bali she thought she had had a ghostly visitation, a premonition of death while she and reilly were walking in the malay bamboo. . . . although she was brought up on the edge of l.a. in a tin hovel that makes trish's appalachian shack sound like a mansion, when she was a child she spent summers with her grandparents on a navajo reservation and picked up their beliefs, which still affect her emotionally—still claim her superstitious allegiance from time to time—even though she doesn't accept them intellectually. . . . her grandmother used to tell her stories about *chindi* and holy people and witches. . . . now she suspects that the evil in some dead person is seeking her out and she wants me to cure her of the shadow that came to her in the night in bali, the tiger behind the flowers. You see, the ancestors did everything right because they were afraid that making a mistake might cost them their lives, and toni feels that she has gone too far, much too far, off the Way.

She may be decompensating; the strain may be too much for her. i'm thinking about some prozac, but i'm also thinking that possibly she might respond to a shaman?

e

To: E-man   Subject: Depression
    9.12.91

I'd be happier with Prozac first. She might be schizophrenic, but I suspect not. And if she hasn't been exposed to Indian ritual beyond the hogans of her childhood, all that rattling about, or whatever shamans do, might scare her. . . .

Go-dot

To: go-dot   Subject: treatment
    9.13.91

No emergency! I think toni's perfectly rational given her origins, lack of formal socialization, and the intense navajo fear of death, so i'd like to see if she comes around to normal in a couple of weeks without any meds. Besides, shamans aren't available by prescription at the neighborhood pharmacy.

The major issue at the moment isn't toni's state of mind; it's what she's doing to me!!! She sits in the chair across from me: she wears long black boots with a couple of inches of thigh showing where her hipbones ought to be; she wears this white shirt that ties at the waist but i don't know why she bothers to tie it, all the buttons are open, there's nothing but bare breast underneath. . . . add gold hoop earrings and long black lashes and you've got the picture. . . . it's all i can do to sit still, given what you call my "vulnerability," but i'm not asking about how to handle my sexual feelings; i'm a grown-up boy, i know how to keep it all under wraps. I'm asking about why i can't get my *mind* off having sex with her?

While it's true that she's everything i ever fantasized, every woman i've ever pinned up on my mental bulletin board, i should still be able to go beyond that. In a couple of months, or sooner, or later, she could start to lose weight, lose her appetite, become cachectic and jaundiced; her belly could fill with fluid as she dies one of the more outrageous deaths, and all I can think of is penetrating the barrier, soothing, smoothing, gentling my way in. . . . as a catholic, even as a catholic turned agnostic, i should be flaying myself with switches . . . and then i'm imagining her breasts again. . . .

yours,
m

Endemann

2

1990

PRIVATE FILE: Do not send.

To: Marc Martell

Subject: SEX AND MORTALITY

When I sit in my office with patients, I say very little but I hear every word. Afterward, alone, I recreate their monologues. I become them; they become part of me. I absorb their mannerisms and their eccentricities. It helps me to understand them and to make interpretations later.

I don't know how to respond to your letters. They're so angry, so open, they make me want to break through my normal restraints and write about myself the same way. Usually, when a patient talks to me, I nod and I empathize, but what can I do in reaction to print?

It's always been easier for me to write about myself than to talk, except with my first husband, Harry. We could really carry on, gossiping, laughing, discussing life, death, the family. But I ruined that—or he did—I still don't understand why it happened. And now there's Elia. We've been married almost ten years. Not introspecting was the undefined pact of our marriage. I was attracted by his silence, reassured by his self-sufficiency. I should have known better, but I didn't. Most people seem surprised when they hear Elia is my second husband. It's as if I've let them down—violated their impression, tarnished the vision they have of me as someone too aware of the subtle nuances of romantic relationships to make such a mistake.

Maybe I'll never be able to share intimacy with anyone but Harry, except in writing to an anonymous world. I wish you could be the intermediary—the distant epistolary friend who brings me out—but it wouldn't be right for me to become the focus of our relationship. If I'm supposed to be supervising you, I can't write about myself to you. I bind myself in the role of encouraging others to speak spontaneously while I contain myself.

My mother taught me how to be an audience. She forced me to learn. I'm sure that's why—except with Harry—I've been the listener. Writing is my affirmation of life. Your E-mail provokes me to make associations to what you say. I want to record for you the voices I've heard, to tell you the stories of the perverse and curious ways people—we—search for love. I can't send them to you yet, but I'll write and hoard my words until I'm free to share.

At the moment, I'm thinking of death and sex because your patient Toni could die a virgin unless you become her lover. Is an act of love the end of therapy? When is it proper for a therapist to touch, to breach the boundaries? When my patient Abel Endemann was dying, I knew.

Endemann's nurse phoned my office to tell me that he would appreciate a house call as soon as possible. I had debated when to visit him. If I paid the call too early, I would have to see him again and perhaps even a third time. That would be awkward and hard on him. On the other hand, I didn't want to wait until he was comatose. When a person is dying, you don't want to say goodbye too often, but it's well to get to the bedside in time to say farewell to a fully conscious human being. As always, Endemann had treated me impeccably by having his nurse call at the right moment.

Although they only knew me by my name as their father's psychiatrist, I could recognize Endemann's children as they sat in exhausted and impatient grief in the living room. Four sons and a daughter by his second wife, all dark-haired, strong, gentle, attractive, talented people in their late teens and early twenties, all looking so much like Endemann that there was no question about the identity of the sixth person, his lover, who was his children's age but blond and slight. Not one of his four divorced wives was there.

The nurse nodded toward the bedroom door. I approached it and Endemann's lover, Nicole, followed me in. "He will understand you and be able to answer you if you climb on the bed next to him," she said in her soft French accent. "He says all the seats are filled and you have to get on the stage to see the play." Smiling and shrugging faintly, she backed out of the bedroom and closed the door firmly.

Endemann was lying curled up on his side in a huge king-sized bed. He was darkly jaundiced, skeletally thin beneath silk pajamas, and apparently asleep. Only a few weeks ago his flesh had been bright, his thoughts active, his paisley ascot provocatively jaunty. The room was dimly lit by frosted art nouveau wall sconces that emitted a mauve light from their delicate lily shapes, as though to provide the right funereal setting. Several long columns seemed to be obelisks but soon were identifiable as stacked amplifiers, tape decks, CD players, turntables, speakers of all sizes.

I took off my shoes and climbed onto the bed. The gray silk coverlet was soft under my stockings. I patted Endemann's most prominent bone, his hip, protruding at an angle. "Hi," I said.

"You," he whispered. "The lady doctor."

"Me," I said. "Hi."

"Listen—" He lifted his head a little, urgently. "I want to tell you. There's so much more music to hear. I won't have time. Listen to it for me. Even Hindemith. Even Wagner."

"I promise. Even Cole Porter again."

He dropped his head back on the pillow and sighed. "Another thing."

"What's that?"

"Hold me close."

I had never touched him before except to shake hands. He was lying sideways again. I moved next to him, spoon fashion. "You always need an arm around you, don't you?"

"Good." He laughed. "You're analyzing. Therefore I'm still alive. . . . Look, shrink, listen. I want to do it once more."

"Do what?"

"Do what, she wants to know. Make love. Fuck. Screw. That's what I want to do. Once more."

"I know."

"She knows." He closed his eyes in a mixture of exasperation and the need to rest from the exertion. "Doctor, shrink, witch, can you help me to do it once more? One more time?"

I stroked his shoulder and his waist, down the protruding hip. We had been through all the devices that had helped him to make love to Nicole: the penile injections, the bandings, the vacuum pump. Even if he had the energy, there was nothing that would work anymore. But though Endemann might accept his mental and cardiac cessation, he would never accept his sexual death, which was synonymous with the extinction of his spirit.

"I've come to say good-bye," I said. "You invited me."

He turned in the bed and hugged me frontally. His breath was fishy and musty with the smell of his failing liver—fetor hepaticus —and his body trembled coarsely, down to his knees. "God, small g god, e e cummings, don't forget cummings. . . . Do you need anything, doc? Do you need any money?"

Endemann was the president of an international agency that represented concert artists. He might have been rich if he hadn't disposed of his assets to his wives. When he first consulted me, he had already done his multiple marrying and divorcing. He believed in total monogamy without infidelity. His principles carried a high price. What he had wanted from me was not emotional salvation but rather the restoration of his potency, the loss of which he thought was connected with his psyche. Unhappily, his psyche had little to do with the problem. The medical workup showed first that he had diabetes, a frequent cause of impotence. Soon after, we found a bowel cancer that had already metastasized to his liver. Given the choice of chemotherapy that would allow him a year of pleasant life with some possibility of tumor regression, and chemotherapy that would destroy his daily enjoyment though it might have an increased effect on the cancer, he had chosen the former. The year was up.

"I'm okay," I said. "No money problems."

"Are you crazy?" He sat up, the strength flowing back into his body, as if my holding him had infused a new energy. "All women have problems. They all need money."

"We've been over that. You pick women who resemble your mother."

"Bitch." He searched his pajama shirt pockets, then pointed to his cigarettes on a night table. Still trembling slightly, he lit one. "She needed money from every man she met. And she brought them all home, six husbands, fifty lovers, twenty gigolos, every last one." Endemann was most alive when he was flagellating his mother.

"On second thought, you could change your will," I said. "A couple of million would help."

"I knew it. You're all alike. But it's too late. The estate people have already gone to bed." He shifted his weight and sat cross-legged; his toenails were dry, decayed, deformed into claws, large and small. "Doctor, tell me this. Have I been monogamous because I hated my mother?"

"Interesting thought."

"I really hurt women every time I leave. I kill them."

"Maybe so."

"My second wife sent me a letter. She said when I left I shot her heart dead. She could never love again."

"Could be." I reached out and pressed a fingertip against the largest clawed nail. "Endemann, we've been over that, too. You had five siblings, but you wanted to be the only one. Your mother should have worked harder to let you know that you were the only source, the only one."

"But I wasn't."

"We all have to feel that we are."

He stubbed his cigarette out in the ashtray I had quickly reached for, coughed thickly, then covered himself with the gray comforter. "Lady. Priest. I don't want your sweet extreme unction."

"Sorry. So you're guilty. Go to hell."

"Hold me again."

I put my arm on his waist. He was very tired. His body seemed to collapse from within. He coughed again and gestured for me to put my ear close to his mouth so that I could hear him. "Is it too late for me to get an implant, doc? One of those things that make it hard forever?"

I brushed the still-thick gray hair with my hand. The back of his head was the only part of him that looked fifty-six years old. "I'll talk to the surgeon," I said. "Meanwhile, I have to say good-bye. You need some sleep."

He turned on his back as I got off the bed. His eyeballs protruded under closed lids; his unshaven cheeks were sunken; his white teeth shone beneath parched, parted lips. He lifted a hand for me to take. "Bye, doc. I love you. Thanks for coming."

I said, "I love you, too, Endemann."

When I called the next day, the nurse told me he was in a coma. A week later, Abel Endemann was dead. I saw it in the *Times*.

PART TWO

BOYS OR GIRLS

Baby Girl

To: go-dot   Subject: beginnings . . .
     9.18.91

Nothing so depressing as a new practice with all new patients!
Starting fresh is rough trade, dr z, rough trade! Everyone brings you
a state of emergency! Can you comprehend what it's like to listen
to so many people's crises one after the other? At least when you're
in practice a couple of years, or even a couple of months, there's a
spread: some patients are better and some are improving, but when
they're all in hell at the same time, the purgatory is unimaginable.
. . . they get their money's worth out of my gut; it eats holes in my
belly to sit still and empathize until either the medication works or
they've talked themselves out— :-(—sad face, sideways.
Maybe that's why i need to play in cyberspace so much these

days; i need an out from all the crazies. The price of the habit is going up: $200 a month to play games and talk to the new breed of on-liners—pretty soon i'll be ordering my supper from the set—am considering drugs, maybe i'll be a hippie in my old age; after all, i'm a californian now, or maybe virtual reality is the answer—tripping without chemicals—but are they at least going to give us a good trip? No way! I read that for a buck we'll be able to rent 4-D helmets at club dv8 and get chased by a pterodactyl and a bunch of killers. Hey zion, what kind of world would a zen monk create? I'm going there.

Tell me, what do you do when the pack is after you to fix them up this minute, this instant, relieve them of their pain? But of course in your practice, there aren't any emergencies; everyone's had their sexual problem for at least a couple of weeks before coming to you, and sex isn't a matter of life and death exactly. . . .

m

To: E-man   SUBJECT: Wrong
    9.22.91

Sex isn't the real reason most people come to see me. Usually they're depressed, they're angry at each other, they're fighting. One of them thinks that if the sex were better, they'd be fine! As if I could press a button to improve people's lives so they'd want to have sex.

I'm looking forward to more advanced forms of virtual reality, too. I'd get myself chased by pterodactyls any day. Incidentally, I have a patient who's having an interoffice love affair on computer: she and her boyfriend don't let on that they even know each other. They met on an electronic memo board.

How's Toni? Any progress?

Go-dot

To: go-dot   SUBJECT: ah yes. . . .
    9.25.91

How's toni? Well, she's stopped wearing the pin-up outfit, at least on a regular basis, which wasn't the way i'd expected she'd progress, but it could be construed as a removal in the right direction.

... and without her makeup, her skin is pale, she has the faintest touch of acne; in jeans and a faded shirt she could be a student or any kid, just hanging out. ... of course, when she dresses, her "day-time" wardrobe is a piece of work—reilly goes on buying sprees —romeo gigli, fendi, chanel; he buys, she wears (or returns the stuff and pockets the money). ... sometimes she looks like the victim of a paris peep show and sometimes she looks as though she just stepped off the yacht and into the limousine; most of the time she's sexy but not enough to draw blood, until I think about her later. ...

As for her mind, it's working away in the direct style of a woman who's learned to hide her intelligence by appearing reductionist: she says How can I know what I want to do with the rest of my life unless I know what I believe about death? (Which is really the point, isn't it? How do you know what road to take unless you have some notion of the destination?)

I'm fascinated by the way she gets to the core of the cosmic questions: she wants to decide whether or not to follow the navajo way. ... even if it's her blood, she doesn't necessarily have to be-lieve, and since we're both in the same theological boat, i suggested she do some research, say, on comparative religion, a job i should have done when my parents were fighting over whether or not i should be bar mitzvah (my father's only—and half-hearted—link to family feeling is jewish ritual; my mother's catholicism is part of her life, like her cooking) and i decided, on no evidence whatso-ever, that i was nothing. ...

Thus, ergo, today we took a tour through the Blue Mosque in Istanbul, the Yemenite Synagogue in Jerusalem, a Zen monastery in Kyoto, and other interesting places in caps on a tape she brought to the session for the start of our psychoreligious phase. Religion has to appeal to me aesthetically first, she said. If the art's no good, the logic won't help; for me, seeing is believing.

I get so absorbed, she's always the one who has to tell me when the session is over. I made her my last patient just in case i got up the nerve to walk out with her, but she always leaves in a hurry to be at the phone for reilly who calls her five, sometimes six times a day when he's out of town. ... so after she rushes out today, after this very different sort of session, i force myself to go directly home, up to the top of the hill, up the antique wood-paneled stairs, and there on the top landing, her face lit by the electrified gaslight fixtures, stands trish, waiting for me.

Do you think she's waiting to throw her arms around me, to say hello, and happily? Do you think her face is flushed with joy to see me? Is she wiping a hand on her apron? Do you think the fluffy strands of blond hair are loose at her nape because she's been near an oven, or a stove, or even a goddam microwave with a slimlife dinner in it?

Right! You've got it, you know the source of the riddle, the question all humanity is trying to answer: why is trish in a fury? Answer: i'm *LATE* and i haven't brought home any *milk* for patti or even a *crust of bread* for anyone's dinner. Trish is smoking a cigarette, but never mind, she's going out alone for chinese food and i can stay home with patti, which is captain's orders for me, just fine, thank you very much sir/madam.

She keeps telling me *i'm to blame* for her temper, for her constant chronic rage, for all the things she does and doesn't do to irritate me—for instance, she's stopped paying the bills—but i can't deal with that right now. She says that if she were a sexually satisfied woman, life would be very much more peaceful; she might even boil some pasta now and then. Not that i'm not capable of sex: i'm quite sure i could keep three women happy all night and through the morning, too, and *i don't think a pot of pasta makes it as a trade-off for my sort of passion*. . . .

marc

To: E-man   SUBJECT: Passion?
  9.25.91

Question: What *is* your sort of passion?

Aphra

To: go-dot   SUBJECT: triple threat
  9.26.91

"My sort of passion" obviously has to wait for its mate because i stopped having sex with trish in her 6th month of pregnancy. . . . i'm not sure what demon took me on, but i didn't want to do it— my erection was there, i wasn't impotent, i simply didn't want to use it—i didn't want her to have me, i didn't want trish and my daughter to have me.

You see, i hadn't wanted to have sex for the past three months as well, ever since i knew from the amnio that the baby was going to be a girl.

I know it's politically incorrect not to want a girl in this day and age; more than that, it's a crime against humanity: girls are as good as boys, girls are better than boys, girls and boys are the same, boys started out in embryo as girls, boys are girls with certain malformations owing to the unfortunate necessity for seed. . . . it's a social/cultural/personal/family tragedy that i had these feelings, but i did. I wanted a boy. More than merely wanting a boy, i didn't want a girl. I actually did not want a high-pitched female child around the house. I did not want dolls in the toy chest. I wanted blocks and bats and trains and balls! You can tell me all you like about how what children play with isn't built into the genes, but i've seen it, in child psych i saw it: some mothers wouldn't let their girls play with dolls—then all they wanted was dolls—they could never be persuaded about dump trucks.

And more than not wanting a girl, i didn't want to make love to trish with a girl in her. . . . i've never explained all this clearly to trish—just told her it was something about her being pregnant, not about her, herself, that brought me down, which explanation sent her off on a series of wild analytic attacks on my manhood: *was i so 19th century that i still had a madonna complex, was i someone who couldn't fuck a mother figure, had she married a mama's boy in a man's beard, or was i just plain afraid of the responsibility of being a father?*

Well, maybe she was right about all of the above, but what use was knowing it to how i felt? Sure i was afraid i couldn't be a good father. . . . what psychiatrist in the history of the world has ever been a good father? We're all shrunk up, contracted—that's why we go into the profession—we know what it feels like to be damaged, so we try to help our patients live the ideal life we never did, or if our goals are not so misguided as that, at least we try to pick up the pieces of the wreckage other people left behind; that doesn't qualify us to be financially, morally, socially and physically responsible for whole new children. . . . all we're accustomed to is damaged goods, seconds, rejects like ourselves. . . . chances are that's what we'll raise, so i didn't have any utopian hopes about my abilities as a parent being any greater than the unwashed norm, but i tell you i couldn't have sex with my wife with that little girl fetus inside her, that's all there was to it, and now that the baby's out, so to speak, i'm still not the least bit interested in trish sexually or any other way, besides probably ruining patti's life by neglect. . . .

So what do you think about toni?

e

To: E-man   SUBJECT: Think?
    10.3.91

I have to spend some time digesting what you've told me about your relationship with Trish. I'm trying to figure out the best way to react helpfully. . . . I'm not witholding. . . .

What you're doing with Toni sounds benign enough, though ideally she should be going to school, or adult classes, or socializing. Does she have any friends?

Do you?

Aphra

To: go-dot   SUBJECT: friends?
    10.3.91

No, toni has no friends except for a few professionals who keep in touch from time to time in case she needs "work" or to see if she has any work for them, and what few so-called friends i had i left back east—the holidays were empty—as far as friends are concerned, san fran is the namibian desert with one lone baobab tree, a vulture circling overhead, and no more water (toni and i have been looking at some south african landscapes and practices). . . . no i have no new friends.

Of course, when i couldn't sleep with trish anymore i told her i still wanted to be her friend and she looked at me as though i'd just told her not to believe in the virgin mary (trish is a devout feminist marian catholic). We can't be just friends, she said, we're husband and wife, we're lovers, we're bound to each other in God, *HOW DARE YOU?* and she started to cry as though i were on the cross and she was kneeling at my feet sharing my sufferings. . . . Dear Mary in heaven, she said, what is your pain? Tell me your pain. . . . and her neck muscles stretched her cheeks into gray hollows of devotion where i used to say i wanted to light candles when we were making love. . . . What are you doing to yourself? What are you doing to us? The tears ran down her cheeks to her chest, wetting her camisole; she reached out to clutch my pajama top as though it were some sacred relic, kissing it, and i disengaged her hand from my shirt, kept her at a distance: Oh my God, I love you, Marc, I love you more than I love life, Mary or Patti, I need you, I need you inside me, I need our love, our worship together, our divinity together, Marc, please, please come back, please make love to me! Why did you take yourself away? Who took you away from me?

Memory

AGE 5

1942

To: E-man   SUBJECT: BOYS OR GIRLS

When I told my psychiatrist that my parents were disappointed at my being born a girl, he minimized my concerns. Most people wanted a boy first, he said. Primogeniture, heir to the business, keep up the family name. Nothing unusual. He was wrong. Harry spent years trying to make me feel secure as a woman. He'd ask me did I know how beautiful I was? His fingertips would float over my cheekbones. He insisted I wear my hair pinned up so he could adore the naked line of my neck. He'd compliment me until I felt I'd had too much dessert, but yet I believed him; he did it so often because I needed it so much. In return, I told him how much I loved to study his expressions, especially his green eyes that seemed to cry with laughter.

But Harry hasn't told me how much he loves me for a long time. Instead of being embarrassed by the extravagance of his delight in my femininity, I remember my childhood: how difficult it was for me to understand that I was a girl. That's why I'm so disturbed by your withdrawal from Trish. I'm not "clear," free of personal confusions. How could you reject your wife and the female in her womb? Something dreadful must have happened to you early in your life, something unspeakable.

And you're driven by rage, which makes my attraction to you hard for me to understand. Why am I so interested in knowing all about you? And why do I want you to be familiar with the deepest memories of my life? Do I need to connect to someone so badly that I want *your* warmth and acceptance, *your* support, *your* help to be me?

I have to be so careful, so guarded not to ask that of you. But if I were to ask it, I'd send you this recollection from my childhood. My memories of the unlikely people who helped me are the happiest, the strangest and the saddest.

Every afternoon at 4:00 P.M., Randy Lee visited Igor Youstavich, the baker. I observed the visits because Igor's room adjoined the family quarters in the big bungalow behind the white stucco main buildings of my parents' hotel.

In the summer of 1942, these two buildings, covering an area of half a city block, dominated the green Catskill hills near the clear Neversink River in brazen, outrageous, gluttonous splendor, at least externally. Inside, a shabby, mismatched disorder prevailed, even then when the establishment was relatively new. One hundred miles away, New York City supplied the guests, boisterous middle-class families out of the ghetto long enough to afford vacation service rather than self-care in cottage colonies; families arrogant with having survived persecution and the Great Depression; families to whom love and food were still synonymous. They did not take survival for granted. Because the guests came and went—locusts eating, ravaging, passing on—I rarely attached to them. The people I knew by name were on the staff: the chef, the baker, the waiters and busboys, the counselors. I knew Igor the baker best that year because his room was so close to ours.

Looking freshly bathed, smelling sweet, wearing fluffy high-heeled slippers, an iridescent headband and a satin robe that revealed the muscular shadows in her haunches, Randy Lee knocked on Igor's door. Her outfit puzzled me because during the rest of the day Randy Lee dressed as a man, in a white shirt, black bow tie and black waiter's trousers. But at 4:00 P.M., visiting Igor, Randy turned into a woman: petite, black, sinuous, frothy, lacy, mincing, shining and heavily made up. I watched the two of them from my post on the stairs of the bungalow porch. I was five years old and I thought I was too small to be noticed.

Igor, in a clean white T-shirt and white trousers, without flour on his hands, without his stained white apron, answered the knock. When the door opened, Randy Lee placed her delicate black hand with its long red fingernails and many gold rings low on Igor's considerable belly. He put both his hands around Randy Lee's bottom and they moved inside together as he kicked the door shut.

Once they were in, I waited and amused myself by letting my head fall back so that I could watch the wasps disappear into their combs on the porch rafters. Their whine mingled with the steady buzz of the bees in the brown centers of the great sunflowers that grew to porch height beyond the balustrade. Eventually, above the buzzing, I could hear grunts and screams coming from behind Igor's door. These were mingled, too, with the sounds of my baby brother's cry for his afternoon bottle. When the grunting and screaming subsided to moaning and sighing, I wandered back into the family bedroom to see if my new brother had finished his bottle.

The baby lay contented and naked in his crib in the large, airy room that also held our three beds, an armoire and a bureau. The floor was steeply slanted, so that when the baby lay at a certain angle, a long yellow arc of fluid could emerge, without wetting the mattress, from that fountainhead on my brother's body that I identified as his "peeper." Sometimes the stream wet me. Most of the time it made a puddle on the floor. Yet my brother's penis, which could create this magnificent golden rainbow, looked like nothing more than a pitted cocktail olive, surrounded by a little doughnut of flesh—not much, but slightly more apparatus than I possessed.

I remember frequently asking my Aunt Janet, who was also my nanny while my parents worked, whether having a peeper meant that a person was a boy. She always answered my question the same elusive way: "Somebody ought to tell you about the birds and the bees."

"Is a peeper what makes a girl or a boy, or is it clothes?" I insisted.

"You'll have to ask your mother that question." Her tone was angry, disapproving. "I don't want to interfere with what's not my business."

Her tight metal curlers, which seemed to strain what was left of her thinning gray hair, and her long pink corset, a cage of stays, made me fairly sure that Aunt Janet was female. Women's clothes were cruel. And she never wore pants to work the way Randy did.

I wore pants—overalls—all the time. And just the day before, at the Italian barber's, my hair had been cut short as a boy's, as usual. I enjoyed the sensation of the clipper when Giorgio cleaned my neck, the smell of the talcum powder, and the feeling of accomplishment when he shook out the blue-and-white-striped protective drape. The clumps of dark hair that fell to the floor were satisfying in their density. "No perfume," my mother instructed when he reached for the bottle of lavender water.

"Get out there and hit a homer," Giorgio joked, slapping my thin back as I climbed off the plank that crossed the arms of the barber's chair and served as my seat. I showed him my puny arm muscle. "Cute kid," he said. "How many years he got?"

"He's not a boy," my mother said. "He's a girl."

"Is that so?" The barber jutted his lower lip. "So why you cut the hair like a boy?"

"It's a habit." My mother brushed a few loose hairs off my shoulder. "She was born wrong. She wasn't a boy. So I started to dress her like one. It's a habit."

The barber looked deeply at me, his old face creased with concern. "A girl is good. Why you make her a boy?"

"You should understand," my mother protested. "You're Italian. Her father wouldn't speak to me for two years because he wanted me to give him a son. So she wears pants. So she looks like a son."

That afternoon, when Randy Lee finished with Igor, I was waiting on the porch. She (he?) looked tired and smelled sweaty.

"Randy Lee?" I said.

"Yes, honey?" She stopped, striking an exotic pose on the porch rail.

"Is a peeper what makes a girl or a boy, or is it clothes?"

She collapsed on the plank bench near the wooden railing as if I had asked her the funniest question in the world. "A peeper?"

I touched my crotch to help her understand what I meant.

"O-o-o-h!" She nodded. "A peepee."

"I call it a peeper because it pees and it peeps out."

She laughed outright. "Where'd you see one of those?"

"On my brother."

"That's right, you have a baby brother."

"Is he a boy because he can pee like a fountain, or because he doesn't wear dresses?"

Randy Lee shook her head. "Why ask me?"

"Because sometimes you wear pants and sometimes you wear skirts. So you must know."

She stayed silent for so long that I was afraid she wouldn't answer, like everyone else. Finally she said the magic words. "Boys have peepers. Girls don't. Clothes don't make any difference."

"Are you sure? I mean, can a girl be a boy with a cut-off peeper?"

"Where'd you get that idea?"

"My mom says I was born wrong."

Randy Lee put her arm around me and gave me a hug. "Nobody cut it off, honey. It's clear as day you're a true girl-child, all the way."

The relief traveled down my body. "I'm glad I'm a girl. But if I'm a girl, what are you?"

Randy Lee tried to explain: "I like to dress up in women's clothes. It don't hurt anyone. But I'm a man, no mistake."

It was beginning to seem simpler. "There's one more thing."

"What's that?"

"Please, could I wear one of your dresses—please? I won't tell my mother if you let me."

Randy Lee seemed about to choke with laughter that she wasn't letting out. She said, "Come with me, little Bo Peep."

• • •

The gallery of rooms over the casino was known as "queer quarters." Randy Lee shared a room with Maxine Jackson and Louis Washington. Maxine was the most beautiful man I had ever seen, strong, muscular, graceful. Louis was bullish, with a short neck, but his personality was the most tender. Neither of them was there.

While Randy Lee was studying the clothes in her closet, I became absorbed in her makeup tray: pairs of long eyelashes, glue, lipsticks, pots of rouge, colored pencils, powder in huge boxes with enormous brown puffs. . . . Her jewelry hung from the sides of the mirror: chains of gold, pearls and strings of what I thought were a million diamonds filled me with reverence.

While she pulled glittering and feathery things out of her closet, I decorated myself with her jewelry and we talked.

"Tell me about the birds and the bees," I said.

Randy Lee cocked her hand on her hip, tapped her foot with the fluffy slipper, and the secret laughter started welling up inside her again. "Why do you want to know?"

"Because Aunt Janet says someone should tell me about them. What happens with bees?"

"Bees don't apply to you, honey. I mean, the bees, they have queens and workers and slaves and all that jazz. That applies more to me. I'm a sort of queen."

"Well, what about birds?"

She inspected a short red satin dance skirt with an elastic around the waist. On Randy Lee it came down to the top of her thigh. I had seen her wear it when she wore a halter stuffed with stockings and danced for the guests after midnight. I took off my overalls and tried it on. It reached almost to my ankles.

Inspecting me with approval, she said, "Birds don't seem right for you either. With birds the man is a real dude and the woman dresses like a dud, mostly."

"So what am I supposed to learn?"

Randy Lee put her shining headband on my shorn head, sat down next to the makeup tray with me and studied my face. "Close your eyes." She crayoned my eyelids and when I opened my eyes and looked at myself in the mirror, my irises looked dark and large under my now deep blue lids. "Birds and bees and people have to make babies," she said. "Girls have a place where boys put their peepers inside. Then babies grow and come out of that place."

By this time, my lips were painted bright carmine and my cheeks were aflame. "Is that what you and Igor do?" I asked.

Randy Lee seemed to flush under all her makeup. She finished the job with a beauty mark on my chin, twisting the pencil as though making the dot on an exclamation point. "We make believe," she said. I didn't understand everything she explained. There were gaps, but I got the general idea. It was enough. As I looked in the mirror, I thought I was the most beautiful girl I had ever seen.

When I walked up to the children's dining room at six o'clock for dinner, some of the guests told me how adorable I looked. They asked if there was going to be a kiddie show and if I was wearing my costume early. As I passed my mother, who was working in the lobby office, she too assumed I was going to entertain in a show. She wanted to know what I was going to perform. I said I was going to sing "Home on the Range."

Randy Lee let me keep the red satin skirt. I hid it under my shorts in my drawer. I wore it whenever I needed to play at being a girl, until I was seven, when my teacher Mrs. McKay, at Public School 70, sent a letter to my parents requesting that I wear dresses.

Sam(antha)

1979

To: E-man   Subject: BOYS OR GIRLS

What could have happened to you to make female babies so dangerous? Your withdrawal from Trish still stuns me. How could you refuse so completely, how could you turn away from her pleas? Not even a hug? No apology? No expression of pain?

I love the way Trish loves you. I wish I could still love a man that way, as I loved Harry. But I can't tell him that now and I can't dictate feelings to you. I've been trained, without interfering or moralizing, to allow you to find your own way. I have to be still, no matter how much I want to protest.

I was confused about being a boy for many formative years. I've never been a lesbian, though I've had plenty of homosexual thoughts. Ever since my divorce, I've been going through a crisis of redefinition. What have I become? The issue of being male or female no longer matters. The question is, how human am I? Will I ever wholly love a man again? It seems impossible.

Loving wasn't the problem for a man who once wrote to me, although he had more trouble with his gender than anyone I've ever known. He used the pseudonym of Sam Sperry and he was a young psychiatric resident who sent me letters ten or fifteen years ago. I didn't invite his correspondence or his confidence. I didn't want the responsibility. I had enough troubles of my own without engaging in therapy by mail. (Am I doing that with you?) I wasn't shocked by him. I was deeply moved by the excesses of his fantasy and by the extremes of pain that he would tolerate in the search for love.

15 June 1979

Dear Dr. Zion:

I have read and admired your recent work and consider you both model and mentor for my life and my literary style. I hope to write about my work someday the way you do about yours. But more than relating to you from the distance of print, I want to talk to you. I want to become your patient. I don't know if you deal with people like me, transsexuals (in my case a man who wants to become a woman), but that really doesn't matter. I've read what you have to say and I trust you with my psyche.

I am a resident in psychiatry and have completed two years of training. I can't give you the name of my hospital; my wish to change my sex is secret. I would have to effect the transformation after I complete my residency, then practice somewhere else. I'd prefer to change the way the plastic surgeon Sally Strickland did, openly, but people might not be as accepting of a transsexual healing their minds as they are of one operating on their faces.

I want to be a woman. That is all. That is All. That has been the immutable simplicity ever since I can remember. I feel I am a woman in a man's skin. I know I don't have to tell you how many criteria I satisfy to convince you of my diagnosis: I have them all as listed in the American Psychiatric Association's *Diagnostic and Statistical Manual of Mental Disorders*.

What I want to know is can you help me while I am going through the changes? Would you be willing to support my case for the appropriateness of the operation if you heard the evidence? The university hospital at Johns Hopkins may require considerable documentation before they will undertake the surgery. I think if I had the support of an authority like yourself, it would benefit my case immeasurably.

Please let me know whether you would be willing to make a consultation hour available to discuss my situation.

Sincerely,
Sam Sperry (Pseudonym)
Box 403
Gulfton, Maine

17 July 1979
Dear Dr. Zion:
You haven't answered my letter of June 15th. I hope that you will consider doing so in the near future. You may recall that I am the transsexual psychiatric resident who wrote to you for a consultation over a month ago. I'm writing to remind you that I am waiting and hoping for you to contact me. This whole situation is beginning to anger and depress me—everyone so unresponsive. Forgive me if I sound off a little. I need to let out some steam.

As you know, many men who eventually become analysts are troubled by their desire to be either female or homosexual, or that's how it seems to me after having had long intimate talks with my fellow residents. These men want to be women, or passive, or whatever they perceive as womanly; they undertake analysis and find out that it's acceptable to want to be "feminine." No problem. Lots of people do. It's important for maleness and femaleness to be integrated within the self—so long as they behave sexually like men (whatever that means—and it usually means putting the round peg in the oval hole). The point is for them to accept their duality without being too much troubled by it. In fact, the feminine self can be empathically helpful. These men work through their problems with their analysts, who often themselves had wanted to identify more with the feminine. They identify with their analysts. They, too, become analysts and everybody pats everyone else's ass, so to speak, all along the chain and it's all polymorphously okay and not perverse at all.

I just want to press my truth one step further and it's not okay. I'm different. I'm a woman in the wrong body. I'm not even attracted to my colleagues, as men, because they are too effeminate, which may seem crazy but I'm sane. I'm not schizophrenic. Some psychiatrists say that all transsexuals are schizophrenic by the very nature of the absurd wish to change sexes. That gets into complex issues, like the question of whether Tertullian was schizophrenic because he chose to sacrifice his intellect, to make the *sacrificium intellecti* in order to have unreasoning faith—to believe in God. Nevertheless, there are certain linguistic criteria for schizophrenia and I satisfy none of them.

Read me; my language is clear. I know the difference between reality and fantasy. I do not repeat; there are no metonymic slidings, no transport from syntagma to syntagma, no neologisms. My body is total, not fragmented; my "I" is not split; I do not thematize and fabulate about the body's universe. My organs do not speak.

Write to me, Dr. Zion. Send me a text. Enunciate, please. I have read your works. You take a risk by demonstrating so much compassion. You owe me a response.

Sincerely,
Sam(antha) Sperry

July 20, 1979
Dear Dr. Sperry:

I'm sincerely gratified by your appreciation of my writing and sorry to have been so long answering you. To be direct, however. I wouldn't want to judge your mental health by evaluating whether you can sustain the cross-gendering surgery. The program at the Hopkins has a protocol sufficient for you to follow. Sweden, too, is accessible. Making such determinations isn't my specialty. I'm not qualified, truly I'm not. I also have serious doubts about the whole procedure, doubts unrelated to whether you're schizophrenic and to the integrity of your desire to change sexes.

I can reassure you on several counts: you're linguistically sane, persuasive, persistent. I'm quite certain that you'll achieve your goal without me, whatever its appropriateness or rationale.

Again, thanks for your generous comments about me. I'm sorry I can't give more.

Sincerely,
Aphra Zion, M.D.

21 July 1979
Dear Dr. Zion:
I shouldn't continue to write to you. I'm obviously imposing. The problem is now I have no one to talk to. I can't see a therapist because I cannot reveal myself in this small town hospital/university complex. I'm on the waiting list for the endocrinologists at the Hopkins. I will have to spend a year or two taking hormones and looking like and living as a woman before I can qualify for surgery. I'm also connecting to a clinic in Sweden to see if I can avoid the wait. I'm tempted to begin the hormone regimen on my own—I can prescribe for myself—but it wouldn't be a good idea to start looking odd to my colleagues.

When I think about why I'm writing to you, I know that I really don't want to plague you about the sex change operation. What I really want to tell you about is my life. I've decided that I'm going to communicate with you whether you are eager to hear about me or not by writing to you (interesting implications about exchange of text and self). You have the option of inviting me to see you, but the truth is I really can't afford either the frequent trip to New York or your fees, which would be too high even if they were low. We get minimal health insurance. So I'll take the risk of writing, in the hope that you'll read my letters. Even if you discard them un-opened, I will still have the therapeutic experience of writing; you can't escape being my confessor, my mentor, my captive and my transference object.

Until I write again—

SS
Sam Sperry

July 25, 1979
Dear Sam Sperry:

Please! I'm not your therapist! You *must* get into the care of a qualified psychiatrist immediately, even if it means traveling. I urge you to trust someone personally. I can't stop you from writing to me, but it isn't the solution for you!

Sincerely,
Aphra Zion, M.D.

29 July 1979
Doctor Z:
Thanks for the encouragement. At least I know you're there.

You see, I'm an expert at having fantasy connections to people. When you're a woman in a man's body, you have to keep it all under your hat, so to speak. So now you're a part of my constellation of lovers, experts, friends and enemies. I drink to our connection. (I drink—I am now drinking—bourbon on the rocks.)

The star of my universe, the pivot and fulcrum of my libidinal economy, is the chairman of the board of our hospital. He's a major obsession, the person I want, the man I will marry (or someone like him). He, of course, is already married, but that's to be expected. There are other problems: I'm quite certain he has an affective disorder: business magnates like him often do. He's manic-depressive, with great leaps of achievement through risk-taking just before he reaches his manic phase. But that's the part of him I love, am fascinated by, want to possess, but only in the way women possess men. I don't want to be the main person. I want the top person to be him. Which is not as passive as it seems, since I give him his power. Without me underneath, he isn't on top. And I have all the traditional ideas about him taking care of me as well, although I hope to be perfectly well able to take care of myself.

He's not a big man. You might not notice him in a crowd. He's more broad than tall, mesomorphic, his muscle spread is lateral and his face is too wide. His eyes are so far apart, it seems that in addition to triangulating on prey like carnivores, whose safety is in attack, he can also see defensively to the side and behind like the plant-eaters, the herbivores, who either freeze or flee. I imagine that the great space between his eyes leaves room for a third eye and I speculate on whether it will be transcendent or demonic when it emerges, as one day I am sure it will. (Please interpret symbolically.) Anyway, when you become aware of him, it's impossible to take your mind off him. He controls every moment of the time he spends with anyone or any group. He provokes, forgives, soothes and provokes again. He mesmerizes with the speed and brilliance of his drama.

I met him because I managed to persuade the house staff to elect me rotating resident-trustee. I'm quite political, contrary to what you might think. I love the struggle for power. It's something I'm always concerned with.

My chairman has raised fifty million for the hospital and medical school in the past six months. He's also president of the Urban Museum and has organized Humanet here. He's astonishing. I have more to learn from him about life and time management than any human being I have ever met. But more than that, I want him to make love to me.

Sam

P.S. It's two in the morning. I was drinking too much when I stopped writing the above and then I fell asleep too quickly and too soundly, the way you do after you drink. Alcohol is a marvelous hypnotic, but you pay the piper at two in the morning when you can't sleep any more.

All night I dreamt about my mother. When I awoke it was almost as though she were here with me, although she died last year of cancer. I can feel her holding me in her arms, comforting me with her little Spanish phrases, petting me, warming me. Maybe it's writing to you that's bringing her image back. I want to tell you about my chairman and here I am at two in the morning writing about my mother.

I don't think I was more than three years old when I had regularly begun to wear her clothing. Everyone thought I was such a cute little boy with my dark curls and my pale skin, but my mother didn't actively try to sissify me. It wasn't really her doing that I felt so drawn to her closet and her makeup table. They were a magnet for me alone. My brothers and my sister couldn't care less. I wore her shoes, her jewelry, her feathered things—a boa, a hat. She was extremely Latin, very chic, very feminine, contemptuous of athletics even though her profession was spartan.

I especially loved her lipstick. I put it on my lips, I put it on the mirror image of my lips, I scribbled it on everything I owned the way a dog defines its territory by peeing on it. I streaked it on my body and on the mirror image of my body and on all my nails, finger and toe, because I was defining myself with it, writing on myself that I was a woman.

My father kept bringing home boy-toys. I know it's unpolitical to make the distinction: it's a farcical position for me because as a woman today I vote that there are no gendered toys, but in that burgeoning consciousness of mine, the trucks and guns in their Western holsters, the miniature cars, the concrete mixers and the electric trains were male, Not Me, foreign, repellent. I tried to ignore them but my father pushed and pushed harder. I just let the toys sit there. Finally he gave up on toys and tried to get me into athletics when I was a little older. He spent weeks trying to teach me to throw a ball. He took my arm and he tried to force me to throw. I let the ball slide down my arm every time. Until one day he twisted my arm behind my back and kicked me with his knee and told me he was washing his hands of me. I was no son of his, I was sick, I was queer, I was going to wind up taking it up the ass and the sooner I left home the better. I ran to my mother and asked her where was a good place to go if I left home, but she said I was only six years old and wouldn't be old enough to go away for a long time. I shouldn't be afraid of my stupid gringo father. She loved me and she would protect me and not allow him to hurt me. After that he stopped bothering me and we never had much to say. I grew up wanting to be a nurse, like my mother. She pressed me to become a doctor and I did it because it was something she had always wanted to do. She cried at my graduation from medical school, and being a doctor made my father a little happier with me, too.

At home, I learned to keep all my possessions private, the evening gowns, my bras, my panties, my high heels, my stockings, my makeup. I still have all my dolls and the clothing I made for them. I'm quite a creative cook and have some talent for art. Most of all, I love decorating. If I wasn't a doctor, I'd like to be an architect/decorator.

I miss my mother.

I want to decorate my chairman's new Santa Fe house.

I'm sleepy.

Goodnight.

Sam

1 August 1979
Dear Dr. Zion:
What I want to describe to you is how I imagine making love to my chairman, let's call him Peter. As I told you earlier, I feel I can write openly to you because you are so accepting in your book, because you, yourself, write graphically sometimes. I want to show you the pictures that really play out in my mind.

I have my glass of bourbon next to me so I can drink in enough strength to tell you about this, though it's not the least bit abnormal. It's not easy to write about sex, even with your example to imitate. I'm also self-conscious because I know that I'm not a modern, self-assertive person. Yet these are the pictures and images that drive me toward changing my sex. To me, they are the essence of being Woman. I never spend a waking moment without thinking of them at some level.

First I want to give Peter power over me. I want him to know that I am a beautiful doctor who would do anything for him, anything. I want to flatter him, touch him, make him feel that I am his physical and psychological slave and that in me he has really made a conquest, as I have in him. Wherever he is, wherever he travels, I will be there in the hotel room, waiting for him. Whatever he wants, no matter how outrageous, I will have prepared. If he tells me what clothes he wants me to wear for sex, I will wear them. If he wants to take pictures, I will pose. Whatever he wants me to do sexually, he has merely to instruct me and I will do it. I lie in bed and fantasize the scenes of my collaboration in the utter extinction of my will. Does he want to be kissed? I will kiss his mouth, taking each of his lips between my lips in turn. I will lick his lips. I will kiss his tongue and lick the insides of his cheeks, Dr. Zion, I will be in such a passion that I will kiss his teeth!

Does he want to be massaged? I'll stroke his body as though he'd just been born and I had to keep him alive. I will stroke the blood toward his heart in the Swedish way; I'll take hours to relax him with the most delicate oils, with every combination of kneading and pounding, petrissage and deep touch known to hands. I will loosen all his tension, touch his pressure points, break up his knots. I will do everything to him, from Rolfing to Reiki. And I will humbly, so humbly, massage his feet, stroking his Achilles tendon, heel, sole and arch with all the wisdom of reflexology to arouse his pelvis and his gonads, engorge them, make him ready for me.

Does he want me to perform fellatio? I don't want to do it in bed, as an equal, side by side, or taking him while he lies there passively, although I would do it if it happened that way. I exist only for the moment when he tells me in his deepest voice to kneel—to genuflect almost—and to suck him. I want to take his massive prick in my hands (for of course it is massive), and wait while it slowly expands to fill my entire mouth cavity so that even pressing it deep into my throat, so deep I can't breathe, even trying to take all of it, my jaw and lips only half cover it. I want to suck him at the end of each stroke, lick his corona glandis, kiss the tip of his urethra and lick it with my tongue. I want to take his balls in one hand and stroke the base of his cock with the other. I want to spread his perineum with my forefingers and run my fingers around his scrotum and up the column of his penis, around the corona to the other side, and back down to the scrotum. I want my finger to find its way into his anus; I want to massage his prostate, Dr. Zion—I fantasize giving him the best blow job, the best oral sex he's ever had in his life, so great he'd have to go to Japan to match it.

Of course, it's all fantasy. I've never even been out in the world sexually because I'm not homosexual. I don't want to have sex with homosexual men, men who now see me as attractively male. I don't have a secret life where I go out in women's clothes for a night. I keep all my feminine clothing hidden. I want to have a relationship and make love like heteros do, not just have sex, homo-style. I want to do it because of desire and connection, because this person brings me life, because I want to share a piece of my soul with him, because he is a real man who relates to women as though they are the grails of posterity.

Now I'm getting maudlin and romantic—I've been drinking my bourbon, as I told you. Have you ever known an alcoholic virgin? Forgive me. Please write.

Sam

August 8, 1979
Dear Dr. Sperry:
   You could possibly get everything you want: your operation, your man—or someone like him—everything. And you might develop a good practice, too. It's up to the world, not me, to decide on your sanity. I don't agree with your concepts of the feminine, among other things, but I still feel friendly.
   I have a question. What physical sensations do you expect to feel after your surgery? What will it be like for you to be female?

Sincerely,
Aphra Zion, M.D.

15 August 1979
Dear Dr. Zion:
Thank you, thank you, thank you! Not for your responsibility—let me reassure you, you have none—but for your involvement.

I won't try to defend the politics of my fantasies of extinction in sex. They are what *I* experience as femininity: being without a penis, a person without a burden, a great relief. I can only hope that other women can be as happy to be female as I will be.

I appreciate most—more than you imagine—your questions about my attitude toward the operation. Dr. Zion, I dream about that operation even more than I obsess about Peter. I live every detail of it over and over in my mind.

I've spent months, for instance, ruminating about whether I want a vagina constructed with the inverted tube of my penile skin, or whether I want a segment of my ileum—or possibly my sigmoid colon—to become my receptor. It disturbs me, though, that the act might feel like having intestinal sex, or worse, rectal sex. As I told you, I'm a transsexual who regards being buggered as a homosexual's idea of femininity. I wouldn't want to go through all this surgery only to be sodomized in my own vagina, so to speak. I'm trying to think it through sensibly.

The easiest approach, I believe, is when two teams operate simultaneously, one putting in the silicone breast prostheses and the other removing the corpora cavernosa and the gonads, and then sewing the skin together to make a vagina. A more complex technique has recently been developed in Oklahoma that requires a skin graft from the thigh to provide real labia, major and minor. I'm going to opt for some variation of these easy procedures, I think. I just don't like the idea of using my colon or gut for sex.

Apart from thinking about which part of my anatomy should become my vagina, I dream about the reasons for my surgery with a surreal ecstasy resembling Salvadore Dali's objects with holes upon holes in holes. I dream about my orchiectomy the way I imagine women dream about giving birth. My testicles will be taken from my scrotum like twins from a uterus. I sometimes think of my testicles as though they were the twin peaks of Mars: symbols of the upper and lower worlds. My sacrifice of their substance will preserve creation. The only way I can be free of my duality is by removing them, by becoming a space, by being Woman.

And my castration. . . . I want it so much that sometimes I am in danger of taking a knife and doing it myself. I wish I could. I wish I had the courage, but then I would lose the skin for my vagina. But I marvel at the men who've done it historically: the *sacrificium phalli,* the act of Origen. Did he just hack it off? My God, he could have bled to death. I wonder how they did it in the old days, without antisepsis, without antibiotics.

Do you know Origen? He was a Christian theologian and teacher in Alexandria in the second or third century A.D. He mutilated himself, sacrificed his phallus to be a true Christian. He literally disconnected from any sensual ties.

I love Origen. That's why your question to me about what feelings, what sexual sensations I expect to have after all of this is over, is so important.

The postoperative studies make a big thing about recovery and pleasure. You wear a dildo-shaped form for a long time, until the vaginal space is firmly created between your bladder and your rectum. And they try to give you a clitoris, too. Some surgeons make it out of a piece of the glans penis; others might use a stump of the erectile bodies, the corpora, that make up the shaft of the penis. And a fair number of post-ops report actual sex pleasure and orgasm.

That's not what I'm looking for, Dr. Zion. That's why your question was so good. I might even ask them to leave out the capacity for orgasm when they fix me. Having one will remind me that I once had a penis.

All I want is the joy of emptiness, the utter transformation into nothingness, a hole, a space, the entrance to eternity. I want to die and be reborn through my aperture. I want the ecstasy of transporting my man through the mandorla, on to his spiritual journey. I don't need orgasm. I don't need physical feeling for that. In fact, the feeling, the sensation, might ruin the ultimate metaphysical moment.

But more than being a passage, for that is, after all, being something, I want to be all submission; I want to be nothing. I want to be that space which is part of a force bigger than I am. Do you understand that like Wotan, Zeus and Jove, Peter is that force, represents that force, is cosmic? I want to be nothing so that all I am is consumed by him. I want to be nothing so I can be transformed. I want to be nothing so I can be redeemed. I want to be nothing so I can save the world.

So you see, my motives are quite pure. There's nothing lewd, common, or ordinary about them. And in the back of my mind, of course, I'm hoping that you will comprehend me enough to support my unquestionable sanity and appropriate motivation without my having to ask you again.

Sincerely,
Sam

31 August 1979
Dear Dr. Zion:
Motivation and sanity have nothing to do with why I want a sex change. The reason is all in the *feeling!*

Thank you for reading. . . .

Love,
Samantha Sperry

PART THREE

GURUS AND MENTORS

Menzes

Toni may be about to lose her livelihood because she's too depressed to keep up the charade with reilly. Her appointment with
me now is right after seeing him, she comes into the office all
smeared with black eye makeup, she looks like she's just been
charred in hell and i usually find that a turn-on, but i was in no
mood for the pleasures of my concealed depravity because today,
first thing, *first goddamthing in the morning,* i got the news.

If there was anyone i never thought would kill himself, it was
menzes walters—his woman called to ask me why he did it! I
haven't seen the man for over ten years and his woman calls to ask
me why he fired a shotgun into his mouth! Not that i wasn't inter-

ested, even relieved in an odd way that he'd done it, but i didn't
need the retribution anymore.

So while toni's growing increasingly depressed, worrying the
issue of when her *real* life is going to begin, and how can it begin
if she dies first, this old son-of-a-bitch letch guru imposes his suicide on me.

You see, the "community" was on a hill near Big Indian in the
catskills; i discovered it when my first wife danah and i were hiking
with the appalachian club two years into our marriage—i took her
walking in the mountains because her mood had been so unstable,
up and down, irritable all the time—i thought the fresh air (not to
mention a symbolic climb out of ordinary reality) might do her
some good.

A small black and white sign said CAMP MENZES ¾ mile; i was
sure it was an orthodox jewish refuge but danah told me she'd
heard it was a non-sectarian ashram for spiritual renewal rebuilt
from an old hotel by the hands and funds of the faithful. Menzes
Walters, an entrepreneurial guru who she suspected was probably
schizophrenic, presided.

Menzes was a small, bald buddha type, with energy and charisma
radiating from even the shine on his head—O:). I felt that he could
tell a rattlesnake to dance and it would rise to do the mambo; just
looking at him brought up thoughts about totalitarian leaders and
the sources of power. . . . menzes had the magic. . . .

The night we explored the camp, after a day of hiking with the
club, menzes himself was sitting in lotus position on a flat stone
near a campfire whose orange light was reflected on his white
robes; he looked like a rebirth out of dipankara via shakyamuni. . . .
the acolytes were submissively kneeling near him, waiting for a
signal. . . . i'd have sworn i was on the set of a bad movie about the
'60's; it was still the '60's in a way, it was the middle '70's: there were
all the open shirts revealing male chests with necklaces under hair;
the men wore an earring, pony tails, jeans; the women had fuzzy
hair, heavy breasts, thick ankles and bare feet or sandals under long
skirts. . . . it was the whole Love scene, but no sweet potsmoke in
the air and no Love visible. . . .

Menzes's large eyes were closed behind deeply convex lids; he
held a black walking stick in front of him like a divining rod. . . . his
arm outstretched, he pointed the stick at the disciples, feeling for
connections. . . . he might as well have been training dogs. (Why do
people respond to sticks?)

Finally the training cudgel came to a halt (he was really professional at making the cane seem controlled by outside forces); it stopped, pointing at a young man who was hiding at the fringe of the crowd. Menzes spoke; his voice was gentle yet it carried and echoed between the mountains in the night air under the firelit stars: *The council has informed me of your death wish* he said. *You must dance for us. . . .* apparently dancing was an exorcism.

The boy moved forward, pushed along softly by the crowd to the space near the stone dais, he shuffled as the group started to clap in rhythm, his awkward stomping and sliding became even less like dancing as the group's clapping increased in tempo; soon he began to jump, yell and flail—if he seemed to tire, the stick waved and the clapping grew more savage—they kept him going, they kept him moving as though to force his heart to give out, as though to make him dance himself to death, and i thought with sudden clarity maybe that was the idea: they could, they could really kill him that way!

But finally he collapsed in a wet heap, heaving, panting, bursting, sweating, sobbing in front of menzes, who touched his shoulder with the stick, a gentle caress of redemption.

Then menzes went into another searching trance while all heads bowed in that intolerable allegiance, the fire crackled and the crickets rubbed their legs impatiently, mosquitoes and moths threw themselves into the flames. . . . menzes lifted his stick and pointed at danah. . . . in his polite tenor voice, he said: *Please allow me to comfort you!*

I expected her to make a nasty remark or ask to leave but instead, as though hypnotized, she removed her hiking boots and walked toward him barefoot. . . . she climbed the rocky dais and sat down next to him. . . . he placed a hand on her shoulder—that was all— after a minute of deep breathing, an effort to control herself, she began to sob, then to cry silently, the tears streaking her cheeks which were sandy with hikers' dust. If menzes was demonic, he was also a genius because with one simple gesture, he had gotten closer to danah than i ever had, than i ever could, and how did the little bald prick know the exact location of my damage???

Of course danah insisted on staying until the end of the ceremony, and when menzes proclaimed, *You shall stay here with us tonight,* offering us a room in one of his cottages as though delivering a commandment, danah accepted without even looking toward me for approval; if i wasn't careful, i was going to get into a real fight with one or both of them.

On sunday, after a hot grain breakfast, we sat on the wooden porch of the main camp building; the sun warmed our knees as we dipped back and forth on old presidential-style rocking chairs, finches and warblers chirped a bucolic message, but i wanted to go, to get out, it wasn't my kind of place, i don't take orders, i think of priests and gurus or any form of hierarchical structure as another kind of fascism.

After we'd rocked awhile, menzes emerged from the dining room: he was wearing a red batik turban and an indian-collared white shirt that showed off his wrestler's shoulders but didn't conceal the belly in his jeans (the roundness made me touch my own flat abdomen for reassurance). I wasn't prepared for menzes's unique brand of concern.

Leaning with one hand over the other on his slender black cane, he told me with great humility, as though apologizing for a guilty verdict from higher authorities, that my spirit was in pain, gnarled and contracted. *Without an enormous effort, greater than you may ever make in this lifetime, I do not see much hope for you* he said, affecting liturgical speech, then turned to danah. *You have love and surrender in your heart.* He paused, overwhelmed by sadness. *But it is not enough.* Thus delivering his vision of us, dropping the negative tarot card on the sunny face of the day, he retreated off the porch and down a path that disappeared around a curve. . . .

Danah spent the rest of the morning doing yoga and meditating with the group; i paced the perimeter of the field where the activities took place. . . . i was waiting for him to return; he had to pass this way on his way to lunch. . . . as i anticipated, he did indeed cross the field later and i walked alongside him to ask exactly what he thought he was accomplishing by making uninvited astrological insights into my life and danah's. He answered that he felt it was his mission on earth to provoke, to awaken, and then, being very skilled, he got me into a discussion of art, beauty, pain, homosexuality, zen, kerouac, burroughs and ginsberg, and finally into the dialogue on writing: how did he know about my writing as both sickness and salvation, how did he know my secret, the incessant compulsive drive to write it all to someone, anyone, him, you. . . .

By the time we finished, lunch was over; we had walked in the woods for a long time and i was under his spell, i could feel the danger beginning, he was catching me in his paternal, charismatic net even as i tried to get the drift of his philosophy and saw it for an outrageous pottage of sentimentality, morality, and drivel. . . . he seemed to have published a number of pamphlets and was plan-

ning to turn them into books, audiotapes, and even videotapes. . . .
his message had repetitively to do with a Love (always capitalized
in his works) that, being in God and man and finding its appropriate place in the Heart (sic), would transform the seekers. . . .

But his effect, his charisma, was the key; his message was nothing
more than a kind of buddhist/christian/cabalist hash with cultic
overtones. . . . the issue was the man himself, provoking, assuming
leadership, having the audacity to take over and act the guru with
such a trite, ancient, unimaginative, and basically conservative platform—he was entirely a charlatan, probably a psychopath—he re-
pelled and fascinated me. . . .

I began to obsess about the processes by which a man, an ordinary man who hadn't even finished his degree at the University of
Pennsylvania (although somehow everyone knew he had at least
attended college), took charge, for even though he was guru and
teacher at a dead hotel on the edge of a deserted mountain and
over a lost generation whose minds had been destroyed by the
chemicals of the '60's, by taking no specific power, he governed
almost absolutely, he lived on his believers' savings and contribu-
tions, and it seemed he took no responsibility.

I began to be so drawn to him, so mesmerized by talking to him
and watching myself become engaged in the grid of his authority
that by the end of the weekend i forced on him a rather large sum
in payment for his hospitality, which i made sure to label payment,
not contribution.

Danah and i became regular weekend visitors to the ashram that
summer and even took our long, two-week holiday there; i pretended that danah's interest drew us, i complained of being forced
to participate in a regression to theocracy, but i was caught, trapped,
obsessed by menzes's emotional authority, by watching even his
body with morbid fascination as he grew more obese during august
and had to have larger new shirts cut for himself. . . . his physical
incongruity with the spirituality he preached kept my almost fever-
ish interest: how did he do it? How did he control everyone, even
me, to serve his own purposes?

His formula for relating to danah and me was always the same:
he began with a spiritually confronting statement to me and then
made a sad, loving, appreciative comment to her; this set me up to
monopolize him in self-defense and for the rest of my stay we
would walk, talk and argue. Everyone who watched us thought we
were deep friends. . . . i found him fat, abhorrent, opportunistic,

fanatical, yet i agreed to be his victim, i accepted his teachings and his wisdom because ultimately he was right about me, the bastard knew me.

He knew that there was a vacuum around my Heart and a contraction in my Spirit which i could almost visualize. . . . i could feel the emptiness surrounding my Heart, a strange absence of blood/elixir, ethereal, non-medical fluid, something missing, my heart shrunken. . . . a tiny, deformed piece of flesh acting as a heart, a cold, small remnant of my heart loose on a pedicle within my chest, flipping up and down with the lub-dup of every second. . . .

The colder i felt inside, the more i found myself focusing on my strange attachment to menzes, an attachment of that tiny Heart fragment of myself that could easily break off altogether, could lodge as an embolism in my soul. . . . maybe it was on account of menzes's guru power that i made my decision to become a psychiatrist that summer. . . .

Danah's mood had been escalating all during that july and i was beginning to realize that she might be starting a manic episode, that my wife might be mentally ill, emotionally unstable—it wasn't altogether clear but the signs were increasing—and suddenly i knew that the mind of the woman to whom i was married was leaving me, going off on some dangerous journey where ideas flew in the icy blue air of madness like bleeding putti children, damaged and lost in the heavens—she was flying, faster than my thoughts could follow—she was on earth, she piled black charcoal on a white tablecloth, she said Look at my beautiful shit; she was in heaven, she reached up to the light between the chasms of a city morning, she said See, the sun is pulling me up, I am rising, I shall eat the white shadow of the moon for lunch, oh Marc! she said, I want to paint the fields of the earth for you, I want to take you with me to the planes beyond the planes and bury us both in ocher and chrome yellow and violet, oh all the flowers are coming out in spring, pink and sky blue and the most delicate new green, we'll be born together from the painted earth, I'll make us a world!

Then she spent money, she bought thousand-dollar western boots, she bought first-class air tickets to taos and santa fe and india, she painted incessantly, her paintings burst with the painful colors of deadly blooms. . . .

She lay naked in the studio, smearing herself with red, like blood, wanting me to fuck her in the paint on the floor, and i did, i wouldn't see, i wouldn't listen, i wouldn't believe, and i got the holistic idea that she would get better at the ashram, that menzes would calm her and cure her.

On a weekend at the end of july, menzes made his usual provocative welcoming remark, but danah wouldn't allow me to wander and talk with him. . . . she took him herself and set off down the winding path, recently paved with pebbles and now punctuated with trees labeled for nature lovers; the ashram was becoming a kind of new age spa/resort and menzes had become known as an avatar: his lineage had increased, tibetan monks sought him, his enlightenment included a resurrection. . . . he carried the cane at all times, everyone did his bidding.

Menzes and danah seemed to be staying in the woods; after fifteen minutes i began a search, but i couldn't find them. The minutes, then the hours, became intolerable. I tried to read, to work on a paper, later i paced the yoga field and suddenly realized that i had given a crazy woman to a madman; he might beat her with his walking stick—or, thinking she could fly, she might run away and dive off the edge of the cliff—what if he let her go? I imagined every conceivable disaster—i could feel my fist buried in menzes's belly; i could feel my knuckles smash against his jaw. . . .

The sweat was rolling down my back, my hair was wet with it and my body was trembling with the guilt of having returned to the ashram with danah instead of finding a doctor to put her on lithium. I was crazier than she was; i brought her there and gave her like a sacrificial offering to menzes. . . .

Finally danah emerged, not from the woods but from menzes's cottage, across the road. How did they get in? Was there a back door? She came out slowly, in full control, her mood seemed calm. . . . she smiled at me with apparent Love in her Heart.

I want a divorce, she said.

Menzes's lower lip was puffy where danah had bitten it—she always bites my lower lip when she's having an orgasm—it's one of her trademarks, a kind of brand, the way a trumpet brands and shapes the upper lip of the trumpeter into a little ball, or the lips of many homosexuals seem branded and configured in a unique, everted pattern, maybe from all the cock-sucking. . . . i watched menzes as he wet his lower lip, then touched it with his forefinger, as i had done so many times.

"Why the hell did you fuck danah?" i said. I wanted to hit danah, i wanted to slap her across the face and see her head jerk to the side, hair swinging, like movie violence, but i didn't; instead i hit menzes, full in the bloat of his stomach; my fist went in without recoiling. "Why my *wife,* you fucker?"

It had been like hitting a mountain of soft dough—menzes went down to his knees, but looked very comfortable there—he seemed to be bowing to an invisible person. . . .

Danah's chin was up and her deep eyes under the wide forehead looked clearly at me; she answered for him passionately, her full red lips forming the torrent of words. *He didn't fuck me. He made love to me. He makes love. He doesn't fuck. . . . For you a fuck is a fuck is a fuck, but that's not the way it is for me. . . .* Her white, oval face was drawn into shadows under her burning eyes as the decibels went up. *I don't like the way you do it,* she was screaming now, *I don't like being told to kneel and suck. I don't like dressing in open-tit bras and g-strings and posing for pictures. You're the one who degrades me, not menzes. You're the one who won't let it be more than top and bottom and B&D and somebody's got to be humiliated. Menzes made love to me and I made love to him and I feel good. I feel terrific. I hear the birds. I want to breathe. I want to run. I want to sing. I want to paint. And I want a goddam divorce!*

Menzes seemed amused and undisturbed by my punch. He stood up and now he seemed to be bowing to me; then with a small smile that plumped his cheeks like a child's, his leg flashed out in a high karate kick to my chest and the world turned sideways, i was down and doubled over, i thought i would never breathe again, the muscles clamped around my ribs and i couldn't pull in a single breath of the green air that buzzed and floated around me, a sharp pain like a wire cutting my lungs in half had begun inside me. . . .

I passed out. . . . when i came to, menzes and an anorexic elderly gentleman whom i took to be the local doctor because of his antiquated black bag, were taping my ribs. . . . i was told that danah had gone, he had sent her home in a limousine to be safely away from me. . . . *And so,* menzes was saying, in a warm, tutorial sort of way, *there's an excellent dojo in the city, not far from your home. . . . My sensei is quite a remarkable man. . . . The martial arts would help with your anger. . . .*

Well, danah got her divorce; she was swinging emotionally high but before she had to be hospitalized she obtained a lawyer, flew to the dominican republic and got it all done—i didn't contest it for a minute.

Instead i went to the dojo that menzes had mentioned and began my white belt student days in karate training; the sensei had, indeed, a remarkably kind way of exercising the sadism necessary to the art, and my anger seemed to lessen under the discipline.

What surprised me even more about myself was that i began to return to the ashram. . . . more than ever i became addicted to talking to menzes, even though i was no longer a special person to him. . . . i had to wait patiently for his attentions, which might or might not be bestowed in the course of a visit, yet i enjoyed watching other people respond to his humiliations, i was drawn in and captured entirely by the perversity of what he had done to me.

And when his audiotapes and videotapes came out under the STARFIRE label, i sent for them and watched them for hours, i found myself trying to achieve the state of purity and acceptance and surrender that he proselytized, i wanted to be whole, he seemed to have a greater message than anyone i had ever encountered. . . . my parents' conflict about my religion had come to this, a focus on a strange, incoherent, impossible ideal that would purify and transform me, simply, directly, i would pass into a state beyond pain and desire, i would be in God . . . through menzes the Father. . . .

I don't think i would ever have been really angry at menzes if i hadn't learned through the network that danah had deteriorated, she never stayed on her medication, she started to drink, she turned up at the ashram and couldn't pay for a room, and he sent her away!

He looked her straight in the eye and told her that he had Compassion in his Heart for her, but no room in his ashram. . . . she hadn't treated me well, hadn't forgiven me, hadn't taught me what he had taught her. . . .

That was what she told me after i sought her out, found her, and hospitalized her as i do now from time to time. . . . her shrinks will contact me, tell me she's out, sleeping in parks, living with some crack addict, abusing drugs, drinking herself to death. . . . i try to get her in control, under shelter, it costs quite a lot. . . . what else can i do?

So when i heard that menzes walters committed suicide, i wasn't really about to mourn the death of a great man. I don't know why the s.o.b. killed himself. He just didn't seem the type for a belated act of conscience. . . .

marc

Memory

AGE 14

1951

PRIVATE FILE: Do not send.

To: E-man   SUBJECT: GURUS AND MENTORS

I'm beginning to idealize you. Why? What have you done to win my respect? You're taking on a heroic dimension. Is it simply your ability to write stories that absorb me? Is the capacity to do that enough to transform you into a channel for higher wisdom?

I respect your honesty about your feelings. And I'm beginning to think of you as the receiver of my thoughts, my recollections, though I'm not sending them to you.

You're on my mind all the time. I fantasize telling you about myself. I don't know what to tell next—the history of a patient with whom I connect beyond empathy? Or do I tell you more about myself? I imagine that you'll help me in some magical way. Is my need so great that I'm creating you?

I've never been influenced by a guru like Menzes. I stay away from charlatans, fakes, pretenders. I don't understand cults. I couldn't give my will to any person. I became a psychiatrist because it's a commitment to a healing idea. After Masters and Johnson, important aspects of psychiatry had to be reinvented. I've tried to find my own way.

What goes on in my mind has always seemed more real than life. Writing to you, communicating in this virtual way, has a stronger reality for me than any verbal exchange or relationship.

I think I'll eventually tell you about all the men in my life. Why do women—some women—like to tell their lovers about their past? Is it for forgiveness or understanding? I've begun to think of you in some ways as a lover; I dream about you. I'll tell you about Jerome first.

Jerome was gentle and kind. He was gifted, brilliant and lonely. He taught. He shared. He kept me company. He kissed me. He helped me to separate from my mother and her hotel when I was fourteen, going on fifteen. I was adolescent—a time for idealizing. I thought Jerome was History in its development and Truth in its becoming. I became. I loved him. He slipped away.

Who was Jerome? Who are you?

Jerome was not my parents' choice of a proper boyfriend for me in 1951. He was twenty-six, twelve years my senior, and either homosexual, basically asexual or simply afraid to be sexual: it was hard to tell. He wore thick, steel-rimmed glasses; his face was eroded by two decades of acne; his nose was outrageously Semitic. He sang in a soft tenor—lieder, medieval songs, liturgical chants—and he also sang strange atonal melodies that he called songs, although I didn't know why. On the piano, he played mostly Bach; occasionally he surprised me with Schumann. But most remarkably, he was a competent professional dancer, his hairy legs fleshed out with substantial muscle. I met him because we performed together at the City Center as members of the same modern dance group. He was also a capable ballet technician. Beyond these talents, he had intellectual complexity and was working on his doctoral dissertation, something about Nietzsche as seen by Heidegger.

In what seemed a moment of high inspiration, I asked Jerome if he would tutor me in return for a summer vacation in the Catskills. When he reluctantly agreed to be my "guru," I asked my mother to give him room and board at her hotel, provided he entertained the guests every so often. She probably didn't hear my requests, but I interpreted her shrug as agreement. "He can sleep with the waiters and busboys and eat with me in the kitchen," I said. She nodded absently.

When Jerome asked me what his work would be, I defined his job as doing dance workouts with me, teaching me the piano and introducing me to philosophy. (Fortunately, I knew I would never sing, so I refrained from asking for singing lessons.)

My mother saw Jerome for the first time as he was eating lunch with me at the long, oilcloth-covered table where all the "help" had already finished their meal. I'm not sure she actually perceived him, but if she did, she made no objection to his presence. I think she decided he was too unattractive to be worthy of notice, much less of sexual interest.

Jerome's philosophic/political project for me was merely to predict the future of the world. I was to think about Nietzsche's concept that in the absence of God, in a world without uniform structured religious commitment, the Will to Power emerged and the dictator became a substitute for the figures of high holiness. Now, in the light of Hitler's defeated will to power, what would come next? Was Marxism going to be salvation or damnation in the next round of events?

He presented this project to me as a gift while we sat on a blanket in a clearing behind the bungalow where I slept. It was late afternoon. Near us a cacophony of frogs spawned tadpoles in the rainwater collected in a deserted concrete structure that might once have been a septic tank. The trees and my line of laundry cast long shadows; the setting sun still burned the dry ground. From his battered leather briefcase, Jerome took a sheaf of single-spaced typed paper. "Cap-Soc one-oh-one," he said, presenting me with his university notes in capitalism and Marxist socialism. His steely glasses gleamed with the promise of a celestial academe to be achieved through labor of the mind. I believe I was to emerge from these studies as a Marxist. I was to understand that capitalist systems exploited the laboring classes and that the rich got richer on an extraordinary margin of profit. The problem was, of course, that Jerome had taken his course before Stalinism, communism, totalitarianism and Marxism became synonymous in the popular mind. Now the solution was more complex. Nevertheless, I was already beginning to feel that in the notes, or somewhere in Jerome, was the secret of universal peace forever.

We practiced our piano and dance exercises, oddly enough, at a neighboring hotel. I never really thought of Lionel's Sunhill as a hotel but rather as a perfect commune. I always spent as much time there as I could. The staff and the owner, Ellie Lionel, knew me and enjoyed my attraction to their place over my mother's. It was an idyllic resort, frequented by teachers, writers and artists, most of whom were committed to socialism and Marxism. But in the summer of '51, to go up to Lionel's was, for everyone in the valley of my parents' hotel, to make a statement supporting Stalin and totalitarianism. Jerome and I went there via a back route, over the parched hills, across rusty barbed-wire fences and through fields of garbage buzzing with gleaming flies.

The room in which we practiced was dim, clean, cool and hung with pictures of Russian (or maybe Lithuanian) peasants in wheat fields; there were gnarled men and weathered women with open white shirts draping across full breasts. Kerchiefs—babushkas—contained their long, thick hair in the wind and sun of the plains.

I was convinced, philosophically, about the inevitability of socialism, even of revolutionary Marxism, but for one dimension: the need for work. My mother, the capitalist, worked harder than anyone in the world, I thought. It was the intensity of her work rather than her meager profit that impressed me: would anyone ever labor so hard to make a barren industry produce in a system that required sharing? I thought not. The revolution could not occur until labor itself was largely unnecessary.

But the logic of Jerome's notes seemed irrefutable, and I considered it seriously as, in black net stockings, tight black shorts and red high heels, I vamped my way through cigarette smoke in a scene we produced for the guests. The show was supposed to take place in a cabaret like the Blue Angel in the Weimar Republic, but the guests didn't understand. They thought Jerome was a Nazi or a Stalinist in his Brechtian leather coat, cap and steel-rimmed glasses, and that he was grooming me to be a whore. They complained to my mother about the quality of the entertainment. They wanted Danny Kaye or productions by Dore Schary or Moss Hart. My mother said Jerome could sing if he wanted, but only briefly. Figaro or Pagliacci or something like that. I was to stay off the stage.

Jerome supplied the texts for my reading: Nietzsche, Heidegger, Sartre, Camus, Marx, Brecht. We listened to Bartok, Stravinsky, Hindemith on the hotel phonograph/loudspeaker system until a temple sisterhood convention threatened that unless we fixed the record player they would check out. I studied his collection of European postcard art: Klee, Chagall, Léger, Moholy-Nagy. . . . I wanted to be with him all the time, learning, experiencing his peculiar pessimism that seemed like optimism as he confronted the problematical. His gaunt cheeks and the great bridge of his nose bespoke an apostolic presence. His mind actually operated. He began to seem a kind of prophet.

At the hotel, no one thought beyond immediate sensuality. The female guests ate and played mah-jongg; their children cried at being overfed; the husbands smoked cigars and played pinochle, bare-chested, on the lawn on weekends. And no one talked the way Jerome and I did, drinking coffee and eating leftover cake until the early hours of the morning in the deserted kitchen.

The important thing, the main issue that I didn't understand, was the gradual transformation of my feeling, the transfiguration of Jerome. I stopped seeing his acne, his hooked nose, his Adam's apple constantly in motion; I did not admit to myself that his dance form was less than perfect, sometimes almost caricature. He represented a world beyond the illiterate, food-centered microcosm of life at the hotel; he belonged to a cosmos where there were books, phonographs, posters and people who (while they might not be better human beings) spent at least as much time thinking as they did eating and sleeping.

"Take the existentialist test," Jerome said one day in the middle of summer as we sat in the direct heat of the sun on the white sand of the beach near the river, a beach that my father had made by trucking the sand to a stony slide, dumping it down the bank and spreading it. "What do you think a hypothetical young man should do: go to war for his country or stay at home—against the law—to take care of his sick mother?"

"That depends on how he feels about his mother," I said.

"Exactly." Jerome touched my bare shoulder with approval, and I shuddered in ecstasy at this recognition. "Remember that everything in life requires individual decision. Don't be tied to abstract rules."

I took his hand and played with it, the way I always played with my brother's hands, spreading the fingers apart and turning them gently. Every part of Jerome had muscle, even his fingers, which had gained their strength from the piano. He kept his nails smooth, clean and rounded. "I think my mother will need me one day to run the hotel," I told him. "My father doesn't do much. Most of the time he's in the city and working at his job. In fact, my mother probably needs me right now. I should be helping to answer the mail."

Jerome's fair skin was turning pink in the sun. "I think we ought to get wet," he said, extending a hand to help me up. We walked down to the river's edge, where tiny minnows swam in the cold, clear water. Jerome hurried in. I liked to wait until my legs were numb and my body acclimated to the chill before I submerged. He swam out to the rock, a warm slanted slab of smooth gray stone near the opposite edge of the narrow river. I followed slowly, swimming over the deep middle of the river, then quietly around the rock so as not to disturb the large, fat gray fish that always lingered, suspended, at its base.

Jerome reached to help me up the rock ledge and I settled down next to him on my stomach, on the warm rock in the sun. As I baked, my body seemed to lose its boundaries. A glow inside radiated invisibly toward him, a circle of heat spreading outward, carried on the rays of light, hovering over him and warming him along with the sun.

"I don't want to spend every summer of my life working at the hotel," I said, "no matter how much my mother needs me."

"It's your choice." His hand had reached out to play with the strands of my wet black hair. "Only you can decide."

I turned over on my back. My cheek was then in the palm of his hand; his lips were close. He brought his lower body next to mine while his hand moved behind my back to tuck me into the hardness at his center.

"I choose you," I said. "I want to spend all my summers with you, just like this."

His lips brushed my forehead. "You don't know me," he said. "I'm an oddity. A loner. I couldn't spend my life with anyone. Besides, I'm almost old enough to be your father."

"Not quite." I laughed and reached to kiss him, but he pushed me away, gently disapproving.

"Don't," he said. "You're a real minor and your parents trust me. Anyhow, there's someone watching. We'd best leave."

I climbed obediently down the rock and we swam back to the beach. When we got out of the water, I put my arms around the thick triangle of muscle where the neck joins the shoulder and kissed him hard on the lips.

"You shouldn't have done that." He shook his head with controlled irritation. "We're still being watched."

"If you have to leave on account of kissing me, I'll never come back here as long as I live," I said.

"I suspect my chances of not coming back are greater than yours. I'm sure that whoever was watching us is headed straight for your parents."

Jerome was right. That night, while we were having supper, my father approached us in the kitchen. Without ceremony, he told Jerome that he wanted him out of the hotel on the first bus after dinner.

For purposes of demonstrating my own attraction to pedagogical guru figures, the story ends here. In life, it went on a little longer: I followed Jerome to the city. My father, incensed at my attraction to the "sniveling communist who couldn't sing on key," followed me. There was a scene where my father located me at Jerome's apartment and threatened to call the police to get me out. I had been there only fifteen minutes. Jerome had been begging me to leave because he wanted no trouble. He was an isolationist who believed only in art. He could never be an activist of any kind, he said. He confessed his total lack of moral fiber and exhorted me again to go before I ruined his life and my own. I left.

But I didn't return to the hotel for many, many years. After the explosion, my father's uncharacteristic and incomprehensible interest in me collapsed. He wasn't hostile. He was simply indifferent. Neither he nor my mother asked me to return then or in future summers. They seemed to disown forever my taste, my opinions, my possibilities for passion. I tried to understand my father's following me to New York. Was it a step on the road to getting rid of me? Slightly more acceptable, perhaps it was a secret jealous lust, but that was a fantasy inspired by too much reading of Freudian theory with no evidence to bear it out. It was certainly not a protective act, because I lived by myself in the city during the next few summers. Why would he follow me into town, leaving my mother to work alone for several days, in order to disrupt a romance that was, if anything, too innocent? Why did he ignore me afterward for the rest of my life?

In subsequent years, I found summer schools. I stayed with friends. I found the theory of communism attractive but not convincing because my experience at the hotel made it impossible to believe that humans had evolved enough to cooperate in the absence of a dictator. I invested deep young passion in becoming an existentialist according to my independent concepts. And even though I thought a lot about it, I couldn't predict my own future, much less the future of the world, as Jerome had enjoined me to do.

Memory

AGE 20

1957

To: E-man   SUBJECT: GURUS AND MENTORS

In 1957, immediately after I graduated from college and eloped to become Mrs. Harry Zion, my husband "took me" to Philadelphia to meet his best friend, John Hardecke. Harry didn't fully realize the self-destructiveness of his mentor and intellectual guru; he ultimately defined John as a martyr, a victim of a society that wasn't worthy of him.

Harry befriends a great range of people, from jailbirds to literati, and supports them with incredible emotional generosity. He has a remarkable gift for awakening qualities to admire, for eliciting self-esteem. Some, like John and me, have lived with him intimately in the city of the mind and felt we were the only ones he nourished. To our surprise, there were always others.

I don't know why Harry teaches us to perceive ourselves as stronger than we do without him. Before we divorced, I thought it was to satisfy his own longings. After considering John Hardecke again, I am sure that Harry idealized us because we needed him so much to think of us that way. Harry's fatal flaw may have been not to perceive the full jealous measure of our love.

Elizabeth's bold print incised the page like the lapidary inscription of an epitaph. It was January 1973. I had been married to my first husband, Harry, for sixteen years. Her husband, John, had died last week. There had been a cremation but no funeral. Elizabeth was writing to Harry and me because she, John and Harry had been so close sixteen years ago that she thought Harry would want to know.

John had had a heart attack. In case we heard rumors, she wanted to state her opinion that John's death was not a suicide. True, he left the hospital against medical advice a week after his first heart attack. Also true that he slipped in the street, fell and suffered a second, a massive myocardial infarction this time. He died in the gutter. But he didn't deliberately commit suicide. His arrogance—thinking he knew more than doctors—killed him. If the insurance company refused to pay benefits, young Harry—who had been named after my husband—would need a scholarship to go to college.

As for herself, she had for many years continued to teach classical guitar at the Curtis Institute of Music and had also taken private students. Now she was returning to her home in Virginia, where life was cheaper. They still had nine cats. Little Rita was demonstrating a prowess at language that had made John proud.

She sent formal good wishes and wrote no return address on the envelope.

• • •

Harry and I were on the train to Philadelphia, where we were
going to live with his parents while he wrote a book with his friend
and virtual guru, John Hardecke. In October 1957, we had been
married only a few months. For me, the best surprise of the marriage—for we had known each other only six months before we
eloped—was Harry's intense desire to be considered a fair and
loving partner, a man who loved women in the particular as well as
the abstract. For this I owed at least partial gratitude to John, who
was the first male "feminist" I encountered. He and Harry had been
collaborating on a book deploring the cultural bondage of women.
The condition of women in our society was a most unusual topic
for a book that aimed to be popular. In that era when there had
been no liberation since the acceptance of women in the armed
forces as nurses and secretaries, it would be the first book of its
kind. Finally getting down to finishing it was the object of our
journey.

As we sat on the long, undivided train seat with its single swinging back support, we breathed the smoke-filled air, the incense of
adulthood. I lit my cigarette with book matches. He lit and relit his
pipe with wooden matches. The bursts of flame and our long ex-
halations punctuated our talk with tribal messages, erotic pauses.

We were an attractive, if disparately styled, couple. Harry was my
first scholar; in him I was intoxicated with literature. Seeming to
emerge from an elite intellectual minority, the Philomathean Society at the University of Pennsylvania, he represented, at the same
time, all New England reading a good book on a cold winter's night
near a warm hearth. He wore tweed jackets, striped rep four-in-
hands or foulard bow ties, cordovan loafers, gray or khaki trousers.
He smoked a large briar pipe, brown, burled, grained, masculine,
professorial. One expected him to be the sort of person who would
calm a crisis, cure the mad dog, rescue the heroine from the tracks,
lead public opinion on campus and experience the love of the
entire academic community. The impression he gave remained the
same after he got his Ph.D. in sociology.

As I recall, I engaged a rather different set of first-sight responses.
I had evolved a personal style that could be identified as French
gamin, even though the clothing came from stalls and shops on
Second Avenue. My early years in masculine clothing had left me
with a strong internal prohibition against soft colors and fabrics,

lace, embroidery, or any item of apparel that might connote innocence or helplessness. My costume for entering sexual maturity
included a man's black French beret at all times, even indoors, and
gold hoop earrings (reminiscent of gypsies or piracy). I wore black
cotton stockings, high-heeled black shoes and a tight black skirt
topped by my striped T-shirt, genuinely derived from the French
navy. My clothes suggested the romance of the imperishable victim,
French schoolgirls damaged by the war, prostitutes, the black market and illicit pleasures taken openly. I wore red lipstick applied
beyond the edges of my lips, smoked Gauloises, talked about exis-
tential dilemmas as both subject and object, and would see only
French movies, with an occasional Italian classic permitted. In keeping with my cinematic preference for the signal costume, I never
used anything but a black garter belt to keep my stockings up,
though I always managed to find a sturdy one made without lace
and resembling a man's suspenders.

Harry's train talk was mainly of his excitement at being about to
see John again. He'd felt it for days, marveling—with that special
capacity for appreciating the exceptional that makes most people
love him—at John's vitality, his language, his ideas, his knowledge.
He exhorted me to imagine a man who could talk in three literary
languages: Sanskrit, Latin and Greek. Indeed, before getting on the
train, before daring to meet John, I applied myself to a review of
Virgil and Latin pronunciation, to a refresher dash through Bulfinch
and to some light scholarship on the early sacred and later classical
lore embraced in Hindu writings. I couldn't do much more than
remember the names of important works.

"You've been talking so much about John," I said to Harry as the
train rattled past all the peaceful little houses that seemed to contain
no thought at all, "I'm really afraid to meet him. In some ways, I'm
beginning not to know whether I'm in love with him or with you."

Harry put a reassuring arm around my shoulder. "I know who
I'm in love with, don't worry about that."

"If John's so brilliant, why bother to be in love with me except
for sex?"

Harry puffed on his pipe. When he drew in the smoke, the un-
derside of his chin formed a small pouch. Even though he was
twenty-five and had no job, I could begin to see him as a distin-
guished gray-haired professor who always retained his boyishness.
"John's a unique person, but so are you—that's why I married you.
I couldn't live with an ordinary mind. He's learned, discursive,

political. But you have the greater genius, you move through the issue and beyond it, you're an artist."

I fell quiet as I always did when Harry nourished me with praise that I hadn't the self-confidence to believe. True, I had written a verse drama that won a prize, I had been art editor of our college magazine, and I had graduated with all the honors I could want, but it was amateur. It was only school, and not even Ivy League.

Harry opened his newspaper to the sports page and became absorbed in the baseball statistics. I closed my eyes, yawned nervously and repeated (with the help of a mnemonic) the great names in Sanskrit literature as the wheels turned in rhythm: the sacred texts called the *Vedas, Brahmanas, Aranyakas* and *Upanishads;* the national epics—the *Mahabharata* and the *Ramayana;* the *Sutras;* the histories of the universe known as the *Puranas* and the *Tantras.* Maybe John and Harry could include some material from the *Kama Sutra* and the *Tantras* in their book. . . . I had my questions ready, too, garnered from my ancient encyclopedia: Did the Sanskrit verb system resemble that of the Greeks? What was the relationship between Sanskrit and the great Indo-Germanic or Indo-Aryan stock of speech? Could John give some examples? Could he recite some mantras? How many vowels . . . The wheels clicked and the air hissed with sibilants, consonants, gutturals. . . . Darkness fell, I was lost in a passage through the caves near Aurangabad, Ajanta, Ellora, or was it Mirabar, had it happened or not, did he make love to me or not, the beautiful Indian guide, would we English ever get to know them, and how would it all turn out, was Forster really homosexual in Phil-a-*del*phia, next stop Phila*del*phia, it was always the same sound, *ba-oum,* returning from the cave, *ba-oum,* even if you cried I see God, it came back, *ba-oum,* wake up we're there, Harry said, we're home.

She encircled me in her arms, enveloped me in her scent of white lilac, pressed the full silk of her dress and the rolling beads of her pearls against my chest, and placed her lips on my forehead for a long time. I returned a small kiss to the rough, milia-studded skin of her cheek. She squeezed my hands until the wedding band, which had been hers and was too large for me, dug into the bone of the fingers on each side. Cupping my chin in her palm, she exclaimed about my beauty and kissed me again, just to one side of my mouth, which she might have kissed full on the lips had I not slanted my head a trifle.

The only person who greeted me with a similar profusion of hugs and kisses was her son, Harry, my husband. From him the affection was healing, something I wanted, flew to, embraced, connected to with all the feeling that I could not express to my parents. His lips were always a welcome, his hand on my chin an appreciation, his joy at my beauty a source of pleasure. I would elongate my body against his to kiss him and breathe with him when we met after a parting; there was always an immediate stirring, a reminder at the center that sex was imminent, sex was present, sexual union was soon to be.

Yet from his mother this same embrace felt strange, intimidating, perhaps false. How could she love me well enough to greet me so warmly? Why should she? I reasoned that my shyness might be related to my upbringing. My parents had not taught me the fullness of affection. My mother kept physically and emotionally distant; my father was personally aloof as well as absent from our lives during the summer and from all but meals during the winter. Perhaps I must put myself to the task of learning closeness from Harry's mother. I should feel affectionate in a nonsexual context. My hesitancy was sickness; her joyous excitement was health. I was lucky to be the recipient of such abundance. I must learn to love it.

Nevertheless, I retreated gratefully to the handshake and quick kiss on the cheek that would always characterize my initial contacts with my father-in-law, which took place mainly at the door to their apartment. Afterward, he picked up my suitcases and ushered me gruffly into the foyer.

For me, the Philadelphia apartment represented a world of love, just as Harry's clothing connoted intellect and caring. This home, with its thick Persian carpets, dark mahogany furnishings, silver picture frames and candelabra, gilded mirrors and a crystal chandelier in the dining room, represented parenting and safety, well appointed, luxurious and conventional. I had never experienced belonging to this kind of home, this kind of parenting, embodied by Harry's mother, who cared by worrying about how things looked, felt, smelled, were ordered. She went to the beauty parlor regularly to coif her thick gray hair; her nails were long and pink. Perfume was ever present. In her home, each piece of furniture fit into its place in the room; every fabric coordinated subtly with the rest. Any object that could shine was rubbed to a high luster. There were no pockets of tarnish, no hidden strings of dust. The garden of ornament was tended, gilded, burnished. The pillows were of softest down. Heavy silver was laid on white damask every night and dinner was served in response to a bell. I was seduced, I was dazzled, not by the riches—because even then I knew that my parents owned more and showed less—but because I felt loved. In spite of my miserly father and my martyred mother. Or perhaps because of them.

Autumn moved by slowly. Each day was the same. We breakfasted in the dining room; then Harry left for John's house. His father, a recently retired fight manager, also left for undisclosed destinations that I assumed to be card games or visits to the ring with his cronies. The daily breakfast solved the mystery of what Harry had been trying to re-create in our small, unfurnished apartment in New York. At breakfast he had attempted to replicate the silver toast rack, the marmalade dish, the porcelain egg holders and the large white china cups steaming with fresh-perked coffee. Once I had casually complained that polishing a silver toast rack seemed like an excessive effort for people without a maid, furniture or any source of income, but Harry had been strong, if not adamant, about "living with grace and dignity."

At breakfast, my mother-in-law was fond of intoning, "I believe in living with dignity and grace. . . . I always use the best silver and china I own, don't you?" I took a piece of toast from the rack and buttered it with an engraved silver butter knife. "Yes, indeed," I said. Her pitch, inflection and fluidity of speech had been so much like Harry's that I shuddered at the mimicry. Yet coming from Harry, the words had always sounded brave, sophisticated, understanding. From his mother, whose origins were in the grace and dignity of poverty rather than the elegance of artifice, the phrase sounded misguided, pretentious. Was there something wrong with me? Didn't mother and son intend the same meanings, the same nuances?

After coffee, after the men had left, there was the daily ritual of preparing for the maid. I found it embarrassingly intimate. I had never been much aware of housekeeping. In summer, the staff at the hotel did it. In winter, the transvestites rotated through our apartment, cleaning mightily. Again, my mother-in-law's words and thoughts reflected Harry, but seemed to imply something else. "It's always a good idea to straighten the bed" was Harry's educational phrase to me at home. But I always wondered why he never went on to make the bed. His mother's version of the same thought

continued, "I wouldn't want Jessie to think we had a restless night."
For Jessie would undo all the beds every day, air the mono-
grammed, lace-trimmed linens in the sun, and change them twice a
week. . . . From Harry I might hear, "I think a person should clean
his own sink and tub." His mother added, "We don't want Jessie
cleaning our private lives." Nevertheless, Jessie rewashed sinks and
tubs every day. This ritual of double cleanliness kept all fixtures
immaculate. If Harry said, "I like to hang my clothes neatly in the
closet," his mother revealed that she had trained him to this so that
she herself could "brush the hair from the shoulders and smooth
the pocket flaps—if men at least hang their clothes up, they won't
get so creased and you can keep them neat."

Gradually, without any superficial damage like roughened skin,
chipped nails or housemaid's knee, I trained as a wife and housekeeper. I even began to take pleasure in the depth of shine on the
columns of the silver candlesticks and the sparkling surface of the
bright-cut silver tea set. I learned what polish to use on the double-
pedestal dining table with its band of rosewood inlay, and how to
make the crystal goblets gleam with a linen towel.

Once every three weeks or so, Harry brought a chapter of the
book home. I wondered, at first without impatience, when it was
going to be time for me to help—to edit or to proofread. Books
took time. When the chapters came, however, they seemed to need
little revision. Occasionally I made a comment or a suggestion;
sometimes I even proposed a major structural change, which frequently would be incorporated and accomplished by the next script
delivery. My part of the book did not seem to require a triangular
conference.

The content of the work was both pleasing and disturbing: it was
a call to women to revolt against the tyranny of cleanliness, of Ajax,
the God of Soap, of Ivory, the gentle white witch. Women would
do well to cease their allegiance to parlors of beauty, to products
that created a false facade, to the insanity that mimicked Chinese
courtesans in the form of long red nails. Women were to abandon
the Sadeian high heel, to study math, to become pilots and priests,
to walk in the country, to stop fussing about the house, clothes,
meals—in short, to stop being Harry's mother. At the time, the ideas
were fresh, even startling, and the writing, while eminently read-
able, was eloquently spiced with scholarship.

My mother-in-law wore a long corset that laced down her back.
When we were invited to family occasions, I pulled the ties tighter

than her husband could with his limited dexterity. Otherwise, she wore it loosely, but she wore it always. By the time the chapter on the necessity of doing away with constricting clothes arrived, a panty girdle had displaced my easy garter belt. Although it created tiny bulges at the top of my thighs, it did support my abdomen better and sculpted a flatter line for my new slim tweed skirt. Indeed, all my old black, victim's clothing was gone, supplanted through my mother-in-law's generosity by cashmere sweaters, a string of graduated pearls and blouses with Peter Pan collars. My high heels were mercifully replaced by British Brevitt walking shoes; my black cotton stockings gave way to expensive nylon. The rest of my minimal black underwear transformed to a pink hand-made lace camisole.

Although they were the essence of conventional, upper-middle-class, imitation-British style, my new clothes were actually rather liberating. I wasn't sure whether I looked more or less intelligent in them: maybe my maverick black seductiveness indicated a more original mind in some way, but I did feel free, light, warm, cozy, caressed by my cashmere. In my Brevitts I could now walk indefinite numbers of miles without foot pain. Even the wrist-length white gloves (with the new gold bracelet-chain peeking out) added a degree of warmth in the cool fall air. And there were no ogling whistles from workmen to worry about. But occasionally I questioned whether or not I liked the softness that was blurring the erotic edge of my sexuality. I looked wistfully at the black artifacts under the new pale silk in my bureau and wondered whether my mind was still as sharp as it had been. How could a change of underwear reduce the mind? I didn't know, but something was missing.

My first meeting with John and his wife, Elizabeth, in no way prepared me for the cataclysm that was to come. Harry's mother invited them to dinner; after all, she said, she had met them before but I hadn't; it was time we all knew each other.

At table, John was a polished guest. His fluent speech, his manners and his style made it difficult to believe that he grew up as a foster child in a series of submarginal Appalachian homes, or that his life now was impoverished enough to justify his radical politics. He could have been a sixties Californian: long brown hair, heavy sideburns, a full beard and a tall, muscular body created by hard labor on the farm rather than at the gym. John's small blue eyes were sharp and undrugged; his slow movements were characteristically southern, not lethargic.

John began by telling my mother-in-law that she was the parent of the most extraordinary young man to have emerged from other lives into this generation. Harry was a gifted communicator: he could bring an audience to tears or laughter at will. Beyond merely speaking well, he could act: he had a perfect ear and could, without mimicry, create individual characters who spoke so universally that listening to them taught all the great life lessons. . . . To be with Harry was beyond entertainment, it was to be in life, to be in love. John's love for Harry was the most overt feeling I had ever heard one human being express for another without any trace of sentimentality.

To define his version of the relationship, Harry invoked the friendship of poets: he was Wordsworth to John's Coleridge. John's mysticism, like Coleridge's, required an earthly anchor. However, John's concept of his connection to Harry involved no minor union of transcendental poets. From his allusions I gathered that John identified with the Indian deity Shiva, the destroyer, and conceived of Harry as Vishnu, the preserver. Between them, the cycle of life and death was complete, all was *lila,* together they danced the cosmic dance toward boundless vitality.

After dinner, Elizabeth entertained us with her guitar. She played and sang the ballads of love and loss, the folk songs that were then still new enough to the world beyond Appalachia to make me cry. Her blue eyes seemed to tear, too, under her pale glasses as she sang the songs she learned as a child in the mountains, of giving her love a baby with no crying, of wanting to be with Johnnie from morning till night, of the four Marys, soon to be three, and of how a certain maid would never marry nor be no man's wife. Below her gaunt face and behind the sinews of her hands on the guitar, Elizabeth's large, half-hidden breasts shook with the passion of the riffs she periodically executed with excited volume. I liked her strength and the freedom of her femininity. When we finally said good-night, I hugged her without reservation.

On what I thought was my day to make an official contribution to critiquing the book, Harry suggested I join him at John's house in the afternoon. Perched on a stool in John's kitchen (which also served as a living room), I swept some counter crumbs aside so that I could put the manuscript down while I picked up John's toddler son, who had begun to cry. Elizabeth reluctantly worked as a teacher. Against her will and better judgment, John took care of the small apartment and the children. To satisfy his missionary belief in role reversal, he had interrupted acquiring his Ph.D. to tend house and write the book. Elizabeth would eventually enjoy working, he was sure; as for himself, deserted by his mother, abandoned by his vagrant father and abused in so many households, he wanted to run his own home as a refuge of safety. Role reversal was the main article of faith in the creed he imparted to Harry.

"I hope you're not learning too much homemaking at Jenny Zion's place," he said to me. "You'll observe all my domestic shortcomings."

The flaws were evident even without my recent specialty training: unwashed dishes, dirty floors, diapers clogging the toilet. But Harry had told me to keep my counsel; John was very sensitive to criticism. I offered his son a zwieback, put him down and went to take care of Rita, the new infant, who was now beginning to complain in her carriage. "So what did you think of Harry's book?" John asked, starting on the dishes. The water splashed loudly, Rita's cry was becoming a wail, and little Harry was grunting in an effort to fill his diaper. No one was making it easy for me to exercise my critical faculties.

"I loved it," I said loudly, picking Rita up and patting her. She grew quiet. "I read it page by page when Harry brought the chapters home. I enjoyed every word." I told John that his prose was an extraordinary blend of the classic and contemporary—brilliant social essays.

The dishes were not done but John turned off the water. Although he seemed to respond to praise, his expression suggested some misgivings about the terms of my flattery. His silence insisted that I speak until I found the precise vocabulary he would consider worthy of his work. I told him that I especially enjoyed the prologue, where he created a case for woman as Earth Goddess, preceding male deities (then a new concept). I was beginning to tire of delivering encouragement, but I kept on. "I haven't read anything with more pleasure since graduating from college." Softly I added that I'd offered very few criticisms as I read each section at home and that I had suggested amazingly few structural changes, but there were one or two essays where the points were out of logical sequence.

The muscle cords on John's neck tightened underneath his frayed shirt collar. He turned to Harry, who had been sponging the countertop. "I didn't know I had an invisible helper," he said.

Harry ignored the confrontation. "But I thought I told you Aphra would be looking at the chapters from time to time."

"Looking at?" John rubbed the back of his neck. "Is there anything more? Does Madam have any other precious thoughts about the book?"

"No," I said, making what I considered an obvious, nonthreatening, secretarial sort of comment. "The manuscript needs to be retyped, that's all. There are typos and occasional grammatical errors."

John adjusted his reading glasses, an academic gesture of intimidation. "Publishers hire Radcliffe girls at two dollars an hour to play pedant. I'm not so sure about Harry, but I can't afford those rates."

Harry dropped the sponge and came to my side. He put an arm around my shoulder and managed to sound cheerful. "A clean manuscript is the price I'll gladly pay for marrying a Phi Beta Kappa." Then he said, "Maybe we should take a break, Aph. Give the real genius of our crowd a chance to collect his emotions in tranquillity."

John took Rita from me. She had fallen asleep in my arms. "You've violated the canon, Harry," he said, "Two people collaborate—three compete." He kissed Rita on top of her head, on her fontanel.

My arms felt empty without the baby. I said, "I think you two should work this out yourselves. I don't think this has anything to do with me."

"It's not your fault." Harry picked up the manuscript. To John he said gently, "I'll submit this as is, if you prefer, or if you reconsider Aphra's suggestion, I'll pay to have it retyped."

That was the last time I saw John Hardecke.

The Woman was submitted without retyping. It was rejected by three publishers. After it came back from Alfred Knopf, John insisted Harry destroy the book. The conversation was conducted on the telephone, but Harry told me later he hadn't protested when John decreed the end of their collaboration. He returned the book by mail to John and learned by mail that John had layered it loosely in an outdoor garbage basket, added lighter fluid and set the pyre aflame—a celebration of their failed relationship. (Several years later, *The Feminine Mystique* defined the bondage of contemporary women, raised consciousness and launched the movement.)

John never finished his Ph.D. He went to work for the government as a public information specialist. At the age of forty-six he had the heart attack that Elizabeth wrote to us about. I've never told Harry what I felt about John or their relationship. I can't hurt him or make him feel guilty. I suspect that John became so dependent on Harry's extraordinary encouragement and vital presence that he killed himself after Harry left him for me, even though so much time elapsed between the events.

Harry doesn't know the power that his loving and enthusiastic good spirits have on people. The dependency they created in me. He brings to friendship and love creative gifts that he focuses on us without any motive beyond making us feel better about life and ourselves. When Harry withdraws his attention from a vulnerable person, the rage at loss may turn against the self.

We had previously sent Elizabeth and John many letters. They were all returned unopened. Although Harry found it a mystery, I understood Elizabeth's silence over the years.

PART FOUR

OPENING
BODIES AND MINDS

Papa et Maman

9

To: E-man   SUBJECT: Analysis!
10.20.91

I'll be preoccupied for a long time with your guru relationship, but right now I don't understand why you stopped having sex with Trish. What happened? I'm left with Trish's view that you reject women and maternity. It's bad technique to tell a person (patient or not) what they feel and why. But unless we sit at our consoles and send messages or talk on the telephone, which presents a scheduling problem, I can't draw you out.
Ergo:

You seem threatened by any suggestion of feminine helplessness. You fantasize the indestructible woman. You desperately want to be nurtured and cared for by a strong woman. Your virility ebbs at the thought of a fetal female or a woman who is growing a large enough belly to need male caution and protection in sex.

Yes? No? Maybe?

AZ

To: go-dot   SUBJECT: well, maybe. . . .
   10.20.91

I thought i had explained but—the concept of a helpless female does send me into a primitive sweat! I find the idea unacceptable, like sharing my bed with a homeless person who hasn't had a bath in a couple of years. *I don't like helpless women!* In fact, i like them so little i want to go on to more interesting subjects, more challenging projects, like, say, creating dynamic female cyborg replicas of aphra zion and anna freud and melanie klein to inhabit virtual reality and cure all mental illness.

That's what's so appealing about toni: she's practically cyborganic. . . . yesterday she was talking about the mind/body duality as it relates to her profession: she says it's complicated for her because she wants to live a true duality, to have a separate body to use (preferably as no-contact visual erotica) to earn a living and perform all the necessary functions; she also wants a mind that can encompass all the important information. . . .

Toni says there are too many misguided females who see the vagina as the interface between mind and body; to her it's just another area where bright women expose themselves to exploitation and soul-rape.

marc

To: E-man   SUBJECT: Why?
   10.27.91

I'm puzzled. You must feel comfortable with helplessness, or how would you have the patience to treat the emotionally injured?

Aphra

To: go-dot   SUBJECT: helpless
   10.27.91

Maybe you're right, but I rarely think of myself as kindly. I went into psychiatry because my father wanted me to be a doctor; he couldn't afford medical school when he was young so the only education of mine he'd pay for was medical. . . . i wanted something else, i didn't know what i wanted, maybe it was to be a philosopher or a woodcarver, but that was the offer, take it or leave it.

Becoming a doctor was the way i related to my father; for the rest he was never home, never there, and besides, i couldn't think of anything better to do, so i went into medicine and then into psychiatry as being the field furthest from what my father had wanted to be—a surgeon—although i might have made a good one. . . . did you know that most shrinks rate body-hacking as their second favorite career choice? When you're really impatient with a disease, you just chop the bugger out, no fuss, no talk, no bother!

I still don't know what i want to be when i grow up; i need a new father to tell me how to suffer the helpless more readily or find something i'd like more. . . . toni thinks i should have been born a navajo farmer, she says the rough land and the seasons would tame me.

m

To: E-man   SUBJECT: Subject
    10.27.91

!!!!!!!!!Are you talking to Toni about *yourself?*

To: go-dot   SUBJECT: questions
    10.27.91

Questions, questions! No, i am not talking to her about myself, i am being a good guru, i am trying to set up the longing: she has to want to connect with me, she has to want to reach out and possess me, even if i don't know who i am myself. Do i have that system right, AZ? (you are aware, of course, that i have been wanting to know *you* better for some time. . . .) and since i'm not your patient, you could tell me a little something about yourself now and then!!!! I'm not paying for your attention to me and i assume you're being friendly, with a weather eye to the future of your clinic, so why don't you break down and confess something? Say a bad word. Tell me if you prefer all-bran to shredded wheat, or bach to cole porter. What music do you like, new age, jazz, latin, african? Do you remember graceland? Do you know zulu jive? I want to know these things about you. . . . How do i know you can help me if you don't tell me things? What, for example, is your cosmology? That's important if you're going to continue this virtual communication with me. . . .

No, i don't tell toni about myself, but i pace the office cage, i climb my tree, i sit on my hillock, i paw the ground and growl every so often—she gets the idea—she comments.

everyman

To: E-man   SUBJECT: Motives
   10.27.91

Does Toni have an ambition?

A.

To: go-dot   SUBJECT: object
   10.27.91

Do you know that you have a compassionate face, with luminous skin and asian eyes? That last year when you talked about your patients in seminar, i fantasized—alone, you and I—well, never mind. . . . at the moment, toni only wants to compartmentalize herself into an android duality for thinking and paid sex. . . . she doesn't go any further than that. . . . but she does go back, she's beginning to connect to her childhood, when her parents would send her to the grandparents' farm in arizona, a farm on one side of a canyon.

She went there summers, with all her cousins and siblings, seven grandchildren in all, to help with the corn, the sheep and the wool-making, to learn to weave rugs like her grandmother, to be out-doors and learn navajo tradition.

And she hated every minute of it! It was supposed to be good for her: fresh air, simple life and all that, but she hated it from the moment she set foot inside the summer hogan! You'd think a kid from a slum shack would like rising with the sun, enjoying the view from the rim, listening to the canyon wrens, but even though the family had four main hogans (one for each season), hundreds of acres of canyonland, and a big herd of sheep, there was not much talk, no tv, and there were no books at all.

Not that toni missed talking—there wasn't any conversation at home, either, except for bouts of brawling—but she seems to need words to engage her, words on tv, words in books.

The main thing she got from the experience was her feminine identity, strange as that may seem. . . . among the navajo, females do

the inheriting and their most important deity is Changing Woman.
. . . toni wasn't in line for her paternal grandmother's farm and she
might not have wanted it if she were, but she says that just being
navajo gave her the strength of being female in a way that most
women can't appreciate.

To go back to our original subject, it's a sense of being competent, in charge, capable—everything but helpless—that attracts me
to a woman. Is that so abnormal?

everymanwomanandchild

To: E-man   SUBJECT: History
    10.27.91

No, not abnormal at all. I wasn't talking about your sexuality. It's
simply—well—how do you help people who need you without
caring about them? We're taught not to become overinvolved, and
yet the most concerned young residents usually do the best treatment. Aren't you curious about where your lack of charity comes
from? Could it have something to do with your mother?

G.

To: go-dot   SUBJECT: *maman*
    11.10.91

For sure, my mother is/was nothing like you or toni, that's a
given. What's my mother like? It's taken time to think about the
answer. I've never quite defined her; her persona more or less
depends on her circumstances which, most of the time, are bad.

Offhand, i'd say her two basic activities are cooking and complaining, both carried out in the french style—her accent grows
heavier every year—you'd think she was the proverbial jewish
mother, except, as I've told you, she's gallic and catholic, which
latter might have contributed to my mistake in marrying trish. . . .
(my father is jewish, but he might as well be a new england wasp
for all the apparent warmth he ever shows. . . .)

I suppose it's on account of my mother that i think all women
are born with a wooden spoon in the hand. . . . the whole neighborhood has an aroma for days after she slow-cooks a roast flavored
with *herbes de provence.* . . . she bakes french bread, she makes all
her own stocks, she loves wine. . . . sometimes she stays up all night,
baking croissants or raspberry tarts or whatever she happens to

fancy. . . . if she weren't so bitter and reclusive, she might have been a famous chef or a caterer, a cookbook celebrity or a tv personality, but she never took the stove out of the house, so to speak. . . .

I don't remember what it was like before my brother got killed, but i divide life into the golden period, before his death, and the black time, after. There's a long black time that i don't remember at all—a couple of years—and then it all turns gray every day, perpetual rain, bitter winds coming up at all the intersections. . . .

In the beginning, in the golden time, she tells me, she would cook for my father when she expected him to come home from a trip. . . . Even though you are a tiny boy, she tells me she said, you can help, you can shell the peas, you can wash the beans, you can mix the batter. . . . she tells me we cooked together all the time; she says she hummed her old french songs when we were expecting him, she would be kind, she would kiss my forehead and i would kiss hers, she would say she hoped i would someday have a wonderful wife to cook a goose for me or make me a beautiful *gâteau*.

My father was a kind of surveyor, an engineer for a large multinational company that built dams on government contracts—he's retired now—i haven't seen him in years. His company sent him on surveying missions to all parts of the globe though he never sent so much as a postcard! I think he surveyed every river (and possibly every woman) between the arctics and across eurasia. . . . his company abused him with travel and low pay but i think he enjoyed it. . . . most of the time he spent at home was during the summer, but sometimes he'd come home in winter, too, to the small apartment in brooklyn, and we'd all sit down to eat on a thursday night. My mother tells how she wore the duty-free joy or chanel or hermès perfume he always brought back from the airport (or maybe the local drugstore); she repeats how he told her she looked lovely, how she told him how much money it cost to make her hair salon-perfect, her nails bright . . . how my father would say it was worth it, and how good the dinner was . . . how he would sleep contentedly that night. . . .

But what i actually remember as the years went by was that she would prepare the great meal, polish the silver, buy flowers and candles, and wait for a doorbell that never sounded. Even though he rarely arrived, she went through the ritual: i think she actually pretended he was coming most of the time. . . .

You heard the bell, Marc? she would ask, making ready to take off her apron.

No, nobody's there, i would tell her.

The telephone, she would say, I didn't have time to take it. He must have called to say he would be late.

I didn't hear the telephone, i would tell her.

Your father is not good anymore, the litany would begin. He used to come home, he used to care, but now all he sends is the little money order. The miserable, tiny little money order. On such pitiful dollars we are supposed to survive in this place, with killing now in the street in this brooklyn, where the truck came and killed your brother like a fly and your father never helped me even to get a little money, it wasn't his son, so what can I do—(she would take off her apron and light the candles for our dinner)—I don't know how to work, what is work, what it is to work, my English is not so marvelous. I add on my fingers for the arithmetic. What can a woman do?

Eventually she complained about everything and everyone: the chicken was bad, the vegetables had no taste, the butcher was cheating, the neighbor's baby cried all night and kept her up, she was afraid to go out in broad daylight, her hair was dead, she couldn't dye it blond anymore, her nails were brittle and ridged, the stove took too long to light, her sister was married to a rich *cochon,* she hoped she never had to see him again. . . . men were all the same. . . . i would grow up to be just as bad as any of them, i would go away to school and desert her, i would die young and leave her like my brother, i didn't help her anymore, i didn't care if she died alone in her bed without a priest, i wasn't eating her food the way i used to, i wasn't giving her enough money from my part-time job, i never kissed her forehead, she was getting arthritis in her knuckles, she could hardly cook, the apartment needed paint, the landlord was a thief, her coat was falling to rags, she had no more perfume. . . .

Do you hear the bell, Marc? I think I hear the bell.

I don't hear any bell.

The telephone, it was ringing earlier. He must have called.

I didn't hear the telephone.

Men, they are all alike, they use a woman's best time, then they choose some kind of work to take them away, they send a little money, a very little paper, not even enough for the dentist. . . .

Memory

AGE 31

1968

PRIVATE FILE: Do not send.

To: E-man   Subject: OPENING BODIES AND MINDS

When you write about your attraction to me, I create a scene: we wander the art galleries, lunch in Central Park, touch and hold. . . . I'm defenseless and maybe you know that I'm unhappy. Have you guessed that Elia measures out the quantity of his emotion as though he's reacting carefully to his temporal lobe epileptics? I've been wearing black like Chekhov's Masha mourning for her life in *The Seagull*. I'm mourning my death in my stirrup pants and my black turtleneck. When I wore black early in life, it was an erotic back-street charcoal. Now I wear black for serving without ego.

Serving without ego. As an intern in 1968, I slept only every third night, when I was allowed to go home. Often I didn't have the strength to leave the hospital. I'd collapse on the bed in my on-call room. The internship hadn't "filled." The hospital had promised two out of three nights at home but hadn't lured enough interns to fulfill the promise. Eight of us had to cover the work of fourteen.

I spent every free moment dreaming about being home. I was depressed not only by the illness and death at the hospital but by the mustard-yellow walls and the watery meats and vegetables in pans on the steam table. Our apartment seemed a luxurious paradise where children's toys created a landscape of primary colors. The odors of real roasted chicken, grilled fish and steak domesticated the air. At home, toddlers—bathed, cheerful and healthy—created their first intelligible sentences, drew their first pictures. Home was a huge hug, an embrace, a happiness where I should have been practicing gourmet recipes and ladling bowls of fragrant soup. Harry would be going to work in the morning. . . .

But Harry would never go to work in the morning. I didn't blame or criticize him. His philosophy was beyond argument, his logic impeccable. Mankind (sic) wasn't created in the image of an alarm clock. After majoring in English literature at college, he had taken a Ph.D. in sociology. He wrote, lectured, taught and championed causes. He refused to surrender the regulation of his time.

Nor would I ever have the patience to be a great earth mother, queen of the kaffeeklatsch. I passed muster in maternity in those days because I'd learned to cook and clean from Harry's mother, but I felt making a home was a job Harry did better. He had fun. I wanted to enjoy it the way he did, but I didn't know how. I enjoyed what the rest of the world called work. I couldn't match his pleasure in life. I didn't know then that nobody could.

Everyone said I was wrong to "leave home." They warned that the children would be neglected, the house would be dirty, Harry would be unfaithful. They were wrong about the first, half right about the second and—eventually—prophetic about the third. As long as the children were cared for and Harry and I stayed married, I was convinced the rest didn't matter. As the sixties progressed, the rules about relationships became more permissive. Besides, my experience and upbringing hardly led me to place any faith in fidelity. I let Harry know explicitly, solemnly and casually—in a quick exchange after dinner one night—that it was all right with me if he did what he had to do and was there when I came back. We both knew what that meant. He said, "I love you. You'll always come first. No one will ever love you as much as I do." I thought I understood him. I thought we understood each other. We never discussed it again.

During my internship, I rarely thought about sex. I didn't have time or energy. But it was unavoidable the night before I performed my first operation: a circumcision. The surgeon who taught me was handsome and talented. The patient was a man of forty who couldn't have intercourse.

Dr. David Starrett's deep, clipped New England voice resounded above the clatter of supper dishes in the hospital cafeteria. He told me he had assigned me to do a circumcision, first case in the morning. It was October 1968. Dr. Starrett was chief resident in surgery and I was an intern on a three-month rotation through his service.

I gulped my coffee and rushed to the library to read a brief description of the operation that I found in a textbook of urological surgery. It was hardly reassuring. Even though there were only two major circular cuts to be made in order to remove the foreskin, what if the knife should slip? What if I cut a ragged edge? What if I went too deep? It was unusual for a resident to give a case to an intern. I wondered why Dr. Starrett had done it.

I had probably gone too far with advertising my love of surgery. I doubt if other medical interns on surgical rotations wanted so much to perform operations of their own, to imitate the surgeon as he (in those days) skillfully passed his instruments through tangles of shining viscera and emerged with the segment of cancerous colon or the stone-filled gallbladder. I wanted to do it, though I suspected it was an ambition I could never achieve. It takes experience and endurance to do surgery. My dual life at home and in the hospital kept me continually and overtly fatigued. Surgical training took more physical endurance than I currently possessed and there was little hope for improvement.

But when I was in the operating room, I especially loved the moment when the field, the patient's body where it was to be opened, was prepared. Made antiseptic with Betadine, the skin lay placid beneath the green drapes on the operating table. Sometimes the rhythm of the heart could be seen, beating from below, spreading pulsations upward from the aorta. Like a conductor at the start of a concert, the surgeon would draw his breath and raise the scalpel; then, in a swift moment almost before thought, the incision would be there, exactly the right size, precisely the right depth. Twice, on easy explorations, I assisted across the table, when the surgeon was quite sure he would need no skilled help and I could peer over my mask into the marvelous geography of the abdomen and identify living organs, nerves and blood vessels. But most of the time, I was stationed to one side and enlisted to tie off bleeding vessels as the fatty yellow layer of flesh was incised, or—even more ignominiously—to singe small bleeders with a hot electric cautery. As I touched the red spouts of blood on the chrome-yellow mounds of glistening fat, the cautery would sizzle, filling the room with the acrid scent of blackened flesh. The job required little finesse.

Once opening the body was accomplished, I was usually removed to the head end of the patient, where I could see very little except for an occasional glimpse through a mirror placed to assist the surgeon, not to educate me. I generally held the retractors, steel tools to pull the flesh or the liver back. The surgeon could then dig out his quarry without disturbing the neurological, vascular and fascial networks that held the anesthetized human being together. When the offending organ was finally removed, sent to pathology, and everything else tucked neatly back into place, I was given the opportunity to stitch up the final layer of skin. To me this was not an inconvenience that kept me in the operating room longer than the attending surgeon; it was a reward for the aching arm muscles, numb feet and irregular heartbeats that always accompanied my long vigils of standing behind the retractors. I loved holding the curved needle in the scissorlike grip of my clamp and pressing it through the resilient flesh on both sides of the incision, then creating the knot with the black gut that threaded through one end of the needle. Most operations required about eight stitches. Creating these was my dessert, as carefully savored as any Proustian made-leine, so great was my delight in creating the neat closure, the track of fine black knots that was the obvious mark and residue of surgery.

It was at night that I missed my husband and children the most. Yet even when I went home, all I did was sleep. My contact with my family was almost entirely at the hospital. We might have supper occasionally in the cafeteria; if one or both of the children were ill, they might sleep on an extra bed in my room so that they could get their hugs and I could observe the fever and culture a red throat in the morning. Both children liked to hang out in the "community room," which had a kitchen and a TV set much grander than the one we had at home. On holidays they might play cards—the older one even tried billiards—with the house staff. I took them swimming in the hospital pool (in that era when the pool and the pool table were mementos of an easier time for doctors). On most nights that year, however, the kids—still in nursery school—were at home with my husband while I was on duty in the emergency room or on the wards.

I couldn't sleep on the night before I was to perform the circumcision. Usually my thoughts disappeared as soon as my body felt the ambrosial mattress. I fell asleep in pure exhaustion before I could even define what I was thinking. But on that night I remember reflecting on sex and surgery, trying to understand what was happening to my sexuality, my thoughts spurred by anxiety about the act that was going to release a stranger from the bonds of a tight foreskin and allow him to have normal erections.

The change in my thoughts had something to do with the work of entering people's bodies. Witnessing people's bodies entered was changing my feelings as surely as had the steady impact of doing physical examinations on every variety of naked patient. The question that night concerned the sacrosanct quality I had begun to connect with a penis entering a vagina. Long before marriage, my life at my parents' Catskill resort had left little to sanctity. After the vows—and well after my departure from hotel life—my sexual and reproductive inner self seemed to belong only to my husband. We lived a symbiotic existence for many years, spending most of our waking and sleeping time together in a haze of warm affection for which I had no precedent. We worked in the same room; we survived on Harry's teaching fees, writing assignments and my meager sales of stories; we had dinner *after* making love. Harry taught me to be close, to laugh, to play. Now—perhaps because I'd left home and left Harry to decide about other women, or maybe because living alone in the hospital was so much like my premarital life at the hotel—I was beginning to feel again that sex was impersonal. It may also have been that I was seeing, visualizing everything about a human being that could be seen.

Penis and vagina were, after all, just membrane, muscle and tissue. They weren't even necessary to individual survival (a comforting thought in case the knife slipped). . . . They no longer represented mysteries about interior, unseen worlds. Those inviolate places where a profundity of skin dwelt in undulating vortices were laid bare under lights and mirrors, scoured of their lingering scents of summer nights, disinfected of poetry, severed from their connection to desire. Where kisses were, now were orifices; where life disappeared to beget life, now were sphincters; where the taste of almonds and honey and apples was, now were lubrication, reflexes and parasympathetic innervation. Beyond the narrowly sexual, beyond those particular insignificant portals to inner space, lay the body, opened rudely to reveal its machinery in a bold light that defined all sexual sensation as purely physical.

The organs of my matrimonial union seemed innocuous, impersonal, unimportant components of the scheme of things. The thought drifted across my consciousness—like a hazy moving electrical sign on Forty-second Street, a message perceived only barely through fog and darkness—that my husband was having sex with other women while I was on duty at the hospital. In the middle of the night, when I perceived the human race as a vast collection of organs in various states of disrepair, the subject of infidelity occurred to me but the answer didn't seem to matter. After a while, after months, even years without enough rest, the meaning of life, the basis for attachment, was something that would have to wait for an answer when the ordeal was over. Meanwhile my phone was ringing and my beeper was going off. I had to get up, after only an hour's rest, to see why someone's blood pressure had fallen to 80 over 50.

· · ·

As I scrubbed my arms and hands with a brush and Phisohex the next morning, I became aware of Dr. Starrett doing the same thing at the sink next to mine. He lathered himself more vigorously than my skin would tolerate and I wondered if I would be clean enough. The energetic sound of the bristles on his arms, so close to me, made me feel as though we were getting up in the morning together and washing at adjacent basins in a hotel room. He was a strong, handsome, competent man who did not allow others to get to know him easily. I almost felt as though it was intruding to be so close that I could smell his after-shave lotion and see the reddish underarm hair poking out under the sleeves of his green scrub shirt when he reached forward to catch the tube of water streaming from the high, arched nozzle.

At first I thought he was scrubbing for another operation but gradually I realized that he was going to be in with me. I felt a short twinge of disappointment and then a surge of relief so great that I nearly broke scrub to hug him for being there. He probably had intended to be present all along but hadn't fully explained. Maybe I wasn't even going to have to cut.

But when we were gowned and masked and gloved, Dr. Starrett gave me the position on the right of the patient where I could cut best. When the general anesthesia was complete, the drape across the field was removed and the organ that had preoccupied me all night was revealed. It lay on the shaved pubis, a quiescent, sleeping, dormant, curved, helpless sausage of flesh that, in a forty-two-year-old unmarried man, had never expanded to its natural fullness. I wondered briefly what entry into the world of normal lovemaking would be like for this penis, for this person whom I had never seen, whose face and breathing tube, behind another drape, were the province of the anesthesiologist. Was he handsome enough for women to help him overcome his inexperience? Would being able to make love reveal new dimensions of life to him? What would the fascination of his virginity be to other women? What was it to me?

Dr. Starrett signaled that it was time to begin by motioning to the nurse to hand me a swab with Betadine for my antiseptic baptism of the site. Soon afterward a probe was in my hand to separate the foreskin from the glans and to break any adhesions that might have formed between the two. After the probe, I was quickly given a dissecting swab to remove any further adhesions that might interfere with pulling the foreskin down and cleaning the coronal sulcus. As I did all this, I was aware of Dr. Starrett instructing me gently and patiently to do a job that he could probably have done in one third the time, even though I was trying to do it as fast as I could. When I had finished cleaning, I held the penis up with a foreskin clamp in my left hand, while accepting the scalpel that replaced the dissecting swab in my right. Dr. Starrett pointed to the correct level above the corona glandis where I was to carry the knife through skin only, all around, leaving a small upside-down U for the frenum.

It was the moment before the incision, the sacred instant before the first cut. I was the holder of the ritual blade; I was the agent of health and manhood; the authority was vested in me as healer, doctor and surgeon to bestow a rite of passage. I was terrified. My jaws clenched as though to keep my hand steady. The blade sank easily into the soft flesh and I turned the knife slowly over the coronal ridge. Dr. Starrett ligated small vessels and sponged the blood, more blood than I had anticipated, and the first cut around the jade stalk was over.

Dr. Starrett pulled the foreskin down again and told me to begin the second incision about three millimeters below the coronal sulcus. I was to go through the epidermis and into the underlying areolar tissue. With this maneuver, the extra skin was cut to form a band, which could then be snipped off vertically with a scissors. I did this while Dr. Starrett continued to sponge and to ligate small vessels. Finally, the two incised circles of skin were ready to be stitched together with small catgut sutures, the job I still loved most.

Later that week, Dr. Starrett sat down with me while I was having lunch alone in the doctors' cafeteria. Over our tuna fish salad, he asked me about my plans for the future. When I answered that I was working hard at trying to make them, he offered his willingness to support any interest I might have in becoming a surgeon. I thanked him. We looked into each other's eyes. We shook hands.

It may have been a failure of character, but a part of me had suspected that the assignment to do the circumcision was a chauvinist exercise with overtones of sexual sadism. Another segment of my logic considered that it was a kind of initiation, a rite intended to humiliate me in some way so that if I retained my dignity I could join the club. I even theorized that, conversely, it might have been a way of worshiping me, a way of symbolizing male subjection to female power because I had been put in charge of the phallus. But when all was thought and done, it had been a test of my competence, and I had passed. I had a friend. A lover, too, if I wanted one. I didn't.

I thanked Dr. Starrett and over the next weeks thought about my future. My first consideration, I told myself, must be my family. How could I be enough for them, ever, if I spent three to five more years in savage training and the rest of my life in an operating room? At home with the children, Harry did a remarkable job of maintaining the structure of a friendly boot camp nursery. He was a dedicated park father, known to everyone at the playground. Parents and their offspring visited our home often to watch his entertainments and listen to his stories. He seemed to provide so much—and our children were so content—that there was no apparent need or room for me. Still, was paternal affection enough? A friend of mine, a man with a wife and four children, a man who had given up his secure job as chemist with a drug company to go to medical school, was planning to train as a surgeon—but he was a man. And even though he was male, entitled in those days not to think too deeply about the consequences of his actions upon his family, other male medical students considered him irresponsible and zany.

I decided against surgery as a career, the formal reason being that I did not feel physically or emotionally able to undertake such a great expense of effort at such an important time in my preschool youngsters' lives. When I returned from the hospital, they did need me: they greeted me, sometimes with loud joy, as often with equally noisy demands and requests. But in retrospect, this was a convenient excuse for the real reason. I'm still in conflict about the propriety of the real reason, although not about its appropriateness for me.

In surgery, the details would absorb me; learning the procedures would strain my memory; learning technical skills would improve my coordination; the sacrifice and altruism would exhaust me; people's gratitude would restore me; malpractice suits would quench my arrogance, but in the end—and I still feel uneasy about it— surgery would not engage my imagination.

Unless I was somehow entering people's minds rather than the rest of their bodies, I was afraid I'd feel robotic. I'd lose interest. I craved the varietal experience of entering other people's psychic lives, which was spiritually different from the warm connection of love given through manual labor. No matter how much I liked to cut and sew, I needed to find work that would enlist my greatest defense against pain: hearing other people's stories. My mother had trained me for the role since childhood.

Memory

AGE 32
1969

PRIVATE FILE: Do not send.

To: E-man   SUBJECT: OPENING BODIES AND MINDS

Do you remember R. D. Laing, a Scottish therapist in the sixties who advocated entering into a patient's illness as the only way to cure it? Colleagues mocked Dr. Laing, but I always felt an affinity with the champion of "the virtue of madness." He failed, but I understood and admired the daring of his approach.

I've never believed I was superior to any of my patients. I've always sensed I had a unique empathy with the distress of madness. I work to relieve emotional anguish with an intensity peculiar to those of us who are never quite certain whose pain we are curing.

I experienced the doctor-as-patient early in my medical training. I credited it to exhaustion, but I knew it was something more than that. When it frightens me, when I almost feel that I *am* my patients, I reassure myself that it's my effort to identify with their common humanity.

The big cat with rosettes on its coat was sitting across from him, a jaguar smiling at him the way animals smile—they cover their teeth and pull back their lips like they want to play. She was sitting totally still in the dry yellow grass, all chest and no shoulders, her legs stiff in front of her, like a queen ruling absolutely, smiling, smiling and smiling. Cats really do this, you know.

His parents had insisted on leaving him with me in the emergency room, in this worst of all places for a trip, and especially for the bad one that they expected. He always went to hell, they said, it was always the same, first the trip through never-never land and then suddenly straight to hell, and that's where he could go permanently as far as they were concerned, no, they weren't taking him home and by the way chlorpromazine didn't help, it only made things worse.

So they signed all the papers for their seventeen-year-old son and stalked out: the tall, thin actress with the bleached hair from whom Kevin got his Irish nose and cleft chin and the short, fat banker who supplied the curly black hair and big eyes with long lashes, and I put him in my "bedroom," the cell of the on-call room where there was a cot, a table and a miniature lamp with a pink shade someone had bought to make the confinement homier. Being with him in the small room felt like being at home alone with my younger brother almost two decades ago, before he died.

Since I couldn't get any sleep on call anyway, I used my cell as a "down room," a place for all the bad trippers with nowhere else to be, only tonight I didn't know who was on the trip, Kevin with somewhere between two and five hundred micrograms of LSD or me with maybe twenty or thirty cups of coffee to keep me up for my fourth day and night in a row because all the other interns were playing sick to study for the medical boards and I just kept working out of some kind of crazy momentum.

I asked Kevin if the cat was still with us and he nodded yes, kind of humoring me, indicating that she was sitting on the floor near the foot of the bed. Her eyes were half closed, sloopy, like she was real content and if we didn't disturb her she probably wouldn't hurt us, although once in a while she yawned and she had long fangs so we had to be careful. He asked if I had any tapes for the player that was on the table next to the bed, and as a matter of fact I had some Mozart flute sonatas that I started playing. Kevin was happy with the music; he wasn't an ordinary acid freak, he went to private school and he thought maybe he'd be a physicist, maybe he'd go to MIT, maybe he'd get the world talking in pictures and making peace. Or at least he'd get the world talking—communicating—but now the music was beginning to turn the pink lamplight different colors and he had to watch them for a while—would I hold his hand while he watched: sometimes hands got really big when they were holding his and could make him feel safe forever.

So I sat with him while the light and the jaguar's spots turned color and the flute was weaving spirals of South American trees all around the cat. My hand grew larger and larger and I didn't even need the shells and flower pictures and squares of mirror cloth that I kept in my drawer to try to induce a good trip, because we were flying. He said my face was flipping back by calendar years and I was getting a year younger with each flip: thirty-one, thirty, twenty-nine, twenty-eight—pretty soon I'd be his age, I was losing all my no-sleep lines and all the laugh lines, and even all my happy lines; he said he guessed I wasn't too happy when I was young and I said he was probably right but I hadn't known it at the time.

He told me to turn out the light because now the movie was starting to pour out of a hole in the black sky, Technicolor streaming out in a cone, coming down on us and covering us in colored light. I asked what was in the movie and he said it was going too fast, a hundred thousand frames a minute, but if he squeezed his lids together the movement slowed and he could see patterns with fireworks bursting between them. I closed my eyes too—maybe I could get some sleep while he was hallucinating—but the patterns billowed out like great sails and began to roll toward me. I seemed to be on the trip with him. I wondered where I was going and vaguely wondered also what my chief resident would say in the morning.

I asked him where we were going. He told me that he had to find Beyond, wherever that was. I wanted to know beyond what, and he said beyond despair, he thought, beyond suffering, but there were a lot of barriers to pass and first he had to read the patterns. So I studied the dots and diamonds and bars making larger shapes, and it was perfectly obvious to me that all the universal truths were encoded in their tribal geometry and that we were Beyond already. But he seemed to think we needed to go on, to pass some further test of the unknown, so pretty soon we were two Chagall figures holding each other's big hands and flying toward galaxies with white cotton clouds turning to doughnuts all covered with pow-dered sugar, and stars twinkling through the atmosphere like Christmas lights against the blue night. He seemed to know I loved to be taught, so he was teaching me orbital space flight as we went along and I understood everything, everything instantly. I could see

that according to the equation $e = \sqrt{\dfrac{1 - b^2}{a^2}}$ our eccentricity was

approaching unity and we were heading out in a virtually straight-lined ellipse toward an apogee that just might possibly be a place from which we would not turn back. You see, he said, the turning point is at the end of this infinitely long ellipse, and if we reach it we'll see Beyond. I told him that it was going to take us forever to get there and he said that was precisely the idea, so I settled into the long trip. I wanted to know some more about what he was going to study at school when we got back, if we ever got back, and he said computing probably, did I realize that soon there might be computers that could solve problems like how did the world start and when would it end?

I said I didn't yet know much about computing except that 702 is 1010111110 and EDVAC started things in earnest and there would probably be a lot of applications in medicine but they hadn't begun yet. What was he going to specialize in? He said he thought he was born to make computers talk to each other because his parents did such a lousy job of it; his talking about his parents made me sure he'd had over a hundred micrograms because you don't get to insight until the dose is high.

He was remembering how, as a kid, he used to send signals to the world from his apartment on the twentieth floor while his parents were drinking and yelling at each other—he sent flares, firecrackers, electric bulbs dropping to the sidewalk—but nobody noticed. Then he stole money for a ham radio he used for erotic communication at all hours of the day and night, and now he was going to make the ends of the earth exchange information peaceably, faster than you could blink three times. When he turned and used his free arm to make a big gesture encompassing the ends of the earth, I noticed that the jaguar was loping behind us, like a pet, her spotted coat looking like collections of stars in a constellation, regular stars, red giants, pulsating stars, novas and even neutron stars, all blinking away.

We came to a kind of crossroads between galaxies, and there were two enormous signs made out of audible and legible radio-light waves, all illuminated from within, like neon, talking aloud and pulsing with light at the same time. One sign said Danger and the other said Bliss, and there were arrows pointing in opposite directions, while bells rang and incense burners smoked underneath us. We were moving in the direction of danger, when suddenly he was streaming away from me, his hand was torn from mine—a gravitational force was pulling him into what was probably a black hole. He was disappearing fast. The jaguar shot after him, catching his foot in her mouth to try to save him, but either way he couldn't survive because in order to save him, she would have to eat him.

The decision posed a complicated problem: Was it better to be destroyed by the black hole or eaten by the jaguar? Was it better to succumb to the pressures of gravity and get lost in time or suffer the living agonies of dismemberment? I signaled the jaguar to let Kevin go. I couldn't bear the sight of his flesh ripped and bloody in her jaws. The hole seemed a kinder death. She opened her mouth. His freed body twisted in the force and elongated slightly as he was sucked swiftly into the food chain of his new universe.

The jaguar tried to comfort me, rubbing her huge head against my leg, catlike, but at first I wouldn't let her. She persisted and after a while I climbed on her back and fell asleep as she loped back to the world we had come from. I felt warm and secure being carried along on her power. The message seemed to be that even a great spirit in the form of a mythic beast could do no more than I had. Losing Kevin wasn't my fault. He was caught between irreconcilable forces. I didn't have to take so much responsibility. . . . After four days and nights of flagellating myself in the sandpit of the emergency room, I felt as if I'd had a vision.

When I opened my eyes I saw Kevin stretched in anguish on the bed. He was twisting and moaning, apparently being drawn deeper into the hole. "No," he was repeating over and over again. "No, please, no, help me, oh God, please, no . . . no. . . ." His face was contorted in fear and pain and he was perspiring.

"Easy," I said. "Take it easy. You'll be fine." But I wasn't at all sure, although my identification with his trip was over. I was rational and lucid and could only hope there was nothing he had taken that hadn't shown up on the blood samples. He went into paroxysms that repeated themselves for the next several hours. Each upheaval raised a new question: Was being adolescent like being born? Was this the pain of freeing himself emotionally from his parents? What were the pains my children would experience?

I watched Kevin and imagined my son, even my daughter, in the agony of some drug-induced nightmare because I wasn't home giving them security by sleeping in my marital bed in the room next to theirs. Harry was there; no one could give more warmth and delight than Harry, but what about the day when one of my children would have red eyes and be lethargic after school, would deny pot, but I'd find the seeds in a jacket pocket. . . . Considering that both were still near kindergarten age, my fear was a bit premature, but still, what was I doing in this chaotic emergency room, allowing other interns to take advantage of me while they studied for our exams? Why was I working four days and nights in a row?

Eventually Kevin fell into a fitful sleep. He was worn and pale and his hair and body were wet. I covered him with a bedspread patterned with drawings of elephants and turtles that I had bought for my son but had never taken home. Kevin woke up when the nurse poked her head in to tell me that she had another patient for me, a flier this time, a kid who jumped out of a third-story window. Would I sign orders to get the blood levels done and the orthopod and the X rays moving? And would I see Kevin's parents? They were waiting for me.

His parents looked worse than Kevin. Apparently they hadn't gone home at all. They'd sat up all night on the dirty white plastic chairs under the fluorescent lights of the waiting room. His father's crushed cigarettes collected in the rusty chrome-plated standing ashtray. His mother's mascara streaked her face. They wanted to know what to do with him, they had tried to be good parents, what did he want, what did kids today want—all they seemed to want was money for electronic toys and drugs—what were they supposed to do? Should they be strict, should they turn their eyes away, was it their fault—they wanted to send him to a psychiatrist but he knew better, he said they needed shrinking, not him, was that true, would it do any good if they went to see a doctor?

Through the window to the ER I could see a nurse waving a pen at me to sign the orders for the X rays. The stretcher-bearers rolled in a new cardiac patient while the ambulance driver signaled that I was needed for a DOA. On the back of an admission card I wrote a name for them: Dr. Roland McGowan. He was a family therapist, they should all go to see him. I touched the mother's hand and the father's sleeve and told them I was sorry, this was an emergency room—I couldn't spend any more time but wished them well.

On my way back inside, I met Kevin coming from the men's room, his face washed, his hair combed. I told him he'd be going home as soon as his parents signed the papers. I said I'd given his folks the name of a psychiatrist for family therapy. He said he thought that was a good idea, better than seeing someone alone, but how was I?

I was fine, I said, why did he ask?

He said that it seemed I'd had a pretty cool trip.

I said I didn't know what he meant. I'd gone along with him because I'd been taught to attempt to feel what was happening so as to be an understanding and supportive presence.

He shook his head. Man, he'd seen his usual colors and lights and patterns and things, but I was like somewhere else.

Like where was I, I wanted to know.

He said I was all wrapped up with this jaguar, it was powerful. Was it my animal, like in a vision quest? I practically had him seeing it too.

When Kevin and his parents left and the heart patient with the myocardial infarction was stabilized, I stopped the chief medical resident, who was doing emergency room rounds after breakfast. I said I was working too hard. I was neglecting my children. I was destroying my marriage. I was being eaten alive. Maybe I was letting the other interns take advantage of me because I had some unresolved guilt about my younger brother's death from polio when he was seventeen and I was twenty-two. His nurse had pulled the plug after I said good-bye to him in the iron lung. . . . The chief resident interrupted me by looking at his watch and saying that he didn't have time to be my psychoanalyst. No one was taking advantage of me. All I had to do was ask. He'd get me covered.

Longford

1983

To: E-man   SUBJECT: OPENING BODIES AND MINDS

Theorists of deconstruction say about stories that it is not easy to distinguish what is in the text from what is in the reader. So, in practicing psychiatry, it is not easy to distinguish what is in the patient and what in the analyst. Even more complex, in writing about doing analysis, it is virtually impossible to know whether one is the imagined reader, the patient, the self as psychiatrist or the self with its own personal history. Furthermore, in the interests of confidentiality as well as with a view to improving the story, one may combine cases, elaborate on the nugget of an interesting plot or fabulate one's own past. Is what emerges fact or fiction? How is it to be presented? How can I best tell the story of Longford? And why do I want to?

Somewhere in my cache of secrets, I've always hidden the fantasy that if I were a beautiful woman, life would be effortless. Men would take care of me—ply me with houses, decorators, jewelry, expensive cars and first-class trips—for the slightest perfumed brush of my attention, the mere permission to caress me. But I know it couldn't be so painless. Men often distrust beautiful women— sometimes even seek revenge on them for the power of their beauty—as much as they admire them.

Consider Toni. I feel sad for her. Men want to conquer women who look like her, even the privileged. Toni defends herself with the Cartesian philosophy of "separating" her mind from her body. That's an anachronism. The mind is unequivocally the part of the body that does God's business, among other things. (Unfortunately, God seems to have a great many mundane accounts to settle.)

I wish Toni demanded less of herself. As I've told you, I risk blurring my boundaries with those of my patients. (I even identify with your energy for life.) I like the Navajo Way, or any mystical catechism that removes differences and boundaries. I used to paint pictures in which you couldn't tell precisely what the objects were: a ship or a landscape? an ocean or a city? The attitude when listening to patients is "floating attention." I try to have that approach to life, to let it happen to me. If I give it a strong J-stroke, I usually go off course.

When reading Navajo ritual poetry, I'm held by the idea of the unified spiritual animal. I'm moved by belief in a song-dance for rain and transforming oneself into the wind, which becomes the rain that falls on dry fields. To be free, Toni should become the wind and the rain.

My identification with—my need to tell the story of—a different patient, another beautiful woman, disturbs me. I don't feel as though I *am* her; I can't write in her voice. I have to write about her in the third person. I can't *be her* in print because I can't make the bridge, the connection of experiencing myself as universally compelling. She was beautiful in the way my father was handsome, cold the way he was cold. Her looks—and her horsemanship— excited male attention, attracted male generosity. But men abandoned her. Her father was alcoholic and disappeared when she was a child. Her patron and caretaker deserted her later. Both men gave her warmth. Both left her without resources. Afterwards, accepting homage was the highest form of trust she could give. She was afraid of becoming needy. Instead she became a woman who cared very little for her own physical self or anyone else's. She split mind and body. She was more willing to risk homicide or suicide, to destroy her body utterly, than to allow herself to use her mind, to think about her feelings.

Perhaps the story begins when I first saw her eight years ago, although it quickly moves to the end of the action when she called me to see her in her hospital room after the terrible accident. . . .

Eight years ago, when Longford came into my office for the first time, I was intensely attracted to her elegance—and even more to her obviously athletic body. I was also shocked by her resemblance to my father as a young man: the sexual appeal of her coldness. They had the same aristocratic, prematurely white hair. Their features were aquiline: proud noses filtering air through narrowed nostrils; quizzical, questioning green eyes with taut lids that defied sadness; thin-lipped mouths, cruel at the corners. Yet all the sharpness was redeemed by the infantile cleft in the chin, an incomplete joining, a doubly rounded memento of embryonic life.

Longford was as impatient then as she is, even now, swathed in bandages and wrapped, almost head to toe, in plaster. "I don't need you," she had said. "That's why I'm here." She swung one long leg, encased in tight denim, across the other. Loops of gold cascaded from her ears; in high contrast to her classic whiteness, her pale, paper-smooth skin, she wore a colorful ethnic headband and an assortment of African animal pins that seemed to possess the feral power of fetishes. She could have arisen out of the sandy dust of the desert, like an apparition on a horse.

I repeated, "I don't need you. That's why I'm here. . . . Does that mean you want to learn to need people, or that you're here in spite of your better judgment?" The parallel muscles on the thigh of the leg pressed against the seat were sharply defined by a lengthy indentation between them. Like my father when he was a young man, Longford was a human version of the Thoroughbred, perfectly balanced, with sleek, powerful haunches and an air of being ready to bolt at any moment. Longford suffered my collection of her demographic data (reason for choosing me as a therapist, age, occupation, recent family history) by playing with a long earring and pumping the firm calf of her crossed leg against the supporting knee. I had the feeling that she was imprisoned in her stall, pawing the ground and waiting impatiently to be turned out.

She had chosen me because she had browsed my book of essays on her last trip to England to watch the Three-Day Event at Badminton. When it was over and she was wandering the bookshelves at Heathrow, she picked up the British edition for the trip back. "I didn't read it all, of course, but I could tell you did more thinking than most of the popular mindmongers. And I do have a sexual problem."

She was thirty-two, had belatedly attended Columbia Business School in her middle twenties and now worked for Morgan Stanley as an investment banker. "I earned a quarter of a million dollars last year," she informed me gratuitously, "and by 1984 I expect to earn at least half a million, even at Morgan Stanley. Of course, if I chose to change companies I could earn a great deal more, but in life, unlike competition, I prefer a low fence with a good clear view of what's next, if you know what I mean." I understood. Most of my male investment banker patients at other houses were earning twice and three times as much. Longford had opted for modesty and convention.

As she gave me the facts of her history, I began to build my private story of her life. I confess that I often have fantasies—usually more or less unconscious—about my patients while they are revealing themselves. Only later does my fiction connect to their facts. How do I know that what they tell me is true? How do I know that I accurately perceive what they tell me?

"I was born in Gloucestershire, you know, near Beaufort," Longford told me. "You can hardly grow up there without understanding horses."

I knew very little about Gloucestershire except that it was the home of the event that had led her to discover my book on her return to the States. Nevertheless, I pictured her being born at Stratton, the home of the duke of Heyland. Not in the manor house itself, of course, but in the cottage where her parents lived. Her father, Timothy Longford, was in charge of all matters pertaining to the duke's horses. Tim saw the world only in terms of horses. It was at Tim's insistence that Longford was born at home: "foaled" would be more accurate. He would not allow his wife to go to an unsanitary hospital where she might "contract the strangles from a contaminated feeding tray." And Tim was also the one who had chosen her first name, Lucinda, after Lucinda Prior-Palmer, the great champion. Longford had dropped it, however, because she tired of the inevitably challenging comparison.

But beyond his concerns about his wife's becoming ill, Tim had a serious disease himself. "My father drank too much. One of the duke's best horses colicked because my dear father had been drinking heavily for two weeks and hadn't been there to notice. The horse died."

In the weeks when he wasn't drinking—Tim Longford was a periodic drunk—he spent most of his time loving his little daughter. He accommodated her in front of him when he rode. As soon as she could sit up she felt most secure astride his horse, her flexible young legs straddled wide, her back against the tightness of her father's abdomen, his arm protectively around her belly. They rode this way through most of the chores of his mornings, she soothed by the rhythmic walking and cheered by the attention of passersby. Sometimes they left the stables and the town to ride out on the meadows. Tim would spur the horse on to take them for a real ride. She could remember the wind in her eyes and hair, the rhythmic turning motion of the saddle and the rushing warm scent of horsehair and muscle as they galloped across the field; her mouth was open wide and she held on to the strong arm and the big firm hand.

The image of Tim Longford holding his daughter fused momentarily with a memory of my own father—once, just once—holding me tight around the middle as we sat in the small open red car of a roller coaster, as we crossed the rounded apex of the track and plummeted—*whoosh*—down into the valley of nowhere. Did Longford have the same vulnerability that I do to the firm, warm hand, the aphrodisiac touch that associates speed with safety. . . .

. . .

When his daughter was five years old, Tim Longford disappeared from Stratton. She remembered the age because it was on her fifth birthday that he had taught her to mount unaided. A famous German horsewoman had done it by vaulting at the age of three, but Tim was pleased with her prowess at five. Since she was a small child who had done all her growing late, everyone had made a great fuss and she had caught Lord Heyland's attention for the feat. "Lord Heyland took pity on my mother and me, I suppose, and gave me rather a great many advantages though he could ill afford it."

I envisioned an older Longford, tall, thin, mourning in the green field near the ring where Lord Heyland (from time to time) supervised the equestrian education of his own children. I imagined his surprise and admiration as she demonstrated her precocious skills, light-years ahead of his own unathletic offspring, who were rotund like their mother, Lady Heyland.

I wondered why his wife allowed the favoritism and concluded that she must have been a practical woman who decided that her husband's interest in Longford kept him from less constructive ways to work out his depression at the disintegration of his fortune.

I could feel Lord Heyland's fascination with the growth of Longford's lean and supple body as she accomplished skill after skill, learned to trot and canter and jump, mastered dressage, as it became evident that she communicated with horses and would become a rider, perhaps a competitor in major events. . . .

I pictured him falling silently, painfully in love with her, unable ever to consummate sexually because of her youth; obsessed with her, neglecting his wife and children, fighting off their growing jealousy as he had the finest equestrian outfits tailored for her— the round visored black velvet riding caps, the dark hunt coats, white shirts, stocks, breeches and shining black boots made to her measurements each year. He sold off his possessions to buy a horse called Be Quick for her, to give her a royal mount, an extraordinary luxury for an adolescent child. I could see him risking everything, losing it all. . . .

Longford interrupted my reverie. "What are you thinking, looking off into space like that? Dr. Zion, you know I'm not here for psychoanalysis. You can't just daydream or fall asleep."

"Actually, I was wondering what happened to Lord Heyland." He was becoming dissolute, alcoholic and suicidal as I forced him to fade out of my mind.

"Lord Heyland lost everything when I was twelve. I don't know exactly what happened, but that was the end. My mother decided to take me to Canada, where she had a sister. He didn't even pay our passage."

"What happened to him?"

"I don't know and I don't much care, really. He always sulked when I was about—and, oh yes—I remember now, in the months before everything fell apart, he used to have me ride with him every day on the path along the river—he kept talking to me—I hardly listened to him. He talked about being more active in the government, perhaps becoming ambassador to some small country and sending for me. It was all perfect rot."

"You never heard from him again?"

"Dr. Zion, at four dollars a minute, I haven't time to waste on the geography of Lord Heyland. I need your perfect attention."

"You have my attention," I said, "for whatever it's worth."

"Good. Lump of sugar for you." Longford was not entirely un-kind. "Now, the problem is that I know a lot about horses but not much about how people conduct their lives. I'm married to one of the richest, dullest men in the world and I want to have an affair with one of the handsomest and most exciting. I wonder if I should get a divorce first—not because of morality but for financial rea-sons. If my husband found out about this affair, I doubt there'd be much of a settlement."

"Sounds like you need a lawyer, not a psychiatrist."

"You're right, I shouldn't bother you with that part of it. The main issue is something else. You see, my husband and I have no sex life. We haven't for over a year. He says I don't know how to love, how to feel love, and that I'm cold, I want everything too fast. I think he's a puritanical, slow-witted, clumsy American who doesn't know a brass farthing about having sex and probably never will."

Disobeying my major rule of therapy, which is never to give advice or tell a patient what to do, I said, "Divorce first!"

"That's fine for you to say, but it isn't quite so simple. You see, my husband supports my riding habit—and it's quite a habit, make no mistake. I could support it myself but basically I don't care to. Child in me, I suppose. I own half a dozen horses. I have an indoor ring, stables, grooms, trailers, everything I'd want, just to maintain things for my weekend activities."

I remained silent.

To my astonishment, Longford's eyes, green as that early spring when her father left, began to fill with tears. She sniffled and wiped her nose with the back of her hand, disdaining my box of tissues. "I'd miss him," she said. "I'm terrified of life without my horses, but I'm even more terrified of life without Stephen. I'm an absolute basket case when I think of being left alone without a man. If I were alone, I think I'd shoot myself. I have a pistol, you know, in case I need to shoot a horse—or an intruder." She patted her purse as though it contained the weapon. "Can you help me? Is that more your line?"

I allowed as how emotional life was more my specialty. I didn't much care for homicide or suicide, though. We made our next appointment.

But Longford never returned for another visit and I never found out what she decided to do except in retrospect. In any event, it was clear she was the sort of person who would probably act first and find out what she was thinking and feeling later. She was not an ideal candidate for therapy.

The auto accident had virtually destroyed Longford and Stephen. Both had concussions but Stephen was still in a coma in the intensive care unit, his condition precarious. Longford had emerged quickly from her coma and now occupied a regular room. She had fractured almost every part of her body: several ribs, her right wrist, her clavicle, her pelvis and the tibia and fibula of her right leg. Stephen's injuries were similar.

Longford's face was quiet and nunlike in its cowl of bandages. She said nothing when she saw me. Possibly her eyes became slightly wet. All I could think of to say was, "What on earth happened?"

"I'm afraid of the answer," Longford replied grimly. "That's why you're here."

"What are you feeling?"

"I feel dreadful. I feel desperate without Stephen. What if he never wakes up? What if he dies? What then?"

Trapped in her bed, confused by her disaster, Longford began to tell me the story. I visited her an hour a day over the next weeks to hear it. Little by little, she told me about her affair. She had decided to remain married. Indeed, she had elected the greatest risk of all: giving up her job to work full-time with her horses and to become a real wife. Her "work," of course, was exorbitantly expensive. Longford was realizing her childhood dream of being supported by a paternal figure. And becoming a "real" wife meant—in the European tradition—time to have affairs, since she no longer chose to participate in the exchanges of the financial market. Stephen was necessary, but Stephen was slow, methodical, unsuspecting, regular, ethical and very busy in his demanding and hugely successful dual practice of international real estate investment and law.

Besides, he had given up trying to elicit from Longford any responsiveness to romance: to firelight, kisses and declarations of affection and appreciation, all those things he had grown up believing women wanted and for which he himself was longing. "He belongs in a ladies' magazine, circa 1950," Longford concluded. "I don't know where he gets his ideas. Certainly not from the men's magazines, where I get most of mine. . . ."

Her lover turned out to be Henri Bequet, the performance artist, who shared her interest in speed; who was as impatient as she was; indeed, whose theme in his life and his work was men's domination of the world (including especially women) by speed, by velocity, by the ability to make not only vehicles but words and images and other particles move at speeds that fractionate time almost infinitely. On stage, he tried to deliver his messages on various subjects in quick bursts of special effects. In life, his motorcycle was his symbol and his passion; his love for it matched Longford's devotion to her horses. It is difficult to tell where my fantasy and the true story part ways, but I picture him taking Longford out for her first ride behind him on his Ducati; she is helpless, not in charge, straddling a mechanical animal over which she has no control. I see them zigzagging deep into a forest or riding with the moon down a long stretch of beach; he always revs the speed up to the point of ultimate danger—that point where the roller coaster races down the steep tracks of the valley—while Longford's hair flies out below her helmet and she wraps her arms and her amazing legs around him as they go deeper into the forest or balance on the hard-packed wet sand near the sea. The ocean rocks gently, the moon stays still, but the dunes slip past, faster and faster until, at the height of the speed, when the stars are a blur and there is only land, sea, space and the loud motor that sounds like death, Henri stops the cycle abruptly. With the rush of the motor still vibrating in their groins and the world suddenly silent as any eternity, Henri slaps the numb skin of his thighs and the ride continues as he mounts her and they finish the trip on the hard sand with the cold sea licking their feet.

In the story that I both remember and imagine, the story of how
the affair with Henri came to an end, Longford invites Henri to the
farm in Millbrook for a weekend when Stephen has gone to Europe
once again. She and Henri have been quarreling on and off for
months, Henri suddenly busy with engagements, rehearsals, creating new performances—in short, success—and Longford wanting
him to be at her disposal as he had been at first, dominant yet
overall totally obedient to her whims.

She has a wish to ride with him along the river path, to walk and
to talk and then to take him out on the meadow. Her father and
Lord Heyland are part of the wish, somehow, but she is not sure
why. Henri wears dark round sunglasses, black disks that reflect
drugs, theater, leather, mystery. He has allowed his auburn beard
to fill out. He had been thin, which disguised his lack of muscle; he
is still thin, but in the snugness of his jeans she can see that he
is flabby at the middle. There are two soft rolls of flesh inside
his T-shirt above his belt. And by Longford's standards, his seat is
poor.

They ride and talk, their sentences punctuated by the clap of
horses' hooves and the swish of tails. The river flows as incessantly
as Henri's monologue: a mixture of postmodern anarchist philosophy and premodern totemist fascism. He denigrates the speed of
horses as a bourgeois remnant of nineteenth-century power games.
"Why would you want to torture a sweating animal when you can
sit in a sports car or pilot a plane?" Poor by Longford's standards,
Henri aspires to more expensive machinery than his motorcycle.
He wants a Ferrari or a Lamborghini. "Today, horses belong to
women," he says. "Men gave them up after the Industrial Revolution."

"Is that your own concept?" Longford breaks into a trot.

"I don't find twenty-five miles an hour a challenge." Henri posts
broadly, conspicuously proud of his novice's ability to move in
rhythm.

"You ride well, then?"

"It isn't very difficult. In 1800, everyone could ride. I don't understand why you spend more money in a year than I make in ten to
prove your superiority over horseflesh."

"You can really handle a horse?"

"Women are simply bent on proving they can bully an animal
bigger than they are. Of course I can handle a horse."

They come to the broad, flat meadow surrounded by a wide old
stone fence. Longford increases to a canter; Henri follows. She

allows him to get slightly ahead, then brings her crop down lightly on his horse's haunches. "Tallyho," she says, laughing softly.

Henri is almost left behind by the sudden burst of speed. Longford watches as he struggles to get forward and in control. As soon as he is comfortable and stretching ahead with the horse, she speeds up to him and takes the lead. "More?" she says in passing. Henri nods.

"Don't if you can't," Longford warns. "I'm going over the wall." It is nearly four feet high, wide and made of stone, but easy for an experienced rider. Longford knows that Henri's horse is a steady old chestnut mare who will do what has to be done, even without clear commands. She also knows that Henri will follow her and that he will probably lose control. (She had expected him to fall after the little tallyho.)

Longford flies over the fence, suspended in perfect harmony with her animal, as easily as though she were a dancer leaping across a narrow brook. Henri takes off well with his horse, but when he jabs at the horse's mouth with the bit as they land, it is clear that he does not know how to jump. He is left behind and thrown headlong into the rocky brush at the side of the crossing.

In the hospital room with me, Longford tells the end of this story. "Henri's head hit a rock hidden in the brush. I've never seen so much blood. His glasses had sliced into the bridge of his nose and the disks were lodged in his eye sockets. His skull was pouring blood." She laid him flat so he could breathe and tied her blue cotton shirt around his head to try to stop the flow of blood. Then she rode back to the stable for help.

Henri died four hours later in the emergency room of the local hospital. While she spoke, I had the impulse to announce to Longford that she had killed her lover. I had the urge to wrap her in guilt like a mummy in its burial cloths. But she was already wrapped in plaster and gauze.

"I didn't kill him, if that's what the absurd look of horror on your face indicates you're thinking," she said. "I merely allowed him to kill himself. It was what he wanted. Why do you think he drove his motorcycles so fast? Why do you think he provoked me?"

After Henri died, Longford found herself needing to spend more time with Stephen, yet resenting every moment. She trusted the exercise and upkeep of the horses entirely to the help. She gave up her cherished autumn event to go with him to Tokyo. But even so, sometimes he went and returned alone. Their accident happened in the late afternoon of the day she drove, herself, to Queens to pick him up at Kennedy Airport. First they planned to stop in New York for him to collect a few things and then they would proceed up the Taconic.

"You're driving too fast," Stephen said, predictably. They wound onto that part of the highway that curved continually and unexpectedly.

"I've set the radar detector. We're perfectly safe."

"You know very well that I don't mean safety from the police. I mean these curves are treacherous." Stephen had taken drivers' safety lessons. "Why don't you let me drive?"

"Because you're tired, my darling. You've been flying for eight hours. And besides, we'd never get home."

Stephen remained silent, his eyes closed in frustration. But gradually his narrow jaw relaxed into sleep. The trip had been long. The time was late for him. Pleased, Longford drove on. Although she was doing over ninety, the radar detector was silent. There was little traffic and rather than driving a car, she had the sensation of the road speeding under her like a treadmill, curving and swinging her from side to side in a mechanical motion that seemed to be generated by a computer and over which she need have no control. Her illusion of safety, however, was soon broken by blinking lights and a bleeping siren. Obediently Longford pulled over and submitted to a speeding ticket. The radar detector had not been functioning.

When she got back into the car, Stephen was awake but pale and rigid. "I forbid you to drive," he said coldly.

"Nonsense. It's my first speeding ticket in over two years. Besides, if you drive, you know, we'll never get home."

"First of all, you're repeating yourself, and secondly, if you drive we'll wind up either in the hospital or in jail."

"Can't we talk about something else?" Longford tried to govern her temper. "How was London?" Stephen had been negotiating purchases and leases for a major client.

To avoid a fight, he made the conversational attempt. "Jergens wants fifteen new stores without any rental increases—imagine, in this market. And Ardway is howling about the New York City commercial rent rise. . . ."

Longford's foot crept toward the accelerator and pressed lightly.

"You're speeding up again."

"I know I am." Her foot pressed harder. The speedometer needle rotated rapidly to the right, over seventy, over seventy-five, over eighty. . . .

"Longford, slow down, please!"

"Tell me something interesting that happened in London."

"This is unbearable. Have you been drinking?"

"Tell me you were robbed in Piccadilly."

"I was perfectly safe the whole time."

"Tell me you went to a sex show in Soho."

"I never go to sex shows."

"Ninety. Tell me something."

"I have nothing to tell."

"Ninety-five."

"Nothing exciting happened in London!"

"One hundred and five."

"You're going to kill us both!"

"Right on. Now or never."

"No, Longford, please—"

"One hundred and ten."

"Stop for Godsake. I love you."

"One hundred and twenty."

They were suspended in speed. Suspended in space. Carefully Stephen tried to edge his foot under the accelerator so that Longford couldn't press it down further. But it was no use. They had left the road. They were rushing into the valley of nowhere. Stephen hugged Longford tightly to him. The car was falling . . . crashing . . . rolling through barriers . . . rattling . . . silent.

Longford is crying and wiping her tears with her good left hand. "I don't know how I'm going to live without Stephen. I need him so much. . . . Oh God, Dr. Zion, what if he doesn't make it? What if he dies? Or stays in a coma forever?"

"You just tried to kill him—and yourself."

"Then it would have been all right." Longford's sobs and tears are uncontrollable. "Then we'd both have gone together and I wouldn't miss him. Dr. Zion, I wanted both of us to die, together, and now it's gone all wrong."

. . .

A week later, Stephen emerged from his coma. He spoke slowly, his speech impaired by poor ability to retrieve the word he wanted. If his body was a showcase for orthopedic handiwork, his mind was a testimony to how little medicine can do for brain damage. The neurologist predicted improvement but could not promise that he would be without permanent deficit. He would probably always be slower than he had been before, though not necessarily less intelligent. It would merely be more difficult for him to communicate and would require more patience on the part of the listener.

Longford's doctor cheerily suggested that she and her husband might like to share a handsome room ordinarily reserved for semi-private patients. Longford refused with disdain. "We never got on before. I should think it would be obvious that in his condition we are particularly unlikely to thrive on each other now."

"Very well," said the doctor. "I'm sorry."

"I don't like obsequious men," Longford said to me when he had gone.

"Do you like any men?"

She shrugged. "Haven't I told you that men are God's mistake that women were created to correct? I neither like nor trust them, and I never shall."

"Aren't you curious even just to see your husband? You did say you couldn't live without him."

"Of course not. If he had died and I had lived, I'd have his fortune. Now all I have is him. He used to be dull, precise, rich and boring. Now he's going to be slow and stupid as well."

"Not stupid," I corrected. "Just slow. Will you be able to live without him?"

"Probably not." Longford fingered her handbag, small and full. There were no tears now and she sighed. "I don't suppose I'll be needing any more help from you."

"That's absurd."

"Ah! A spark of rebellion! You're improving, doctor. And you're probably right. I shall need you again, but I don't need you right now." She bade me good-bye and urged me to charge for my travel time. I considered staying to argue the issue of her need for me: so far she had virtually killed one man and maimed another besides herself. It was also clear that she was able to feel emotion of any sort only at the point of loss. But she was so cold and irritating as to be, perhaps, beyond salvation—by me at least.

I threw my scarf around my shoulders and picked up my bag.

"Good-bye, Longford," I said. She opened her purse, searched it with her left hand for a long time, then removed a case from which she proceeded to extract her makeup and apply it to her incredibly unblemished skin. I watched, transfixed, while she painted herself as a nunlike medieval Mary, all smooth innocence.

When I started again toward the door, she called to me. "Doctor," she said, "what time is it?"

"About a quarter to four."

She rang for her private duty nurse. "I've reconsidered. Please stay for tea and discuss something with me."

"I'm sorry," I said. "I officially start work in the afternoon at four-fifteen and I have to get back to the office."

"Will you see me tomorrow?"

I considered, then submitted. "I have an hour between two and three."

"Of course," she said. "At your convenience, doctor."

Longford was being so polite as to be deferential. It was unlike her, except for those moments when her mood shifted abruptly because her need for Stephen overwhelmed her indifference to him.

"Would you mind giving me an inkling?" I found myself asking, in spite of the patient who would soon be arriving at my office door. "What made you reconsider?"

Longford studied me with a detachment that lay just on the surface of contempt. She said that when she opened her handbag, she had been relieved to find that her small revolver, which she always carried with her, had been confiscated by hospital security and replaced by her makeup kit.

"Wouldn't being without your revolver have made you feel more insecure?"

"It made me feel safe from myself," Longford explained.

I offered the homily that aggression against the self was usually displaced anger at someone else.

Her contempt emerged openly. "If you had been paying any attention at all to me, you'd know that I would never kill myself without killing someone else first, or at least trying to."

I persisted. "Then why did you feel safer without the gun?"

"Because, dear doctor, as you were leaving, I had the most profound desire to fire my handgun at you, right between the eyes, as it were."

"I see," I said, sitting down. When I had let some silence pass, I asked, "What made you want to shoot me?"

"I don't know." She smoothed her covers and stared at me.

A cup of amber liquid had somehow found its way into my hand. Her nurse was holding a tray that offered milk and sugar. "How do you take your tea?" Longford asked. And then she said, "I'm afraid I've begun to feel as though I need you."

PART FIVE

FATHERS AND DAUGHTERS

Reilly

What happened to my mother? She left the old apartment in Brooklyn and moved into Manhattan with her sister and brother-in-law, but she still complains life has been unfair to her even though she has the use of everything her sister owns.

Toni never complains, her depression seems improved, and she never spends a cent of what she considers her own money—it's all in the bank against the time when she'll be free to leave reilly; i think she keeps her sexual feelings in the same safe deposit box, storing them up for the future.

Whose life makes more sense?

Incidentally, toni told me reilly's secret: he has an obsessional lust for his daughter. Toni looks like her, so he buys the same clothes for both; then he masturbates in front of toni while saying his daughter's name. Sometimes he touches toni and calls her carol, but he doesn't want any response from her; that would be too much like incest. I still don't know how i'm supposed to stop imagining reilly's hand (my hand) on the flesh under toni's thin silk blouse. . . . she doesn't remind me of my daughter or my mother or any relative, she's incest-free, she's unconflicted for me. . . . you haven't been any help, dr z, and toni knows why i keep my biggest notebook on my lap (as though i'm ever going to forget a word she says)!

You know, when virtual reality really gets going, prostitution may become archaic—think of it—reilly could have a disk made for his hologram-projector out of an old picture of his daughter; he could put on his headgear, his data gloves, his sensitivity suit, and then he could go to it. Would that be reality or fantasy? Would it be a crime? You could almost literally fuck anyone whose picture you owned —i'll bet that would change the porn trade and maybe put *us* out of business, too! I'm trying to think of an excuse for taking toni's picture for use as an old-fashioned glossy page until VR comes along, but that would probably lower my already borderline score for entry into psychoheaven.

mm

To: E-man   SUBJECT: Cooling
  11.14.91

At Payne Whitney in the old days they prescribed cold showers for randy patients. What's the cure for the patients' doctor?

Go-dot

To: go-dot   SUBJECT: infancy
  11.14.91

She gives me everything. . . .

e-marc

To: E-man   SUBJECT: History
   11.14.91

Ah, you see, the golden time . . . the magic mother . . .
   Considering Toni's problem, did you mention the possibility of
incest in her background? Have you explored it? Why isn't she more
intimidated by eccentric sex?

                                               Aphra

To: go-dot   SUBJECT: herstory
   11.14.91

Compared to her life experience, reilly's "eccentric sex" seems
safe and luxurious: toni's father was a wandering swede from
nebraska who migrated to cattle country and found that driving
herd suited his alcohol habits, but eventually he couldn't even
do that. Toni doesn't know how the intermarriage happened, but
it did; his two sons followed in his footsteps, only they never
worked at all except for odd jobs. . . . the three of them used to go
to a bar where all the itinerant cowboys hung out to get drunk
every saturday night (and as often between saturdays as they could
pay for).
   Toni was the youngest; she had nowhere to go or stay but home
in the trailer. She and her brothers had slept on the same trailer
bunks—plastic mattresses in a hot tin can, no sheets, ever since her
mother died when she was six and they lost their house—she was
used to their nakedness, their alcohol smell, their sweat, their erections, their dirty underwear, their talk. And she was also accustomed to their using her backside or her belly or her chest as a
rubbing surface for coming off. She says they occasionally tried to
get inside her but she found she was safe if she kept her legs tightly
closed. They wouldn't rape or sodomize her. They only wanted
some warm female skin!
   She thinks her father participated in the rubbing off when she
got older, but she doesn't know for sure—she kept her eyes shut
during these episodes—she didn't want to see her brothers, she
didn't want to talk to them, she didn't want anyone who ever did
that to her to be alive in her mind. That's why she became attracted
very early to the concept of emptying the mind. And now, as far as
she's concerned, her brothers and her father are dead. That's what
she tells people: my brothers and my father died trying to save a

policeman from the drug dealers, she says. They got caught in the crossfire.

m

To: E-man   SUBJECT: First....
11.14.91

It's hard to imagine what Toni must feel. Sex therapy is out of the question but we've agreed on that before. So far, you've obeyed the primary rule of the physician as healer: First, do no harm. Now what *good* are you doing?

Go-dot

To: go-dot   SUBJECT: foremost
11.14.91

I listen to her. Nobody ever has. And i think i've been a model of discretion, if not therapeutic skill; toni hasn't a clue about my life, my feelings, or my fantasies, which i share with you, as honestly as i can, so they don't spill over.

Why am i so fixed on toni? Why do i imagine that i'm reilly, masturbating, looking at her, owning her? And why, ever since i heard the story, do i imagine myself as her brother, drunk, stinking, stupid, coming off on my sister's naked ass? I've even masturbated to that fantasy....

Remember, trish and i don't have sex—should i get into yet another relationship to reduce the sexual pressure? I don't want to mess up again, but i'm going to need someone soon—i've been celibate for two years!

So it's better that you're on-line, you're print, you hardly have a body anymore.... i still remember your body, though the memory is fading; i'm not sure i could tell you this face to face but i have a need to say it, i want to write it: i remember the frailness of your wrists and ankles, the small waist, the adolescent chest, the whiteness of your skin under black hair.... i thought that if i had sex with you i'd probably be too big for you, but after i read your book i was sure you could satisfy any man, you know all about sex, you're a certified sex guru and i wanted to fuck you because then you'd be out of my fantasy life—you don't belong there—i need a woman like toni, a woman who is built for sex, a big woman, stronger than i am....

Miss America

1986

PRIVATE FILE: Do not send.

To: E-man   Subject: FATHERS AND DAUGHTERS

Toni may never recover from her brothers' and father's perversity, but I sincerely hope she makes an adjustment. She seems to have resilience, intelligence and ingenuity. You've described her in such a way that I have confidence in her future. I have nothing to say here that I haven't told you in our correspondence beyond my admiration for her.

Is incest *ever* forgivable? I always had difficulty convicting Oedipus. He was separated from Jocasta at birth. How was he to recognize his mother? I wouldn't convict any couple that had sex without knowing they were related. To me that isn't a moral issue, although it may be a subtlety of the family romance. The deaths in Oedipus's story are the real tragedies.

Incest between adults and children, or in any abusive relationship, is a disastrous miscarriage of human feeling. There are sexual atrocities that test my most benevolent beliefs. I wasn't able to erase the past when an incest victim came to my office some years ago. I could only relieve her depression, help her kick her addictions. The damage was irreparable, and yet this bizarre, suffering woman may have been a tribute to how the best in human nature can emerge in spite of the most extreme abuses of nurture.

The year was 1986. Wearing purple silk shoes with clear plastic high heels, black net stockings and a lynx jacket, she lurched into my office. Her father called her Miss America.

■

You see, doctor, my father thought I was Miss America, he'd say there she goes, Miss America, and I'd walk around the pool in my bathing suit and high heels, sometimes my mother would put a satin ribbon across my chest, she'd say you're too good for those junky pigs out there. I'm so beautiful I really am gorgeous, my hair's practically the same red color as when I was a kid, and—I think my father—I can't remember—it's all so fuzzy with the heart necklace he gave me if I would let him touch me there, but maybe he only gave it to me, I don't know, but anyway I decided to let John Malo paint me but at first I wouldn't let him touch me.

No I said it makes me very nervous to be touched, that's why I get my headaches, I wake up with my head being hammered until I'm blind, I take fifteen Seconals a day that's a lot less than I used to take and twelve Motrin and about half a dozen codeines and it's all because I'm so beautiful, Miss New Jersey America, and I'm so successful, I'm the most successful art collector in New York because I make painters, I find them on the streets in Soho and I love them so much, I love each and every one of my lovely painters and their lovely paintings, I have an eye, I know my art, but that's because I'm made of plastic, I'm a piece of art.

You see, doctor, I'm a sort of a combine, you know a Rauschen-berg thing part real, part with paint slurped all over me, you could hang me up on a wall.

Probably it all started with my father, he thought I was Miss America—stop looking at me like that I'm not crazy even though I'm coming to see you and when you see a shrink you've got to be crazy but there's not a thing wrong with my mind. You wouldn't believe it the way I talk, nobody does, but that's my gorgeous charm, I am a really savvy art connoisseur, it isn't my business but I want to make it clear take me seriously because I can sling the semiotics of the privy and the problems of naming heterotopia but that is not what I am here about.

My father thought I was Miss America, there was this presence in my bed, sometimes I think I can feel him from behind I hate to think about it his finger in my little crack I don't want to face that I just lay there I didn't say a word, maybe I take more than fifteen Seconals sometimes, I stop counting, when I make a big buy from a big collector then we all celebrate, I have been buying Malo like crazy especially since he went neo-Jencks, it's so wild this market, it's the toughest in the world, so much stress, so much stress, no-body knows that the bodies in his pictures are all mine and the faces are me forty years ago in 1942 when my father and mother were under the umbrella at the side of the pool and I thought I was Miss Rita Hayworth America in my red lipstick and my white bathing cap, that's why I'm keeping my body up, because it's art, I'm a thing, a valuable thing.

My face is mostly made of silicone inside, I had it added drop by drop to take away those wonderful lines that are so marvelous for character and make you look like a hag and men say you look gorgeous you earned every line and then they fuck some tight-assed stewardess. When you're fifty-six it all falls down especially when you have a thirty-year-old painterlover, but I never had a face lift, I don't need one thank God and Dr. Cherney did my tits, they look just like Tom C.'s beautiful sexy girls, Malo doesn't know about the job because they came out soft you can't tell, I'm practically a ready-made, I have plastic laminates on my teeth, Duchamp couldn't have done more, I'm a bleached redhead siliconed laminated thing but Malo paints me like Miss America twenty years old, you know what that does for me?

Well on account of my father probably on account of my father I could never stand anyone even touching me, I hated to shake hands and one day Malo he's so cute, he's such an adorable little painter, you should see him, doctor, I love his little face with his two big sort of Indian eyes and his wonderful classical nose, I love his two earrings on one side and one on the other, he said he wouldn't touch me, he would only touch me with his brush on canvas, an act of the imagination, if I would take my clothes off for him he would preserve me forever, I would never grow old no matter how many sins like the picture of Dorian Gray, so I said yes I would do it if he didn't touch me except with his mind.

So he started painting me in his studio and pretty soon he got this complexity, he said it came on him slowly like a disease, he said he had never been interested in sex before and if he ever got interested he said he thought it should have been men but it wasn't anybody at all, but now he said he was starting to get hard while he was painting me and I said please stop my head was hurting and I couldn't pose for almost a month. He got depressed, he said the sex went out of him so I felt safe and started to pose again because I wanted to buy more paintings and get him started becoming really famous; his depression went away and he started to talk about my body again, it was to die the things he said about wanting to lick the spaces between my toes and massage the back of my neck and suck my earlobes and wouldn't I just let him kiss my closed eyelids because he now knew that he loved older women and nobody else.

So then, doctor, my headaches got worse again and I decided to sell some art to give Malo more money, I decided to sell one of my Jeff Koons sculptures, Mrs. Diamond wanted it right away but I reneged, I love Jeff Koons, I love him so, she couldn't have it and now it's gone up up up, it hit the sky and she's buying it for triple the price, isn't it crazy me so rich with beautiful art in my little townhouse? So my asthma started squeezing my lungs and I had to start the prednisone inhaler, it makes me even more nervous than the Seconal, I hate all my stuff, I know I'm an addict in addition to all my diseases, and all I was thinking about was why didn't my mother know that her husband was shadowing in and out of her daughter's bedroom when it came to me that she must have known about it, she dressed me up for him, she kept me at home away from boys for him, she set it up so that he could get all of me he wanted, she put a little love seat in my room so he could sit with me and put me on his lap, but maybe she didn't do any of it and it's all my dreaming, I'm a great dreamer, that's why I know who's a great painter and why I'm so rich.

Well Malo made a vow that he would cure me of my father, he

said he would get rid of him, he would exorcise him, pull him out
of me to let love go in, and then he stopped talking about his sex
feelings for me, he got into reading some downtown Eastern tantric
books, he began to paint me now not just as if I was young you
know but as if I was immortal, he said I was a goddess, caryatid to
the world, I was the core of a Corinthian column, he made of me a
pediment, a portico, he put me on a plinth, he painted himself
painting me, himself a little skinny man in baggy pants, me now
Miss Universe, Miss Galaxy, Ms. Alpha and Omega, and my father
was disappearing because I was everything, the earth and stars and
matter everlasting, and one day he said look and I looked and he
put his hand on the breast of the goddess painting he made of me
and I felt it—I felt his touch on my breast like being brushed by a
beautiful star.

It took a long time, we would lie together and the star would
begin and I would expect to get my headache but it wouldn't come,
I would feel this space heating up inside me, Malo would tell me
let it move upward, let it go slowly up your back up to your waist
and we stayed there more or less through the winter when a dead
pigeon didn't smell on the rooftop near the studio because it was
cold and the snow was coming down outside the studio window
while the heat was moving up through me. We lay naked on our
mat for an hour a day and the hot spot started to get bigger and to
move up my back, some days the sun shone on the orange mortar
of the gray brick, the shadows of the houses outside divided the
buildings in half, sometimes at the corners, sometimes across, and
the shadow of a chimney fan was a giant prick, a white bowl of
green ferns in a window caught sunshine on its belly, the same
sunlight that was moving up my back and going into my head as
the spring came and buds started on the trees of the terrace he had
outside his window, a bird singing on an antenna drove the light
into my eyes and sinuses and down to my lungs and I was breathing
okay for the first time in years.

Finally when it was summer I could send the hot star all around
inside me and I began to want Malo to move more, to do something, to do anything, I began to be all open, he was painting me as
Ishtar and Astarte and Aphrodite, no more Miss this and Ms. that,
but the real sex stars. I was open, I was mythic, I decided I wanted
him inside me and one day he nuzzled in as cozy as a clam and I
pulled on his two earrings and touched his nose and he said with
tears in his lovely limpid eyes, oh his lovely limpid eyes bringing

up tears for me, he said I love you no matter what happens remember I love you and I care for you and I'm inside you forever now, remember me this way we have a long way still to go.

So then we began another journey, we had nothing but time and money and I was getting to be the Apotheosis of New York in the paintings—god—I sprouted wings, I was glorious maiden form only sexual as hell and Malo was teaching me to fly with my body, get ready to soar by squeezing the warm space up and up and through your head, squeeze me in, take me with you take me into you take me up through your brain, take my penis in your brain then squeeze it out of your body squeeze it out as hard as you can push it out get rid of it give birth to it, then squeeze it in again and take it up and around once more. . . .

We went to warm islands, we swam in green bays and I was taking him around inside me all the time his energy was healing everything even the time that I can't remember when I was terrified my father's dick was going to kill me because I couldn't breathe with it shoved into my mouth, and even though nobody had ever taught me how to pray I prayed to Moses to set us on fire like the burning bush so I didn't ever have to breathe again and that's why my asthma got so bad whenever I had a sexual feeling after that, I was afraid to die because he stayed in there so long everything went black, blacker than the dark in my room, and when I woke up or came to he was gone and I wasn't even sure it happened it was a bad dream I'm a big dreamer I always wake up dreaming I can't breathe. I didn't know how to tell my mother about my dream. I told Malo never to put it in my mouth I had a neurotic fear of dying and he promised he would never do that to me.

The spring started again and Malo said it was time for me to come but not like those little blips they record on the sex meters but really come the valley way and I didn't know what he meant, I wondered, I got scared because I'd been in the valley before, the valley of the shadow of my father, the valley of the shadow of death and I told him I didn't like that word so he said it was really more a drawn-out way, he made a little drawing to show me the lovely beautiful radiance that would come out of my head when I pushed the energy up and that was releasing my spirit from my body and how I could pull it down again while he did the same thing with great breathing—if we did it hard enough we would get to a plane of ecstasy and another and another and another until we were part of the cosmos until we were the cosmos itself, until we were in cosmic orbit he said spinning with no little slug-feet to stop us, no little wire brake on the rocket to unwind our force and float away.

I clenched I squeezed I pushed every muscle in my body with all my might and the orgasm was suddenly there in my nose in my lungs, pouring through my head, reaching out all across space in waves on waves on waves of blue flowers until it was so intense I thought I would explode or fall apart in tiny burned-out pieces of star or fragments of nebulae, I asked him to help me stop it please it was too much for me too much I wouldn't live until the morning and he drew breath and yelled out loud and after all that time he came, he came with splash on splash of hot white joy inside me I began to shake and laugh and cry and my orgasm kept going on with my head thrown back and him holding me and petting me and smiling me down even though it wasn't all over it was just the beginning.

That was pretty good for an old fifty-six-year-old piece of art, don't you think, doctor? I mean, we carried on and on and Malo began to get into the world of art, Mary wanted him and Leo and all thr rest of them wanted him, too, and even though they got him five figures he wanted six figures, he wanted real fame so the prices could really start upping in the stratosphere and I put him on a long string and let him fly because he wanted to show big-name and I was sure of him and how he loved me and I wanted him to have everything.

Well, one absolutely magnificent Bruno Civitico day when the sun was a golden shower of Zeus on a white linen morning I went to his studio and the mat wasn't down for us. He was eating peaches. He offered me some tea from his old gray pot, the steam rose in the bright cool air, and he said he was sorry he didn't feel any more sex for me, he didn't feel anything except love for me anymore. I didn't believe him I said you've got to be kidding you're my whole life and he looked at me with the flesh sucked into his cheekbones and he waved a limp hand with half a peach in it and he said he wasn't challenged anymore and the feeling had gone away but he would stay with me if I wanted. I asked him if all his energy had become spiritual the way the book said it should but he said no it had all been just the challenge and the ride and the excitement and now that he was there the trip was over, but he wouldn't desert me ever and we could live together as friends if I wanted, but he said it in a way that made it clear he really didn't want to be around me and I felt like ripping the bloody earrings off

his earlobes and slashing every painting he ever made of me and
tearing up the photographs of me by the pool that he used for my
face, I don't know who I want to kill more him or me, my asthma is
back and now I've got arthritis, my poor little fingers get red and
stiff in the morning and I'm too mad to call him to massage me,
doctor, do you think I should live with him as an unfriendly nurse
just for the company, I'm little Miss America dying with my headaches in my townhouse full of art, my silicone is falling, I'm a drug
addict, I can hardly talk clearly my mouth feels full of mush, I've
taken eighteen Seconals already today, I can't walk steady in my
high heels anymore, look at the roots of my hair they're all yellow,
please help me, doctor, I'm a gorgeous tiny thing, a beautiful piece
of art, I'm so lovely, such a good sweet person really, please, what
should I do?

Patti

To: E-man   SUBJECT: Incest
  11.30.91

You like large women, but you lost interest in Trish when she
got big, when she was six months pregnant. Aside from your feelings about me (thank you), which we can explore later, what do
you feel about your tiny, helpless little girl? I've been thinking about
fathers and daughters.

                                                              Aphra

To: go-dot   SUBJECT: helpless?
  11.30.91

Patti's a really bright bundle; she might even be a genius: outer-
directed, verbally identifying the world. She doesn't say See dog,

See bird, like other two-and-a-half-year-olds, she says See big brown dog. See white sea gull. See gray pigeon. And she never cries unless there's a very good reason, she knows all the neighbors and their children by name, she doesn't like any TV she can't understand, especially cartoons; she prefers to be read to from books, with explanations from the reader!

marc

To: E-man   SUBJECT: M-hm. . . .
11.30.91

That's what Patti's like, that's a good description, but what do you *feel* about her?

Aphra

To: go-dot   SUBJECT: mother
11.30.91

I don't know, exactly. I know it *hurts.* You see, i think she feels toward me the way i did to my mother when i was her age: when i was a toddler i remember my mother's perfume smelled so wonderful—i used to imagine that i was close to her, i wanted to be wrapped in her warmth instead of shivering between the cold sheets in my new bed which felt too big for me, and sometimes she would take me in her bed in the middle of the night, i remember the satin of her nightgown, the rough lace at the edges, the smooth round silky warm flesh spreading out on the mattress. . . . i was interested in the creases where all her parts joined, i wanted to see if she had hinges because i had no extra flesh the way she had, but she never let me explore after the first few times. I used to love the way she smelled in the morning, too, sharp, like wet salt.
You ask how i feel about my daughter and all i can manage is a sensual summary of my physical relationship with my mother.

marc

To: E-man   SUBJECT: Daughters
11.30.91

How you felt about your mother is a good way to build a bridge to how you feel toward Patti. You started to say it was painful—

Aphra

To: go-dot   SUBJECT: mother
 11.30.91

I haven't finished about my mother; years later, after the black
period, or my depression, or whatever it was, i reacted to my
mother with a kind of nausea: she always touched me a lot, i could
never respond, my chest constricted, my skin felt raw.

Marc, she'd say while touching me, your tie is not correct, or
Your collar is crooked, or Sit down, I want to tell you about my
childhood in France, and she'd try to hold my hand or she'd place
a confidential palm on my knee and i'd pull away or sit there rigidly.
I don't know what precisely was the matter, but after the black
period, i couldn't bear to touch my mother—i went cold on my
wife when she was pregnant—maybe my mother was too seductive
with me. . . .

marc

To: E-man   SUBJECT: Feelings
 11.30.91

Maybe, but *what do you feel toward Patti? What happens between
the two of you?*

A.

To: go-dot   SUBJECT: happening
 11.30.91

What happens is this:
Daddy, she'll say, *read Babar;* i prop myself up next to her on
pillows at the head of her bed and i open the book with the little
elephant holding his tophat in his trunk on the cover. I like elephants; they seem like important fun because of ganesha. I ask patti
What's the name of another elephant in stories, a very good elephant? Patti smiles, her front teeth digging into her lower lip as we
go through the familiar ritual: *Babar and Celeste.*

That's true, but who else?
Babar and . . . Babar!
Come on, you know the answer—
Babar and—Babar n'nesha
Good girl! Good job!
She smiles and claps her hands for herself. I read aloud:

IN THE GREAT FOREST, A LITTLE ELEPHANT IS BORN.
HIS NAME IS BABAR.

Inevitably, the sickness starts: i ask myself why i feel so agitated, my chest is tight, my gut seems twisted; why does reading to patti send pins of anxiety through me, pins that seem to prick at my skin as preparation for peeling it off?

HIS MOTHER LOVES HIM VERY MUCH. SHE ROCKS HIM TO SLEEP WITH HER TRUNK . . .

Patti's thumb goes into her mouth, she sidles up next to me; she wants me to put an arm around her shoulder. My arms feel heavy, immobile, i've lost sensation in my hands, the book may fall.

Daddy, rock Patti. Rock Patti in trunk.

Daddy's arm hurts. Daddy can't.

Daddy hurt arm.

May I read to you, please?

Read me about Babar.

HE IS A VERY GOOD LITTLE ELEPHANT.

Babar good e'phant.

Yes, and Patti's a very good little girl.

Patti good girl. Daddy rock Patti.

I can't.

Daddy rock Patti with trunk.

No more Babar.

Read more Babar.

I said no more Babar.

Kiss? Kiss? Kiss?

My mouth is dry, my heart is floundering in my chest; her baby skin is so soft, softer than lips, softer than eyelids . . . softer than the sexual skin on toni's thighs. . . .

Go to sleep. I don't feel well.

Daddy kiss Patti goodnight!

I can't!

Read more Babar!

Go to sleep! I said it's time to go to sleep!

She looks at me reproachfully, sucking her thumb; maybe she'll fall asleep peacefully enough. I get up, stand at the door and try to be a comforting presence. I dig my nails into my thumbpads to counteract the pain, the anxiety in my arms.

I have so much work to do: i have to enter patient visits, medicare demands an accounting for every single visit, i have to send out a billing—you'd think trish would help me, she's the one who's good at bookkeeping—i have to answer my e-mail, write to you, get out to cyberspace, my body feels more real extended through the monitor, reaching people in the matrix; i know i'll feel better when i'm touching the keys at the terminal.

Sometimes i feel like Case, you know, the hero of *Neuromancer,* with a load of toxin sacs in my blood waiting to disintegrate. I feel like they'll spill if i have to be human, warm feelings will melt the membranes and the toxins will kill me!

Maybe it's all right that i don't hug her, can't kiss her, maybe she understands, she seems so bright, it doesn't seem to be hurting her intelligence, it isn't doing her any harm.

The sobs begin, the muffled sounds that herald patti's crying, and then she starts calling in that funny cracked hoarse voice of hers that sounds more like a blues singer than a two-year-old child: *Daddy, tell story! Daddy, don't go 'way! Daddy, don't close door. . . . Daddy, come back. . . .*

I pull the door softly behind me, leaving a small crack for light, and head down the hall. *Daddy . . . daddy . . . open door . . .* she's screaming now. *Daddy-y-y-y. . . .* She'll have to stop, she'll just have to cry it out, there's no other way, she'll have to get tired sometime. Maybe she's a goddam spoiled brat after all!

Amy

16

1990

PRIVATE FILE: Do not send.

To: E-man   Subject: FATHERS AND DAUGHTERS

My father was a faraway star. No doubt about his distance. I see
him as cold, implacable, unreachable. So did my mother. And yet,
was he, really? Probably not. Probably not that much more than
anyone else. He came home most nights. He dutifully ate supper,
read the newspaper and listened to the radio. I'm sure he would
have talked if my mother hadn't filled the silences with her recita-
tions of victory. He might have been a good conversationalist. He
was charming with other people at the hotel. And he did teach me:
to ride a bike, to swim, to skate, to draw—what little he knew of

architectural rendering—and math, he helped with that. He's the reason I've always loved my teachers.

I always felt a stirring, a movement beneath the ice, life flowing there, undetectable. It was as though he was putting in his time, waiting for his real life to begin. His sister, who raised him, always described him as a loving child. Her Freddie. They slept together until he was sixteen. No one owned an individual bed in those days.

It's a mystery. Why do I present him as heartless?

And why do you present yourself as irresponsible with Danah, withdrawn from Trish, cold with Patti? It isn't possible. Marc Martell can't be that bad.

I don't know what will finally happen to the daughter of one of my patients, a girl named Amy. Her mother had an indefinable illness and wilted away from her husband. Amy may grow up to feel abandoned by affectionate rather than distant men. By comparison to the possible disaster for Amy, I consider that I had a secure childhood.

———

Doc, do you know what it's like for a man to bathe a little girl? Do you have any idea? Amy's four. Last night I gave her a milk bath with bubbles; she said my hand looked huge like the statue's hand in the park, you know, the Hans Christian Andersen made for kids to climb on his lap. I tickled her with my big bony fingers, I kissed her tiny neck under the ponytail and then I ran my hand down her spine over where she has a little too much hair. Her skin was softer than any skin I've ever touched, softer even than I remember my mother's, softer than the skin on all Morrissey's inner spaces.

How does she know how to get me to the heartbreak point, my little four-year-old vixen? How does she know how to bring me to the edge when she stands up naked in the soapsuds and looks at herself in the long mirror near the tub and asks me what I think of her lacy soapsuds nightgown? The suds are all torn in big holes, she says, and dips herself again and again in the milkfoam to come up, eyes shining with love and laughing in the steamy room so I don't want to leave any inch of her unkissed? Who taught her how to lie on her stomach in warm green water when the suds are low and look over her shoulder to her little round bottom rising out of the water and say to me, Daddy, there's a part of me sticking out, it's my elephant, I say I don't see any elephant, she grins, Oh silly, it's my heinie sticking out, and I want to kiss the round woman that is becoming, but instead I tickle her toes and talk about little piggies going to market but she knows. That's a baby game she says. Look, I have a beard, and she sculpts a foam beard under her big eyes and on top of her pointy chin, she figures out how to make a mustache and space for her lips by blowing and licking and then she says, I look just like you, I'm a daddy kissing his little girl, and kisses the little foam-feet that just went to market—kids are pretzels.

And what do you do when you wrap her in a soft white towel and rub her dry through the terry, rub the bath-warm muscles and the curves and she puts her arms around your neck and grabs your ribs with her feet and says, You're my daddy forever and ever and I love you and you will never go away and leave me, never never never, you'll stay home forever and ever and ever, you won't leave me not even for one night and I don't want a new mommy, I like my old mommy best.

So how do you kiss your angel girl good-night and tell your wife you're going to an architectural symposium for the firm and instead you take yourself across town to fuck Ellen Morrissey? What kind of man is that? What am I made of inside? Doc, I love Morrissey more than anyone else except Amy. Strange, me loving such a big woman, maybe the most abundant woman I've ever had the guts to walk the streets with. I mean, my mom was a big sweet warm messy paranoid schizophrenic, we've talked about that; after rushing to church to talk to her voices she used to come home and kiss all of us and feed us some slop, and finally they took her off to Creedmoor. God I was ashamed of her and now I love this monumental woman, she belongs in the Greek room on the first floor of the Metropolitan Museum, early Greek more like the Egyptians, she's such a colossus but she feels like a child when she trusts me and cries to me.

She says my build is really tremendous like her father who just died last year, and I'm also big like her two brothers who got killed in Vietnam when she was small. I don't mean to be narcissistic, doc, but I am built—even the women look at me when I work out. Anyway, I'm it, I'm all the men in her life, she cries all the time when she tells me that.

I take her to the park on Saturdays sometimes, just like Amy. I tell my wife I have some plans to check and I go over to Morrissey's apartment. First I fold her things from off the floor and I always hope to find some underwear—I love to wash it, I love smelling it and squeezing the soap through it—and then I wake her out of her moaning and move the books away from her legs—she falls asleep reading—I kiss her until she wakes and smiles for a minute, she has a cherubic lower lip, one of those with two little marbles in the middle that have never really closed, I wake her until she turns her face to the side on the pillow and runs her fingers through her hair, and then I gather her breast in my two hands and lick her nipple and slowly press my teeth around it harder and harder until the tears wet her pillow and she says stop, it hurts more than remembering. Then I suck her into my mouth, fill my mouth with her softness—have you ever seen how much breast babies get into their mouths?

In Central Park, Morrissey likes the rocks. She's heavy on her feet, like a peasant woman who has to keep climbing the mountain even though her heart is no good, and yet she's this blond cradle of sensibility, she's a poet, that's all she does, she has an inheritance. Tell me about the bedrock again, she says, in that voice that breaks on the vowels with the pain of being alive, it always gets right to me, tell me why you can build skyscrapers on Manhattan. So I tell her about the three layers of Central Park, the gneiss on the bottom and then the marble, and the schist on top, all we see is schist, and how the park was once mountains with peaks that we see only as small outcroppings after the cycles of upheaval. And what is schist made of, she wants to know. Sugar and spice and mica-bearing bands alternating with layers of quartz and feldspar. No, it's made of words, she says, everything is words. And we say the words of the intersecting minor rocks, amphibolite and granite and granite pegmatite, the pools of rock that were forced into the fractures, we say the words of the names of the rocks like a chant in the sun of Central Park on Saturday and maybe next week she will give me a poem about them to keep in my desk drawer at the office.

She leans back on a rock seat and her hand pushes back the

sunlit winged hair, my head is in her lap, my skull on the wide columns of her thighs, I want to build buildings on her thighs, Solomonic pilasters, she is all Pompeii and Herculaneum, she is a peristyle garden and a pool of Eden in her bed when my hands are on her hipbones and I am kissing her labia and I have to raise my head to see her face.

She cries when we make love, she tells me that no one, no one loves her and forces her the way I do, she makes me feel a sexual leviathan, I fill her vault with all my flesh and spirit; I love you, lave you, lavish you, she says, her blue eyes always running with black mascara, I privilege you, she writes.

We always buy balloons in the park, she has to have four red ones, it's funny to watch her try to skip like a child, she's so heavy, her breasts bounce in the T-shirt under her jacket, I want to walk behind her and hold them up, I want to be inside her walking behind her while the bicyclists wearing Mondrians go by and a man with a bowler hat and cane doesn't notice.

FAO Schwarz is just below the park: 1990 is Expo year, salute to Japan, I love Japan, believe it or not I won a big competition there last year, now everything is Eastern in toyland. The good green dragon flies along the ceiling, time flies on the happy moonface, doll robots rush clock hands around the dial, the ballerina lifts, the teddy meditates in his hot Zen balloon, we rise laughing on the escalator, we float high toward childhood, she wipes her eyes, I'm really a little girl from Ohio, she says, buy me a toy on the second floor where they sing, I wanna be loved by you.

So I buy her a porcelain doll for five hundred dollars that looks like her, blue eyes and winged blond hair, but Morrissey is no doll, she has all these contradictory features: square jaw, cherub lips, fine-chiseled nose, great blue delft eyes that are someday going to crack with tears.

When I am fucking Morrissey I can feel my cock reaching her cervix which is placed at just the right angle to be pushed, I smash up against it, knock the wind out of her belly, she groans me into a frenzy until I reach her womb again and again, because she can take so much I seem to come again and again without coming, sometimes eight or nine times in a row and by this time she is screaming, she's sobbing, she's soaking wet, she's stiff as a board with her orgasm that has become one long orgasm, maybe never to stop until I push her legs back and spread her wide and thrust into the tightness of her ass, her eyes flood open, the first time I did it she hit me, and that's how I finish in my baby Morrissey, that's how my sweet big-little girl likes me to say good-night.

Sometimes we go downtown to the Lower East Side and buy marzipan and chocolate ice cream and Danish pastry, we stuff our mouths and eat and kiss and wipe and walk, it's wonderful to be with someone who doesn't worry about her weight.

You know, the last time I saw my mother alive was before they reformed the state looney bins, she was crouching in the hall with her skirt up around her waist, her big white butt shining in the light bulb light, she was defecating brown turds on the floor and some old geezer was watching her and laughing and scratching his pecker until I called the attendant. That's a funny thing to remember, it's probably important, I never really said good-bye.

I want to marry Morrissey, doc, I want to live with her without shame, I want to have her child-woman self all day, I love the way she talks, I read her poems between the deals I make, the calls, the faxes, the conferences. The business is really taking off—we're building a new hotel in Moscow, I'm going to be traveling a lot, I want to take her with me, would it be so terrible to leave Amy with her mother, doc, I have to leave home anyway?

It's getting late, I have to go home, I have to take care of my wife, she'll be waiting in bed for me to bring her tea. She stays in bed most of the time these days, no one knows exactly what's wrong—Epstein-Barr syndrome, depression, bad blood—who knows? She used to be such a dynamo, but her career never took off and she doesn't seem to care about a second child. I bring her tea and I kiss her forehead, sometimes I bring her a cookie and ask how my skinny little girl is tonight, won't she eat something for Daddy, she's wasting away, is the doctor sure she's not anemic?

What do you suppose is the matter with her, she feels weak all the time and sleeps a lot, the depression pills aren't working but no one can find anything, I have to wait on her hand and foot, like a baby. I'm tired of taking care of little girls, doc. I want a big girl like Morrissey, I'm not ashamed of wanting a big woman anymore, I want someone who can take care of herself—a grown-up independent woman—I need an adult, doc, do you think I'll ever get there, do you think I'll get to Moscow with Morrissey?

Listen, I know our time is up but before you kick me out, before I go, one more thing. Another problem, women are always falling in love with me, I don't know what it is. Anyway, don't fall in love with me, doc. We don't need that. Okay? Even if I bring you a rock or a Popsicle.

Memory

A G E 8

1945

PRIVATE FILE: Do not send.

To: E-man   Subject: FATHERS AND DAUGHTERS

Survival was the goal of my paternal grandfather's life. Religious persecution had nothing to do with his focus on living rather than dying. He was the last of nine children, all born to a family in Vienna. The other eight perished during infancy. Only my grandfather survived. To improve his karma, the rabbi's wife raised him. He wore gold bracelets, a gold necklace and white linen changed daily until he was a man. He was granted every request, no matter how trivial or difficult. He lived. He also became rigid, narcissistic and demanding, hardly capable of taking care of himself, much less being a parent. But he had a beautiful voice and he sang the value of life.

By comparison to *his* father, mine was warm and loving. My father accepted the food my mother served without complaint. He worked. (My grandfather never understood the concept.) He gave money to his family for food and clothing; he ate together with his children rather than requiring separate service. He assisted my mother's efforts to be a hotelier. He taught us what skills he could. And with all this, I experienced him as someone I never knew at all.

I watch her sitting in my past, the little girl who is and was me; in the instant of recollection more than four decades disappear, time vanishing into time. The magical power of age can extinguish decades with the signal of a wish, roll back years faster than any computer, review old visions coded deeply in the memory of most important moments. I am eight years old. My black hair is plaited into two braids that hang behind my shoulders. Under my deep-set brown eyes, as if chalked in, are soft gray crescents that smudge my pale city skin. I am sitting—I sat—in the fourth seat of the first row of desks near the window.

"Roll call," Miss Eichner announced. "Sit on your hands in silence, please."

On the first day of classes after summer vacation, this year's teacher was taking attendance in the usual fashion at our school. Her green eyes under amber brows scanned the rows of desks as we placed our palms under our buttocks, our knuckles pressed in pain against the hard wood seats. We sucked our lips inward and bit them into the line that signified our intention not to communicate with any other member of the fifth-grade class at Public School 70 in the Yorkville section of Manhattan in the year 1945.

"Lotte Auer?"

"Present."

"Hans Bohne?"

"Present."

"Henry Buckholder?"

"Present."

"Eric Clausen?"

"Present."

I wondered whether to say "Present" or "Here" when my turn came. "Present" sounded refined, but although "Here" was only a grunt, it was somehow more eloquent. Neither response expressed my real state of mind at school. I lived in three dimensions of time at once. In addition to the dull present, there was the shining future (imagining the arrival of my new two-wheel bicycle); there was also the crystalline past (thinking about "The Snow Queen," a fairy tale I had read yesterday afternoon).

"Lise Ehring?"

"Present."

"Joseph Fischl?"

"Present."

"Karl Geiger?"

"Here."

"Christa Handwerker?"

"Here."

The Snow Queen
A Tale in Seven Stories
First Story

"Deals with a mirror and its fragments. Now we are about to begin, and you must attend; and when you get to the end of the story, you will know more than you do now. . . . " The first page of the fairy tale went on to say that the mirror reflected "every good and pretty thing as almost nothing, and magnified every bad and good-for-nothing thing so that it stood out and looked its worst. Scholars thought it showed what man was really like."

"Rolf Heinemann?"

"Here."

Rolf was a large, inert boy who was often left back with the same absence of plan that had pushed me two years ahead of my grade. I found myself staring at him as though seeing him through the dreadful mirror. His blond hair fell in oily strands across his forehead; his teeth, coated with a yellow-green scum, were too widely spaced; a wetness of spittle collected at the corners of his mouth; his blue eyes seemed colorless, with a white ring around the iris.

I tried to clear my vision of the mirror's effects by squeezing my eyelids together and then opening wide, but as I looked around, not only Rolf but all my new classmates seemed deformed. Their faces were speckled with sores, their shapes were bizarre: big heads on small bodies, large feet and hands. I tried to forget the mirror and think of the bicycle, the gleaming new wheels that soon would be mine alone and not my brother's. It was to be a girl's bike, with the center bar slanted down. Best of all, my mother had said that my father was going to teach me to ride it. But the vision of myself riding high on the bicycle did not suppress the demonic aspect of my adolescing classmates. I was seriously afraid that a fragment of the mirror had entered my heart: in the story, the mirror had smashed into hundreds of millions of billions of bits, one of which could enter a person's heart and turn it to ice.

"Gabriel Heinz?"

"Present."

"Antonio Izzini?"

"Present."

"Walther Kohler?"

"Present."

"Aphra Gold?"

"Here."

Miss Eichner tapped her list with the eraser of her pencil. "What sort of name is Aphra?"

People were always asking me that question. "The original Saint Aphra was a Christian martyr," I explained. "She was the patron saint of female penitents." My mother had chosen a name that began with "A" after my grandmother, Anna. She had selected Aphra so that I might remember her own martyrdom at being a woman—and possibly suffer it myself.

Miss Eichner's eyebrows slanted quizzically. "And what sort of name is Gold?"

"It's a Jewish name. My father says a long time ago a ruler re-named all the Jews and gave them nice names, like Gold and Silver, if he liked them."

"I see. . . . " Miss Eichner smiled. "Mark Konigsberg?"

"Present."

"Elsa Kraus?"

"Here."
"Mary Rozito?"
"Here."
"Anna Luther?"
"Here."

Rolf's eyes were focused on me with an intense vacancy. After roll call, when we lined up at the front of the room to get our permanent "size places," I was glad to be the smallest and, therefore, first in line. That meant Miss Eichner would usually be close to me when we marched to assembly and recess. Rolf would be far away, at the back of the line.

The bicycle was navy blue with silver trim. The handlebars were brilliant chrome. Zoli, the Hungarian doorman whose name was short for Zoltan, accompanied it to our apartment when the delivery boy brought it from Rappaport's toy store. "On the seat of this bicycle only a queen will sit," he said, taking the bike from the boy and wheeling it into our dining room area, where he propped it against the wrought-iron railing that became its permanent home.

Our apartment had what was known as a dropped living room. As you entered from the hall of the first floor, the dining room was on a platform; two steps down was the living room, furnished with my mother's treasures: several small Persian carpets (with designs suitable for playing hopscotch), my father's English-style mahogany kneehole desk (never to be touched by anyone else), and two pastel sketches of Venice acquired on the honeymoon in Havana (the lantern hanging behind a stone arch and the bridge across a canal were, perhaps, the most romantic fantasies my parents ever had). There were also two important pieces of furniture: a wine-red mohair sofa with a mountainous down pillow (where my brother and I wrestled every afternoon before dinner) and a deep, spacious green-striped chair (where my grandfather sat until he died and where I now sat to read "The Snow Queen" and other tales).

The bicycle leaned permanently against the wrought-iron railing between "dining" and "living" because the apartment house provided no basement bike rack or any interior space for it. Yet compared to the other children in my class at P.S. 70, I lived in a luxurious—indeed, a palatial—home, a house with a doorman, a home where every room had windows, a box-style apartment where parents and children slept in different quarters. For Yorkville in the forties, while clean, was very poor. The German majority had not prospered as much or immigrated as early as my family, which arrived in the late nineteenth century; there was also a sprinkling of Italians, Armenians, Hungarians and Czechs who spoke mainly their own language. The children in my class slept in corridors, the central windowless compartments in railroad flats, where only the front room and back kitchen had windows. The room my brother and I shared faced directly on the street and had a whole corner of casement windows, below which a ledge enclosed a small garden.

My mother made a litany of telling me that my classmates had no rooms of their own, only dark cells to share, but that their lives (and mine) were a whole lot better than hers as a child. Her mother, my grandmother Anna, tossed mattresses on the floor in all the rooms of their railroad flat over the dry goods store. My mother's two brothers and three sisters slept on any unoccupied mattress they could find. I was to remember that I was one of the most privileged children in the world because I had a cot of my own and a room with a window. I came to believe that I was, indeed, among the economic and social elite.

My father returned home for dinner at seven almost every night of the week except Thursday. Occasionally he was late, but on Thursdays he had evening conferences in Brooklyn and stayed the night at his brother's house. He was a civil engineer in charge of waterways, the chief engineer in fact, and it was hard to discuss matters with certain contractors and government officials during the day. My mother felt relieved of cooking that night. We usually celebrated with delicatessen. But on most other nights, in the hour between six and seven, he usually shaved, bathed to cleanse himself of "germs" and dressed in a clean shirt, the trousers that he wore at night and his dinner jacket, gray wool with gray corduroy lapels. With his slender build, prematurely white hair, erect posture and fine-boned face, he seemed to me the epitome of cultivated elegance. As we sat down, he would switch on the radio for us all to listen to Lowell Thomas and the seven o'clock news. Then, ceremoniously, he would open his dinner napkin (he insisted on cloth) and place it in his lap. My brother and I followed suit. We started on our grapefruit sections. The rest of the meal was waiting in the kitchen: chicken soup with homemade noodles, veal chops, potatoes, apple pie baked yesterday. I always felt that the hearty food was incongruous with my father's genteel inner anatomy, but he never complained. We had a four-course dinner every night he was home. Whether or not he arrived on time, my mother always prepared for him. She ate before we did so that she could serve us. She returned to the kitchen to prepare the next course. Her shining black hair was pompadoured in front and rolled up in the back to keep it off her neck; in the autumn heat her strong, broad back and the ample frontage—the imposing ledge of bosom inside her apron—seemed to steam along with the hot food.

Lowell Thomas's voice was funereal as he discussed the death of Franklin D. Roosevelt on the eve of victory. Among other quickly reviewed headlines were Simpson's troops at Magdeburg near Berlin and the opening of Buchenwald. I tried to imagine a world without FDR and without the threat of extermination. I couldn't conceive either.

My mother returned to the room, carrying two plates of soup. "The bicycle has been here for three weeks," she said to my father, setting the first plate down in front of him. "When are you going to teach her?"

"Please, Nettie, I'm listening to the news," my father replied.

After serving my brother, she picked up the used fruit saucers from the flowered tablecloth and complained that all my father ever listened to was the news. "Listen to what's going on around you instead of drowning us out with the news."

"Nettie, the President is dead but Lena and Sam might still be alive. They only went to camp two months ago. Who knows where they went? Maybe the other camps will be opened soon."

My mother stood at the head of the table, her black hair now a halo of angry doom. "You're like the Germans, you're the Führer, all you know is your routines, your dinner, your news. Maybe you'll give us appointments when we can talk to you."

My father flushed, his neck rising out of his long, thin body, his shoulders tightening. "Will you be quiet and let me listen? What do I have to do?"

"You're going to teach her right after Hebrew school on Sunday," my mother continued. "If you don't get started, the bicycle will be too small for her before she learns to ride it. You'll teach her this Sunday after school."

"That's enough." My father raised a long, neatly manicured finger. "No more. From now on, no talking at supper. No talking, period. Silence. That's an order."

My brother, who was a genius and attended Hunter College Elementary School kindergarten (for which, as a female, I had not been tested), got up from the table. "Where do you think you're going," my mother asked. "You didn't eat anything."

"I don't feel good," he answered, rubbing his eyes under the thick round glasses he wore for his myopia. "The news makes me sick. Even good news makes me sick."

"You're making the children sick with your news. Why do we have to hear it at dinner?"

My father's hand trembled as he continued to eat his soup. "The war in Germany is almost over," he said. "Now we have to finish Japan."

My mother shook her head. "I'm not interested," she said. "War is never over."

On Sunday morning a black swastika appeared on my window. It fully occupied one of the casement panes. As I awoke I thought it was an enormous spider; then I recognized the design. It was a painted cross, really, with tails at right angles to each end of the cross. My mother said that someone drunk on Saturday night must have climbed the garden ledge and painted it on the glass. My father drank his orange juice thoughtfully and asked me if there had been any trouble at school. I told him that school seemed okay. He warned me to be careful and stay away from the German kids. Some of them were hoodlums. I said I didn't know how I could do that, exactly. My mother got some turpentine from the superintendent and washed the swastika off.

That afternoon my father folded his newspapers on the dining room table, switched off *La Gioconda* and went to the hall door with instructions to me to take the bicycle and follow him. My heart thrust at my chest. I wheeled the bike through the door and held the handlebars while my father picked up the rear wheel to get us down the few steps to the lobby. Zoli smiled at us with Hungarian joy. We proceeded into the sunny street.

"I'll hold the bike up while you get on," my father instructed. I climbed onto the seat. My left hand on the black rubber handgrip almost touched his left hand. I could sense his right hand on the seat, near my bottom. He rolled the bike forward slowly. I felt perfectly secure. My father, who hardly ever spoke to me, much less touched me, was instructing me and protecting me physically at the same time.

"Now put your feet on the pedals and push." I did as I was told. The bicycle moved faster. He had to trot to keep up. "Push harder," he said. The bicycle sped ahead and now he was jogging behind it, his hand still on the seat. "Pedal harder!" I pushed as fast as I could and he was running as I rolled halfway down the block. "Now slow down," he called. "Keep your feet still. Push the pedals backward to make yourself stop." I reversed directions and the bicycle slowed to a halt. Breathing quickly, he looked at me with what almost appeared to be approval.

While he was catching his breath, I decided to ask a question. It was risky but he seemed in a good mood. "Why doesn't a bicycle fall down when you're riding?" I asked. "Why does it stay up on only two wheels?"

"You tell me," my father said.

"I didn't tip over because you were holding me."

"But I wasn't holding you at the end."

"Then how did I stay up?"

He smiled, pleased with himself, pleased with me. "You didn't fall because the faster a bicycle goes, the more stable—the more it stays up straight. You have to pedal hard to keep things going in this world. Now, what do you do if you think you're going to fall?"

"Go faster."

"Right. And which way do you turn when you're falling? You turn into the fall and go faster. You have to go with it to go against it, counteract the fall with centrifugal force. Well, it isn't as simple as all that—there's more about the steering angle curve, the forkpoint, the torque—but that's all you need to know for now." He pulled one of my braids with what was, for him, a show of affection. "We'll do it a few more times now and again next Sunday, and then you're on your own."

At school, Miss Eichner announced that there was going to be a new subject in fifth grade. The Board of Education didn't require it until the seventh grade, but she thought it was important that we study current events now. We were all to go home and listen to the radio and read the front page of a big newspaper, not a tabloid. Then we would talk about world news in class.

When our first lesson in current events began, Miss Eichner asked for volunteers to tell anything that they knew was going on in the world. In our school, the only time you raised your hand to talk was to be excused to go to the bathroom. The authorities felt that silence was necessary to keep order. No one was in the habit of volunteering. Miss Eichner made the request again. I felt my hand going up, as though someone else were raising it. Miss Eichner inclined her head expectantly toward me.

It wasn't easy to talk. My father had frequently told me that girls didn't need to talk; they only had to know how to diaper babies. While my mother had no objection to my conversation, she never seemed to have time to listen. I took a deep breath and jumped into the abyss of public speaking by saying that Franklin Delano Roosevelt had just died at the age of sixty-three and that Harry Truman would be the next president.

"Good." Miss Eichner beamed. "Anything else?"

I thought about Sam and Lena and my cousins who might possibly still be alive. "The American soldiers are letting the prisoners out at Buchenwald. There may be no more"—it was a big word—"persecution."

Miss Eichner looked quickly around the room. She seemed frightened. She shook her head. "We don't know about all that. About the Catholics and the Jews—it could be true—it could be stories. Just stories, that's all." Miss Eichner's eyes searched for another volunteer. The class sat with lowered heads, mutinous, sullen, angry. Rolf raised his hand even more slowly than I had. Miss Eichner recognized him and he lumbered up to standing position. When he was on his feet, he stared at me for a long time. Then he sat down, as slowly as he had stood up. No one else volunteered.

At recess after lunch I was leaning against the school wall, my face up to the sun, my eyes closed. I wasn't big or strong enough to play pummeling ball games with the boys, and the double-dutch clothesline jump rope that the girls used turned too fast for me to get in. It seemed to me that the shadows of trees were moving across my face, although there were no trees in the schoolyard. I opened my eyes. Rolf was standing above me, his large body wavering. "What do you want, Rolf?" I asked. His big hand lifted, then lowered again. "What do you want?"

"*Jude,*" he said softly through the spaces in his teeth, his upper lip lifted in contempt. "*Jude,*" he repeated.

I moved away from him as my father had instructed.

· · ·

My second. lesson on the bicycle was an even greater success than the first. My father was obviously pleased with my natural aptitude. I was so excited to be near him that my feet pedaled as though I were an infant kicking with delight. The warm flesh of my father's hand pressed against my back; his chest leaned across my shoulder as he held both handlebar and seat; his panting increased as I pedaled faster and he had to let go of the handlebar. The feel of the seat between my legs, the motion and the faint fresh smell of his shaving soap thrilled me with a delirium of craving. I wanted him to start me again and again; I could have done it with him all day. When he got tired, I felt let down, abandoned, alone. I wanted to continue the new feeling forever, the ecstasy, the soaring, the high. Instead, I had to accept termination, frustration, sorrow. I wanted more. I couldn't have it. I was on my own. The teaching was over.

After school on Tuesday of that week, Zoli helped me out with the bicycle so that I could try riding it entirely by myself. He was too fat to run with me, but he held the bike up until I got started. I pushed hard on the pedals and to my amazement began to roll down the street, light as air, all alone. A few more really strong strokes and I was gliding, passing buildings, dogs, people, who then became a blur as I was suddenly tied onto my reindeer, darting toward Lapland to find the Snow Queen, over briars and bushes, over swamps and plains, through the big wood as fast as we could go to rescue my love. The wolves howled and the ravens screamed while the red lights quivered up in the sky as we went faster, faster, faster, leaping across the cold sky, crashing into a huge bright star and falling . . . falling . . . falling against the sidewalk as the voice yelled "Jude!" and the big hand rubbed my face into the cement. Behind Rolf, through the hot blood leaking into my eyes, I saw Hans and Eric and Karl. They were throwing things at my head, pieces of metal, pieces of wood, a bag of garbage. A foot kicked my stomach, my chest, my mouth. "Dirty Jew whore," the shoe-voice said. "No more lies. No more current events." Suddenly I felt very cold and dizzy and far away. When I opened my eyes, I was warm and wet with blood and comfortable in Zoli's arms as he carried me into the apartment.

My Uncle Morris, the doctor, was called to look at me. He found that my nose and three ribs were broken. He taped my chest and ordered me to stay in bed for a week to make sure there were no aftereffects of concussion. If I got too drowsy, I would need an X ray. I was lucky I hadn't lost any teeth.

As soon as I could talk I asked about my bicycle. It was gone. There would not be another. It was too dangerous. After a week, my parents sent me back to school with an admonition about keeping to myself and not talking to anyone.

For months after the beating, when I came home from school I locked myself in the bathroom for at least an hour, partly to keep myself from wanting to ride the bicycle, which had provided wheels for Eric's new crate-wagon, partly to be sure no one would follow me in and hurt me. I didn't initiate talking in class for several years. No one noticed my muteness. You got graded only on what you wrote. During supper at home, we listened to the end of World War II in obedient silence.

PART SIX

EROTIC EDUCATION

Soma

To: go-dot
12.8.91

SUBJECT: teachers

Once upon a time, my mother read to me in french, *Le Petit Prince, Les Aventures de Pierre et Jean,* she spoke only french before the truck killed my brother. She kept us near her apron, hand-raised us as though we were in the parisian suburbs instead of brooklyn; that deepened the darkness after donny's death, when she chose to speak only english, chose to leave me mute in the echoes of what seemed a foreign language.

I wondered what death was. I thought it must be like a cold; even though it didn't make me cry into a handkerchief, i wondered if i'd caught it.

People say that their memories don't go back as far as the third year, but i truly remember that time, the year before death came; everything after that in my early childhood has vanished, but that was the year my mother gave to teaching me: *l'alphabet, les chiffres, les couleurs, le triangle, le cercle, le petit chien, voilà l'avion....*

Later my father taught me arithmetic; when i was much older he taught me math (between dinner and the airport). He gave me real insight into geometry, algebra, trig and calculus—whatever i was having trouble with at the time—he bought me my first slide rule. I still have it, not that i need it anymore.

My brother taught me best: how to walk, run, climb, jump, throw a ball, wrestle (he never hurt me), make funny faces, build a sand castle against the waves at the beach in summer: those memories are perfectly clear because the sunlit images, the highlights in the photographs, blacked out so abruptly; suddenly the world froze into grayness, snow filled the screen and i crept along the ice, looking for a horizon, searching for the golden keyhole, trying to crawl back into the magic past, but it had disappeared, everyone was gone, there was no one to show me where to go, no one to teach me.

Later i always tried to be close to my teachers; there's something erotic but more than erotic in it, a transference back to that shining time when everyone taught me.... and now you're involved in that golden grid, that data mesh of childhood cobwebs, gleaming, and i search for you down the long tunnel.... i don't know the code to bridge your silence, to reach you, because i want to reach you despite yourself, i always want to reach deep into any woman i'm involved with, to gain entry so irrevocable that i can never be shut out or denied again.

I remember my philosophy teacher at college, sophia maggio, soma we used to call her, she looked a little like toni but emotionally she was like you, just this side of being clerical; all philosophy was based on her italian catholicism: she postulated a First Cause and went on from there to other questionable hypotheses like sin and absolute virtue. She'd never married but lived in a large, immaculate, almost empty apartment, perfect for the parties she never held, on the top floor of a building on the edge of campus.

Walks and meals with sophia were a ritual of health and cleansing; in her indeterminate (late?) thirties, she was tall, broad-based —she wore flowing clothes and jewelry to follow her curves: long necklaces below dangling earrings, ankle length skirts that hung like sculpted drapery in motion—she seldom dated (although there was campus gossip about a failed engagement).

She was consumed by a life of teaching, service, contemplation, but male students in her class often began the semester with perverse comments about her anatomy; women sought her out as a strong feminine, even feminist, presence on the humanities faculty.

I'd try to feel absolved after we walked at the hour of vespers, then climbed to the roof above her apartment and watched the lifelight flicker into the town below us. . . . she brought our meal up there—brown bread, fruit, cheese, wine—she gave me my taste for the "vegetarian slush" trish objects to. . . .

But absolution felt more like temptation even though Sophia once confessed very tactfully and carefully that she'd never before met a young man who aroused *maternal* feelings in her as i did; she felt sometimes as though i were a son or a favorite nephew, and when i came to her door she'd greet me in a rush and then she'd stop herself with both hands outstretched on the door frame, as though waiting for me to kiss her as a filial toll for entry.

But i was not her son, i couldn't honestly kiss her as a son, and i stood still until she stepped back. She'd lower her eyes, as if in gratitude for my self-denial, and we'd hug lightly in benediction, but i could feel her heart beating, i could see the flush at her throat, and even though my experience was limited to women who were children by comparison to sophia, i was almost certain that the heartbeat would make something happen someday—i didn't know when—i didn't know why not now. I began to feel held up at the door, kept out, locked out of the room. Sophia's "tenderness" began to seem an esoteric form of torture, but i kept visiting. . . .

Over the next year, i met my first wife, danah, who was funny and strong and gave me everything she had without reservation: sex, money, love, her car, her apartment—even her old exams! She wasn't "nice"; she could be rough—bitchy—but life with her was bright, sharp, alive, challenging. (I didn't realize it and neither did she, but the first manic episode of her manic-depressive illness was beginning.)

We three became friends during the period that might be called an engagement; there were dinners and movies together—sophia's gold cross always gleaming on the olive skin over the heartbeat that i could almost see in the shadow at the base of her neck—but our private meetings continued, just the two of us, for coffee, for walks down the *grande allée* of oaks in the evening after classes; always there were the long philosophical and theological talks—about appearance and reality, ontology and epistemology, god and good, culture high and low, the one hero and the many faces. . . :

And always there were the unacknowledged tremors, the moments of erotic unfulfillment that bound me to her, fastening my mind on her, keeping me wondering what she felt, why she felt it and whether i should break the tension.

I was surprised when she offered us her apartment for the wedding. It was large enough to hold all our friends, it was a simple, white, quasi-monastic sort of place; we accepted.

The day of the wedding, i came in the morning to see how it looked, to see what i could do to help (danah was busy trying to get a hairdresser to do something for her hair that she could do better on her own).

Sophia must have spent her month's income on flowers, white roses and lilies in festoons, in vases, on trellises and in clusters; one small bouquet of red roses lay, like the single touch of red in paintings—the tiny figure in the corot landscape, the hat in the venetian gondola—at the feet of the small bronze statue of saint theresa that stood on the sill of a leaded bay window, background for the little pulpit where the judge would stand. . . . the flowers were still partly closed; on this bright day they would blossom perfectly by afternoon. . . .

She greeted me, stopping a foot away as always at the door. I'd always seen her dressed for school; i was unprepared to find her barefoot, her long black hair still wet from a shower, her white terry robe tied loosely at the waist. . . . she looked like an artist's model (matisse?) between poses, her hips and buttocks squared above the roundness, her robe casually fastened, soon to be opened again. . . .

I left my sandals at the entrance, offered a hand; she took it, saying openly that today she wished she were younger, today she wished she were the bride.

I held on to her hand as we went inside. The white flowers contrasted with the darkness of sophia's skin. We walked between the rows of gilded chairs, like bride and groom, down to the reading stand in front of the leaded bay window, and then she turned to me, her eyes round and brown and warm with all the great questions, her robe thick with wetness, her breathing slow and shallow. . . . our lips moved closer. . . . she kissed me hard. I stood still, holding out until she had almost given up, and then i finally returned her kiss, crushing and violating her mouth with it.

She shivered in delight or pain or both, then touched me below as i slipped my hands under the lapels of her robe, cupped her breasts, pinched her nipples too hard as we kissed. . . . she opened her robe and let it drop off: it was hotly july, she was naked underneath and she sank to her knees on the small figured carpet that danah and i, bride and groom, would soon stand on, she began fondling me, stroking me, kissing me, the penitent at transgressive prayer. . . . she pulled me down on top of her. . . .

Make love to me, make love to all of me, she said. Even my soul.

I kneeled above her, my face close to hers, our bodies far apart. I said Fuck love.

She lifted herself on her elbows and began to slide out from under me. I drew back to let her go but she stopped moving. She lay perfectly still, waiting. I told her she didn't want real blood love, she was looking for sin, for a sick victory. Today i was getting married, i was taking holy vows! Did she want to spoil it for danah? I asked her Should I always remember today as my wedding day to *you*?

When she said please, i went in and then i don't know how many orgasms she had, repeating Yes yes no, Fuck you, Don't, Yes now more, and then Oh my God as i hiked her buttocks up under me and pushed furiously deep into the tightness between her haunches. . . . her voice broke, her head turned aside, the sweat ran under the crescents of her small breasts with their pale nipples that had never known pregnancy, her belly heaved where the dark soft hair began high near her navel. . . . we moaned and thrashed and i rode her hard, punishing her ass with the frenzy of my crisis for all my long waiting, for my betrayal, for her generosity.

You're evil, she said sitting up; she kissed my belly and wrapped her arms around my bare knees, then held my hands tightly in hers as if to protect herself from me. You're Milton's Satan, she continued, as though she thought i'd enjoy the role.

Aphra, *you* know i don't enjoy morality games. I'm not baptized and that may be why i've become the whole stinking unwashed conscience of the jewish/christian world and i said: I'm not Satan, I'm Paul the biblical letter-writer and you're a cocktease and this isn't a goddam ethics poem, it's a movie. This is the last tango at ann arbor, only i didn't use butter. . . .

She repeated how i was evil, evil and vile, and how now she hated me, and i told her if there was original sin around here, it wasn't mine. I told her she wanted the flesh without having to commit to it. I told her i would never again fuck a woman who didn't make it clear right at the start that she was willing, i wouldn't even kiss a woman unless she wanted sex openly; she'd have to ask for it, she'd have to dress for it, and she sure as hell couldn't give me any mother/son sister/brother stories. I only wanted one small piece of data: was there a single woman in the world who would take responsibility for herself?

She let out her breath in a sharp, deep sound of mortification and bit the back of her hand hard enough to draw blood. I touched the blood with my forefinger and spread it on the gold cross at her neck. The caterers were ringing the doorbell. . . . she quickly pulled on her robe and tied it securely. . . . i deliberately avoided her during and after the wedding. As it turned out, we never spoke again.

Memory

AGE 19
1956

PRIVATE FILE: Do not send.

To: E-man   SUBJECT: EROTIC EDUCATION

At the University of Chicago in 1955, the exam on the hundred great books was—astonishingly—multiple choice. The question on James Joyce's *Dubliners* was: What coin did the young narrator hold tightly in his hand while he was on the way to the fair in "Araby"? I didn't remember. Joyce was the first of the hundred authors I read; his stories seemed the most accessible. Almost a year had gone by since I was spellbound by the pages. I'm sure I didn't guess correctly because the right answer, a florin, which I looked up later, seemed like an Italian coin to me when I had to choose.

What was graven in my mind was the *end* of the story. "Gazing up into the darkness," Joyce had written, "I saw myself as a creature driven and derided by vanity; and my eyes burned with anguish and anger." That last line stayed with me long after it proved useless on the exam, because it also described the end of my first love.

Why are we so often disappointed or humiliated by first love? Sophia gave you admiration, support and eventually her body, but it was too late. That year, Dean Culverton tried to be my friend as well as my first lover. He betrayed me for reasons he perceived as the only alternative to betraying himself. I thought I would never forgive him. Although, like you and Sophia, we never spoke again, soon after I left him, I did forgive him. I wrote a play indirectly about our relationship. It was a verse drama in which society destroys itself in war as it feeds on young love like a bird of prey. Maybe that's what writing has been—a way for me to forgive—my lovers, my parents, myself.

Ever since I can remember, I've had a variety of imaginary relationships. The people are real enough; only the communication is imagined. I pick someone—or perhaps I am selected in some mysterious way—and the person becomes my mental companion for anywhere from a couple of months to many years. You're my muse now, Miss Bonner, because I'm having some difficulty starting to write a play for your course, Playwriting I. Don't misunderstand: I want to write a play—that's why I registered—but I know very little about the theater. The plays I've seen in modern language seem pretty tame, if not dull. *Death of a Salesman, Our Town,* assorted musical comedies—compared to Shakespeare, even compared to Marlowe or Ben Jonson, they're almost simplistic. Were people who lived a couple of hundred years ago that much more complex than we are? Can people who are alive today in 1956 really watch current drama, even the good stuff, without feeling they've heard it all before, and much more eloquently expressed?

By the way, do you know that I'd like to cut my hair the way you do, short in front and long in the back? But even though I'd prefer to be different, I'm not the experimental sort. I've always worn my hair long and straight, without taking any chances on being shaped by some pioneering scissors. But I have such a small forehead that I do think I'd look much better with the hair around it full and wavy.... Your hairstyle is theatrical, like your voice. You must have wanted to be an actress, but instead you teach playwriting and literature....

The point is this: I'm back in New York now after spending my junior year at the University of Chicago, where I had a love affair that ended badly. That doesn't sound interesting enough. Try this: I had a tragic love affair with an actor/poet that ended in disaster. Redundant. If it was tragic, then of course it ended in disaster. That's what he kept saying at the end, over and over, redundantly. He had "breath-pressing premonitions of disaster." He was right. And now I want to write a play about it all, but how to put it together?

First of all, conversational dialogue won't work. We didn't talk much, really. All I remember is the phrase about breath-pressing and "What's for dinner?" and "While you go to the library I'll go to rehearsal." Once he told me that my weight was beginning to climb "up there." So I ate puffed oats and skim milk for breakfast and Ry-Krisp sandwiches with lettuce and tomato for lunch and lost ten pounds almost instantly. That's a miracle, but not material for a play.

We spent most of our time together making love. While that was very exciting, it's hardly a plot. But there is one scene that I'd love to put into a play, just visually. The stage is dark and empty. One street lantern glows in the fog. We stand in the portal of a Gothic arch—the university is quite Gothic—and even though we don't even know each other's names yet, we are kissing passionately. I'm still a virgin, but I'm sure that he will be the one to know me first. I think it will probably be tonight. I've even unzipped him to touch the wonderful hard hot part that is going to enter me for the first time—you can't show that on stage of course—but the stage lights play on us and on the splay of the doorway, the piers, the tympanum, the archivolt, the trefoil, the gable—moving upward to the pinnacles and spire and down again to us coiling and uncoiling in the cold black night under the yellow lamplight in the fog....

What I want to tell you is that it took forever until we found a place to make love. I couldn't go back to his room at International House because women were not allowed, and he couldn't come to my room at Gates Hall because men were not allowed, and we both knew that we didn't want to get caught outdoors in the shadow of the architecture of religion and scholarship.

I'd like to work that scene in, somehow, because our feeling is so brilliant, like Chartres at night, illuminated from within, the stained-glass windows glowing like lanterns. Yet the actual university was as drab as Elsinore in a black-and-white *Hamlet*.

Probably that embrace would be better in a movie than a play. The camera could move up along the flights of the flying buttresses and suddenly the scene could burst into the burning-bright jeweled glass kaleidoscope of my imagination. . . . Well, that first kiss was important and it has to be in the play somewhere, yet the whole relationship was quite out of character for me. I don't know how we met. I think he followed me around and asked me to have coffee with him. I wasn't even sure he was a student; he was so much older. I'm nineteen now, so I was eighteen then, and Dean was twenty-seven. That was his name, by the way: Dean Culverton.

What do you do with your time? Somehow I don't think you go out with men. I didn't see your disfigurement at first; it's not that obvious but the effect could come from the scar across your forehead that you conceal with makeup, or the way your eyebrow rises quizzically as a result. As I've studied you in class, I've begun to wonder. I somehow can't imagine you kissing a man or a man kissing you. I think of you as going home and having dinner— some cereal or a salad: you're so thin—and then you go to the theater with a woman friend. You've chosen to teach women. Your voice speaks to us as though we were your collective lover. You caress us with your vocal cords. I want whoever represents me in the play to project as you do.

The next thing my first lover and I had to accomplish was to find a place to be alone. We knew it wasn't going to be a quick liaison, which is why we didn't leave campus and go to a hotel. Besides, I couldn't imagine giving my virginity (if that can still be said to be a gift) to someone in a hotel room. I more or less grew up in a hotel and it would feel strangely incestuous to have sex in a place that reminded me that much of home. I thought I needed a reassuring, comfortable sort of apartment to free me for my first experience.

I didn't give up my dormitory room (I couldn't), and Dean didn't give up his, but we did take an apartment about twenty blocks off campus. I had twenty-five dollars a week as an allowance, which was more than ample to pay the rent, buy groceries and pay for the odd lunch at the student cafeteria for both of us. Dean didn't have to spend any money, which was a good thing because he didn't have any. I don't think he ate much more before he met me than the snacks provided to the university's acting company. He was on some sort of scholarship after having spent seven years in the navy. He never answered any questions about why he'd been in the navy or where he went while he was in. All he told me was that he liked the job because he could read incessantly, thousands of books. He'd wanted to absorb all the world's knowledge. He had read all the authors I ever mentioned to him; the hundred great books that were such a chore for me took him about two weeks to review before the exam. He barely needed to read for the course we took together (English Philosophers from Bacon to Mill. . . . It turned out that we were enrolled in the same program for an early master's degree in English literature). He had only to refresh his memory. I couldn't imagine anyone reading John Stuart Mill on utilitarianism all the way through for pleasure, but he had done it on his own. He was so well read that I didn't even realize that his main interest was acting. It took him only about two hours to learn the leading man's lines for a whole play, to memorize them completely!

Another scene that ought to be in my play is our apartment. I can't quite see how to work it into the plot, if I ever get the plot straight, but that apartment was perfect for the stage. We had a kitchen, a living room, a bedroom, bath and garden on the ground-floor rear of a one-family house converted to small flats. It must have been furnished with stuff that was secondhand during the Great Depression; the Salvation Army would probably not accept it now. The walls were so cracked and sooty that it seemed as though a set designer must have worked on them before we moved in. Old throws covered the round arms of the once plump club chairs in the living room; dust rose to choke us when we sat down. In the kitchen everything stood on legs: the stove, the refrigerator, the sink and the chipped enamel gateleg table. Water came slowly out of the faucets; the gas didn't work on two out of four burners, and the refrigerator didn't make ice. The cupboard was filled with mismatched green Depression glass and crazed china; the linoleum floor had spots worn through. There was even an old Philco radio in a cabinet that must have come from a Broadway stage set. It didn't work no matter how many times I forgot and turned it on.

But we had taken the apartment mostly for the bed: a high iron bedstead with clean, inviting-looking linen and a thick goosedown coverlet. We were in that bed ten minutes after I'd paid the rent and security and the landlady, smiling as sweetly as any crafty crone in a Dickens novel, had shut the door. Unfortunately, we could never use the bed after the first night. By morning we looked like victims of some exotic tropical disease. Bedbugs. We brought blankets and linens from our dorm rooms and camped out on the floor until my first lover found us a tiny cell right near the university that he could keep nautically clean.

Integral to the tragedy was that our only truly romantic moment was the first kiss. Any further adventure was all imagination. But the mind may be all there is. When I am seated on its winged silver horse, it doesn't matter if I'm being eaten by bedbugs in a rooming house or making love on a sofabed in what might have been an old closet. My first lover could make my illusions seem real.

You can do it to me too. Miss Bonner, when you read aloud in class, you excite me, especially when you read something I've written: a sketch, a description, a slice of dialogue. You've read four of my practice pieces aloud. It makes me feel as if you love me. I can't describe what happens to my body when you do that. I feel as if you're filling me with sunlight. But even when you read poetry or something else that's not mine, I feel loved by your voice. Yesterday, when you quoted Lorca, I wanted our minds to melt together: "If you can believe that a tree may be changed into a puff of smoke because I tell you it can . . . " you read, "then we have created a miracle of belief, a theatre image that has charmed or deeply moved us both . . . if I have created well, you will always carry with you the magical and enticing forms and rhythms."

Dean Culverton's voice also enchanted me. When we were making love, he would speak a kind of poetry into the darkness where all the poems he had read collided with one another. He had rather too strong a passion for alliteration—but I overlooked the awkward phrases because of his tenderness. Meaning didn't much matter when his sibilants were linking us in the night: "The swan sound of souls sleeking across the sun," and so forth. That I couldn't usually get the meaning was irrelevant because Bach or Mozart or Beethoven came through the static of the white Westinghouse portable radio I had brought from home. The themes wound around us as we wound about each other; my first lover's consonants rained on my eardrums in the soft autumn, and it didn't matter whether anything ever made sense again.

He stroked me, too, with his hands and his penis in a rhythm that

I thought would last forever. I could never again be without desire for that fullness to move inside me.

How do you live without it? I simply can't imagine you making love to a man. It's even difficult to imagine you making love to a woman, but I can conceive of a woman making love to you, a large woman, not me, not like me, someone you'd enjoy voluptuously but also someone I'd like to be. I can see myself as a large woman making love to you, or you as a large woman making love to me—one of us would be wrapped in the other's breasts—but together, in reality, we'd be two scrawny pullets. To put a kinder light on it, we'd be like two young boys having their first experience with homosexuality and jostling each other's elbows.

Dean Culverton was probably the most beautiful man on campus, if not in the world, at the time. I didn't even know it, oddly enough, until I saw him on stage. I was accustomed to seeing him in his perpetual navy peacoat and the blue jeans that in those days were not cut to emphasize narrow hips. I had never studied his body objectively; he had merely seemed slender, long-muscled, well proportioned. On stage, as a soldier in the antiquity of Christopher Fry's play *A Phoenix Too Frequent,* he wore a short golden tunic, leather sandals cross-laced over his calves to the knee and a blazing Roman helmet topped by a grand cockade. I suddenly perceived him as a star, a triumph, a prize. He had such exquisite thighs, a sentiment shared with me by Doto, the bawdy maidservant in the play, and by Dynamene, the heroine. How could I have allowed him to spend so many days and nights rehearsing the kisses that were part of the play? While I watched, I felt the bloodlust of my jealousy rising. . . . In my drama, I want to show a performance of a play within a play, like *Hamlet.* Within a day of having made love to me, he had been kissing Dynamene. . . . "O, most wicked speed. . . . Within a month, or ere those shoes were old/With which she followed my poor father's body/Like Niobe, all tears. . . ."

Strange, but I have that same pang of jealousy whenever you mention that you go to lunch with Mary McCarthy. You and she. She and you. Everyone together, excluding me. I'm outside, studying. I'm a student of everything, master of nothing. I feel I'm shrinking as I sit alone in the audience and watch him. The humiliation seems something I'll never overcome. I realize that he's the leading man with two of the most seductive women I've ever seen in the flesh. The play's action takes place in a tomb. The heroine, Dynamene, is supposed to be mourning her husband's death, while

Doto, her highly erotic servant, practically attacks my lover. His name in the play is Tegeus (the British pronunciation of *tedious*?). I am furious.

> I love all the world [says Doto, rising]
> And the movement of the apple in your throat.
> So shall you kiss me? It would be better,
>   I should think,
> To go moistly to Hades.

But Tegeus is reflecting on the pure, unambiguous loyalty of Dynamene to her late husband, Virilius:

> ... We'll put a moat of tears
> Round her bastion of love, and save
> The world. It's something. It's more than something,
> It's regeneration. ...

You see, six men had been hanged that day. Tegeus is supposed to be guarding their dead bodies outside the tomb where Dynamene is mourning her dead husband. One of the bodies disappears while Tegeus is dallying with Dynamene and Doto. The point of the play is that Dynamene blithely offers her husband's corpse to replace the missing hanged man so that she can have Tegeus's living body. So much for true love.

The idea is occurring to me that perhaps I should write a tragic verse drama. I'm not sure why. I suppose I'd like to write verse but I don't think I could do comedy.

Soon after we began to make love earnestly and regularly— usually after I cooked dinner and did the dishes—I suddenly woke up one morning with a 104-degree fever. I had to be admitted to Billings Hospital, where they put me in quarantine. I think they thought I had tuberculosis. That would be a good scene for the play too: me in white isolation, doctors and nurses in masks, gloves and gowns moving in and out all day and night, my pale face upon the pillow, my cough (Mimi from *La Bohème,* Emma Bovary, et al.). The fever progressed, moving up to 105. There were alcohol sponges and grim looks exchanged after the second week. Finally, perhaps suspecting that I was about to die, they allowed me a choice of one visitor, just to look in. My parents had been notified, but they were too busy to fly out. So I chose Dean, who was allowed in, masked and gowned and carrying in his gloved hands a rose preserved forever in a glass bowl. After a few seconds, he cried out in anguish, put down the rose, tore my plastic isolation curtain aside and broke quarantine by kissing me moistly while the nurse obligingly, I thought, left the room for a few moments.

I thought the nurse was a friend, but she had actually gone for a doctor and a urinary tract catheter. My lover, caught in his act of rebellious intimacy, was brusquely asked to leave. The next thing I knew, my bladder was being catheterized. By the following day I was diagnosed as having a urinary tract infection: what they cynically called "honeymoon cystitis." The nurse told me that I'd sure had them fooled: I didn't look old enough to drink from a cup, much less have sex. I was a wild and tricky one, now, wasn't I? The administration was certainly going to hear about this waste of money.

I can't figure out how to put all that in stage dialogue either. I'm leaning more and more toward writing a verse drama using Fry's rhythms.

The rest of the Dean Culverton story was savagery. The hospital contacted administration, which contacted my dormitory. Housemother and floor mother convened to report that I had, indeed, been absent from the dorm for a long time. (I found this particularly cowardly on the part of the floor mother, since she was the one who taught me that if you lifted your legs quickly after entry, the penis would slip in with a very satisfactory pressure.) I was sent to the school psychiatrist, who tried to elicit my unhappiness. He wore a tweed suit, smoked a foul pipe and studied me in the dimly lit room from a recumbent position in his leather chair as though I were a human specimen for an unspeakable experiment. He kept asking about my parents and whether or not I was homesick for New York. I had not much thought about New York, except sometimes to be reminded of it by small objects (for example, in our first apartment the Depression glass was just like my mother's). Was I angry that my parents didn't come to Chicago when I was sick? I hadn't thought about it. No, I wasn't homesick at all. And no, I had not had intercourse with any young man. Absolutely not. I had done other things, of course. The other things Dean and I did were quite normal and ordinary—no corpses, no beatings, no enemas, no feces, no sodomy; no, no costumes, for Godsake, he confined his acting to the stage. No, he did not wear my clothing. What was this, an ecclesiastical trial? The other "things" we did, characterized by numbers, were quite enough, quite, quite enough, and very ordinary.

After we had been seen by the psychiatrist, Dean said that he, too, had undergone an inquisition and, as we agreed, had not confessed to intercourse.

Next the dean of students asked to see us. For the interview, my Roman soldier wore a suit he must have owned since adolescence and a child's bright green tie. I was vaguely ashamed of his clothing but we held hands through the inquiry. The dean said that our academic records were satisfactory and that I would not be expelled. (That had never occurred to me as a possibility.) In any case, my lover could not be expelled since he had broken no dormitory rules. I, however, was sentenced to a 10:00 p.m. curfew and required to log my whereabouts during the day. I was to remain on campus (meaning I was not allowed to visit our little room off Ellis Avenue). I had cost the university a considerable sum for my hospital visit; I required surveillance.

All this, of course, was very different from home, where my parents would have seen to it that I had bus fare to take me to the hospital, and when I returned, cured, they would have nodded hello. When I actually went back east for Christmas, I arrived at the same time as a letter telling my parents that I had committed serious sexual improprieties, including having daily—and sometimes twice daily—intercourse with a man to whom I was not married.

My father did not react at all, but my mother took the opportunity to display her turn-of-the-century vocabulary; I'd heard her use it on chambermaids and other lazy females at the hotel. She called me a whore, a Jezebel, a harlot, an ingrate and a slut. This sent me into a rage, but somehow I wasn't angry at her. She could hardly have reacted differently. I wasn't even angry at the school. All the rage was directed at Dean. I looked at my mother, shook my head and looked down at the floor. "Men," I said simply. "Men."

She stopped cursing and studied me expectantly. "Men are beasts," I said. They were the same words she had spoken all her life.

"I never wanted you to be a girl," my mother confirmed. "I never dressed you in girls' clothes and I never gave you dolls." I finally understood. It wasn't better to be male. It was merely safer to be a beast than a victim. My mother was silent for a while, then told me to stay away from the bastards. Sex wasn't worth the price.

When I got back to Chicago, I asked Dean how the school had

known for sure that we'd had intercourse. My gynecologist—a female and the only one in Chicago who would fit an unmarried woman with a diaphragm—had told us that there was no way they could know for sure. The cystitis could have come from anything, even a toilet seat. How were they certain enough to send a letter? Could I sue them?

Dean didn't seem interested in pursuing the mystery. I persisted. "My parents received this perfectly monstrous two-page letter, single-spaced. It described everything, *everything*, even our frequency," I said. "How did they know? I didn't tell them. They could have threatened to burn me at the stake and I wouldn't have told them." My voice rose. (This would be the climactic scene in the play: the great confrontation.) "How the hell did they know?"

Dean sighed and averred as how maybe men and women thought about these things differently. "For a man it's not as big a deal," he explained. I stared at him as he went on about how he'd slept with maybe a hundred or more women while he was in the navy, stopping at ports and whatever, and he just hadn't believed he had committed any crime by having sex when he fell in love for the first time with an elegant spirit from another world who also cooked for him. Besides which, the psychiatrist had accused him of being gay. "That cocksucking, motherfucking son of a bitch," Dean concluded, rolling out the vocabulary he had learned aboard ship.

Slowly I said, "You told him."

"What was I supposed to do? He called me everything from a fag to a pimp."

"You even told him how often." I sank down on our tiny sofabed. I'd been playing Juliet when I should have been playing Pamela. A woman had is a woman ruined, but the man who has her proves his virility.

Is it so bad to be thought of as homosexual? How do women feel about it? I think about you—about your life as a teacher—and I think you are probably a lesbian, or if not a lesbian, a woman of unfulfilled sexuality. I may be dead wrong. But why would it have been so traumatic if he had left them thinking he was queer? They would have to prove it before they could expel him, and then I don't think they could get rid of him unless they could prove he'd committed sodomy or seduced other male students.

So I stopped having sex with Dean. Even though he was still handsome and begged in alliterations that he stole from Dylan Thomas, I couldn't join him. The wings had fallen off. And now my parents were into my sex life. Maybe I had come to Chicago to keep them out of it.

I'm back here at school in New York now. I wrote Dean a letter from home at the beginning of summer vacation. I told him that I would not return to Chicago in the fall. I cried on the letter but could manage only one tear; when this dropped on the paper I forced it to run down the page and streak the ink. I wanted him to think I was violently distressed. I was. I sent my diaphragm, neatly tied in a little packet, back to the address off Ellis Avenue, as if I would never wear one again.

I won't, either. Not until I've found out who and what I am, without a man. I'm upset that my all-female college has been en-rolling male students, accepting elderly World War II veterans and men who served in Korea, too. They've taken over all the student offices.

Maybe I'll become an English professor, like you. Maybe I could become enough of an actress to teach. I have a column now called "Powder and Paint" in the school newspaper—drama criticism. I'm art editor of the school literary magazine. I hope administration isn't too unhappy about my changing the format for seven hundred dollars more per semester. Print needs pictures. Pictures need print. But I don't think I'll be an artist. I've decided I'm going to write my play as a verse drama. Who knows? I could win the Blanche Colton Williams Playwriting Award and then go on to the Nobel Prize. After reading all those hundred great books—all those people: Darwin, Thackeray, Dickens, James, Hardy, Plato, Joyce, Fitzgerald, Dreiser, Sterne, Richardson, Boswell and all the other male immortals—Christopher Fry, who wasn't on the list at all, influenced me most. (Was Jane Austen the only woman who ever wrote a great book?)

My drama will take place in ancient Greece. The hero will wear a golden tunic and a splendid helmet, and he will betray the heroine. But that will be merely the thread on which a social message is hung. Plays have to be about something more than love. They have to have world meaning. The world terrifies and infuriates me. I don't know why men fight wars instead of poverty, starvation and disease. I think the elders betray the young and send them to ritual slaughter for territory, the way old Greek nobles used to kill their firstborn sons to prevent battle over succession. Isn't there some other way, or is it a rule of nature that everyone betrays everyone else? That's what the play will ask.

How will I betray you? I can't imagine, though I'm sure I will, somehow. I know I won't disappoint you with my verse drama. Will I betray you if I marry a man? I doubt it. I don't think you care whether or not I have sex with men or marry them. Perhaps I'll betray you by never telling you how much I admire you. You are a center for me, a teacher, a critic, a scholar, perhaps a poet, a woman by herself! But you know that. . . . You must know I adore you, because I sit there in the front row, looking up at you, listening to you, loving you. . . .

The real betrayal would be never satisfying your encouragement and your belief in me. If men and life get between me and the promise you believe I have. If I can't persist in spite of all the odds. I'm not a person who can sit in a garret and produce unrecognized masterpieces while everyone else is rushing about and hustling life. The fruit on the carts, the colors of the market umbrellas, the flowers for sale and the smell of bread and cheese will always tempt me. I don't think I will be very good at rejection, hunger and loneliness, even though you've given me so much spiritual sustenance. Or perhaps I won't be eager for pain because what you've given has informed me of a different sort of world.

Memory

AGE 36

1973

PRIVATE FILE: Do not send.

To: E-man   SUBJECT: EROTIC EDUCATION

Dr. Cranston Kerry was as devoted to serving others, and in as disorganized a fashion, as my mother. Come to think of it, he reminded me of her. No intrusion on his life was too small to merit immediate attention. He was incessantly busy, almost too busy on the telephone to listen to me during my visits. I was young; it never occurred to me to request my rights. I didn't know I had any. Older people (he was forty-five?) talked to others first.

In fact, my mother had seen him before I did. Harry had set up her consultation on the recommendation of a college friend. She needed to talk to someone when my brother died. After two visits, she dismissed Dr. Kerry's services as helpful but unnecessary. She would take care of herself. She always had.

I went to see Dr. Kerry because I felt tired all the time. Bone tired. Exhausted. I functioned. I took care of everyone in my family, my husband and young children, but even though I was physically healthy, I couldn't stay out of bed any longer than necessary. He identified my malady as depression due to suppressed rage. This was helpful. I came to realize that I was angry at—as Dr. Kerry called him—that "editor, or teacher, or typesetter or whatever he was" for reneging on a promise to publish a book I had started in his class. He'd also attempted to seduce me (into seducing him) and then never responded to me again because I resisted the connection. "If only you were a little more aggressive," he had said.

Feeling abandoned, I couldn't finish the book. I made a youthful vow never to write again unless someone asked me to. The business was too subjective. But what else was there for me, when writing was all I ever wanted to do? (Of course, the world may have been saved a lot of ecological damage from the sacrifice of trees to satisfy my muse.)

Dr. Kerry's diagnosis helped me to resolve my problems, to make new decisions and difficult choices, but he, too, infuriated me.

I told him my mother's attentiveness to me seemed lacking. He told me what a wonderful character she was and how much he liked her. The week after I informed him I was applying to medical school, he wanted to know what I was doing with the rest of my life: would I remain a housewife and go back to writing? When I was accepted, he had forgotten that I had applied. If he had known, he said, he would have discouraged me. It was going "from the frying pan into the fire." I reasoned that if I passed my exams, the school would grant my degree. They wouldn't renege the way my teacher/publisher had. Grades were objective. No seduction was involved. No whimsical opinion, either.

Dr. Kerry's distracted attention and my intermittent feelings of being neglected didn't prevent me from falling in love with him the way I always do with anyone who offers any serious attention to my psyche, who listens at all, who reads me. I had to go through with him what I went through with the teacher, only I emerged feeling as though I loved humanity. Dr. Kerry did a good job.

As I look back, perhaps I should have examined his religious

beliefs before I asked of him what I did. I may not have paid
attention, either. In the end, we had a peculiar role reversal. I didn't
understand his feelings—his confusions, his sense of inadequacy
—until he asked for my help. When he did, I shouldn't have felt a
sense of triumph.

Your voice is, more than ever, too loud, the midwestern twang
overlaid by a gruff Bostonian affectation. And you are too big, embarrassingly large and obvious in a restaurant. You have to choose
restaurants with space to lean your crutches so they'll be handy but
out of the path of fellow diners, space to heave your bulk into a
chair, space to wave those overdeveloped simian arms at the waiter,
at the friend across the room, at the heavens to corroborate the
folly of humankind.

"How are you, darling?" you ask, and I am as always humiliated
by the word, which connotes more condescension than affection: it
is not a word used to a wife or lover, not a word casually used to a
prestigious woman. It's more like patting the elevator man on the
back or putting an arm around a nurse, which I know you've done
often in your medical career. . . .

On the other hand, I think it was better having had you as my
first psychiatrist than some small-framed graylocks who trod the
mule's path to sanity. You never plodded carefully along, ever. You
got one leg blasted off in the war, you committed follies, you've
been married four times and had six children, you despise the
establishment and still survive within it. . . . I think if I'd had the
conventional bearded pedant for an analyst first (instead of second), I'd have become a cipher. There's a part of me that still wants
to hang out behind the door, in the powder room, in a closet while
the party goes on. I doubt you've ever had that feeling.

So I pick at my roll and tell you about the years in between
seeing you and this present moment: I saw you, when was it, 1959
or '60 to '62 or '63, something like that, at least until the year before
I entered medical school. And now it's 1973 and I've been in prac-

tice almost two years. But I'm thirty-six years old and everyone thinks I've been practicing a decade longer. That's helpful.

You order a bottle of expensive burgundy that you say needs to breathe for a while before we can drink it; I've read that "breathing" does nothing for wine but I don't contradict you. A new glass of red wine in a clean crystal goblet at a good French restaurant always makes me feel sexual. It's the sight of the wine, I tell myself. It isn't you. But I felt aroused, too, while I was dressing to see you this morning. Why? Hadn't I long since transformed my sexual feeling for you into something more appropriate? How is it possible to feel sexual toward an overweight amputee who behaves as if he is the only person in the room, and as though I am an old office girl to whom he owes a treat?

Flushing, reaching awkwardly, almost slapping me, you put your enormous hands over mine, in full view of everyone in the restaurant, and you bring my knuckles to your lips. You tell me, without modulating so others won't hear, that I was right about everything, about your third wife who wasn't intelligent enough, and your fourth, who isn't sexual enough. Once this sort of confession would have fed my fantasy like a horn of plenty; now it is a signal to beware fatuity. There was a time when any revelation of self might have set me to wanting to become part of your family tree; now I am still numb from the series of sensible, appropriate rejections that certain patients must suffer. I like the public display of your affections even less than the belated tribute, although it does feel good to have been right about your absurd marriages.

I move my hand away from your fingers and cup my wine. You drink, indicating that it's now ready to be sipped. On top of my uneasy self-satisfaction, an old anger has begun to spread, like the hot brandy on top of a dish to be flambéed. It sits there, ready to be ignited, but for the moment I have forgotten what started it, why it is there, like the penetrating aroma of the wine in my nostrils, beginning the intoxication although I haven't sipped a drop. You tell me that my having become a doctor still profoundly amazes you: while I went to sessions with you, I had never even mentioned I was applying to medical school, never told you my anxieties, never explained the identification with you. Suddenly I was a student; as swiftly, I had graduated. Now I was actually practicing. Did everything go on in my mind outside the sessions? How did that work? As I begin to answer, your attention wanes and you're off on another subject: you tell me that you yourself are practicing biofeedback now. You don't have to listen to the damn patients as much. You just let them lie there and control themselves. The Buddhists knew how to do this a long time ago. I never tell you about my habits of private thought because you are really not interested.

A waiter flames a duck à l'orange for a diner across the room and my anger puffs in the flame-burst. I remember now: it was all about Nadine, almost ten years ago, and I swore I would never talk to you again. Yet here I am, at what appears so far to be a lunchtime seduction. And you go on, talking incessantly as you did all through my therapy, about yourself, focusing now on your increased interest in Eastern medicine since your year in California.

Nadine was my best friend while I studied for medical school, which was my desperate solution to finding an identity and an income after being unable to finish a novel. My children would someday need college tuition. Writing was too chancy to depend on for that. Harry had published a book, but there wasn't much money from it. Keeping humanity healthy seemed a more rewarding profession. Its importance relieved my guilt for not helping my mother at the hotel. Besides, I was good at taking tests.

As for Nadine, she had had a rather dubious finishing school education, even though she had always wanted to be a doctor. Her parents had not felt medicine to be an appropriate career for a woman. Now we had both taken the minimum premed courses to qualify: two years of chemistry, a year of physics, a year of biology. Together, we had made straight A grades. Even with our A's, admission was not guaranteed. Women usually numbered between two and five in a graduating class of a hundred or more. Women with children were generally excluded by policy, with rare exceptions. I would have to do well enough to be an exception.

Nadine was a Jewess from South Africa. Were she from almost anywhere else, I would say simply that she was English, or French, or Venusian, but since she was from South Africa, her Jewish identity was important because she looked black. Although her skin was of an unidentifiable paleness, her jet hair fell in corkscrews. Her tall, thin, bony frame was loosely articulated in the way that makes some black adolescents appear effortlessly agile; she had long, flat feet, narrow sandpiper legs, angular buttocks and a body that elongated to a head inset with eyes that shone like onyx wet with tears. Although the overall impression was that of a mulatto urchin, Nadine's features, when you looked closely, were chiseled on the classical European model: firm, square chin, slightly aquiline nose with flaring nostrils, full mouth.

When Nadine and I studied together, we engaged the basic sciences with the intensity of acolytes. I led the worship, but Nadine kept us in balance. For organic chemistry, the idea I conceived was to answer every problem in every textbook that had an answer guide. I bought all the books I could find at Barnes and Noble; there were also a few to be had from the school library. We spent the nights before each weekly quiz learning the problems and remembering the route by which to calculate our answers. Out of the hundred or so problems we did each week from six textbooks, our professor always chose one. When we began the term, I characterized him as too unimaginative to create his own problems. I was right. We never missed.

But on Saturday mornings, no matter how much we had to do, Nadine pulled me from the textbooks and my chores with the children and insisted we go for a walk in the park or along the river. On these walks, she would tell me fragmentary tales about South Africa. She felt as though she were dying a slow death of asphyxiation now in this city. Her face would contort with the pain of it; her voice, with its odd accent that always sounded to my naive ear half English and half Australian, would choke on the city's stale air. "I can't understand this climate!" she was forever exclaiming. I loved the way she said "can't." It sounded like "Kant" with the *on* sound spread over an incredulous octave. Her voice and body worked so hard at everything she did, there was no energy left to create any substance beyond bone and the excited transparency of her skin.

I never quite comprehended the climate "at home." It was bracing and dry; it was subtropical; it was hot as the Sahara—all on the same small tip of the continent. Sometimes Nadine told me about riding a horse bareback in the veld, which seemed to be a dry, coarse, grassy place high in the mountains. She was racing toward sunset, clutching the horse's mane yet leaning back because her legs were long and strong enough to keep her locked to its belly; she was whooping and yelling her freedom. God, she was *breathing.*

Or sometimes she was riding more slowly in the bushveld, through the thin wood where rain, captured by the Drakensberg, did not fall and where grasses could not grow; ambling along, she meditated on wild pomegranate and bitter aloes, on mimosa and acacia, stunted, as she would be stunted if she did not leave this place.

She had chosen to leave with Jacob, the American doctor who had come for a vacation and to visit his family on the warm, south-eastern shore. Why did she go south that week? An aunt's death? Her father's business? They had kissed among the orchids and the arum lilies and the white everlasting flowers and he promised that he would help her continue her education in America. He could virtually guarantee her admittance to one of the best medical schools in New York: he was on the staff. And if she came to America with him, she could be more useful to her family. She could send them money from abroad; she could invest her own funds more wisely abroad, too, before civil strife destroyed the economy. He was insatiably in love. Her smile, her laugh, her freedom, were all he ever longed for in his otherwise narrow, compartmentalized life.

So Nadine left the southern languor, the mangroves, the palms, the baobab and the bombax trees, and went back home to Durban to prepare for the wedding. In six months, Jacob returned to South Africa and they married, she in her grandmother's—also her moth-er's—dress, reputedly made in Russia by her great-grandmother, seamstress to nobility, possibly to the czarina. Her dark, grieving eyes shone beyond the antique lace and the intricate seed pearls; while they were on the first lap of their honeymoon she told Jacob that in America she would like to become a practitioner to the black people who lived in that part of the city called Harlem, because there were so many here whom she loved and did not want to leave. Jacob kept his doubts to himself and listened as they rode up the mountains to say good-bye to the plains she also loved. On the way up, she wanted to show him every kloof and krantz, rand and ruggens, kop and kopje. He loved her speech, and the strange Dutch words that had passed into her vocabulary to describe the mountain terrain, as much as I did, I think. . . .

"Do you remember Nadine Ulrevsky?" I asked you, in the middle of your explanation of the relaxation response, which was putting me to sleep as effectively as it did any patient. I had used the technique on myself ever since I read about it in an antique issue of the *Reader's Digest*. You stopped talking about yourself long enough to say you didn't recall, exactly. Familiar name, you thought. Was she a patient? Had you referred her to me or had I referred her to you?

I reminded you that you had not, as yet, referred any patients to me, not even the poor ones who couldn't afford your mechanized magic.

You wanted to return to your topic, or—failing that—to your favorite monologue, not changed in all these years, on Jane Goodall and her maternal apes. You believed that everyone in society was a sort of mother to someone else, even policemen. I liked the theory and was sorry you had given it up for biofeedback electrodes. But I refused to be deflected. "Don't you remember Nadine Ulrevsky? You must, really."

You downed your glass of wine and the waiter poured another. "Wasn't she your school pal, the one who wanted something, I forget what?"

I had sat outside in your waiting room while Nadine told you what she wanted. You were my friend, my psychiatrist. I brought her to you. She had nowhere else to go. I had no doubt that you would help her. I was sure. All you had to do was sign a piece of paper.

At first you and Nadine talked in civilized tones and I couldn't hear, but soon the sobs had overtaken her voice, sobs punctuated by screams of despair. I still believed in you. I thought you were putting her through some sort of test. But Nadine had understood your character better than I had when we discussed whether she should see you. She didn't have much time.

"I'm seven weeks pregnant," she observed, "and he won't see me until the middle of next week. That probably means he won't clear me for an abortion."

"Don't worry," I told her. "I know him. He's wonderful. He's liberal. He'll say you're crazier than a bedbug and you'll get your abortion. You'll have time."

Pregnant women, then, were not allowed to go to college, much less medical school. The authorities feared legal action because of, say, a miscarriage on a stopped elevator, a fall downstairs, a birth in the bathroom. At medical school, they felt the schedule was beyond the capacity of any pregnant woman, all of whom were generally forbidden to exercise. Wheeling patients from floor to floor or running infected fluids to the lab was not for a gravid female. Not to mention all the disease contact she would have: tuberculous patients, the sputum of people with pneumonia, the rectal material, collected on a gloved finger, from the jaundiced victims of infectious hepatitis. . . . No, pregnancy was not allowed at medical school.

"How on earth did you manage to get pregnant?" I finally asked Nadine, not without disapproval. It was, after all, puzzling that she would defeat herself this way, when contraception was so simple. She said she didn't want to explain, but I pressed her. I was her only good friend, after all. She broke her code of privacy and finally told me that she and Jacob had not been getting along at all well lately. She had been spending too much time studying. He was angry and jealous. "I kept reassuring him . . . there was no one else . . . I was with you. . . ." Nadine hugged me tightly and laughed as though she were crying, like a child in distress.

"There was no one else?"

"Oh God, no. I've never been with anyone but Jacob. He was my first, and I think he will be my last."

"What's the matter, Nadine? Oh, Nadine . . ."

She collected herself and sat down on the edge of a huge chair in the emptiness of the vast college lounge where we were talking. Her lids lowered as she checked for strange listeners, then looked down at her trembling hands. "Jacob is a doctor, Aphra. He knew exactly when I was ovulating. He decided that he did not want me to go to medical school because it would deprive him of a wife. He raped me to prove it. Three times."

I was sitting in your waiting room and listening to her voice rise as she protested your refusal. "I'm not crazy," she was screaming through the office door, "but I want you to call me crazy. I'll take my chances with the medical school finding out. I'm not crazy, I've wanted to be a doctor all my life, please say I can't stand it emotionally, please, my husband raped me, I'll hate the child, please, oh God, please, I just want to go to school, Aphra and I were accepted together, do you realize what a miracle that is, I'm only twenty-six, I'll have lots of other chances to have children."

"At twenty-eight you'll be an elderly primigravida," I heard my trusted doctor tell her. "You're a perfectly normal woman. Have the child and go to medical school next year."

"I can't. Jacob won't pay for it now or later. He saw to it that I was refused at his school. At least if I don't have a child, I have a chance of working to earn some of the money."

The screams gradually lessened. From a loud wail the sound

became a regular low moan of exhaustion that pulsated for a long time until Nadine was finished. After five minutes of silence that seemed an eternal rest, Nadine came out of your office. Her mouth tightened in a smile, but her eyes raged.

"I heard it all," I told her. "There must be another psychiatrist who can help."

"I don't want any more of your bloody mental doctors," she said. "But it isn't your fault, Aphra. I don't blame you."

"What are you going to do?"

"I know someone. . . . He'll take care of it."

"A doctor?"

"An excellent doctor. Don't worry."

"But I *am* worried. . . ."

"Look," she said, with amazing equanimity after her storm, "the same thing will happen to me whether it's legal or not. If it's legal, I can have my insides poked in a hospital operating room. If it's not, someone will poke me in his office and I'll have to take a taxi for him to meet me in the emergency room. That and a thousand dollars cash make the difference. So don't worry, and I'll meet you in anatomy class."

When she put it that way, I felt almost betrayed by her total control and understanding. We kissed and I said I'd call that evening.

You thoughtfully held your snail, your escargot, in the holder and poked the slippery body of the gastropod mollusk with a tiny fork that seemed an absurd toothpick in your immense paw. "Now what did your friend want?" You dipped the embryonic curve of the flesh into the garlic-butter sauce and popped it into your mouth. Memory returned and your features brightened. "I remember now, your friend what's her name. She wanted an abortion."

I ate a few cuttings of my endive salad. "You didn't help Nadine," I said.

"That depends on how you look at it." You ate another snail and followed it with a mouthful of French bread dipped in garlic butter. You chewed the bread, revolving your mandible in wide arcs. Droplets of grease collected at the corners of your lips. "Your Nadine was a very strong person. Had what it takes: guts, rage, lots of bone and gristle. They get that way, from the abuse. Beautiful, too, for a colored girl."

A sharpness cut through the wall of my abdomen, a slice of fury.

"Nadine wasn't black," I said, not that it mattered. "She was a white Russian Jew. Her family migrated to South Africa two generations ago."

"Had some color in her, then," you said, shrugging. "Whatever happened to her? What kind of doctor did she become?"

I wanted to jump out of my seat. I wanted to pace up and down the restaurant, kicking the chairs. I had a fantasy of tying your white napkin around your neck until your face turned red. Instead, I told you, "Nadine Ulrevsky has been dead a very long time."

I went to the first assembly for medical students, where we were instructed to keep our hair cut short and to wear neckties at all times. The dean also mentioned, looking directly at me, that people over the age of twenty-seven could not usually remember enough to pass examinations. I was twenty-seven. After assembly, I went to the bookstore and bought all my books new. I didn't have time to look for bargains. The children would be waiting for me at home. The next day, I started classes. I kept in touch with Nadine but was not able to go to see her immediately at the hospital near the East River. A private obstetrician had induced the abortion, just as she had planned, and had admitted her that same day. But recovery was not going well. There was fever and pain, in spite of antibiotics and medication.

On the third day, I was able to visit. Jacob had not been there. The room was empty of flowers except for the small azalea I had sent. Her relatives were all in South Africa, of course. The lone plant emphasized that she had no friends except for me. That was why she had been able to devote herself so exclusively to studying. I held her hand for an hour as she intermittently tried to make lively conversation, cried, slept and cursed Jacob.

I will never know exactly why Nadine did what she did after that day. Did the doctor give her some dreadful news? "You will never be able to conceive a child, I'm sorry to have to tell you. Your uterus was irreparably damaged. . . ." Or perhaps her fever rose uncontrollably and she went into a visionary delirium, throwing off her white coverlet in the middle of the night and walking, as if in her sleep, to the huge Gothic window on the twenty-fourth floor of the hospital—amazingly easy to open, even for a weak young woman. . . .

Or perhaps she went into severe postpartum depression, the way you can when your hormones send you into a fecund ecstasy, and then suddenly—after you rip the little ball of flesh from its mooring —the levels drop in the bloodbath that follows; the sadness grows in a dark mantle between you and the world, shrouding you in desolation. Maybe Nadine pulled the mantle over her head, a cape of darkness in whose womb she alone existed, opened the window wide, stepped on a chair, crept out and let go ... let go ... let go. . . .

You finished your bread and slipped the stem of the wineglass between your fingers. "What did she die of?"

"She committed suicide on the third day after the abortion. Jumped out of the window of the twenty-fourth floor."

You cupped the wineglass, cradling it like a breast, running your fingers along the roundness. You said, "I'm glad as hell I didn't sanction the goddam abortion. I'd have felt like I murdered two people, not just one."

We ate our way through the grilled salmon luncheon in relative silence, although you kept repeating how young I looked, how fresh, how work always seemed to agree with me, how sexy I always seemed to be. Why were you stroking my psyche now, ten years after I had done my best to channel my unruly sexuality to two-legged people capable of chasing me, or at least of truly being paternal, maternal, filial, or otherwise loving. . . . I decided to tell you about my family: My son was in high school. I didn't know whether to permit him to play football. My daughter seemed to be gifted in several academic areas. My practice was thriving. My husband was happier with my work than he had been with my education. Now we had an income, but it all went to pay tuition. There seemed to be no financial benefit for all the effort. How was your family?

You took time to slice the smoking tip off a Havana cigar and light the other end before answering. The smoke made my eyes tear and my throat feel rough. Then you ordered a cognac, drank it in a swig and ordered another, which you cradled.

"Family is why I invited you to lunch," you said, finally. "It's about Betsy, my eldest daughter. I need your help."

I sat perfectly still, listening intently as you told me that you didn't like what was happening to your child. She was married to one of the new yuppies; the couple seemed to spend their lives acquiring material possessions and taking drugs. It all looked smooth on the surface: perfect apartment, perfect country house, even a yacht being built in Rome. (Can you imagine all those Italians rubbing and scraping a boat for my daughter to float around the world in?) You were worried. Perhaps it was no longer your proper concern: Betsy was twenty-six. Even though I was a decade older, I was not an intimidating older person; maybe I could help her to acquire some of my values. She was not enough of a student to go to medical school, of course, but maybe she could do something in health or education, or maybe she could even be helped to get a job to enhance her self-esteem. "I think you'd be the perfect person to guide her," you said.

I wanted to continue to be ambivalent, critical, nasty at heart about your unresolved countertransference, your professional chauvinism, your awkward mistakes, your errors of judgment, your self-exoneration from the crime I considered you had committed. I wanted to deliver a sermon on what a poor father you had obviously been, with all the confused philandering I imagined you had done in search of the sexual and intellectual acrobat you'd need to keep up with your nonconformist attitudes.

Instead, I stirred my espresso without putting any sugar in it. I lifted the demitasse to my lips. "Of course I'll see her." A curious satisfaction settled on me. "Is Betsy in town? Will you be asking her to call me?"

"She's at home. Her depression is increasing, I think. She'll probably call next week." It was the ultimate confession.

I promised, "I'll do the best I can."

PART SEVEN

SADISM

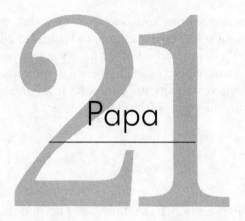

Papa

To: go-dot
12.19.91

Subject: distant constellations

The more i write, the less you respond. I thought we both understood this isn't psychoanalysis! I regard our communications as a
conversation between friends—an opportunity for me to express
what's on my mind to a more experienced colleague—you, who
guides and shares. If you were to collect and quantify the time it
took to read everything i've ever written to you, cover to cover,
would it consume an hour?

I appreciate the ingenuity of your questions, the directness by
which you seek to lead me to self-discovery, but frankly it would
mean a great deal to me to know you think of me as a peer, or at

least a person for whom you have a regard that transcends the professional! You could take a minute to write something now and then, like how you are and whether it's winter in new york and if there's even a tiny ripple of excitement in one small chamber of your psyche when you get an e-missive from me—in brief, the sharing of intimacies that is friendship.

marc

To: go-dot   SUBJECT: koan
12.21.91

It's almost 48 hours since i sent my last note, and still no response —this is like clapping with one hand—non-response to e-mail as a form of analytic silence: do you have any idea of the feelings it's beginning to generate? I haven't even had an m-hmm, much less an mHmmmMMmm from you in what seems like weeks!!!

:(
marc

To: E-man   SUBJECT: Mhmm—
12.22.91

Hmmmmmmmmhm.

Aphra

To: go-dot   SUBJECT: more
12.22.91

Your sitting on the fence in this relationship is a real pisser. I have to have more from you if you aren't my analyst or my supervisor. Maybe it will be hard for me to give up my imaginary position as your favorite neophyte, maybe i'll have to give you some time, think about *you*; i'm selfish about wanting all your attention for *me,* but then i could be imagining that i'm the one getting all your attention, i could be hallucinating that i'm getting any, really, for that matter. . . .

Tell me something. You should have caught on by now that there's no longer any privacy in the world.

m

To: E-man   SUBJECT: Apology/apologia
12.22.91

I'm sorry—in a way, I don't quite know how to be friends in print. I'm not ready yet to finalize my *mea culpas,* though I want to. You see, it's possible everything I thought I did right in life was absurdly wrong. My villains weren't heroes, but they weren't evil either.

I have the same collection of injustices you have. It may be perpetuating a pattern for me to keep them to myself a while longer, but I'm collecting my tales of woe. Someday soon I'm going to polish them up and present them to you as my great apologia-for-her-life. Then maybe I'll live up to my name and we'll both learn something.

So please go on.

The weather in New York is almost cold enough for Christmas.

A.

To: go-dot   SUBJECT: toni's egg
12.22.91

I'll wait. A part of me doesn't want to give up the luxury of thinking and writing just about myself. That part of me, you understand, is keeping you out, hogging cyberspace, making it all a one-way street. That part of me—the cold, narcissistic s.o.b.—enjoys the thought of you squirming among your unrevealed selves, wondering which one is safe to wander in the liquid architecture of other people's psyches, in the babel of cyberspace, to come softly to me, finally. . . .

And maybe i want to hear more from you to relieve me from telling you about toni, who's building up a rage. Why do all women eventually want to do it to me? Her depression is starting to crack, like an ostrich egg, and the big bird is bursting out. To tell the truth, i was losing interest in her, she'd sit in the office, legs up on a hassock, boots crossed, and just look at me for the whole hour. . . . she's an expert in not having anything to say: her indian reservation family, as she told me, never talked beyond noting it was light or dark or time to throw sacred corn meal around, and her mixed live-in family drank, had sex, or fought—speech, in the classic sense of emotional or intellectual exchange, was not in her training—so she's been sitting around, looking sullen for the past god-knows-how-long, but now the furies are unleashing:

At me.

At men.

She says "you" when she talks, as if i did it. You, she says, and she's right, too, she's absolutely correct, You see me as if I'm some goddam sex robot. You'd kill me if you thought I'd resurrect so you could do it to me again.

Warm feelings? she says. You have got to be in fairyland. . . . and then she describes the nightmares that happen in the sex world that made her decide she'd never let any flesh inside her; nothing ever, not one finger. You'd chew me up alive, she says. You'd gouge me with knives. You'd carve my bloody cunt with razor blades. You'd tear my ass with your prick and not care if I could ever hold my shit again. You'd sear me with hot plates and irons and butts. . . . I've seen it all. You'd ram it down my throat till I passed out, maybe till I died. You'd fuck my eye-sockets if I sold you my eyes. Tell me about warm feelings. I've got a very good deal with Reilly, a very good deal. He doesn't touch me. He doesn't twist a hair on my head.

So i nod mhmm, and she continues, What the hell am I doing here anyway? She says she came to therapy because she was unhappy about wanting to do something more with her life and I could keep my sentimental sexual advice for someone else, thank you; the only people who were ever going to get inside her were the surgeons to cut the tumors out, if that ever came to pass. . . .

So why do i get myself into the same situation again and again? Danah, sophia, trish, and how many more, and now toni. . . . i've been thinking lately that i need the rage, i want to see the rage, i want to get it out there in primary colors because i know it's inside, i don't know if a person can be trusted until i know what the anger is.

You see, they never fought: my parents never had a really defined argument. It was a relationship almost like toni's with reilly because toni is paid to be positive all the time, to build reilly up, never to argue, never to tell him what a blowhard asshole he can be. My mother cooked and cleaned and waited and suffered; my father came and went according to some mysterious rhythm governed by foreign forces; i used to wonder if he was a double agent, he was so smooth, no matter what happened, my father maintained his composure, no matter what, no matter what, except maybe—once—

Ordinarily, when he came home (never more than a few times a month), he'd enter without ringing the bell or announcing himself and he'd head directly for the shower, after which he'd change into his supper clothes and I'd watch him stand at the radio he'd moved to the corner of the living room where we ate. He'd turn it on loud enough so no one could talk and we'd listen to our dose of disaster until dessert. My mother would serve us, course by immaculate course, while the world fought all the filthy battles on the airwaves.

One night he couldn't take a shower because the water heater in the basement had broken down; the water ran cold in all the faucets and he was extremely uncomfortable: he was hypersensitive to "germs," he needed his daily wash to cleanse them from his body, to take away their implications of sin, disease, decay, and exposure to the illnesses of the common people—he was elitist that way— he revered medicine as god but couldn't conceive of it as a hands- on profession, unless one was wearing surgical gloves, and i sup- pose i identified with him in the end by entering psychiatry, which is mostly hands-off.

It disturbed him so much to be able only to wash his hands and face that i didn't think he would stay home at all, not to mention that, in addition to everything else, my mother was staying in bed. She wouldn't move, she said, the pregnancy was terrible, her feet were swollen, her breath was short, my father would have to serve himself.

With my mother moaning softly in the bedroom, he heated the soup that was on the stove and put a low flame under the cassoulet that she had prepared earlier. He ladled my portion of soup, send- ing a run of tomato liquid down my jeans and onto my sneakers. He was coordinated in other ways: he could draw a picture of almost anything, but he was so inept at the stove, it must have been deliberate.

By the time we began the cassoulet, my mother's moans were growing louder; when she groaned deeply, i jumped up to run to her, but my father lifted his hand in a priestly gesture of restraint. You stay here, he said, I don't want you in there. . . .

He set his napkin on the table as my mother began to scream, then resolutely pushed his chair back, stood up and walked quickly to the bedroom, which was separated from the dinette by a tiny square of hallway. I remained at the table, but as soon as he had gone into the bedroom, i followed and stationed myself at the gap between the door and the frame, from which i had a full view of my mother from her feet to her head.

She lay under the light patchwork quilt, her belly reaching up like a camel's hump, her face sweating, her hair in wet snakes on the pillow. Oh, God, she whispered between screams, the baby comes, the baby comes too fast!

Can you make it to a taxi? my father asked, and my mother desperately answered No, no, a taxi is no use, I know it's coming, I feel it, there is no time, *YOU MUST CALL THE EMERGENCY!*

My father dialed 911 but the ambulance didn't come in the next five minutes, or the next, and something strange was happening to my mother: it seemed as though the camel hump under the sheet was moving, turning, shifting, as though the baby was doing a dance inside her. The sounds of her agony grew louder and then suddenly her pain eased, her belly seemed to flatten out and she was pushing in long, retching pulses, the mountain was gone, the baby was arriving between her legs. My father helped to spread her knees so the baby could come out and before i turned my face away i had seen it: there was the top of the head with what looked like a flat tube pressed against it; behind the tube was blood; the head had hair, my father tried to pull on it but he couldn't get a grip, then slowly the forehead came out all by itself, then the face, and finally, the whole head. I looked at the baby and i could have sworn it looked back at me before i shut my eyes tight and gagged and pressed my forehead against the door.

My mother was screaming, she was screaming at my father and kicking him, i was trying not to watch but it seemed like they were fighting, and then my father pushed hard at my mother's thighs and held one back with his forearm while he tugged at the baby's chin, but nothing happened, and then he rotated the baby's head, like unscrewing a jar, and a shoulder appeared, then the other shoulder, and then the rest of the body slipped out like a delayed glob from a plastic squeeze bottle. The baby was born, slippery and silent, into my father's hands. It didn't move, it was blue, and there was no cry. . . .

The ambulance team arrived; they tried to do some artificial respiration and to put oxygen in the baby's lungs, but even though they got the baby to look pretty pink, it didn't breathe or move and they wrapped the baby up and we all eventually got in the ambulance and went to the hospital.

When i studied obstetrics at medical school, i figured out that my mother had probably gone into precipitate labor—the contractions may have come on as a swift surprise (i remember once a baby got badly damaged dropping out of a patient who was waiting around at the hospital)—but, as you know, even if a woman is safely in bed, the contractions can come so fast and so strong that the cord may be too compressed to bring the baby enough oxygen to survive.... another possibility, too, could have contributed to the disaster: the "tube" i saw on top of the baby's head might have been a prolapsed umbilical cord, pushed into the birth canal by the head and flattened too much to allow the blood to flow through, also starving the fetus of oxygen....

Later that night, we came home without my mother—they said she was resting comfortably and was going to be fine—they had to take precautions about infection.

When we got home, my father wanted to take a bath. The problem was getting enough hot water to do it. We started to fill up pots of water and heat them on the stove. He didn't need a whole tubful: a few inches would be enough, and we could add cold water to the boiled water to make it go further. When the first batch of pots was boiling, my father started me on assembly-line trips to the bathtub.

I was still thinking about all the blood, the blue baby, pink when i last saw it, the screams, the ride through the streets and hearing the siren from inside; i could see the reflection of our flashing red lights on the cars we passed.... i was kneeling and holding my mother's hand while my father sat on the vinyl seat on the side and looked out the back window, and then there was the hush of busy nurses at the hospital, my mother on the stretcher, disappearing into the elevator.... where did the baby go?

Between trips i asked my father Where did the baby go? He said he didn't know. If it was alive, i decided, it must be near my mother; if it was dead, they probably threw it in the garbage.... i tried to picture the trash can with a baby in it: they would have to put it in a bag, not a see-through bag, but maybe a potato sack, with some plastic over it. Did you bury a dead baby or throw it away? Maybe we would have to have a funeral, or at least a burial, the way people did for dogs, but maybe it wasn't dead, maybe all the machines at the hospital were keeping it alive.

Is the baby dead? i asked when the question didn't seem an intrusion on our efforts to provide for my father's comfort.

My father shook his head slowly and shrugged; he looked at his hands: there was blood encrusted in the cuticles. I thought he might get sick looking at them, i thought about all the blood on the sheets in the room where my father had closed the door—he wasn't going to clean it up—*he wasn't even going to go in there.*

The third round of pots would be the last; they were the biggest and the handles weren't protected with black plastic—we needed a dish towel to be a potholder—i pulled a folded cloth from the drawer and said, I think the baby is dead. It didn't cry and it was blue. I think we waited too long.

My father wrapped the dish towel around the handles of the steaming, heavy pot—as he handed it to me, the pot tilted swiftly forward, toward me, and the scalding steamy water splashed on my thigh, over the tomato stain—it was so hot that i dropped the pot entirely and the boiling water spilled on the floor.

God damn you, my father said, and then amended himself. Godammit, goddam pot!

The burn brought involuntary tears to my eyes. I know now that the pain was a scar i would bear for life, wounding my marriage and my fatherhood, but i could neither complain nor speak to him. He sat down at the kitchen table while i stood in shock in the puddle of spreading, smoking water; he pointed a long finger at me; his voice was cold but reasonable. It was a baby girl, he told me—a baby girl, a girl—and then in one of his rare moments of fatherly intimacy, he said, Only a girl.

22
Joseph and Hugo
1991, 1952

To: E-man   Subject: SADISM

You tell stories. I do, too. We're both epic poets *manqués,* re-counting our journeys through the terrors of childhood. Was your father's neglect responsible for your sister's stillbirth? Did he deliberately scald you? Or was he upset, distraught, unfit for crisis?

And my mother: was she a callous parent or merely a feisty person consumed by the battle for everything she achieved?

Why do I persist in wanting to tell you the stories that are a plea for help I should long ago have outgrown?

When will you be ready to give up your sagas?

When will I?

• • •

Whenever I have a patient whose sadism is the problem, I remember Dr. Hellinger's lecture, delivered to our third-year class during my psychiatric residency. He was a respected analyst, a bent older man with the soft voice and Viennese accent that usually signified a personal familiarity with the Holocaust. His talk was on utilizing the self in the transference as a nonjudgmental agency of healing. He warned us that now that we were seeing patients we should know what we were thinking, what associations we were making to our patients' stories. If we were unaware of our reactions, they might inhibit our work with disturbed aggressive or sexual behavior. He emphasized that most of us had led sheltered lives, cared for by our ethnic mothers. We had probably been our parents' favorites and gotten everything we wanted because we were smart enough to go to medical school. We were all, Dr. Hellinger warned, overly protected, provincial, prejudiced, spoiled. When our patients spoke to us of shocking matters, we had best take pains to be clear; otherwise we would probably do more harm than good.

"What I don't understand is why my head is so full of bloody scenes involving cruelty and the like. That and my sexuality, or you might say, the lack of it, in a practical sense—those are my two problems."

Joseph Brightson was a small man in antique tweeds and an old, tight-fitting woolen sweater. Yet although his clothes looked as though they ought to smell of dung, sweat and wildflowers, the odors of the English countryside, they carried instead a gentle odor of cooking spices: rosemary, thyme, sage, ginger, garlic. They emitted the subliminal message that Joseph Brightson would be as delicious to taste as he was to smell. For Joseph owned and was the chef at an expensive French restaurant on nearby Madison Avenue. Born in Dorset, a seacoast area of southern Britain, just across the channel from Normandy and Brittany, he was entirely the antithesis of the chef I knew for so many years, Hugo Munka, who dominated the kitchen of our summer hotel. Tall, rounded and muscular, like a heavyweight boxer gone to fat, Hugo always seemed to smell of blood and, maybe, tears, for it was rumored he was a sadist. Hugo was born in Chicago.

"You mean you fantasize sadistic scenes?" I asked Joseph. He nodded.

"What are they—what sort of activities do your fantasies involve?"

One of the minor cruelties that Hugo enjoyed was to use a silver service cup to scoop boiling broth from its steamy aluminum caldron and pour it on a waiter's hand, often with no apparent provocation. He had only contempt for the young men who came to the hotel to earn their tuition during the summer. They were not professionals.

"My fantasies are like the cinema," Joseph explained. "To be honest, I couldn't begin to tell you about them if I hadn't seen that film about the cook, the lover and all that. It made me feel quite normal."

We both laughed. I pressed him further. With only a trace of his country accent, soft as cowslips and wild orchids, he explained that most of his initial scenes were like the opening of *Blue Velvet,* only they took place in Britain, generally in springtime. "I spent my childhood in Dorset, near Lyme Regis, not where they filmed *The French Lieutenant's Woman* but more inland, where you'd hardly know the nineteenth century had ended—that's where the fantasies are set."

"What happens in your fantasies?"

"Well, in my favorite, I'm standing near a church, in a country lane along a meadow lined with white hawthorn and Queen Anne's lace, like a regular bridal bower, when in my mind a young boy comes sauntering along—" Joseph paused. "Do you really want to hear this? It's frightfully perverse."

My mother had told Louis Washington, the tender transvestite who waited tables in the children's dining room, to keep the children out of the kitchen. It was dangerous to allow them to escape through the connecting door. The kitchen was a "madhouse," waiters running with large trays of food on a slippery floor, inscrutable drugged Orientals chopping, mixing, frying; derelict alcoholic dishwashers scrubbing enormous pots, and Hugo, presiding in his whites, filthy at the belly where the roundness came up against food and steel. There was a story that Hugo had been discharged quickly from his last job, told to disappear because he had done something—no one knew exactly what—to a young boy.

"It's my job to listen," I said. "As long as you haven't committed and are not planning to commit any cruelty that our legal system would punish. I would want you to go to the police with that."

Joseph quickly and strenuously denied any such act or intention. "It's all in my mind, which, in some ways, doesn't make it less real, you know."

"I know." Joseph's clothes really did have an extraordinarily appetizing odor. I considered whether it would be bad policy for my husband and I to try his restaurant without announcing ourselves, but without hiding, either.

Joseph continued. "Well, if you truly believe you have the stomach for it, what interests me is cutting off bits."

"Bits?"

"Bits and pieces, appendages, things that hang on. You know, fingers, toes, noses, sometimes arms and legs, that sort of thing."

"Genitals?"

"Yes, of course. Especially genitals."

"More or less dismembering?"

"Yes, that's the right word for it. Not your Jack the Ripper treatment—slicing up—but cutting off, disjointing, letting the blood pour out of all the holes, all the vessels, all the exits."

I remembered the expert joy with which Hugo used to work with the second chef to separate animal parts with knife and cleaver, dismantling lambs, calves, chickens, sections of cows. When I was thirteen, I had elected to try my strength by waiting on tables. Watching Hugo work as I moved in and out of the kitchen taught me a great deal about the use of knives, large and small.

"What sort of feeling do you have when you are 'cutting off?' "

"Oh, it's quite happy, quite ecstatic really, like a surgeon. I do it so swiftly my victims hardly know what's happening; the knife slips across the sinews into the joint and the arm's right off, or I just cut round the loose skin where the testicles hang, and they're off, zip, clean. I get quite excited by my expertise, yes, quite excited, the joy is part sexual, naturally."

"I thought you said you lacked sexuality."

"In a practical sense, yes. I would never admit this to anyone but you—I've never had a partner. I suppose that's really what I'm here to see you about. But I do get some excitement from these fantasies. I'm quite ashamed, of course. Humiliated, really. I'm only telling you because I hope you can help me to dispose of them, cut them out so to speak."

Although his tone was understated, Joseph was beginning to perspire with the intensity of his thoughts. . . . When the sweat poured down Hugo's cheeks from beneath the high chef's hat in the heat of the great iron stove, the waiters grew wary. If one angered him by trying to stack too many main course dishes on a tray, he would reach across the serving counter, which was level with the man's fly, grab the trouser cloth and the soft flesh contained within it, and twist hard. If the waiter became enraged enough by the pain to make a move toward retaliation, or if any of the men on line behind him raised a fist in sympathetic protest, Hugo would lift his largest cleaver to achieve discipline. His ultimate control over the speed of service and the quantity of the portions could make or break a waiter's summer.

Joseph Brightson's fantasies all involved young boys whom he would overpower, carry to the local churchyard and mutilate on a stone coffin as though it were a chopping block. His morbid imagination, stimulated now by postmodern films, had been fused early by the tales of Dorset's author, Thomas Hardy, whose places of miracles and murders, or both, set the tone of Joseph's reverie. The image of Angel Clare carrying Tess D'Urberville, wrapped only in a sheet, across a swift river on a moonlit night, to the empty stone coffin at the Abbey church—carrying her and perhaps intending to murder her—all this had blossomed into Joseph's own peculiar style of imaginary butchery. But why boys, and boys only?

Hugo's more active brutalities were performed not on men but on women, who seemed to cling to him. His coterie included his wife, Emma, several chambermaids, a female guest who saw her husband only on weekends when he came from the city to visit her and the children, and the town madam, who left the brothel to come and service Hugo herself. One could only imagine what signs he left on women's covered bodies, but his mistresses did not try to conceal their marks, his black-and-blue mementos on their arms and legs. The female guest seemed to display the bruises on her thighs, especially at the bathing suit line, rather proudly. There were also stripes from Hugo's belt and the occasional black eye or bruised cheek.

Much as I would speculate about these signs of violence and why they were not only tolerated but apparently sought, I wondered even more at the condition of Emma, Hugo's wife. Once, I thought in confidence, she opened her blouse to show me the marks on her chest. The pale skin of her sternum, the fairness visible above and between her breasts, was covered by cigarette burns in various stages of infection, suppuration, healing and scarring. Later I learned that Emma unbuttoned her blouse to expose her disfigurements to anyone who would look. She described how Hugo punished her this way any time she complained of his infidelities or anything else. She was helpless, she wanted to leave him, he was a tyrant, a demon, a devil, but where would she go? What would she do?

"I seem to be a prisoner of my fantasy," Joseph said, rearranging himself in my office chair. "I can't seem to get beyond it."

I asked him why he fantasized only about boys. Did he have any idea what limited the surgery to young males? He didn't know, beyond the fact that they had, in his view, more to cut off.

"What associations can you make? What comes to mind?"

"I'm having a thought, but it doesn't seem to belong to the subject. It seems to be the opposite."

"Go on."

"The thought is that I don't much like women. My mother and sister were a pair enough to ruin any man. But I do like boys; I enjoyed most of the chaps at school. Why would I cut them up, and not women?"

"In an odd way," I said, "it seems to be all right if you cut up males. You're not really acting out of hatred."

Joseph looked at me quizzically, as though I were an extremely odd person. "It's true that I don't feel any anger when I'm cutting them up in my fantasy, but I assume I must be angry somewhere."

"What are you feeling?"

"I think I'm feeling a kind of—a kind of love. This psychic stuff is very paradoxical, isn't it?"

"Very."

"Then you understand it?"

"Not yet." I now understood with Joseph that the dismemberment fantasies were not accompanied by feelings of hatred or revenge but rather by a pleasurable, even loving sexual excitement. In my scheme of belief, sexual excitement always signifies a healthy impetus at some level. It was possible that the surgical fantasy represented or displaced some positive emotion.

"When you're finished cutting off all the young boy's parts, and his orifices, his holes, are running with blood, what does he remind you of?"

Remaining silent, his eyes closed, Joseph thought deeply. Suddenly he smiled, illuminated. "Why, he reminds me of a girl, of course. I've turned him into a bloody female." The insight seemed to relieve some deep distress. He started to laugh. "A bloody, menstruating female!"

We nodded at each other for several moments as if to confirm the existence and the importance of this idea, this connection that had not existed before.

To his next session, Joseph brought along his private photographs for me to see. He had arranged them as a series in an album. Although they seemed to be of different women, they were actually all of himself in a variety of costumes. In a bizarre way, they reminded me of Cindy Sherman's art photographs of herself in assorted historical disguises. Joseph had posed for his own photographs, in all the classical costumes of seduction and betrayal. He assumed the exaggerated postures, in drag, of the young schoolgirl, the miniskirted housemaid, the nurse with tight uniform, the vulnerable housewife alone at her swimming pool, the bride, the nun and the quintessential whore, head down, bottom upended, legs with stockings and garters visible, half a woman, half a carcass.

Joseph's body, padded at the chest, seemed to belong to a strong, athletic, dominant female, even when he dressed as a nymphet. "I took all the pictures with a timed camera and developed them myself," he explained. "No one but you has ever seen them." He further offered that the surgical fantasies aroused him but he never used them for satisfaction. For ejaculation, for release, he masturbated to his photographs. Yet in spite of the costumes, he did not think of himself as a woman. Just as the dismemberment fantasies contained no conscious sadistic urges, so the photographs of himself cross-dressing reflected no conscious desire to be female.

Hugo didn't like my work clothes. To dress like a waiter, in a pair of black trousers, a white shirt and a black bow tie, seemed perfectly reasonable to me. For a woman to wear service pants in 1952 was unusual. Even the Wacs had worn skirts. But I didn't want to feel like a waitress eking out a living. I wanted to feel like a waiter working his way through school, although the identification was absurd since my parents would easily afford my college tuition.

As I set my tray down on the stainless steel counter to be filled with plates of meat, vegetable and potato, Hugo said, "I don't like your pants."

Long trained in silence, I didn't answer.

"You didn't hear me." His voice echoed across the kitchen and up to the chimney rafters. "I said I didn't like your pants."

"Hugo," I said with as much managerial authority as I could muster, "please, the guests are waiting."

He tapped his ladle against the side of the pot and motioned me to move to the back of the line. The men behind me shuffled uneasily.

"Serve me, Hugo," I repeated. "It's my turn."

"Move to the back," Hugo insisted. "I told you I didn't like your pants." His eyes seemed amused at my helplessness. They crinkled in laughter at the corners. For the faintest instant, the most ephemeral space between the particles of time, I felt a lightning scorch of heat, a rush of rage so powerful I could have killed him. Ashamed of my helplessness, I quickly moved to the back of the line. I never fought with Hugo again.

For a few days in May, Joseph went to Paris to attend an international hotel and restaurant convention. He sent me an envelope with a postcard and a gallery brochure enclosed: the brochure had a picture of a face and a hand by Rodin, seeming to be done loosely in clay. It was from an exhibit of sculpture depicting the body in parts, pieces, or sections: *Le Corps en Morceaux.* Joseph's message on the card was, "I've met her. In front of a few loose feet and a head fresh from the guillotine. Her name is Anne. Fondly, Joseph."

By the time I received the envelope, he was back in my office, explaining. "It's an amazing coincidence. She's an American sculptor. She's very strong for a woman and I love looking at her, Dr. Zion. I think I'm in love, really, madly in love. I can't wait until she comes back to the States in two weeks. I don't know how this psychiatric process works, but something is happening to me."

I said I thought it was a good thing to be in love.

Although Hugo made it impossible for me, I didn't quit. My service was slow. Often I had to combine two plates in one to create adequate portions. To compensate, I took a smaller station, served fewer people. The experience mattered, not how much money I earned. I found myself talking more to Emma, Hugo's wife.

"I don't know what's gotten into him," Emma told me. "He's getting worse, drinking more, he thinks I'm having an affair with Marty the lifeguard, my body is all bruises and sores. Last night he tied me to a post and beat me with branches from a tree. My skin looks like a road map."

I said I thought she ought to go to the police. Maybe they would do something to restrain him. She thought it was hopeless; something was driving him and nothing would stop the fire of his jealousy. Besides, maybe the police would put him in jail; how would the hotel make the season without a chef?

I told my mother about the situation. She said it wasn't her business. Her business was to feed the guests. People had the right to do whatever they wanted, in private.

Joseph Brightson beamed with his happy decision. He was going to show his sculptor friend his costumes, but only after he had impressed her with the restaurant, his knowledge of French cooking, his interest in art and films. After all, his fantasies were not unusual, these days. Everything was mutilation, bits and pieces, now. Movies were made like ratatouille, with time cut up like aubergines and courgettes, the forties, the eighties, the sixties, all run together in a soup. Who could make sense of what was happening? Maybe Anne would understand. Maybe she would even see his photographs as art. If Mapplethorpe had an audience, why not Brightson? Should he show her the photographs first or the costumes themselves? He had already told her about the fantasies, which no longer seemed so terrible since they were a route to being excited by a woman. The fantasies hadn't seemed to bother her at all. She said, on the contrary, she hoped he wouldn't be sick when he saw the lifelike flesh of her sculpted pieces of abused and mutilated women. Of women after breast surgery, too, after mastectomies. She wanted the world to see how it was for females.

One night at the start of the second week in August, Hugo came late to dinner. He was more obviously drunk than I had ever seen him, his eyes glazed, his hands slow and trembling, his speech thick. There were long scratches and gouges on his bare forearms.

I told my busboy and the waiter at the next station to cover my guests. I had only two tables. It wouldn't be a lot of work. I had to check something out.

Hugo's shack, occupied privately by him and his wife in deference to his importance at the hotel, was dark, as was the thin, twisted path leading to it. I called to Emma, who usually rested during dinner hour, but there was no answer. The front door was locked.

I made my way around to the back door, the route to a small separate bathroom added to the shack as an amenity for Hugo. It was open. I entered and made my way across the bathroom and into the bedroom, to the light switch near the other door. The floor was sticky.

When the light went on, all I saw was blood. All over the walls, the bed, the bureau, the chair. And the floor—I had been walking in blood: the soles of my shoes were thick with its coagulated softness. The same anger I felt when Hugo laughed me to the back of the line scorched me again, only this time it nauseated me. My heart seemed to be beating in my fingertips as I clutched the rusted iron bedstead to hold myself up, to hold the retching down.

Emma's head lay on the bloodstained pillow. Her mouth was ajar, her blue eyes stared at the ceiling. Her bleached blond hair surrounded her face in bloody ringlets. Dried blood covered the stillness of her lips, her teeth, her tongue. I walked to the side of the bed and lifted the rusty wetness of the spread: Emma's body, hacked, cut up, divided into segments like meat made ready for refrigeration, lay underneath, all the parts in proper anatomical alignment.

Holding my stomach, gagging, screaming, tears and saliva pouring out, I ran to find my mother in the office. "Hugo killed Emma," I yelled. "He cut her into pieces. He chopped her up in the shack. There's blood over everything. Come and see."

My mother shrugged, barely slowing down her typing. "Why do I have to see? You just described it to me. Calm down. Is Hugo working?"

I pulled a Consolidated Laundry towel from the pile of extras she kept in the office and wiped myself with it. "He's serving dinner."

"Good. After dinner I'll call the police."

I sat down on the small couch near my mother's typewriter. My shoes still had blood on them and I wiped the edges of the soles, then threw the towel in the wastebasket and tried to breathe more slowly. My mother, although short and broadly buxom, had an elfin

VIRTUAL LOVE • 239

look at times, with dark hair in a Victorian roll and a gentle face. Her small blue-green eyes, however, were all business. Hardly missing a click of the keys, she went back to responding to inquiries and confirming reservations. She was a human machine at the typewriter. Form letters were too cold. She preferred to answer all the mail herself, with personal interest and without secretarial intervention.

As soon as dinner was completely served, at 8:45 P.M., she picked up the telephone.

Joseph could hardly contain his good news. His smile was as broad as the sunrise over the English Channel and the Cobb, the ancient curved stone wharf in Lyme Regis. "I've done it," he announced. "I've had sex. I put it inside her and I came. It was very nice, very nice indeed."

"I'm happy for you," I said. "But how did it happen? What was different?"

"The costumes were just the right size for her. I showed them to her and she loved them. Thought they were art. Thought my pictures were art. She asked if she could try one on—the costumes violated feminist principles, but it was also important not to be bound by any principle. I said of course, so she chose the dominatrix in leather with boots tied all the way up her thighs, like Place Pigalle, only she didn't need breast pads, and she looked just like me. It was like having sex with myself, it was easy, it was wonderful, and I owe it all to you. The best part was her bleeding. She was menstruating. It was my greatest secret fantasy come true. I got blood on my penis. I'm not a virgin anymore. How did you do it, Dr. Zion?"

I said I supposed my training and my mother's influence had something to do with his fulfillment.

The police were putting handcuffs on Hugo while everyone stood around watching in the kitchen. They told my mother that he would be held in the local jail.

"But you can't take him away," she said. "What am I going to do? I have four hundred guests to feed."

"I'm sorry, Mrs. G." Elmer, the town policeman, shrugged apologetically. "We have to lock him up."

"But you can't take him away. No one has accused him. I only said his wife was all hacked up. I need him."

Elmer and his colleague looked at each other. "I'm sorry, Mrs. G.," he repeated. "We have to take him."

"How much will it cost to get him out on bail?"

"Mrs. G., for your own protection, even if you could get him out, the man is a murderer."

My mother said, "But he's already committed the murder. It was that business between him and his wife. She was a crazy masochist. She drove him to it. I saw her burns and her whip marks. I guarantee, he's not going to do it again. . . ."

Who had helped Joseph? Was it me, observing, questioning, judging, finally screaming (if only to myself) that Hugo was a maniacal beast from whom I, if not Emma, should have been protected? Or was it my mother, calm, pragmatic, the ultimate philosopher of individual responsibility? The matter was difficult to decide. . . . And what was Dr. Hellinger talking about when he warned about the consequences of overprotection? Was a secure childhood and being the darling doctor son of middle-class European Jewry a hindrance? Did one need a Holocaust to become nonjudgmental?

People say they are surprised about being able to talk to me so easily. They feel unusually comfortable with me. Why? Both of my parents were basically unavailable, my father absent, my mother wrapped so much in her own domain as to expose me to violence and murder without concern. Perhaps the answer has more to do with whether one is frightened by a person than with one's ability to judge an action. I could not avoid fear by running to my parents for protection or comfort. I had to learn to deal with my own terrors. It is difficult to shock me. That is as much a grief and a loss as it is a professional advantage.

PART EIGHT

THE SHARDS OF MARRIAGE

Eros

To: E-man
1.3.92

SUBJECT: Only a girl

Self-examination should never end, although the capacity for it does wear down. I don't know why, but your mail—outrageous in its self-indictment—stimulates me to reflect on events I haven't thought about in years.

It can't be that we're simply products of similar generations, even though you're younger than I am. When I read you, I feel all the old resentments spiraling up from the stews, the old houses of hell in my past. And further, I suppose I've never understood what it was to be a male, like you, influenced by the same set of beliefs that devalued women in my early years. Only a girl, indeed. How much harder, in a way, for a man to relinquish a superior position than for a woman to gain mere equality. Your father sounds like an archetype, a template, a die stamping his intaglio image on all our fathers, the men of that generation. I feel as though I know him.

I feel as though I've been there, lived through his remote narcissism, dealt with the world where his self-occupied ghost occasionally came snarling out of the mist. . . . I understand. . . .

News: The intimacy clinic becomes a true possibility. The chief has decided to push. (One of my old patients made a huge contribution.) It seems right for me now: my children are adults; I need to fill my empty nest with a new enterprise. But the new clinic can't be a simple fix-it center. Most sex problems turn out to be affectional disorders that we can't touch with easy-does-it therapy!

Aphra

To: go-dot   SUBJECT: collector's item
    1.6.92

You go on in your happy little world—son and daughter busy, husband perking away at his science, patients grateful for all your kind attention—while i'm here on the other side of the world being scalded on every surface of my miserable neuroanatomy. How do you do it? How do you walk through all the insults and defeats that i know you must receive, you must—we live in the same professional worlds—how do you do it without being furious all the time? Why don't you do battle? Are you blind, or is the Styrofoam packed around your perceptions, too? And why am i picking a fight? I have enough miseries of my own without adding to yours.

I'm on edge because i think trish and i may finally be through—i can only bear so much—she did the worst, the most unforgivable, almost the unnameable. . . .

She can't bear my having any pleasure. I don't give her the two pleasures that mean the most to her: clothes and sex, *her* order of priority; would you believe that there is anyone alive today who thinks that what they drape on their backs actually matters? With all the world streaming in rivers of blood, this woman thinks whether or not i fuck her *means* something!! You understand: when you listen to people complain all day, when you worry about them killing themselves if you turn your head, it's hard to come home with a missoni sweater in your left hand and a box of no-fat flowers in your right and long to screw your wife with your rocket of romance! Dammit, the only thing i want at the end of the day is a long, sweet smoke. . . . i want to sit and fondle my stones, which may sound like masturbation: maybe it is, but what i mean is that i want to caress my art, just the way freud did. . . . he brought it to the dinner table. . . .

I know i'm too big and too young, but sometimes i feel just the way that savage old man must have felt looking back at the ages. Have I told you about my collection? It means everything to me, *everything*, all my thoughts of immortality mixed with the memories of my mother's perfume in my bed, my memories of erotic bliss in the time before i could tell the time, when i was suspended in the terra cotta flight of tiny eros, his boots on my feet, his amulets at my waist. . . . i have spent my soul acquiring my art, just the way freud did: i pay for it with two hours of my work a week—it's why i work—if i can't work for art two hours a week, what use is life? Do i want money? Do i want armani suits? If i can't tithe my income two hours' worth a week to feed my ecstasy, why live?

Last saturday i came to the big moment: i'd saved my money for months and months, put it away in the mahogany box with the falcon-head handle, counted it every week to see how close i was to the total, changed old bills for newer ones, smelled the sweaty green paper and was glad, exultant, thrilled, overcome with joy in spite of my sedentary position in life as toilet for the world's emotional waste. I was happy because chi soon yang (the west's version of robert lustig, freud's dealer) had been saving the piece for me and today i would go to buy it, just as though i were walking the streets of vienna from berggasse 19 to wieblinger strasse; i would walk down the hills of san francisco until i came to his little dark shop, where he had buddhas and bodhisattvas, bottles and reliquaries, jars and hydrias and lekythoi. . . .

I bought my piece of destiny that afternoon: it was a white stone double of freud's baboon of thoth, something i've wanted ever since i started. You see, the baboon was supposed to be the spirit of thoth, who was scribe to the gods and represented all things intellectual. . . . i need a smart woman, aphra, i need a goddam colossus. . . . who is it going to be, toni, you, who is it going to be?

Well, i came home with my treasure, the lunar symbol on top of his head, just as though he were sitting on the corner of freud's desk; i was showing it to patti who was playing in her room while trish took a shower. Patti liked it. See the monkey, she said, See monkey sit. . . . i was teaching her to say baboon. Ba, i said, ba ba ba. . . . Ba ba ba, she repeated.

Trish came in from the shower, her cotton kimono wrapped loosely, her face flushed and hair curled by the steam. She saw the heavy white stone that i was helping patti to hold. Her eyes narrowed, her chin quivered with rage. How much did that piece of junk cost, she asked. Exactly how many dollars? How many? You promised—you swore you wouldn't buy any more art this year! Suppose I get fired? Who's going to buy this stuff? There's no market now; you're the only rich man in the world and you're buying!

I wanted to tell her that the world hadn't quite come to an end yet; someday my collection would send patti to college and buy her wedding and her house and everything else if i absolutely needed to sell it, but i couldn't be convincing about that because it's hard for me to imagine selling it, even for patti's benefit—and trish was not to be stopped—her voice was rising. . . .

Your rocks mean more to you than we do, old rocks, dead history, you sit and jerk yourself off with them, you give more love and intimacy to your goddam rocks than you've ever given to me or patti and i hate your rocks, i hate your objects!

She was crying, her arms folded tight, but she loosened one to wipe her nose with the inner elbow of her kimono as she paced back and forth. It isn't enough, trish continued, that we feed you and shelter you and clothe you; it isn't enough that you have an extra room to house that ragbag of monstrosities while patti sleeps in a closet. We don't do enough for you, helping you start your practice without loans, but you have to spend our money on monkey statues! You said you couldn't contribute to the house until the practice got going: all you could pay was your office rent and your lunches and a couple of dinners out—okay, I bought it—but that thing cost thousands and thousands of dollars, if it isn't a fake, which it probably is. I thought you'd given up collecting until we got on our feet and you were paying your way. . . .

And i told her i might as well give up living as give up collecting, i couldn't make it through the day unless something was to be got for it, some *thing,* and, besides, what was she so exercised about? She could claim her half of anything i collected after we married, and she knew very well which pieces i'd bought and when; it would all be part of the divorce settlement.

When i said divorce, all the shower steam seemed to dry on her —she went cold and pale—she asked me if i would take care of patti for the afternoon, she had some errands to do, so i said sure, i planned on that anyway, there was a big computer show for kids' software, maybe i'd find her something to learn the alphabet with. Trish said plain old books had been enough for her and all her ancestors.

Patti had a great time playing at the computer fair: it's amazing how fast kids can learn with the programs and the encouraging sounds and voices; she must have been just ready because she learned practically the whole alphabet that afternoon. When we came home, she made a beeline for her books to see if she could read the letters, and i was marveling at the miracles of technology that could teach a kid so much in so short a time—though i think patti is a kind of genius—and i thought i would go have a look at my new object in the study (maybe the baboon of thoth had decreed this sudden burst in patti's intellect), and that's when i saw the note on my study door in trish's printing. It said:

DON'T LET PATTI INTO THE STUDY. DON'T GO IN IF SHE IS WITH YOU.

I supposed that trish was on one of her neatness kicks again. . . . she was a periodic slob, or periodic compulsive cleaner as they say in the textbooks. . . . she's hell to live with for months on end, throwing her things around, letting dishes pile, buying new stuff instead of cleaning the old, but then she goes on a rampage of order and cleanliness that would stun the visigoths. I opened the door.

At first i couldn't see why trish had left the posted note: everything was in place, the room was in order. And then i saw the space on the bookshelf where my hydria had been. Of all the motley trinkets of attic art i'd been able to acquire, this had been my favorite and the best. . . . i'd saved for over a year and made a trip to London to acquire it: a small terra cotta water jar from early greece, classically proportioned, with oedipus drawn seated before the sphinx, red and brown glaze on a black background, resembling freud's little vase. . . .

But where was it? Was trish so angry about money that she had decided to remove it for sale? I sat down at my desk chair to think about it, maybe to write an e-letter to you, and that was when i saw the black scar on the wall opposite the empty spot on the shelf; looking down from the wall scar i saw the fragments of my water jug.

It was in perhaps hundreds of small pieces, broken beyond ordinary repair; after trish had shattered it against the wall, she'd obviously used a hammer to complete the job. The old terra cotta formed a powder on the carpet. I walked around it, kneeled down, sifted the ancient sand through my fingers—i caressed one or two remaining shards—i couldn't believe . . .

It must have been someone else, maybe a patient crazed by negative transference; someone had gained access by false pretense and in destroying my oedipal vase had also symbolically destroyed me and psychiatry—that was it—that was why trish had left the cryptic note, she didn't know the answer, either.

But i was fooling myself. Trish had done it. She was too practical to destroy the whole collection; she knew where her settlement or her alimony had to come from so she chose just one piece, the one that meant the most to me, the one she hated as much for its implications of male phallic supremacy as for its importance to my identity with the profession and with freud as shaman, if not as philosopher. . . . she broke the vase, the pot, the container, the symbol of woman that i came as close to loving as i ever come close to love. . . . i used to caress its wide rim and the narrowing of its body down to the stepped foot. . . . and now there was only a jagged edge of sphinx's wing reserved in a patch of red ground, a fragment of flight preserved, a remnant of transcending femininity. . . . i picked up the shard, rubbed my thumb on the smooth side of earthenware wing like a child with a security object or a woman with a rosary. . . . i remembered broken things: my brother's body, my fragmented childhood, the shattering absences of my father. . . .

My collection was a failure, my marriages disasters, my paternity was a sham. Who was i to haunt the dark corners of the world for the sacred relics of other men's gods?

My eyes had begun to water and burn in the antique dust when trish peered in.

You left Patti all alone in the kitchen, she said.

I know, i answered, I had thought I'd be right back.

She stopped in the doorway and i knew she was looking at me but i couldn't look back. I felt her eyes on my head as i remained kneeling in the dust, bent over my loss. . . . i felt her hatred on the wave of her vision. . . .

I hope you got the message, she said, I just hope to God you understand: I don't want you ever to buy one of those things again unless you're paying for this household and for Patti's education.

My hand squeezed the shard in my pocket until i knew it had drawn blood. I said, I don't see where it's written that the man pays all the bills, but I was happy to give you everything I had in New

York. You made us move, remember? You needed to come west to work. You know the practice will grow.

I could see the rage rising as her throat colored, then her jaws and cheeks reddened. You never gave us everything, never. You gave a huge tithe to your art every month, it was impossible for me to put anything in the bank: three—four hundred a week, month after month—I had to watch it turn into stone: I had to watch your inferiority complex and your identification with Freud turn into ugly pots, grotesque heads, one-armed statues, I have to look at that garbage, I have to clean it carefully—

I told you never to touch it. I said I'd clean it! Don't you ever touch it again!!

Is that an order? From Herr Freud, himself? Well, I'm going to touch it. I am going to touch anything I damn please in this house because you don't touch me! You haven't touched me for three years and that's goddam long enough to be without contact, doctor, I mean what kind of psychiatrist never fucks his wife, never even tries. . . .

She grasped the small clay statue of eros around its waist and picked it up as if ready to lash it against the shelf. I sprang up from my crouch and grabbed her wrist, held her arm down with my right hand, squeezing hard to make her loosen her grip so i could collect the statue in my left. She pummeled me with her free hand, she kicked my shins and ankles, if she had a knife she'd have plunged it in my back, but i kept squeezing, kept preventing her from throwing eros, and when she finally let go of it, i twisted her arm to force her to the floor, neatly, neatly, the way i'd learned to do it from the sensei. . . . she kept screaming, now about how she was going to publicize my brutality, and finally she was just screaming for help, yelling as though i'd attacked her—i couldn't stand it—i reached out to put the statue down in a safe place and then my free hand arced toward her face; the shock of the slap silenced her.

Take it easy, i was saying when i noticed patti sucking her thumb and watching us, her eyes big as the black pools of memory where this scene would remain with her forever.

I let go of trish—she could destroy my whole collection, i didn't care—she could take eros and fling him to the winds, and the statues of artemis and athena and demeter, too, because the deed was done and hades had opened up for patti. . . . men were not to be trusted, would never be trustworthy again. . . . i wasn't any better as a father than i was as a husband. Maybe worse.

Memory

AGE 39

1976

PRIVATE FILE: Do not send.

To: E-man   Subject: SHARDS OF MARRIAGE

In the seventies, I remember attending academic conferences where movies of group sex, homosexual relations and intimate heterosexual encounters were shown as "educational films" to great professors who dignified major chairs. Cleansing impure thoughts was the purpose: sex was good, not bad; sex was public, not private. Sex was the great equalizer; sexual relations were a form of democracy in which everyone had a desirable body. The sin was lack of pleasure. Yesterday's inhibition and guilt were to be swept away and replaced with freedom and joy. Equals and unequals, teachers and students, employers and employees—all were leveled in the new sexual economy. Sex at the office made work more tolerable. One or two therapists had even begun to have sex with their patients as a form of special assistance. No one had yet been censured. Both men and women often felt diminished if they couldn't enjoy sex indiscriminately at love-ins. I remember a child of fourteen whose mother had just had her fitted with a diaphragm and sent her to me because the girl felt pressured. Could I help her to loosen up and enjoy men, menstruation and maturity? I thought, not yet.

Harry and I had our hazy pact. It made me feel part of the times. I didn't know if anything had changed now that I was "back." In any event, sexual jealousy was considered bad form, like throwing your tennis racket at the net.

At the height of the revolution, when sex clubs and spas for spiritual sex were indistinguishable, my life changed. No one, in fact, betrayed, hurt or surprised me. Harry's love remained unaltered. We were as close to being perfectly happy as any couple could be. Then I received a telephone call that sent me in search of hidden worlds.

At first I thought I was searching for something in Harry, but he was only a decoy, a bird positioned to fool a hunter or another bird. To try to find what I was looking for, in an internal dialogue, I told and retold my problem to my old psychiatrist, as though I were lying on his couch and he wasn't interrupting me.

What am I doing here again? I wish I knew, exactly. I wish I understood the metanarrative, if you know what I mean. Actually, you probably could have predicted I'd be here. You probably knew that someday I'd be on this couch telling you my husband has been having sex with other women for the last decade or so, the end of the seductive sixties and now the sexy seventies. You probably knew about it all along; you treated his best friend, so it must have come up in the conversation.

But that's not the issue. The question is, why am I so disturbed? I mean, it's not your usual case of wife at the stove, man on the rove. This is no tattered old monogamous hegemony. It isn't as if the sexual revolution hasn't been perfectly clear to me and as if I couldn't have told you exactly when he was out having sex, if not with whom, had I chosen to take notice. What I'm here trying to deal with is my bewilderment, not my surprise. I'm not shocked and I don't feel what he did was immoral. I just looked the other way. He did what most other men in his situation would have done, considering the whole world was one big sex party, only I had something else to do that night. I'm the oddball, not him. So why am I obsessed, why is it in my head day and night, like a boa constrictor or a medieval dragon or a fish, swallowing everything in sight?

Years ago you pointed out that I was an obsessional sort of person. I get a fix on something, become preoccupied; it's all I can think about. You remember those psychological tests you had me take? The woman I drew looked as though she was trying to keep her balance. Well, that's me. I'm always forcing myself away from the idea that consumes me. I push myself to eat and clean house and exercise and do all the dailies that make the world go round. I love everyday life; I'm in love with it when nothing distracts me, but when something is on my mind I forget there are other things to do than think about it.

My obsessive ideas were always grand, good and beautiful. The concept invading my brain felt holy and perfect. It was usually attached to some difficult goal: a profession, a painting, a poem; as often, it focused on loving a man: whether I loved him for his greatness or I wanted his greatness to love mine was always unclear. But obsessing was never unpleasant. I always held a world of light, of joy, happiness and fulfillment, in my mind.

And now this. The feeling is painful but the process is the same, taking up all the space in my brain. I don't know what to do about it. I keep opening and closing his desk drawers, working my way through his papers, reading every line of print, every bill, every stub, every note. I can't stop. I hardly do anything else when he's not here.

I can understand that you need a little more history: how I found out what was going on. I certainly didn't seek out the details. One night Harry came home late. More accurately, he came home early in the morning, about 4:00 A.M. He'd never violated normal hours before, and it occurred to me that he hadn't expected to find me home. It was clear he'd been drinking—unusual for him. I'd told him I was going to visit a woman friend on Long Island—one of those rare nights when an old friend had so much to say she'd asked me to stay with her. My children were weekending with their grandparents. Then at the last minute, she'd called to take a rain check because her daughter was ill.

I said nothing to Harry. I didn't want to ask where he'd been. I knew more than I wanted to know from the musky smell mingled with alcohol.

The following morning, Saturday, he went out early to do some errands. I was sleeping late, recovering from my sleepless night, when the telephone rang and a gentle tenor, soft and long-suffering, asked my pardon for interfering with my morning but there had been no choice. He didn't want it to come as a surprise when the newspapers announced that he was naming my husband as the corespondent in his divorce case. He told me his name: even I recognized it as belonging to a much-married folksinger.

The days that followed seemed calm and rational. I felt no unusual emotion except for the gradual onset of the need to search. The owner of the dulcet vocal cords and the errant wife were stock characters, people in a bad movie. I loved Harry. We understood each other. We had a perfect marriage.

When you suffer obsessions, your mind goes into reverse and you keep trying to pull out of the sandpit, but nothing happens. The wheels spin, taking up energy, sapping your strength. My obsession is that I'm looking for something. I don't know what it is but I have to keep looking. At first—a few weeks ago—when I initially found out, I felt that what I was looking for belonged to my husband. I thought perhaps it was on his body and I kept studying his skin. Occasionally, I could see someone else's presence in the little graphics imprinted by nails or teeth. But what I was looking for wasn't on his body, because the marks didn't stop me from searching his papers, datebooks, records, that tantalizing trail of his life in the jumbled receipts he keeps in his pockets. I found quite a few messages relating to his sexuality. I found one clue, the letter "O," in his datebooks, going back for years and years, summer and winter, even when we were in our summer cottage in the Berk-shires; and another, going back a shorter time, a "T." The letters, probably short for names, and the dates, helped me to understand his problems with travel and vacations. But even placing names and dates and times, being able to recollect what he was doing at all those hours as compared to what he said he was doing, didn't satisfy me. They didn't relieve my need to keep looking.

One day I found the greatest artifact of all. I was sure it was what I was searching for. I had been spending the morning inspecting his papers again. It was Sunday and he was out for early tennis with his friends (an activity that could be used without fear of my calling to check up). Actually, he didn't need ruses. I never knew exactly where he was, nor could I easily find out. One of his life principles has been to have no structure. I think he made a blood oath with an old friend that neither would submit to any institutional sched-ules; his friend eventually died of submission or rebellion, or both, but that's another story.

Anyway, he was playing tennis when I found two file boxes I hadn't even noticed, though they sat on the floor right next to his desk. Harry's activities generate a lot of paper: he gives time to a great many organizations. He lectures or runs seminars. What he discusses is mostly politics or drug abuse or sports or anything at all. Sometimes he gets paid; more often he donates his time. He loves to talk. He can be astonishingly funny but he isn't a monolo-gist. He loves anything from a dialogue to a decalogue. He really enjoys kneading ideas with other people and coming up with the surprise wisdom or the veiled verity. He always gives credit for the verities to other people, which makes everyone feel good. Probably I have gotten credit for more eternal truth than anyone since Moses —but back to the file.

As I said, the two metal boxes sat casually at the side of his desk. In one, manila folders containing short manuscripts were stuffed so tightly that I had to wrench them loose. They were entries to be judged for the various awards that civic and religious organizations frequently choose Harry to deliver after he selects the winner. Harry likes to give prizes. The other box was filled with letters of praise from fans. Near the front of the box of letters, I found one written by a woman who seemed like she might be the person whose husband had called to inform me—in those innocent coun-try cadences—that he'd had it with his wife, and so had Harry. She wrote about herself as a woman whose life was a series of hard-core porn scenarios, ending her solicitation with "I like to fuck anyone who has anything to teach me about ideas." As pleasantly melodic as he was, I felt faintly irritated at the balladeer for running out of educational material.

For days and nights I pored over the hundreds of manuscripts and letters, taking out a few at a time to try to figure out whether the authors were his lovers, his sex pals or his friends. Eventually, I tired: Most of the people who wrote their hearts' stories or sent grateful letters of praise seemed more troubled than brazen, more unhappy than malignant. Even if he had had sex with some of them, I found nothing to envy in their written communications. And there weren't many sexual aggressors like the woman with an erotic fetish for ideas. Of course, he could have met other women, at random, who did not connect to him through admiration for his social commentaries or his skills on the lecture circuit, but I lost interest in the particulars. I had no intention of exposing or harming anyone. I began to realize that if I wanted to know about the women, it was in order to understand my husband. And if I wanted to know about him, it was in order to comprehend myself.

I began to try to elicit more information, not about whom but about why. He gave a standard answer to my questions. The gist of it never varied no matter how often and from what angle I approached the question. He said—he says—with profound patience, "Men and women are different. I didn't expect you to understand. I was surprised when you seemed to. I didn't want to hurt you. You're the only woman I love, and I love you uniquely. No one has ever had or will ever have more of me than you have. And no one will love or understand you more than I do."

Every time I get this explanation, I feel as though I've been blind-folded and turned around three times.

My obsession continues. I've gone over and over the files. I've studied every piece of paper he owns. I must be on the fourth or fifth rerun by now. Examining certain papers is a ritual; certain drawers have begun to feel like reliquaries, the items like sacred objects in a velvet-lined box. These are his medals, his old coins, his French money from our long-ago trip, his sentimental objects.

What am I looking for? Who am I looking for?

Last night was the worst. Harry was out later than usual. I imagined he was probably discussing my reaction, how he wouldn't be able to see whoever it was for a while, if ever again. I could almost hear the conversation. He would probably feel virtuous when he came home. Thinking of his virtue, I recalled that I had recently bought a pair of scissors, expensive and sharp.

The brushed-steel blades gleamed in the lamplight as I took the scissors out of their case. I flexed the blades open and closed a few times and listened to the sound of the edges grinding against each other. For an instant, I considered jabbing the points into my abdomen but dismissed that Oriental thought. Suicide should be premeditated, not impulsive. Instead, I found myself moving toward his closet, a mahogany armoire built a hundred years ago to fit the space in our bedroom.

His newest blazer was a wine-colored Paul Stuart bought on sale in a spirit of celebration. I pulled the sleeve out of alignment with the rest of the clothes, as if searching for the price tag. The jacket had been extraordinarily expensive, even on sale. The thought of the price—that our money went to clothe him for the seductions I fantasized—stirred my fingers to move, and fighting the thrift bred into me by my Depression-oriented background, I cut off the sleeve at the underarm, the scissors slipping easily across the fabric.

Releasing the sleeve from the body of the jacket seemed to release something in me. I began to laugh. I thought it would be clever to hide the loose sleeve in the other one, to be discovered the next time he wanted to wear the blazer, but the scissors kept moving. I cut off the other sleeve, then the pocket flaps, the buttons, the collar. Soon I had dismembered his entire wardrobe, the pieces lying around the bedroom like severed limbs on a battlefield. But when the scissors stopped and my hand ached with the hour of effort, I felt no better. I began to experience the desire to go through his papers again.

I forced myself to sit down in the middle of all the rags I had created and tried to elicit meaning from all the jugged clothing, the arms and legs and buttons and pocket flaps. Was it simply and obviously that I was mad as hell and had cut off all the hanging parts, whose symbolism one didn't have to be Freud to interpret? I remembered a chef, when I was an adolescent, who literally butchered his wife because he suspected she was having sex with the lifeguard at my parents' hotel. We thought he was a man obsessed by rage, a sadist. Could he possibly have loved her?

I thought about what I had fragmented. Heavy tweed jackets, bought years ago, during Harry's English literature phase, before he studied sociology. Then, the master had fancied himself a cross between an eighteenth-century Grub Street hack, a nineteenth-century Romantic poet and an early-twentieth-century country gentleman with manor house and library. Good-bye (sadly), Anglophile. . . . Light blue-and-white seersucker suits, summer apparel for the cultivated man seeing his editor in town, for having luncheon before taking the train (1925) to Gatsby's on the express West Egg line. Farewell, dreams of intellect in luxury. . . . Two gray pin-striped suits, one antique, one gaining vintage. Formal dress for the man of estate, the community pillar—indeed, the community totem. Adieu, ritual male that I never was. . . . Finally, the assortment of daily jackets, out-of-shape boys' sizes, absurd tweedy attempts at staying young, too small, the triangle between front button and trouser line always showing. How many heads had cried on those lapels? I should have kept the ritual suits; probably they were the only ones uncontaminated by his liaisons.

I sat quietly in the circle of clothing parts and marveled that no blood accompanied the murder I had just committed. Except that my husband wasn't dead. I was. Or at least the part of me that had lived through identification with him.

How could Harry have loved me when he had sex with other women? Or if he loved me, how could he have loved *only* me? He was too warm, too giving. He had to love others. And I couldn't imagine him playing sex games, using women as objects. Either way, the truth was difficult. Harry hadn't deceived me about his affairs. He'd deceived me about himself.

Jung says an obsession is a way of being possessed by the unconscious, a way of being torn up into chaotic multiplicity. Osiris was torn to pieces by Set. Giants in legends are ripped limb from limb. The Maenads pulled Orpheus apart and threw his lyre and his head, singing, into the Hebrus.

It will be a long song down the river before I believe that anyone else in the world loves only me.

Memory

AGE 41
1978

PRIVATE FILE: Do not send.

To: E-man   SUBJECT: SHARDS OF MARRIAGE

The limousine and uniformed chauffeur were waiting for me outside my hotel in the French Quarter. It was the same limousine that had driven me and Elia there early that morning. I was in New Orleans to accomplish three gratifying missions at the same time: One was to attend the American Psychiatric Association convention as the guest of honor at the opening luncheon, where I was to give a talk, "Sex in America." The second goal was to appear on a talk show to promote my recent book on human sexuality. New Orleans was not a scheduled stop on my book tour, but since I would pay the airfare and hotel room to attend the psychiatric convention, my publisher arranged interviews on Louisiana TV as a prelude to the rest of my trip.

My third undertaking, venture, project and enterprise was to have, or at least begin, an affair. I didn't know with whom, or how long it was going to last. I'm not even sure that "having an affair" was the correct label. After almost two decades of a monogamy to which my husband had not been a party, the end result was that I wanted to have sex with another man. A strange predicament for a well-known sex therapist, in whose anatomy it seemed at the time everyone might be interested. It occurred to me that sex-for-its-own-sake might be best with a stranger. I'd then have the choice of never seeing him again. But I didn't have the plan all laid out. I only knew that this moment could possibly be the peak of my professional, if not my personal, achievement. While I hadn't yet seen a divorce lawyer, I knew I would accomplish that as soon as the excitement of my career success died down. Meanwhile I wanted to have sex as a rite of independent celebration. I told myself it didn't much matter with whom.

I had begun to realize on the plane that this was an underlying purpose of my trip. I had my illumination when I saw Dr. Elia Petrov seated next to me. He occupied the place near the window. I had made my reservations too late to deserve anything but a middle seat.

"Perhaps you'd like to be next to the sky," he offered as I sat down. In fact, I would have enjoyed a window seat, but I felt it would be taking advantage of him to accept. "I prefer to sit in the middle," I lied. "It's less drafty. I always catch cold from the ventilators on the side of the plane."

As he moved his underseat bag quite thoroughly out of my way, I noticed its lineup of neat contents: a tape recorder with earphones, a ring of keys on a hook, a folding diary at least two inches thick, notebooks with color-coded tabs and a beeper. All were arranged within easy reach on top of the case. It was an impressive statement of the man's organization.

"What brings you to New Orleans?" I asked politely. "Are you crashing my psychiatric convention, or is there some other sort of meeting?"

"I've been honored by your society's invitation to give the Berman Lecture," he explained in his formal way, suggesting an aristocratic Chekhovian childhood. "My topic is aggression and the temporal lobe."

I remembered then that his specialty was studying the effects of tumors and malignancies of the brain. He had something in common with psychiatrists: an interest in altered conditions of the mind.

I knew of Dr. Petrov because he was head of the pathology department at my hospital, but I knew nothing about him beyond his title, what he looked like and that he had been born in Russia. He seemed a most unlikely type to make a lifelong study of aggression. Thin, neat, obviously perfectionist, he appeared to be the sort of person who would rather not kill the buzzing mosquito. Still, he had become the department chairman at one of the most competitive medical institutions in the world.

We exchanged a few further pleasantries, odd bits of information indirectly revealing us to each other, hints implying emotional conditions and liaisons. When I complimented him on the neatness of his carry-on bag, on how everything fit into such a small, tidy space, he said he took pride in having minimal needs and occupying minimal space. In fact, he still lived in hospital housing, in a one-bedroom apartment, although as chairman he was entitled to a rather grand three-bedroom, which he might take someday if he ever required more space.

I took this to mean he wasn't married and had no children. If there were children by a previous marriage, they would have needed at least a bedroom for visiting, even if he was a child of czarist Russia who had been raised in Communist self-denial.

When he asked whether I lived near the hospital, I told him I intended to move closer. "Actually," I said in a burst of revelation, "my husband and I are separating, so I'll probably move out of our Village apartment and come uptown to be near the hospital."

Dr. Petrov nodded and I could feel him absorbing my information into a compartment of his palatial mental file. He smiled at me as he reached for one of the thick folders he was carrying, the galleys of a neuropathology textbook he'd just completed; he showed it to me and I was impressed. I liked the way his long index finger turned the pages for me. He had a uniquely masculine sort of delicacy. I liked his thin physique, so different from my husband's square stockiness. I approved the way the buttons on his shirt closed with plenty of room between the fabric and the abdomen beneath. I also enjoyed the shape of his bow tie, which echoed the shape of his dark mustache. I even told myself I appreciated his excusing himself to work during the trip. He put on his earphones, turned on his tape and checked each page of the text, making tiny,

legible ciphers in the margins. He had an elegantly organized style
that might be very easy to live with, I thought, in comparison to my
husband's *modus vivendi,* which was orderly but never meticulous,
or even sufficiently clean to do without a housekeeper. Harry might
be neat enough to stuff all his business papers in one big drawer of
our armoire. Dr. Petrov would probably color-code the papers,
periodically weed out expired documents and even clean the
drawer from time to time with a wet cloth. . . . Dr. Petrov probably
knew, too, the best way to stack a dishwasher to prevent break-
age. . . .

When I asked Elia Petrov where he was staying, he surprised me
by naming my hotel. Most of the doctors stayed at the Marriott on
Canal Street, where the convention was held. From the guidebooks,
I had elected the Royal Sonesta on Bourbon Street, in the French
Quarter. According to the book, it would provide a more authentic
New Orleans experience. When I told Elia I was being picked up
by my publisher's limousine and offered him a ride to the hotel
from the airport, he accepted, remarking that academic publishers
never provided such perks to impoverished department chairmen.
He carried my bulging suitcase until we found my driver and then
again after we emerged from the car. At the desk of the hotel, the
clerk presented us with a single registry card. Dr. Petrov and I
glanced at each other and smiled. Then I quickly requested two
cards. We had to reassure the clerk that the rooms' locations across
the patio from each other didn't really matter, but we both preferred to face the pool. . . .

My schedule for the day included a TV talk show at eleven, for
half an hour, followed by the APA luncheon address at one. On the
two subsequent days that I would spend in New Orleans, I had a
relaxed southern schedule of one TV show a day, which gave me a
chance to attend some of the sessions, even listen to Dr. Petrov's
Berman Lecture. Then I'd be off to Chicago and points west.

I'd been on local New York television enough times in the past
to know that the New Orleans station was treating me very well.
The cosmetician paid attention to the unevenness of my features,
made my cheekbones emerge, softened the thick bridge of my
nose. A young man kept me company until I was ready to go on; he
came to the set with me and arranged the microphone on my suit.

The show's host was Marlene Blaine, in whose warmth I believed
that day. In spite of something absent in the sheer blue of her eyes,

I felt she wanted to be there with me. She enjoyed me in lilting Delta syllables. I found myself talking much faster than usual, smiling, even joking, not easy for a psychiatrist accustomed to suppressing humor. Under the klieg lights of southern hospitality, I was surprised to learn I was more of an actress than I'd ever had the courage to be in New York. I'd hardly stopped smiling, when I was in the limo again and the chauffeur was driving me to the Marriott, where I was to give the luncheon address. I decided to leave my TV makeup on.

For the address, I adopted a more professorial pose than I had on TV, where I knew the camera occasionally noted that I had good legs. As a prop at the luncheon I used my new tortoiseshell glasses. I lifted them on and off to make my points, as though to look issues more squarely in the eye. Over two thousand people overflowed the tables, but the acoustics were perfect. Many had just checked into their rooms and had seen me when they inspected local TV offerings. They applauded for a long time before I spoke and quieted quickly when I put on my glasses as if to read the talk I had thoroughly memorized. Elia Petrov sat at the honorary table nearest my microphone. He nodded encouragement.

I said we were all aware that in the seventies, human sexuality was the arena where the most far-reaching revisions had been drafted, revisions that challenged not only custom but also theology. I said we all supported the idea of sex as a positive force creating joy rather than perpetual sorrow, guilt, shame and penitent labor. But I stressed that even though sexual behavior had changed, sexual morality was still an issue. The rules governing human attachment and loyalty had not disappeared with the absence of venereal disease. Impelled and inspired by my recent experience with Harry, I delivered an impassioned defense of my book's thesis that sexuality reflected personality and character, and that in today's atmosphere of sexual freedom, the issue was not whether to have sex but rather with whom and why. Our legacy to future generations might be that there were no separate rules for love, for life and for sex.

The number of people in the audience intensified its enthusiastic reaction. When there was laughter, it thundered through the density of the crowd. Heavy rumbles of approval punctuated the speech. And when I became oracular, the awed hush was as deep as in any cathedral. I suddenly knew what it was to have power over a mass of people, to have a response fill a space so completely that souls seemed to join. At the same time that I felt myself extinguished in the horde, I also felt myself magnified, larger than life, part goddess, part woman, at one with those old times when human beings did not know whether they were deity or dross, and made mythology of the mixture. I might have been Athena, exchanging her shield for a podium, or Diana, holding a microphone instead of a bow and arrow. For a moment, I was the bodhisattva appearing in female human form to enlighten the world.

And at the back of my mind, in that spacious recess where the unconscious plays with personal history, I had the inarticulate feeling that I could probably have any man in the room I wanted, providing he was at the convention without his wife.

In early May, the month of the psychiatric convention, New Orleans was quiet, still recovering from winter carnival. Mardi Gras was over, the costumes put away, the dancing frozen until next year. As I wandered along Royal Street, I tried to breathe in the heavy peace of the humid air, to relax in the late afternoon's slanting beams of subtropical sun, but the day had been too intense. The flight from New York, the world of TV moving in fast frames of makeup, lights and rapid talk, the massive luncheon and the sound of the crowd still cheering and applauding in my mind's ear, had left my nerves tingling with an unfamiliar pain. I felt as taut as the lyre strings in the design of the cast-iron balconies that I passed; I felt stretched to my nervous limit, like an emotional athlete recovering from an Olympiad of stress. And yet I wanted to make love— no, not to make love, to have sex, to exchange heat and fullness and wetness with someone, to find one erect penis in a world of those glistening lingams to slide inside me and make me come until I was exhausted.

I went back to the hotel, but I didn't take a dip in the pool, because paradoxically I wanted to avoid meeting other psychiatrists. If Elia Petrov and I had chosen the Sonesta, other doctors might select it also. I didn't want to talk. I didn't want to flirt. And I couldn't close my eyes to rest. So I put on my new sandals, tucked my small monocular scope in my pocket in case I saw birds or interesting details, and set out on a walk. Alone.

The streets of the French Quarter were lined with balconies. As I walked, I kept looking up at these fantasies in iron to see someone, to catch an inhabitant glancing out, taking the air, revealing himself.

No one seemed to use the balconies at this hour. Perhaps no one ever used them at all anymore, but I could imagine families sitting out as in a Goya painting, or lovers climbing up and down by rope in the dark night, even today. Lovers. . . . The idea of finding a lover, of having sex, was on my mind, had been on my mind ever since I arrived. Who would the man be? Who would reap the release of my tension? Maybe a Creole, a French-Spaniard, possibly enriched with African blood, would appear from behind one of the hidden doors set into crumbling plaster at the side of an L-shaped house. Maybe it could all happen without the civilized arrangements, the dinners, the drinks, the endless explorations of circumstance that inevitably go on between people in the trade of human feelings. Having an affair with another psychiatrist would probably be a busman's holiday of revelation and recrimination. . . . But after all the long nights of trying to understand why Harry needed other women and why he took the analytically absurd position that sex usually happened merely for its own sake, that very same deceptive and complex simplicity was all I seemed to want now: a release, a stranger slipping an arm around my waist and leading me upstairs to an old Creole bedroom filled with nineteenth-century antiques, ancient damask, polished silver hiding behind bare ocher outer walls. . . . I wanted to lie there with my Afro-Mediterranean stranger and listen to the rustle of the old garden, where sweet olive and jasmine lofted their scent and oil jars contemplated eternity, while in the distance, far, far away, a mournful saxophone set the sinful mood.

I saw him before he noticed me. He was focusing his camera on a building embroidered with wrought- and cast-iron balconies, more iron than I had ever seen on a single structure. Even though the house attracted tourists with cameras the way human confections attract great masses of insect life, I had somehow never perceived Evan Prescott (known to his friends as "Press") as a camera enthusiast. I had assumed that, like Harry, he was too interested in people, their histories and conversations, to pay much attention to the visual properties of architecture. (Harry's travel photos usually included me in the right lower corner of every frame. I ruined the composition, but Harry found landscapes or architectural wonders meaningless unless a person inhabited them.)

I debated attracting Press's attention. On the one hand, I didn't want to talk with anyone at all. My mind and my vocal cords were too tired. All I wanted, I thought, was to exercise myself into the oblivion of sleep or, alternatively, to have sex with someone until I was so worn out I could do nothing else but sleep.

On the other hand, Evan Prescott had attracted me from the moment I became aware of him during my residency in psychiatry. It had been a major moral effort to establish a friendly, nonsexual relationship with him, even though I'd become expert at deflecting sex and turning it into friendship during all those years when I was surrounded by men in medical school and at hospitals.

Like Harry, Evan Prescott was one of the talkative people in the world: expressive and energetic. Like Harry, too, he was subtly seductive, charming and known for his attentions to women. We had become friends during my second year, when he supervised my in-patient caseload. I diluted my sexual feelings by inviting him home to dinner several times, by putting him under Harry's spell instead of weaving my own enchantments. The maneuver was successful: he and Harry liked each other. Harry thought it was good for me that Press and I became what he called "pals," lunching together to gossip about the hospital and, later on, to discuss mutual referrals. Over the years the perpetual teasing possibility that this relationship offered seemed to keep both of us cheerful, though other events in our lives might be trying.

I started crossing the street to avoid him, to keep my old morality out of what might be a new, more flexible life, but somehow he caught sight of me. "Aphra," he called. "For Godsake, it's Aphra!" As he walked toward me, he waved a large arm, signaling me closer. Following his instruction, I moved toward him, seeing myself as in quicksand, drawn inevitably into the past when I wanted to move to the future. I was Alice-in-Wonderland on her treadmill, not going fast enough even to keep up with the present. In the instant of walking the few steps to meet him, I saw myself, too, as a photo he might have taken: there was no doubt I looked good in the short, clingy jersey dress into which I had changed from my lecture suit.

The hug of greeting caught me into Press's muscular warmth. A sudden rush of pleasure dissolved the boundaries between his chest and abdomen and my breasts and belly. It was a feeling of relief, so intense it resembled gladness at being rescued from some nameless disaster. I hugged him back.

"It seems like years since I've seen you," Press said, slipping his camera somewhere into the depths of his pocketed vest and increasing the strength of the hug. "You're a very busy woman."

Affectionately, he disengaged me and inspected me from toe to head—my sandals, the tight jersey, the flush at my neck, the hair wisping from the Japanese pick and shell that held it tightly back.

"You were sensational!" He smiled and shook his head admiringly. "I've always been impressed with you as a sex therapist but I've never suspected you were so concerned with ideas."

We walked down Royal Street and came to the Vieux Carré, the old square itself, facing the Cabildo, the Presbytère and St. Louis Cathedral. The formality of the elegant buildings, offset by the street artists' brightly colored canvases on the flagstone pavement and against the park fence, suited the duality of my mood. Part of me wanted to cross-examine Press to see if, after all these years, he had the faintest idea who I really was and what I thought. The other part cared only that he was paying specifically masculine homage to some segment of me, although I couldn't say for sure whether that segment consisted of my pheromonal aura or my relationship to Harry. It certainly wasn't my mind. I asked what he got out of my speech.

Press put an arm around my waist and steered me toward the French Market. "You were awe-inspiring," he told me. "You made us all believe in you. What you said didn't really matter—something about sex as joy—but what counted was that you had us spellbound. You were splendid!"

I simmered for a while, realizing that he hadn't comprehended my talk, or made any effort to understand it, but perhaps what he said was true: the words didn't matter; the feeling counted. I might question the depth of his connection to me, but he had other virtues. At the moment, I felt every motion of his hip as he put his arm around me and joined my step.

Later we stood in the dusky stalls of the closed food market and made the inevitable comparison to Les Halles, which I had seen on my first trip to Europe. Press said that, speaking of food, Harry and I had an invitation to dine with him that evening.

"I accept happily," I told him. "But it would be rather a long way for Harry to fly."

We met for drinks at the Desire Oyster Bar, part of the Sonesta Hotel (where it turned out Press was also staying), yet very different from the marble, crystal and mosaic that reigned in the entrance hall. A dark-ceilinged, old-style pub, brightened by red leather seats on bentwood chairs and by too many lights on the ceiling fans, it opened directly onto Bourbon Street. Before Press arrived, I settled on a margarita. Since Harry never drank anything in those days except scotch on the rocks, nor did he approve of any mixed drinks, the margarita was a concoction that I'd had only as an adolescent.

When Press arrived at the bar, twenty minutes late, the menu, written in white paint on the mirrored walls, had begun to grow slightly fuzzy, glittering, more refracted than usual. We were silent for a while, drinking the edge off our hunger. He ordered a straight chilled vodka. I studied him, as he studied me, face-to-face and via our reflections in the mirror. His hair was black and silver, full and wavy above thick, deeply black eyebrows. And although his name and his voice marked him as among those inexactly elite Americans who might have gone to Harvard by rights derived from the May-flower Compact, his face betrayed origins among the Mongol armies who ravaged Europe from the east. Yet all the coarseness had been bred out of the features. What was left were the high cheek-bones, a fine, small nose and full lips over even white teeth. A fold of skin, rather like a mandarin's beard, ran from under his chin up along each side of his mouth when he smiled and ended below each cheek in two outrageous dimples.

Press held forth about New Orleans beverages: there was a pow-erful guava plant brew called *le petit goyave*. . . . Absinthe was born of wormwood. . . . The old Monsieur Peychaud served bitters and brandy in a double-ended eggcup called a *coquetier.* Thus origi-nated the word *cocktail.*

From drink he went to love and death, especially the rise of the feisty Madame Pontalba from the death intended by her father-in-law after he shot her several times, then killed himself. Finally, when the world was floating along on salt-sweet tequila with no mooring place, Press allowed a lengthy silence, then asked, "Why didn't Harry come down with you? It isn't as if he has a regular job. . . ."

I tried to talk as though Press were the last of a long series of people I'd told, instead of the first. "Harry and I are separating," I explained.

He took both my hands and lifted my fingers to his lips. "It's hard to believe. . . . I thought of you two as the perfect couple. . . ."

I ordered a second margarita.

Even though Galatoire's offered the best regional cooking in New Orleans, I could barely eat. I slowly and steadily drank from the bottle of wine Press ordered, not touching much of the shrimp rémoulade or the cream-covered fish that later appeared on my plate. By the time we reached dessert, I had told Press my whole problem: How was I supposed to believe that Harry loved only me when he had sex with any lost, lusty, lonely creature who wanted his thrill? And with others who wanted much more than that. In the end, I didn't care so much about his acts of infidelity. I had no reputation to lose. Most people expected sex therapists and their spouses to be promiscuous (i.e., liberated), so it was no great embarrassment. My anger seemed to rise more from Harry's affirmations of loving only me. Harry couldn't have sex with other women without loving some of them. I felt like an old friend of his, a man named John Hardecke, who probably killed himself because he'd had to share Harry with me.

Press listened sympathetically. He'd heard similar stories many times before from his patients (and probably from his lovers). He knew exactly how to hold my hand across the table and guide me through the tale, like taking me down from a bad trip. He even expressed the professional suspicion (like mine) that there was probably something more to my anger, something that had to do with my past, maybe my father. . . .

After dinner, we wandered along Bourbon Street and listened to the jazz, coming in riffs from behind half-opened doors. I could feel a sadness collecting somewhere deep in my chest, filling the same place that the saxophone I'd imagined seemed to penetrate. The melancholy and the music formed a channel inside me, running a sorrowful rhythm from my deepest center to the surface of my skin. The liquid improvisations grieved my expulsion from Eden into this world of neon and—behind those half-closed doors —topless dancers, sending whiffs of their perfumed, silken flesh out to the street on bars of woodwind melody.

We followed a ululating trail of notes into Mahogany Hall, where I diluted the tears inside me with cigarette smoke and a hot, sweet drink made of coffee, brandy and spices.

Press smiled and said I seemed to be feeling better now that I'd gotten it all out.

The swimming pool in the center of the patio lay flat, reflecting the moon and one small yellow safety lamp. The rectangle of the pool was like a celluloid picture frame on a reel of old movie film. It kept sliding away from me, while another frame moved up in its place. The world rotates that way, out of focus, thrusting away from me, when I'm drunk. Press pulled the rain protectors from two lounge chairs and I sank down on the foam cushions of one of them. He moved the other directly alongside it, like pushing twin beds together. Settling in, he extended his hand toward me. I took it, the tips of my fingers curling around the edge of his palm so I could feel the hair on the knuckle side.

"My room's down there," he said, pointing to a pair of French doors that opened onto the patio directly across from Elia Petrov's room. The light in Dr. Petrov's room was on behind the soft draperies.

"And I'm right there," I said, pointing to my room, which was a few windows away from his.

"Coincidence," he murmured.

"Coincidence," I repeated.

"Predestination?"

I shrugged, closing my eyes and trying to make the world stop turning as I relaxed into the lounge. Holding hands with a man in a hotel setting was like being at home. Most of my early sexual experiences were at my mother's hotel. And yet I felt alienated, too. The vast majority of my sexual life had been spent in my bed at home with Harry. I was in exile here, in exile from Harry, from myself, holding a man's hand for a security I didn't feel, trying to keep my world from rocking too hard. My mind wandered to the problem of making sense out of the impending divorce from Harry: it was foolish; we got along so well. He was really very much like Press, easy, affectionate, comforting. Harry talked a great deal, but then I was so silent most of the time. And while it might be a joy to be married to someone like Press who earned more than Harry, it wasn't strictly necessary. I earned enough to keep us going.

Press had turned on his side. His free arm was gently caressing my waist and moving down over the curve of my hip. Then he suddenly stood up, took my hand and led me off the patio. We went into the hotel and down the interior corridor toward our rooms. His room was the first we came to. He stopped, found his key and started to let us in. I stayed at the threshold. He looked at me, speaking an invitation without words.

I answered, "I don't think so."

"I'm not sure I follow you," Press said. "What don't you think?"

"I think. I know. I want to say good-night."

"I don't understand. . . ." Press leaned against the entrance wall near the door, crossed his arms and posed. "You've told the world how to do it in your books."

It was a curious moment to be concerned about his reading habits, but I had to know. "Have you read my books?"

"No," he said flatly. And then, without the slightest self-consciousness, he told me that he hadn't read "the first one because it was kind of heavy going." "The other" he'd looked at, "enough to give me the idea. There's so much to read these days."

I had the sudden, irresistible conviction that I could measure the full depth of what he might mean to me by his answer to one more question. "What books do you read through and through?" I asked. "I mean page by page?"

He cocked his head and raised his extraordinary brows. The dimples appeared. "Light stuff—for escape—Robert Ludlum."

I nodded and began to look through my purse for my key. He walked me to my door and then kissed me on my forehead. The kiss felt more like a slap. I knew Evan Prescott would never have lunch with me again.

Before undressing, I opened the French doors to let the night air ventilate my room instead of using the air conditioner. Across the patio, Elia's light was still on. He was probably up late proofing his book. Neither Press nor Harry had that kind of dedication. Press had done just enough to get along and Harry worked only if he couldn't find anyone to play with.

Dr. Petrov was thorough and conscientious. If he had been my friend for all those years, he'd have read my books word for word, from cover to cover, maybe more than once. And I was somehow sure that if he ever made a vow, a commitment or a promise, he would honor it. Nor would he ever be twenty minutes late for a date unless the airplane couldn't land.

Elia Petrov's room number was imprinted on my memory from the awkward moment at the registration desk. I dialed it and got him on the phone. "This is Aphra Zion," I said in response to his worried hello. "I was having a little trouble sleeping and I happened to notice that your light was still on. . . ."

PART NINE

BROTHERS

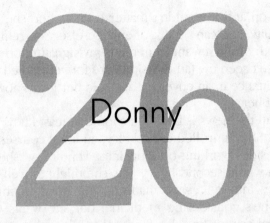

26

Donny

To: go-dot   SUBJECT: vision quest
   1.13.92

Couldn't take another millisecond in what passes for civilization; only artifact i miss here in utah at bryce canyon national park is my computer, which crashed on the plane (meaning that it went down even though the plane stayed up). So i'm writing in a notebook i bought at the airport; either i'll send you the pages or i'll type them into the wire when i get home to my desktop, wherever home is and whenever i get there.

Everything's so much in flux, i had to spin out of it, i had to take a break, i had to look at canyons to remind me that rocks and rivers go on even if life might as well stop. I don't think it would matter to anyone but my mother if i jumped off sunset point into the jaws of the canyon and it wouldn't matter even to her: she's so caught up in self-pity, she can't think of anyone else. She reminds me of trish: all both of them want from me is my signature on a *check*. My mother hasn't seen my father's signature for years; the last time, he left her a pittance in an envelope and told her it was now *my* job to take care of her.

But not all the news is bad: you should at least know that toni is doing well. She's enrolled at berkeley, auditing courses in physics and bio, besides working on a business venture. . . . she's thinking if she has a whole second life to live, she might as well pack three or four lives into it. . . . she's made up her mind to finish college and then she's considering medicine, but she wants to feel the pulse of real school first. Reading pop philosophy, even stephen hawking, is easy; writing equations is something else—except she's a superbrain—the concepts and numbers come to her the way visions come to prophets. If trish could calculate as fast as toni, she wouldn't need me to help support her.

And since she took up meditation, toni's stopped talking about herself; she says her past was too sordid to waste the present discussing the details. Now she's disappointed when i can't show her heisenberg's uncertainty principle in mathematical language, or do similar honors for schrödinger's cat. She thought all doctors understood quantum physics, considering the relative and transmutable nature of disease. I'm her fallen idol and i love every minute of my degraded state because i couldn't handle a dependent erotic transference. I almost lost interest when she wanted to stay and talk to me in california instead of flying to bali. In this goddam era when women don't know whether they want michael jackson, iron john or jack the ripper, toni knows.

Which is why i can't get her body off my mind, can't remove my brain from her ass and breasts and legs: in my fantasy she's slugging it out in the male world for me, the supreme phallic mother earning an income and supplying me with plenty of great sex besides. I want an infinite breast, as the old analysts might say, and i'm also aware this is a ludicrous fantasy that has dried out every time (however briefly) i've tried to suckle it. . . .

But toni is beginning to play out my fantasy for her: be careful of your neurotic entitlement—your patients may satisfy it. She even has a scheme for making money! She's made contacts through reilly's pals to establish an on-line computer sex-talk service, like phone sex, only typed on screen, for literary erotica only. . . . to avoid being called pornography the product uses well-read women with seductive voices to discuss sex scenes in works by henry miller, anais nin, old d.h. lawrence, james joyce, et al. . . . men sign on to hone the finer points; there's also a panel of men for female on-liners, as well as respondents to both sexes for gays and lesbians.

Toni sees no reason to leave the sex business if it's legitimate and doesn't involve her body; she plans on discussing subjects like, say, why henry miller enjoyed fucking june's ass, or proust's masturbatory habits, or the tame perversions of the marquis de sade. For toni, sex unseen and unfelt is a specialty; why shouldn't she make money on it? She knows every line about sex ever written, i think. The trial marketing has been done and it looks like a go with Compu-Mail in a couple of months. . . .

Meanwhile, she has to extricate herself from reilly and, while she gives me credit for the whole scheme, she's made the decision not to hang on as a paying patient once she's out of reilly's clutches. He plays a penny ante game of possession by keeping her twenty or thirty thousand in debt—buying gifts on her credit card and taking his time paying—but she'll probably be able to sell off enough stuff to clean it up. An interesting sidelight is that he could have hung on to her by paying college tuition instead of helping her with business, but even though toni is his look-alike daughter, educating her would feel like incest to him! He refused! So he's going to lose her altogether. Lots of hypocrisy, paradox, even irony in the sex business. . . .

The question now is do i go out with her? The guidelines on sex with patients are getting tougher every day, as i'm sure you know: it used to be that if a person stopped being your patient, you could have sex; then there was a two-year, then a seven-year biblical wait, and now some people believe sex is never appropriate. But i can't do more than wait until she's not my patient. The fantasy is in place: going for the gold ring of being her first and only real lover! And, of course, the fantasy is also that no matter what kind of broken down son-of-a-bitch i turn out to be, she'll resurrect me. I need a female model to be a man. I guess i don't trust men, and toni's perfect because with her vaginismus, she's like a man—you can't get in—i wonder if i'll lose interest in toni when i can get in, or if it's really her dependency i fear. Maybe i'll eventually find out what kind of character i am. Victor Frankenstein's monster committed murder because he was too ugly to be loved; i commit whatever it is i commit (sin, emotional sadism, acts of unfulfillment) because i am fiendishly attractive (sic) and my heart is made of such inconstant stuff: sand, pebbles, volcanic fragments, quartzite cobbles, that i can hardly keep it focused on beating regularly, much less obeying a lifetime contract for taking care of someone, although toni may be a woman of such vibrance and vigor that she'll ignite me in the heat of that tectonic crucible and harden me in her image (bryce is affecting my metaphors). . . .

So why do i still want the all-powerful mother-father figure, what drives me, why am i always looking? Must a woman be strong to withstand my evil? Is what i really want a woman tough enough to survive my abuse? Do i think i'm so bad?

I'll probably never make it to be patti's broken clay—fate of the father—i don't know if i'll even qualify for visitation rights. Trish will probably accuse me of abandonment and get sole custody. But she wants me out of the house now, soon, immediately, yesterday. . . . that's why i'm here at bryce, touring the quickly dead. . . .

Toni once told me i should see bryce, that even though she's not paiute, her grandmother collected legends and told her how Coyote, the great god of the paiute underworld where mankind came from, killed all the wicked after a flood drove everyone to the surface of the earth. He petrified them in "the place where red rocks stand up like men in a bowl-shaped canyon. . . ."

So i'm here to see if old Coyote will do it to me; maybe he'll look at me with his wolf-dog eye and finish me off, once and for all. My lawyer says it's better for me if trish moves out, but i couldn't make it in the same house with her even for another week. I stole all my art (freud ferrying his collection to england, away from the nazis). . . . it's in my office now and i don't know what i'll declare it's worth to the divorce court, but at least i have it!

So you can experience the majestic and awesome nature of my thoughts, the at-one with the universe that i feel while i tour these ancient canyons. Actually i'm jealous of the tourists and hikers because they seem to be in states of primal ecstasy: the world is a picture postcard experienced as a divine slide show. Families, birders (not many birds here in winter), buddies and lovers all tramp the canyon with such innocence. . . . one character took off his backpack, rolled in the sand and snow and said he was experiencing rebirth from the womb of the great mother. . . . he's going to need a shower to relieve his sandy wet crotch.

Toni has supplied me with peyote. It's her opinion i should go on a vision quest and maybe she's right. She gave me some loose instructions about not eating for four days and insisted on pressing the buttons on me by leaving them in an envelope with her check on my desk, but the truth is i'm too depressed to eat anyway and i never had a good trip with LSD, so what do i want with peyote for my enlightenment? But i'm getting deeper into canyon mysteries; i've been alone out here for a couple of hours now and i always fall victim to hope when i'm alone. Maybe i'll never reach the peace that comes with knowing one is part of the great chain of Being; i'll never be at one with Being or comprehend Dasein or get away from all the petty shit.... but i do want to sit under a bo tree and get to the bottom of it all; i need some kind of rite of passage and even as i talk i'm eating toni's medicine and wanting to roll down the side of the canyon in a final orgasm with her, or with you, or with anyone who represents the great goddess, because i need a woman, i need Woman, i want the Ultimate....

Just walked along the rim of the canyon for a way: colors are brightening, shapes forming, sunset beginning and maybe i'll find revelation in psilocybin.... old Coyote is watching me, he's sitting there on the caprock and looking at me across eons, across eighty million years, striding the time after dinosaurs, prowling the Wasatch formation, pawing its gravels, sands, silts and clay, foredooming me now and forever because all my demons are right here: all these dead "queer people" are my past and my future looming at me, raging, glowing red with the fire that makes ashes out of everything i touch.

The guidebooks talk about the canyon's towers and pinnacles and steeples as though it's a christian shrine, but all i see are bleeding pagan bodies in states of decay; the books describe whimsical figures, the pope, queen victoria, albert, but all i see are sculptures on the gates of hell: a sphinx, cyclops, argos, hydra, gorgon, typhon —giants in grottoes, chimera on caprocks—thor's hammer will fall on me....

Old Coyote's gaze is beaming at me across the millenniums and i feel as small, angry and helpless now as i did when i was three, after my brother was killed; maybe that's how i always experience life, but bryce elicits it, peyote elicits it, i feel as though i have no choice but to be eaten by the wild animal; now, now, this moment, this instant, bryce is immediate, bryce is haptic: to see is to touch,

and right over there is Truckdriver, lumbering out of the earth;
Truckdriver raged at my mother: What kind of a goddam Frenchie
whore lets her kids play in the street?

I think the driver would have killed my mother and driven away
if he could, but the women in the houses heard the screech of
brakes, came outside and moved toward the flattened, bloody body,
still twitching as i, sitting next to it on my tricycle, stared at it. They
came in an ant army and converged on Truckdriver and me; i was
picked up and carried into someone's living room where they sat
me on a small green sofa and turned on a big tv for me to watch
bugs bunny, only my brother didn't bounce back up after he was
smashed. I wanted to tell them that bugs bunny was a lie, but i
stared at the cartoons the way i had stared at my brother's blood
coming out of his mouth. I figured out that bugs bunny didn't get
hurt because he had no blood; blood was bad, i never wanted to
see blood again, not then on animals to eat, or later on women. I
could never become a "real" doctor, even to please my absent
father. I managed to seduce female students into doing all my
bloodwork during my training.

Truckdriver is directly across on that promontory, his trousers a
couple of eons long, wrinkled with dolomite ledges and sandstone
drippings, frozen white ripples of time—and Coyote is still staring
rays at me—he wants me to look at the scene again, he will never
tire of making me replay the scene until i get it right. He watches
me watch myself riding down the block on my tricycle; my brother's
supposed to be keeping an eye on me but he isn't looking; he's
playing with his friends: they're all bending down over something,
maybe it's a marble or a cricket. . . . I'm pedaling along the lumpy
sidewalk where the grass grows between the cracks. . . . it's difficult
to ride from one stone to the next without stopping to lift the
tricycle, but beyond the sidewalk the smooth street beckons, velvet
black with oily tire marks. *Maman* has told me never, never, never
to ride in the street. Donny isn't looking, *maman* isn't watching; he
shouldn't be looking at bugs. *Maman* would hit him if i told her
that he wasn't watching me. . . . Why do i like it when *maman* hits
him? She will hit him hard, very hard. . . .

The soft black pavement is so smooth, i'm rolling fast on top of
it, i'm a car going past all the other cars, honking my horn with
them and everyone is calling my name, marc, marc dammit, get
over to the side, get out of the street, get over here this instant,
now, get off the street! But no one can catch me, i'm riding faster

than all the cars, i'm zooming, i'm a motorcycle, an airplane, a helicopter, i'm flying down the hill and swerving off to the side, i'm hitting the curb as the big white truck screeches by and everyone is yelling stopstopstop. . . .

The orange Truckdriver is walking back up the hill. I'm sorry and i want to tell *maman* not to hit donny because i've been bad, i rode out into the street on purpose when donny wasn't looking, only now he's crushed like a bug or a fly or a cricket when you hold it to pull its legs off. . . .

I'm coming down now and donny is dead almost forty years. . . . beyond are the keyholes, the windows in the rocks, the dream i had of looking at you through a keyhole: classical, conventional symbol woven all across the sky in a mesh of windows, a wall of windows in the rock, a wall of holes, a place where all the keys fit (frost wedging on both sides of the ridge enlarges the niches at the joints; in time the skyholes form).

In time i remember the days, weeks, months, years after the accident when i stood at the skyhole, wanting to get into my mother's bedroom, needing to get in, begging to get in! From that small aperture i could see her solid roundness in the bed, mostly her ass filling the shape of the keyhole with its two softnesses, one atop the other as she lay on her side, the soles of her feet echoing its shape below; i watched her, too, as she grew thinner and smaller and her buttocks stopped filling the keyhole; she never took food.

They didn't have anti-depressants then. She slept it out in her bedroom as i stood there, eye to the eye into my mother's space, her body, her bottom, her bed, the flowered quilt, the filthy pink slippers on the floor; when she turned over, she showed me the open mouth of her sleep, in which she might have been dead but there was no blood. . . .

I kept my vigil day after day and at night, too, though i could see nothing then. During the day they sometimes forced me out to play in the backyard, but i wouldn't stay long. I had to return to my keyhole, to the view of her leg, now crossed, now flung out to the side, now drawn up; sometimes she would draw her whole body up into a fetal crouch, she would moan and shake and yell about how she should have been out there in the street where the big trucks and the bad drivers were!

I stood at the keyhole in the next room until my legs ached and i couldn't see through my tears, and then i curled up with my blanket on the floor near the door and every night i called out to her, i pleaded with the persistence of prayer—*maman* please come and kiss me goodnight, please, please—but she never opened the door.

And one day i screamed at her, *maman* please let me in, i have to come in, i have to, do you hear me *maman*, i hurt in my head, please *maman* i'm sorry i made donny dead, please let me in, come and hit me i'm a bad boy, please, please, please or i'm going to be mad at you, i'm going to hit you. You're bad!

And finally i gave up, just as it is written in bowlby's textbook, the rage turned into apathetic detachment, something grew hard in my heart. . . .

And then one day she finally did stand up in her nakedness, her gray skin hanging over her bones; she put on her blue bathrobe and her pink slippers, came to the door, opened it and looked down at me.

Who is it that is there? she said. I heard a knocking.

I didn't answer her. I hadn't knocked for a long time, days maybe. In the next room i lay on the floor, sleeping the way she did. . . . she walked through the doorway and came to me as i lay there. . . .

Is that you, Donny? she said.

I kept my eyes closed. . . . she knelt and stroked my hair, sniffled, kissed my ear and buried her face in my neck. . . .

Poor Donny, she whispered. Now you are all alone.

I didn't want her to stop hugging and holding me so i let her call me donny and kiss me and feed me and put me to bed. I let my name be donny for a long, long time after she opened the door.

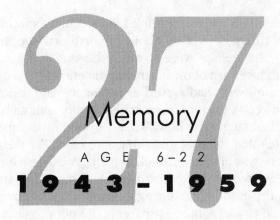

Memory

AGE 6–22

1943–1959

PRIVATE FILE: Do not send.

TO: E-man   SUBJECT: BROTHERS

My brother died when he was seventeen. I was five years older than he was. He died of bulbar polio that immobilized his chest; he lingered in an iron lung for three months after he was stricken. The last time I saw him was at the old Willard Parker Hospital in Manhattan.

We had spent at least a dozen of his seventeen years inseparably together; we never fought that I can remember, except once, toward the end. His name was Thomas. When he died, I was eight months pregnant with my first child. I named my boy Thomas after my brother. My recollections, going back three decades to the birth of my son, and five decades to the birth of my brother, are often confused between the two. I think I am writing about my brother. Sometimes I may be writing about my firstborn, too. It's hard to remember. The feelings were so much the same.

I began to take care of my brother at the end of my sixth summer when my aunt, who had served as my nanny and, briefly, as his, died. I didn't cook for him or wash his laundry, although I did iron it. My aunt had taught me how. When I ironed my brother's cotton overalls, I felt that she was still taking care of us. For the rest of the chores, there was always a nameless maid, Polish or Hungarian, to do the "heavy work." I was entrusted with merely "watching" my brother all day at the hotel during the rest of the summer and after school in the city in winter. My parents did not consider this inappropriate. It was what an older sibling was supposed to do. My father's sister had raised him and his two brothers; my mother considered herself the parent of her six-sibling family. Indeed, I was lucky I had only one child to attend. My brother was mine to do with as I pleased. I had only to be careful that he didn't get hurt. In the world my parents came from, children worked at home or in the family business as soon as they were old enough to perform tasks. I was six years old, almost ready for school and, therefore, capable of responsibility.

The grass is almost up to my chin. I have to cut a clearing with my machete, my jungle blade (my dinner knife). I trample the grass too, to flatten it so the stalks won't pierce the cloth; then I spread the green-and-white-checked flannel blanket over the clearing. My brother is eager to come out of the wicker stroller (mine, not long ago) with its cracked leather seat; he reaches for me and I lift his heavy roundness with all my strength. We sink down on the blanket together; the grass yields to us. A green dragonfly sails by. The cool air coats us with clear blue light; the river moves along the morning.

I touch his arm. The skin is softer than my skin. I lie sideways next to him; we play at touching faces. He closes his short fingers around my nose, grabs my earlobe, clutches a handful of hair. I separate his fingers from the hair; he reaches to put them inside my mouth. He explores my teeth. I try to imagine what he is thinking: hard white stones in the soft place where sounds come from. I suck his fingers gently, pretending to devour them. He opens his smiling mouth wide with the pleasure of being devoured. He pokes at my eyes; I close them against the probing; then I kiss all his fingers, his forearm, the crease in his forearm, his shoulders. I bury

my head in the fold between his jaw and shoulder that is his neck.
I shake my face and make a *z* noise. He giggles and gurgles at the
tickle of the vibrations; his mouth opens again in a wide chasm of
delight. He seems to have two chins, one on each side, with a deep
cleft between. My mother says the split will make him handsome. I
kiss both his chins. I raise his thin white undershirt and kiss his
little chest with the two tiny nipples on it, shining. The mound of
his belly glistens, pushing against his navel. I kiss it, marveling at
the firmness. I can see his bird's eye diaper getting yellow and wet
while I kiss him and I undo the pins to change him. His penis,
growing larger now, is still reassuringly there. It doesn't disappear
inside him or fall off. It makes me feel good; it's a kind of toy that I
know, somehow, I mustn't play with. But I like to look at it and
watch it get larger and smaller.

I change the diaper, put the wet one in the bag hanging on the
stroller and turn my brother over on his belly. That's his position for
sleeping. He settles down, his head turned to the right after a few
trials on each side, and brings his thumb toward his mouth, touching
his lips. I lie down on my back and watch the sky beyond the leaves
of the stand of white birch trees that provides a dappled shade.

The clouds form animals, soft, puffed, silent, still—yet moving
across the sky like horses on a slow carousel. Most of the animals
are mothers. The babies are tucked into the mother cloud or they
are little fluffs following behind. They look like the creatures I've
seen at the zoo with my father. Maybe they are the ghosts or the
souls of the animals in the cages: the mother elephant, the hippo-
potamus with three little hippos behind her, the lioness stalking
the horizon.

I leave my brother sleeping and walk to the edge of the river. I
look for bulrushes, to make a basket for him. What did it mean, in
the story about Moses, that his mother made a basket of bulrushes?
There are no plants near the Neversink that can be woven into a
basket. Maybe I could put him into one of the chef's big pots, like
rub-a-dub-dub. But that would sink. Besides, a pot would be too
heavy to carry down to the river. I would look for a basket that I
could possibly line with twigs and leaves. It would be fun to see my
brother float safely down the river, like Moses.

When I return to the blanket, I lie down to sleep with him. The
flies keep me awake for a while. I brush them off his white undershirt, his legs, his hair. I fall asleep watching the flies. In the distance, the small birds—the swallows and the swifts—hurry to feed
their young.

An hour or so later, I wake to his crying. He must be thirsty. The bottle of water that I have brought for him has spilled into the bag but there is enough left to pacify him. I watch the water level go down as he drinks. When there is only a little left in the bottle, I pull it out of his mouth and drink it. I am thirsty too. It comes out in a sharp stream from the hole in the nipple, faster than I thought it would. I feel that my mother would not like my drinking my brother's water. He is a baby. His thirst is more important than mine.

It is evening in the old bungalow. The fireflies make tiny traffic lights in the dark air. Crickets and katydids scratch and whistle like washboards and teapots. My mother has put us to bed while she is getting dressed to go down to the card room to play poker with the men. When she leaves the bedroom, the smell of her gardenia perfume lingers as a comfort. The crickets sound louder in the silence without her and I can hear the bullfrogs. Tired wasps tap on the window screens. My brother begins to cry, as he always does soon after she leaves. It is the signal for me to take him out of his crib and into my bed. We will sleep together, always waiting until the adult has departed before uniting, until I am well into my teens. I kiss his hair and watch the moon starting across the sky. The man in the moon looks like my aunt. He also looks like my grandmother, who has gone away, like my aunt, to the place called death. I like feeling my brother breathing. They told me you stopped breathing when you died. I try to hold my breath, but I do not die. I always have to give up and start to breathe again.

My brother is two. He is much harder to watch because he can walk and run. Most of the time I hold him tightly from behind, my arms crossed around his belly because I am afraid to let go. "Be careful, a car might hit him," my mother says. "Watch out, a truck might knock him down," my father warns. "Stay off the road," they both say. Keep him busy.

I make myself into a bridge for him to climb over. Sometimes I am a tunnel for him to cross through. Sometimes I am the truck that hits him and knocks him down and we roll on the grass, laughing. We play that game often. In the city, we begin our long custom of wrestling on the living room sofa before dinner. We pretend to be ferocious wild beasts, tearing each other apart. I like to be a jaguar eating him up. Every night my mother calls out from the kitchen for us to stop that fighting. We groan and growl louder. We clap our hands to make believe we are hitting. She never comes out to investigate.

When he is three, I watch my brother while we play in the street after school. Zoli, the doorman, watches me watching him. But I have a problem. I have made a friend. I am eight years old and I have learned to play hopscotch with Mary Rozito, who lives up the block and is in my class. We draw a big rectangle on the sidewalk with chalk. We divide it into eight spaces and number the spaces. We fold and hammer the top of a tin can to use as a "potsy." Then we take turns pushing the metal disk forward into a higher-numbered box by hopping on one foot. The potsy slides along the rough sidewalk with a pleasant metallic rub, almost a tap. I am addicted to the sound.

Zoli doesn't let us draw on the sidewalk in front of the apartment house. We have to play in front of Mary's house, which is half a block away. In return for accepting his rule, Zoli agrees to watch Tommy, but not for more than ten minutes. I check the time carefully on the Mickey Mouse watch that my mother bought to keep me entertained when I had the measles.

After ten minutes, I look down the block toward our doorway. Zoli's blue uniform is protruding from it as usual. I don't see Tommy.

I walk to our house and ask where Tommy is.

—I don't know, Zoli answers.

—You were watching him.

Zoli shrugs. —My job is doorman, open and close doors, not watch babies.

Zoli opens the door for Mrs. Posner. They talk about dog-walking. I start running around the block to see if I can find my brother. I am not used to running. My chest hurts. The tears start, deep in my throat. I pass a thin woman in a shawl.—Did you see a little boy? She has seen no children.

When I return to my house, I run in to tell my mother that maybe we will need the police. In our apartment, Tommy is sitting on the floor of the kitchen and playing with alphabet blocks. My mother is teaching him letters. She is angry at me. Very angry.

—I told you never to let him out of your sight.

I feel the tears coming up behind my eyes.

—Where did you go? I told you to watch him.

—Zoli said he would watch him for ten minutes while I played potsy.

—Zoli? That slob?

—He said he would watch.

—Zoli's an idiot.

The tears were making a wet path into my mouth.

—What are you crying for? I saw the whole thing. You would rather play than watch your brother.

—No, I wouldn't.

—You're a liar.

—No, I'm not.

—You hate your brother.

—No, I don't.

—You're jealous of him.

—No I'm not.

—You fight all the time.

—No we don't.

My mother picks my brother up and kisses his forehead, as though to protect him from me. —That's enough. Go do your homework.

That night I dream I am guarding my brother in front of my house. I am watching him very carefully. Even so, he jumps away from me, into the street. A big gray car runs him over. His head rolls down to the East River. I run after his head to try to catch it. I can't. It rolls into the river. I wake up. I've been bad. My brother is dead. I feel miserable. To feel better, I pretend I am still sleeping and redream the dream over and over again, giving it a happy ending each time. I catch the head and put it back on his body. He is alive and well.

During the next years with my brother, I mainly teach him. He learns as quickly as I can find subjects. In the beginning we name the simple things that come after *house, car, table, chair, grass* and the like. We do the zoo animals, common flowers, basic trees and insects, musical instruments, types of cloth, makes of cars and trucks. He isn't satisfied. He sees everything in the way that it is the same as or different from everything else, and he wants to know not only the names but the systems for naming. We go to books, guidebooks, field guides, maps of the heavens. I learn with him. I am no longer the teacher. We learn exotic trees. We name the trees in Central Park, which has become our savannah, our veld, our wetland, our rainforest. At the Seventy-second Street entrance, alone, we worship a Chinese elm; on the other side of the road we pay homage to the black alder, the mustard-yellow dogwood behind the benches (twigs are paired), the pin oak, the Norway maples, the flock of Japanese cherries, the weeping birch.

We learn rocks. In the spring, we study birds: the myrtle, the ruby-crested kinglet, the warblers that we are, amazingly, able to see without binoculars. I hug him the day he spots an ovenbird, walking busily on its pink legs. He bows to me as though I am Allah the day I spot an indigo bunting. We like to track the carpentry of woodpeckers. Our favorite bird is the nuthatch, doing everything upside down. We try to imitate nuthatches by hanging from trees.

At the hotel we follow spring wildflowers and the stars. He brings me buttercups. I gift him with blue chicory. At night we strain to see the rings of Saturn through a crude telescope that he makes. Some nights we sneak out to the field with blankets and identify stars all night. In August we lie on our backs and watch the Perseids, the shooting stars, live out their short glory. The stars provoke us to talk of God. At first the talks are short. But we are both sure there is something transcendent. Otherwise we wouldn't feel awe. Later, our talks get richer. But I don't know about God and there is one thing I won't teach him, late at night when we are hugging and watching the stars, and he is eight years old.

—Tell me about fertilization.
—Plant or animal?
—Human.
—What can I tell you that you don't already know? Men fertilize women, that's all.
—Could I fertilize you?
—Probably not. You're not old enough.
—If I can't fertilize you, can we practice?
—Don't be silly.
—Nobody's watching. Teach me how.
—No, I can't.
—Then how will I learn?
—From a girl your own age.
—Suppose she doesn't know how?

I tousle his hair and dive at him, wrestling. He fights back very weakly. —You two ignoramuses will just have to figure it out by yourselves.

I consider showing him the secrets I already know about other people's sex lives: the special places in the fields where guests hide to have sex outdoors, the rooms above the casino where Randy Lee once let me see an orgy, the shack where the chambermaids do it for money and the rooms on the top floor where the girls who work as counselors take more than one boy in a night and sometimes more than one boy at a time. I have prowled around and I know a lot. But I don't want to spoil our hugging and kissing.

When he is almost twelve and I am not yet seventeen, we still wrestle every night in the city. Over the years, we have moved from the sofa to my bed, which is bigger. We wrestle with fierce intensity now, sweating out the arm holds, the Indian grips, the tickling, the swift maneuvers. His body is becoming long and muscular, hard and strong. I have stopped growing and am soft and thin. I know that he is stronger and I suspect that for some time he has been allowing me to win, to pin him down and make him give up, even though he can hold me down easily. One day, when I think I have him firmly pinned, he pushes my arm aside, turns me over, giggles and pins me down. —Say uncle, he says, laughing. —Say uncle, oncle, ongili, unculo.

I don't want to be angry but I am. I can't get out of his grip.

—Say uncle, he insists.

—No.

—Say it.

—No. You can pin me all night. I won't say it.

—Uncle. Say it.

—No.

His face is close to mine, panting, smiling, conquering. I lift my head, straining my neck. Suddenly I kiss him on the lips, touching them with my tongue the way I have learned to do with other boys. He backs off in surprise, letting my arms go.

—What'd you do that for?

—I couldn't help it.

—That's not fair.

He sits disconsolately at the edge of the bed, his hands tight in his lap. —I didn't mean anything. I crawl close to him and put my arm around his sloping shoulders.

He shrugs.

—I'm sorry.

He punches the palm of his left hand with his right fist.

—Oh, come on. I said I'm sorry.

—Okay, you're sorry.

—Buddies?

He shrugs again.

That's the last time we wrestle. It's also the end of sleeping together, even though we've been tapering off for a couple of years. Which isn't the end of everything, but it feels that way.

During his late adolescence, our communication all but stops. When he goes to high school, he is away at Horace Mann in Westchester all day. At night we do our homework. As soon as I graduate from the local city college, I elope with my romantic Anglophile and move out of the house. After a while, Tommy and my husband begin a tentative relationship based on discussing history, politics and sports. I pretend not to be jealous, not to be melancholy, but even though new ties are forming, a union is missing from my life.

The real end comes later. It visits us in the virus that paralyzes Tommy and takes him to a hospital that I am not allowed to enter for months because polio is especially dangerous to women early in their pregnancy.

—Hey, buddy, I say to the brown hair above the bony white face that emerges from the iron lung as though the machine is his body. His face has so little flesh that the cleft in his chin isn't there anymore. He can't talk. I think he sees me. His eyes still seem to have intelligence.

I lift my tentlike blouse and show him my belly distended with child and jutting from the cutout in the maternity skirt. It's like getting undressed in public and he can see my underwear through the cutout but I don't care. I want him to see me. I wouldn't care if I was naked. I wish I were naked. I want him to know more about life than he is ever going to know. I want to teach him.

—The baby should be born soon. You're going to be an uncle. His eyes go out of focus. —Uncle, oncle, ongili, unculo, I say loudly. He falls asleep. I don't know whether he has heard me or not.

The last time I see him, two weeks later, they have taken him out of the lung. He is lying in a sort of rolling wooden deck chair out on the terrace overlooking the East River. He is covered with plaid blankets. If he can breathe on his own, I think, maybe he is getting better.

—Hey, buddy, they finally let me back in! His eyes are two vacant circles of darkness. There is no intelligence. He seems to stare across the river into the sun. —Do you hear me?

No answer. No motion. Only the sightless gaze across the polluted river to the dirty yellow buildings that look like a prison. I stare across the river with him. I try to see what he is seeing. Ugly buildings. Blinding sun. I position my face so that I can look deep into his eyes to bridge our separation. I bore into the black space of his pupils. All I can see is the reflection of my own face on the lenses of his eyes, my features distorted by the convexity. The vision of my face is brief. I disappear from his eyes. His lids pull back. His frame shudders. I realize that he has stopped breathing.

They put him back into the iron lung. Breath and blood course through his body again. But his awareness is gone. His mind, the part of his body that I have been allowed to love freely, is destroyed by lack of oxygen. It has been gone for some time.

I want to hold his hand, touch what I can of him, but his arms are inside the lung. There is nothing left but his face. I hesitate—there are rules about not touching—but make up my mind to disobey. I kiss his dry, hot, still-living lips, but not as a farewell, not good-bye. Even though he is in his final coma, it seems too soon for that.

PART TEN

BURIALS

28
Lekythos

To: E-man
1.20.92

Subject: Stories

When you wrote about your brother's death, I thought about *my* brother, my family. You know, we haven't spoken face to face for more than six months! Would it help if we actually talked? Should I phone you? Do you want to call me? Or maybe we should wait until we meet again when you come to New York. . . . I think I've reached the point where I want to be right there to absorb your reactions.

I have to stop—my mother just called to tell me my father isn't feeling well, some kind of indigestion. I have to run over to see him just in case it's serious. Why is it that sometimes I think I became a doctor just so he'd appreciate my attention?

Aphra

To: go-dot   SUBJECT: vacuum
  1.20.92

I hope your father's all right. I know you're upset and you had to leave, but i can't believe that what you wrote is the sum of your answer to me: you can't respond fully so we'll talk later at some unspecified time when i come to new york. Why not when you come to california? Why not when you pick up the phone and call my office? What's wrong with reaching for me? I need a friend. I need a companion in cyberspace. What goes on with *you*? Why can't you express a human feeling like, say, i hate my father—the son of a bitch had a gorgeous, brilliant daughter and all he did was use her for a night nurse.

                                        Pissed.
                                        marc

To: E-man   SUBJECT: Attack
  1.21.92

My father's really sick. I had him admitted to the hospital. He was having an MI, which was what I was afraid of when I ran over there the last time I wrote. He's coming through it fine, and I think he'll be all right, but he has a bit of an arrhythmia.
Which doesn't mean I'm not offended by your note, but if you apologize, maybe someday I'll tell you everything you want to hear. You must think I'm the original ice queen. I'm not.

                                        Aphra

To: go-dot   SUBJECT: peace
  1.21.92

Sorry! Consider this my apology. If you're too preoccupied, i'll stay off the screen altogether for a while.

                                                            e

To: E-man   SUBJECT: Thanks
  1.27.92

My father's stabilized and the crisis is over. I go to the hospital every day. The intern who wrote up my father's admission physical described him as a construction worker. So everyone's been treating him like an exhausted hard hat. I straightened it out with a Post-it note on the front of his chart, and when last seen, my father was explaining the hydraulics of his blocked IV to a respectful doctor.

How's Toni?

Aphra

To: go-dot   SUBJECT: A+
   1.28.92

Good. I'm glad things are going better with your dad. I wish i had a daughter like you.

How's Toni? She's on my mind, as usual, so i think i'll continue if you promise to tell me someday how such a nice all-american girl came to be a shrink who specialized in subterranean sex. . . .

Toni has me squirming in my chair and i don't think i'll be able to hold out even until next week. She speaks to me in that exotic voice at the lowest possible female pitch, the same sensual voice for whatever she says, whether she's contemplating heidegger, hawking or heisenberg, it's always the same and it always stimulates, in its tearless, indestructible way, that vulnerable cusp of my anatomy. . . .

And now she's become quite intimate: that's an aphra zion way of putting it—*om mani padme hum*—she's begun to describe what she thinks it will feel like to have intercourse with me, she's becoming fixed on the idea that it will happen: Doctor, she says, I've begun to have erotic sensations. I twist in my bed at night. I take my pillow between my legs and pretend it's your body. I reach down and touch myself and you're the one who's touching me. . . .

She describes her feeling as only a beginning; she knows it will grow until she can no longer contain it. . . . she says that soon she'll reach over to me, unzip me, and it won't be the mechanical act it's always been; it will be something that she wants to do because she feels i am the right person with whom to do it. . . .

I described erotic transference to her, told her that she should take the feeling she has for me and give it to someone more worthy and appropriate, and she laughed at me. I've read all your infantile books, she said, all the stories written by men who don't know what it is to be used for sex, to be sold for sex, to have sex removed from your brain and body so that you become a robot of the intellect, and I tell you, this is no transference. From whom was it transferred?

Her hypothesis is that sexual tenderness is a genetic predisposition, like walking or talking, that can be destroyed by abuse. She finds herself fortunate that she never allowed a man to violate her interior; she was lucky, actually, to meet reilly who took care of her without demanding very much more than one might take from a child. . . .

Toni considers that reilly's relationship with her would hardly have constituted incest with a daughter! From her point of view, in spite of his cheap tricks, reilly is a good man, someone who has helped her to want to become more trusting, so if there is transference, he's the original and i'm the person to whom she should transfer the trust, but her main thesis is that i'm simply the first man who hasn't seen her as his property, who doesn't want to buy her or use her, and that in itself excites her. . . . she says she finds me attractive. . . . and, of course, i feel guilty about wanting to have her without charge, about having every desire she believes i don't have —if she didn't have the power to sue me i'm almost sure i would abuse her—but my self control, the fact that i never come on to her, seems to liberate her. . . .

warily,
m

To: E-man   SUBJECT: Right
1.28.92

Don't!
The professional prohibitions against relating sexually to a patient couldn't be greater. New rulings all the time. It's never appropriate. *NEVER.* Psychologically, given your wish for a strong woman, you should be careful not to seduce Toni into seducing you.

Aphra

To: go-dot   SUBJECT: yes
1.28.92

Thank you, but I'm afraid you're spinning your own fantasy about me as a seducer! I'm telling you my THOUGHTS, lady. . . . Even the catholic church only gives a couple of hail marys for *thoughts!* When in my life have i ever acted out my own fantasies to hurt anyone else? Admittedly, i fucked a friend the night before my first marriage to someone else, but it was her conquest, not mine. I've never been unfaithful. I had a wife who nearly killed me with her infidelities and i still try to take care of her. I've done everything i could to be reliable and responsible: i gave up my practice to satisfy my wife's need to move, i work the most insane hours, i write endlessly to you and get nothing but platitudes back. . . .

marc

To: E-man   SUBJECT: Who am I to you?
  1.29.92

Whatever you think, I haven't been your analyst or supervisor, but I'm not sure I could have accomplished more if I had been. I know you're miserably stressed by your divorce, starting a practice, relating to patti and everything else. I'm trying to be patient.

Aphra Zion, M.D.

To: go-dot   SUBJECT: can't stop
  2.14.92

I haven't written to you in two weeks, which is redundant because you know i haven't sent any mail, but it's no use pretending. I'm so used to talking to you in print that i can't stop writing. I don't know why I'm feeling so critical.

The news is that a few days after you told me your father was sick, my mother called telling me that my father was also in the hospital. She wanted me to come to new york to see him right away because he might not live very long. . . . i told her i had no intention of seeing him until after he was dead—not until they lowered the casket (i couldn't sit through a single eulogy)—and only if i could celebrate that she hadn't died first. So i may be in new york to talk to you someday soon if he dies. Will you talk to me if he dies? Will you listen to me?

marc martell, md

To: E-man   SUBJECT: Yes
  2.14.92

Yes.

Aphra

To: go-dot   SUBJECT: A+ for me
       2.14.92

And as far as toni's concerned, i've been a model of sexual self-control. I didn't get down on my knees to lick her when she told me what she wanted to do to my prick, and i didn't fuck her ass the last time she walked out of the office waving it. I kept my hands off when she elaborated on rubbing her breasts against my belly....

                                                               m

To: E-man   SUBJECT: Mhm.
       2.14.92

I'd say something supportive of your self-control and I could consider commentary on your vocabulary, but I'll just continue listening.

                                                               A.

To: go-dot   SUBJECT: other
       2.14.92

I also want you to know that i know my rage isn't really at you. You haven't actually done or said anything to me that i can indict as inflammatory.... it's everything else that's bothering me....

                                                             marc

To: E-man   SUBJECT: Mmm...
       2.14.92

Hmm—mm!

                                                           Aphra

To: go-dot   SUBJECT: negative
       2.24.92   transference?

I don't know what's going on with toni: she's been missing sessions for almost a month—it's unlike her—she's always been totally reliable; she's never canceled without calling.... when we began therapy and she told me that she was a kept woman, formerly in the trade, i asked if her profession's sometimes intrusive demands on her time might interfere with scheduled appointments. Her answer was that although she experienced herself mentally as rather a quantum hussy (being everywhere at once), in daily life she preferred a newtonian approach to time, regular and predictable!

She'd been moving toward quitting therapy, as i've told you, but it's uncharacteristic for her to be irresponsible, not to tell me very clearly what's happening. . . .

m

To: E-man   SUBJECT: Eternity
   2.24.92

As you may have come to realize, the best course is usually to wait and see.

A.

To: go-dot   SUBJECT: nature
   2.24.92

I'll try to be a mountain. . . . How's your father?

marc m

To: E-man   SUBJECT: Mortality
   2.24.92

He's getting worse. The doctors give him another few weeks. It occurs to me that we have to be very careful with our feelings about each other because our fathers are terminal at the same time.

AZ

To: go-dot   SUBJECT: me
   2.28.92

On tuesday morning i got a call from toni to say that she had to stop therapy because her funds ran out. Reilly has suddenly decided to end their arrangement. She'd been refusing to be involved in his credit ploy; she had declined to be with him or talk to him beyond certain stated hours; she had been selling the clothes he bought her to second act shops and some had been seen at charitable functions around town. . . . even though her literary sex-talk show was scheduled to air within six weeks, she didn't feel she should use her savings for therapy. . . . and now she's invited me to dinner. . . .

marcmarcmarc

To: E-man   SUBJECT: ???
   2.28.92

Are you going?

                                     Aphra

To: go-dot   SUBJECT: !
   2.28.92

yes. . . .

                                       (m)

To: E-man   SUBJECT: ???
   2.28.92

To her apartment?

                           Aphra Zion, M.D.

To: go-dot   SUBJECT: !
   2.28.92

yes. . . .

                                       (m)

To: E-man   SUBJECT: 0
   2.28.92

I'm sure you know what I'm thinking.

                     Aphra Zion, M.D., F.A.C.P.

To: go-dot   SUBJECT: re:0
   2.28.92

i'm thinking the same thing. . . .

                                  (mm)

To: go-dot   SUBJECT: . . . .
   3.9.92

So i went to toni's for dinner and in the end, it doesn't much
matter what any of us think, does it? I haven't written for a while

because i was too shaken up by seeing her, and now i can't even tell you about what happened. . . .

marc

To: E-man   SUBJECT: re: . . . .
   3.9.92

Tell me.

Aphra

To: go-dot   SUBJECT: #
   3.9.92

Toni's dead, aphra. . . . dr varnhos the oncologist called me this morning to ask if i knew anything about her funeral plans, which i did because she'd left me with instructions: she wants her ashes with me, in one of my urns. . . .

marc m

To: E-man   SUBJECT: Loss
   3.9.92

I care about Toni. And you. If you are ever ready, tell me what happened.

Aphra

To: go-dot   SUBJECT: ethics
   3.9.92

When i saw her, at first i thought she looked great and i made up my mind that if it happened, it happened. Her sense of humor was going strong and she joked about maybe we should be limiting ourselves to postcards for the first three months after therapy ended. . . .

She didn't tell me about her death sentence until after dessert and coffee. She let me carry on about her incredible wall-to-wall books and all her indian and navajo artifacts: blankets, rugs, masks, pottery, hopi kachina dolls, zuni fetishes—she allowed me an asinine discourse on deconstructing the native american myth without hitting me—and then she got up and began to set aside things that she wanted me to take home because there'd be no one to give them to me after she died. . . .

She'd bought a big canvas carrybag for her things. I watched her moving around without thinking about what she was doing, without letting the meaning sink in because she hadn't yet told me in so many words, and i wondered if i was going to be able to keep control. . . . i thought not. . . .

My arousal seemed like a permanent fixture, nothing could put me down, but i gradually began to see that she was really sick: her forehead was perspiring; her makeup gave her the flushed, sexy look; her arms—particularly her wrists—were quite frail and incongruous with the high-style Versace disciplinary leather she was wearing, which she hadn't worn for a long time. . . .

She explained that it had been difficult to make decisions these past few months—she wanted to get rid of reilly not because she was sick, not to get sympathy, but the way she would have if she had been well—she never wanted him to know: it was a matter of pride to step away from that life on her own. . . .

And she had decided to opt for quality of life rather than the latest chemotherapy—the shorter the better—who was going to care when her hair fell out?

And finally, she wanted me to put her ashes in one of my beautiful antique jars because she wanted to love me, she wanted me to remember how much she loved me; maybe it was theatrical and operatic and tragic, but tonight was all there was for us. . . . she needed me to make love to her tonight. . . . she knew i wasn't the type who made conventional love, she'd been around every kind of man. . . . *SHE ACTUALLY KNEW ME* without my ever telling her, she knew that if a woman accepted me, put me in charge, let me dominate—fetishes and all—i'd give her everything. . . . and i could have fucked her all night, i was sure i could have gotten inside her no matter how tight she was.

But i didn't want to—and then, i couldn't—

She was sick, she was weak, she needed me, and i was pissed at her for dying and revolted with myself. So I gave her the party line about psychiatrists having a holy commitment to celibacy with their patients, and how exploring feelings was more important than drowning in sex. I even threw in spirituality and how it would be better for her to die without sex confusing all those issues.

So we talked about eternity and time. She wanted to cling to every second of every good, painless minute on this earth. If there was a way, she'd place amulets of extra time on her body, in her clothes, under her skin. She was—finally—navajo, she did not want to die, she wanted divinity now, in foam and cloud and mist and rain, to come to her soaring. . . .

   She asked me to kiss her, or hit her, or tell her what to do, what to wear, whatever i wanted. . . . i held her close in my arms, i felt her trying to hold back her cough, but even as our lips touched, i had to fantasize someone else. . . . i imagined kissing you, aphra. . . .

marc

29

Loss

AGE 55

1992

Marc and I met for dinner the night before our fathers were to be buried. As the headwaiter at Nirvana led us to our table near the great glass window overlooking the park and skyline, Marc told me that Trish had remained in San Francisco with Patti instead of coming east for the funeral. I seated myself on the banquette and tried to make it appear normal that no one in my family was comforting me. "Everyone had emergencies," I explained. "Right after my father died, my mother had to rush immediately back to her hotel to answer mail and cook for the maintenance staff. She's returning tomorrow morning for the funeral. And Elia's working late tonight so he can get free tomorrow afternoon."

Marc broke off a piece of crisp flatbread and dipped it in yogurt-and-tamarind sauce. "You're lucky to have a busy mother. Mine is too depressed to get out of bed."

Neither Harry nor Elia would have considered eating at Nirvana. French restaurants, from La Goulue in our neighborhood to Lutèce, provided the wine and herbs of celebration, but Harry was addicted to the camaraderie that accompanied American bar food and Italian pasta; Elia's preference was for ocean fish in expensively sanitary chromed environments. Marc and I shared a taste for other ethnicities—Japanese, Thai, Indian and Mexican food—which marked us as aboriginal New Yorkers, but neither of us wanted to eat in a cellar kitchen or a storefront.

At Nirvana we were safely aboveground. It was good to see Marc after our long correspondence, to see him looking strong, bearded and healthy in spite of all his anger, to feel again the attraction that I'd never acknowledged to him because we'd known each other so briefly before our epistolary relationship.

We sat among the turbaned staff, surrounded by mirror-cloth hangings that defied evil by reflecting it off tiny, shining disks. The room seemed to hover in the lucency of the setting sun outside the window; the elephant Ganesha and the Buddha promised the golden joy of wisdom and compassion; bodhisattvas and various heavenly consorts waved multiple arms in ecstatic blessing. Our fingers twined over wine and rice and saffron and cumin and curry; they interlaced with shared grief and gladness. We laughed about the worlds below and above that had conspired to bring us together. Now our fathers were dead, unburdening us, removing the pall of all paternal restrictions. Were we freed, the way children were often freed, by the loss? In the background, a sitar conjured thoughts of reincarnation.

"Do you suppose your father will come back?" I asked Marc.

He smiled. "*Papa* the phantom visitor might arrange it. He traveled all the time."

"My father could probably engineer it too," I said. "He was an expert on waterways. But I can't imagine that he'd want to return if he didn't have to. His life with my mother was punishment enough for two lifetimes."

Marc drank the last of his first glass of wine. "Tell me something." His eyes narrowed with a quizzical aggression. He asked, "Who am I to you? What member of your family do I represent?"

Although I hadn't reflected on it before, I knew the answer. But I couldn't accept the implications. Marc said again, "Who, Aphra?"

How could I tell him that he resembled the parent I loved least, a woman who could suggest love and promise support, and then take it all away? He reminded me of my mother especially in his convictions of abuse and martyrdom. What did that say about my creating him as muse, being obsessed by him? Why would I risk exposing myself to his capacity to perform acts of emotional cruelty?

The waiter refilled our wineglasses, and Marc drank while I contemplated composing on a napkin a drawing of myself as a tiny, mythical medieval beast who wanted love more than anything but would bite off her own tail before asking for it. And then I realized that my reticence was as much a hostile act as his failure of affection. I hurt people as much by what I didn't say as Marc did by his sudden withdrawals. I ate quietly, sifting my thoughts, allowing them to blend into the core of self-knowledge. It seemed ordained that my life would go on in secret. I had never told my parents about Harry before we eloped. And my psychiatrist hadn't even realized I was interested in medical school. Nor had I told him how much I needed to talk. He would squander our time by talking excessively to me or sitting in restless silence because I couldn't initiate speech. After our sessions, I sat for hours on the straight-backed bench in the lobby outside his office, crying my tears of frustration, tears that I was holding back, even now. Once he saw me sitting there on his way out and asked, with a tenderness that surprised me, "Is it that bad?"

Marc pulled at his chapati and used a piece of the bread to help guide his rice onto his fork. "You won't give in, will you? You won't trust me with anything. But I tell *you,* I tell you everything. Why? Let me explain: You remind me of my father because you hold everything in. I hate you for it, but at the same time it makes me want to get to you. To get *in* to you. To get it *out* of you."

We seemed to be suffering from the same disease with different symptoms. If he really needed to reach me, as a surrogate for his father, then I ought to be generous enough to try to give something to him, even at the risk of pain. It would help me, too. Almost inaudibly I told him that as a part of the work of my own transformation I'd been writing to him in secret, that he was a special sort of muse. I had the manuscript in my office. I told him I wanted him to read it. Tonight.

My office is a large, dim sort of place that looks like a men's club. It also looks like Freud's consulting room, but my imitation was not conscious. Only after I saw a photo of his office did I realize the resemblance. Actually, the room is more romantic than Freud's since it has a working fireplace rather than a huge stove.

I moved toward my small hidden kitchen to start some coffee but Marc asked if I had any scotch. I poured a jigger for him and while I was loosening the ice decided to join him. We touched glasses before drinking, more as celebration, it seemed, than as a specific for grief. But my hand trembled and turned cold as I drank. Did I want to help him by trusting him with confession, or did I want to conquer his rage with sex? Did I like him as a person, or did his destructive energy and vitality mesmerize me?

Marc asked when my husband was coming home. I told him that Elia's "emergency" work on temporal lobe epilepsy could go on into the night. In fact, Elia was coming home in the early hours of morning with increasing frequency. I was aware that he had a new female assistant, a young molecular biologist who followed his research with avid and meticulous interest.

Marc picked up the resentment in my voice, raised his eyebrows and nodded. I contemplated giving him my chapter on Harry to read first, the one where I learn that my first husband was chronically unfaithful and I cut up his clothes instead of killing him. I could also show him the one about meeting Elia and taking refuge in his methodical goodwill. Marc didn't press me for reading material.

"I think you know I've been married twice," I said.

He nodded. "You have two children also, don't you? How did they take the divorce?"

"As well as could be expected." I downed a large swig of the scotch. That was the hardest part—what I couldn't face, what I couldn't even write about.

"What would you expect?"

I didn't want to tell him. I wanted to keep it all inside, where I didn't have to look at it. I didn't want him as my psychiatrist, either, but the scotch enhanced Marc's skill at emotional invasion, his talent for trephining hearts. I said, "I didn't know what to expect— that they'd go on with their lives without noticing, maybe."

Marc's silence and another deep swallow of whiskey encouraged me. "My children are more successful than any parent has a right to expect. They're totally driven. My daughter's on full scholarship at Harvard. Renaissance art. My son is a tough, aggressive litigator. Maybe it sounds like I'm complaining about good fortune, but it isn't what it seems."

Taking a long drink, Marc looked around the room as if to find an exit. He noticed the small collection of antiquities that were accumulating on a shelf behind my desk and studied them: the Theban sphinx, the human-headed bird, the reproduction statue of Imhotep from the Metropolitan Museum.

Once started, I found it hard to stop. "My children—although they're far from children—love Harry. They wanted me to be happy in my choice, but they could never understand my choice. They think Elia's a cold fish, and he is. He hangs around under a rock waiting for a woman to love him, and when one comes along he swims off to another rock. The kids want me to go back to Harry. Although he's always had a lot of women, he made it clear that he's waiting for me and he'll never remarry. My children *like* his women and they feel I should forgive their father. He calls and visits and spends time with them, much more than I do, but they want us to be a family again."

Marc fondled the Theban sphinx, his thumb passing over the vague, chipped mounds of her breasts as though they pacified him. "What about you?"

"I don't think I could ever forgive Harry," I said. I moved closer to him and picked up the statue of Imhotep to polish it with the oil of my thumb pad.

Marc put down his drink on top of some papers on my desk. "Did you know there's a legend that if you rub Imhotep's bald head and make a wish, it will come true?" He went on. "Imhotep was an architect of the pyramids, originally vizier to the Egyptian king Djoser thousands of years before Christ; he was eventually identified with magic and with Aesculapius, the Greek god of healing."

Imhotep was also a male figure that Marc was asking me to caress the way he was caressing the breasts of the sphinx. He touched the edge of my palm near the statue, which was seated in my hand. His intention was clear and, as a sex therapist who invented ways to help people pass their first obstacles to intimacy, I admired his strategy. "Make a wish," he said. I closed my eyes and gently rubbed my forefinger over the smooth round black ball that was Imhotep's head. I lifted my face and wished for him to kiss me as he had imagined kissing me in Toni's moment of emotional extremity. He had once said that he never kissed unless he was willing to have sex. As I'd hoped, but not entirely expected, I felt the warm firmness of his lips on mine.

But I couldn't relax. Was seducing Marc what I needed to complicate my life even further? I slipped out from behind the kiss and busied myself with making a fire in the grate. I didn't know what I wanted. I believed that sex was a good thing, in itself, and that I clearly needed a satisfying experience: I was atrophying from sexual boredom with Elia's monotonous routines and I thought that even Freud would have condoned my wish to have mutually creative sex, or at least to get properly laid, but Marc's questions had interfered with my libido, usually perfectly clear in its demands no matter how muddy the outcome.

"If you're not interested in sex, don't you think that building a fire is pushing the envelope?" Marc asked.

I ignited the newspaper and watched the smoke curl upward, followed by the leap of the flames whooshing into the cavernous chimney. The kindling ignited like a fiery breath of afterlife, with the roar of a spirit, a ba, suddenly bursting from confinement in the body. . . . I wondered if it was my father's spirit taking flight, which seemed (after wine and scotch) a perfectly reasonable consideration. . . . I knelt and watched the fire for a while in a kind of alpha wave trance. . . . I drank the last of my whiskey and slowly began to unbutton my sweater. I said, "I was thinking about my father."

I cried while we made love. It's easier for me to cry when I'm doing something. I don't like people to notice. I don't want them to think I need anything. I didn't want Marc to think I needed him. My father trained me not to admit I ever needed anything from anyone, because he never gave me anything. And yet I couldn't figure out exactly why I was crying. It felt like grief but I was sure I wasn't mourning for my father. His death was not the immediate cause, even though images of his death mask—cheeks sunken, beaked nose prominent, eyes closed—were beginning to form. I wondered where the body was (on a table in the funeral home? in a big refrigerator? in the casket already?). My tears kept emerging but they did not seem connected to the poignancy of loss, to my keen sense of being deserted now. He had left me long ago. That was an ancient wound.

The flames of the fire died down and the room began to chill. When Marc finally slept, without holding me or lying in my arms, I knew that I was mourning for Harry.

30

Funeral

AGE 55

1992

My father's funeral service was graveside, in Queens, near the waterway whose underground installations he cared for, near the dark brass plaque that had his name on it at the edge of the East River. The snow was falling on the gravestones and monuments, whiteness nesting in the crevices of the chiseled inscriptions and banded on top of the tombstones like clerical collars. The rows of graves stretched to the horizon; the flutter of falling snow covered the mounds of earth over all the stilled bodies lying obediently in their long queues.

I didn't want to be buried in Queens, even though my brother was there and a space waited for my mother. I didn't know where I was going to be buried. While I was married to Harry I assumed it would be in Philadelphia with his family at a pleasant suburban cemetery, but where would I go now?

Harry's arm was around my shoulders, hugging me to the chest of his old trench coat as the rabbi spoke words of generalized praise above the noise of traffic on the nearby highway. A group of men from my father's office attended. I had never met any of them. One delivered a brief speech on Frederick Gold's impeccable honesty and reliability. That was all.

The males in my life were collected at the service: Elia pacing, writing notes in his nervous hand on a small piece of paper tucked in his prayerbook; my son, the image of his father, with thick sandy hair and a ruddy complexion that always suggested delight; to my surprise, even Marc was there, standing at the back of the group, at the edge of the gazebo where the eulogy was delivered, almost obscured by the gently drifting flakes. I had noticed him when I adjusted my son's scarf before he carried his grandfather's coffin to the grave site. I thought how kind—and how uncharacteristic—it was of Marc to attend my father's last rites on this day when he had a funeral of his own. Had he read the location of my father's in the daily notices?

No one commented to me that it was odd for Harry to be the person by my side at the funeral. He was the father of the family; he was the one my father accepted as son-in-law. Harry's tears flowed as the prayers were said, as the rollers moved and the casket was lowered into the ditchlike hole surrounded by Astroturf. I had the curious feeling that everyone there but Harry was unreal, shadows moving in a poem about snow and death. Only Harry among these shades was alive, his warm blood coursing through his heart, his face wet with memories, his fingers crushing my coat in the anguish of loss. I would need Harry to help me remember my father properly, to remind me of kindnesses I never observed.

With Harry's arm around me, wrapped in the passion of his sorrow, I suffered an odd fear of being buried in a solitary coffin. Last night, Marc had fallen asleep so separately from me that it had been like being buried alive and alone. I wondered if a double casket could be fashioned for Harry and me. We'd lie the way we used to rest in bed, his back tucked against my belly, my leg across the broad muscle of his thigh. I wanted to spend my death untangling the hair of his chest, his back comforting the length of my body. Or, in the reverse position, he could stroke my hair and shoulders as I lay on my side, until his hand came to rest between my breasts as we drifted in our final sleep. Our skin was always silken together at night. . . . The dreams we dreamed were happy. . . .

I was crying, too, when the rabbi threw dirt on the coffin. The last prayer was being spoken when Marc came forward. He knelt, picked up the rabbi's spade and thrust his own portion of earth and stones resoundingly on top of the wooden lid. The rabbi looked askance. Who was this man? What rights did he have at this funeral? The Astroturf rolled back over the grave like a pool cover and the ceremony was over.

"What was his story to you?" Marc wanted to know. "How the hell did he have two families without anyone ever knowing?"

But we didn't have time to talk about it then. The limousines were ready to take us home to our various boroughs. I found a place for Marc and his mother in the car to Brooklyn. As the cortege drove home, the snow fell on the East River, melting into the water. It descended softly, too, on the aqueducts and treatment plants, the fluids and effluents of the living and the dead that flowed under the bridges and toward the sea. Softly it descended on all five boroughs, spread beyond vision, their cleanliness tended with care by the chief engineer. It continued to fall on my father's grave for many winters before we resolved ourselves to his nature.

mérite for his services to *la santé*. . . . i mean come on, give us a break. . . .

Was he like that with you, too? Did he keep the seine and the loire and the dordogne and all the rest of the rivers safe and clean for france?

How are you? How's elia? What are your afterthoughts about *us?*

I've placed toni's ashes in a large urn—a krater, really—that i think she would have liked. She's on my top shelf.

m

To: E-man   Subject: Father
   3.21.92

I can't imagine my father buying pâté and wine. It's inconceivable. Once, years ago, in the summertime, he took me out to Le Refuge and selected a bottle of burgundy. I was surprised that he knew what to order. He'd never done it before and he never did it afterward. At home the only wine we ever had was sweet—for festivals. The closest we came to pâté was chopped chicken liver. My mother would have flayed him alive for spending the price of pâté. Especially in dollars, since obviously he never went to France. My father, a Francophile? It's too much, Marc. I'm having trouble with all my realities. The world is turning around so fast I don't know where I am.

My father took care of the East River. He knew more about aqueducts and sewers than any man in the history of New York, not that he passed the knowledge on. But he did explain grade tunnels, rock and concrete and cut-and-cover aqueducts, and the city pressure tunnel. Once he took my mother and me on a visit to the Ashokan Reservoir. My mother didn't see what was so interesting about a lot of water, but I thought the white jets, aerating and purifying in the sun, were beautiful.

And sewers—that was why he was so germ-conscious. The poor man spent enough time in sewers to catch ten plagues. He could really wax on the relationship between grit chambers and sedimentation tanks and sludge. And he was truly worried about storms and overflow onto the beaches. Drove him crazy with frustration that the city wouldn't listen. Once he drew me a whole flow diagram. Did you know that as late as 1850 files of slaves toted buckets of filthy human waste across the city in the evening to empty into the river?

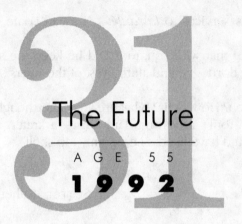

31

The Future

AGE 55
1992

So how the hell did he manage to have two families without anyone finding out? I'm still frozen in the snow, aphra, i'm stuck at the casket. The last time i saw him, he brought home a tin of *pâté de fois gras,* the real thing no less, from sarlat, and a couple of bottles of saint-emilion that he said he carried in his arms for us across the ocean. He complained that the dordogne river was degenerating just like the caves at lascaux and rivers weren't meant to be exposed to anything more polluting than swimmers....

Maman cooked for him an incredible *navarin* of lamb that night, for us both, and he actually came out of himself enough to tell us that the french government was going to give him an *ordre de*

Am I beginning to idealize my father?

Elia and I have agreed to separate. No trouble. He's just a fish swimming downriver, if I haven't talked enough about rivers yet.

Aftereffects of "us"? Well, I seem to be writing to you about myself. Directly. That's a first.

I expect Toni must be happy in her new home, though I can't imagine she enjoys what she hears.

A.

To: go-dot   Subject: filth
    3.21.92

It's all very well for you to idealize dear old dad, mucking about in the sewers for humankind, but as far as i'm concerned, dying of a heart attack was too easy. I wish one of them, my mother or yours, had done him in!

Because you didn't suffer any real lies, aphra, all he did was deceive you, he didn't feed you falsehoods, he just hid his affair. . . . do you know what it feels like to have lived a whole life created by another man's dirty secret?

Do you know what it feels like to realize you're a bastard? Do you know anything at all about pain? What are the rules for bastard brooklyn street urchins, huh? Am i still trish's legal husband and patti's legal father? Was my mother a real mother, or was she a depressed, incompetent, infantile whore, the way all the neighbors whispered she was?

How do you justify having troubles about your "realities"? Try mine.

Sorry.

m

To: E-man   Subject: Pain
    3.22.92

You're right. I have a lot of special mechanisms that defend me. I don't get angry the way you do. I distance myself. I write. I have saviors and redeemers. I believe the future will be better. And I don't tell everything.

But you're wrong, too. Yes, of course you're outraged at suddenly not having a legal parent, but look at what you've acquired. What you've "gotten in" to. You now have a whole new family, and I won't accept thee being holier than me. Or holier than Danah, Trish or Toni! Or holier than your mother, who tried so hard in a world dominated by self-centered, self-pleasing men. In fact, it's time you got off your psychological ass (if I may be familiar) and started appreciating Trish and being good to Patti. You're not going to do better with anyone else. The two of them will always be there, even if you go sneaking around like your father (with a woman who sneaks around like *her* father). That's adultery, not to mention incest. It seems to me you could sell a couple of antiquities and buy yourself a decent analyst since I'm not sending mental health on the cheap by E-mail anymore. You really do remind me of my mother, with all your complaints.

I'm sorry, Marc. Maybe I'm falling into the trap of screaming at you like every other woman you've known. For myself, it's nice to know I'm human, and I'm glad—thrilled—to have someone to wrestle with on the sofa again. I can't be distant anymore. I have to pin you down and tell you that even though you're a good shrink, maybe better than I am, I wouldn't guarantee you're a kinder, more honorable person than your father.

A.

To: go-dot   SUBJECT: yeah, well. . . .
   3.24.92

So i read a bedtime story to patti tonight and i hugged her and i kissed her when she cried—and i kissed her and i hugged her when she cried some more—and then when she kept it up too long i got mad at her, i didn't sneak away. . . . she seemed to like that and she went to sleep. . . .

And by the way, incidentally, nothing important, but did you notice last week i made *love* to you? While you were weak? While you were crying? When we both had lost our fathers? When I felt alone, too?

So i think you ought to go back to harry.

m

To: E-man   SUBJECT: Aqueducts and rivers
   3.26.92

I've always wanted to look at all the reservoirs in the neighborhood of the hotel. The Neversink, the Rondout, and maybe go up to the East Delaware and the Schoharie, too. I'd like to follow the Neversink River down to the Delaware River. I'd like to understand how the Delaware Aqueduct works, picking up water for New York City from the West Branch and the Croton and the Kensico. I'd like to do that in the spring. With Harry, because he listened to my father talk about it.

And then I'd like to go to France. I want to walk along the Seine at night; the lighting in Paris is the most romantic in the world. I want to take a bicycle trip along the Loire and stop at all the châteaux. And canoe down the Dordogne and drink wine with pâté in old Sarlat. . . .

Most of all I'd like to feel the warm Provençal sun in the mountains of the Lubéron above the Durance. I want to remember love among the green grasses and the red poppies, and the wind in the yellow broom under the blue sky. I want to go there in memory of my father because he had so little. I want to go there with Harry because he asks so little and loves so much.

And I did notice that you made love to me. You even said, "I love you." That will have to suffice for all time because it came from you as the father I couldn't reach, as my martyred mother and as the brother I taught. In virtual reality, they all exist in you. And I give you virtual love, too, from everyone you've seen in me: your brother who died for you . . . your helpless mother whose heart was locked . . . our father. . . .

Your sister,
Aphra

About the Author

AVODAH OFFIT is a psychiatrist and sex therapist whose novel affirms that the quest for love motivates all sexual relations, no matter how eccentric. *Virtual Love* takes that quest into the realms of the new communication, the virtual reality of electronic letter writing. There, on E-mail, in this inventive form of epistolary fiction, two psychiatrists reflect on their erotic lives, think about their patients and . . . fall in love.

Dr. Offit's *The Sexual Self,* published a decade ago, appeared in various editions throughout the world. It was a critical as well as a popular success. "This book is wonderful, strewn with wit and insight and written with compassion and sensibility," said *The New York Times.* "This isn't pop psychology. It is instead a book full of complex ideas and concepts, presented in language that's easily comprehensible, a pleasure to read." After the publication of her second collection of essays, *Night Thoughts, Reflections of a Sex Therapist, The New Republic* identified her as "the Montaigne of human sexuality."

She has contributed chapters to major psychiatric textbooks as well as articles and interviews to mass market magazines: *Vogue, Mademoiselle, Glamour, Self, Bride's, Cosmopolitan, Harper's Bazaar.*

Formerly Director of the Sexual Treatment Center at Lenox Hill Hospital, Dr. Offit practices in New York City and is a Clinical Assistant Professor of Psychiatry at Cornell University Medical College. She and her husband, Sidney Offit, have two sons. They summer in Water Mill, New York.